THE PALE TIGER

最高机密

MIKE HARRISON

THE PALE TIGER

最高机密

First published in 2020 by
Matthew James Publishing Ltd
Unit 46 Goyt Mill
Upper Hibbert Lane
Marple
SK6 7HX

www.matthewjamespublishing.com

ISBN: 978-1-913230-07-4

Typeset in the UK

SUNDAY

SUNDAY 22ND SEPTEMBER, NIGHT-TIME

ABOARD THE USS HAY IN THE SOUTH CHINA SEA

The port-side lookout gripped the guard rail with both hands as the deck lurched to starboard, the ship shuddering under the impact of the wave. He screwed up his face, the rain still lashing across the heaving surface of the sea, great black slabs of water looming up out of the darkness, crashing against the destroyer's hull. He shook his head, water dripping from the hood of his storm jacket, his eyes stinging from the spray. He steadied himself, peering into the night, the wind-whipped crests of the waves skittering over the surging ocean. He lifted up the night vision binoculars, scanning his quadrant. Just the rain, thundering down out of the roiling clouds, the dark sea, flexing its salty muscles.

A crackle in his earpiece. 'Report in.' The boatswain's mate of the watch.

He lowered the binoculars, cupping a hand over his earpiece.

'Clear aft.' The hoarse rasp of the aft lookout.

His turn. 'All clear port.' He blinked again, eyes burning in the biting wind.

Silence.

'Starboard lookout, report in.' The boatswain's mate, an edge in his voice.

'All clear starboard.'

The crackle of the PA system.

He glanced at his watch. 0321 hours. Another 40 minutes in the weather. He rolled his shoulders, feeling the spray trickle down his neck.

He glanced up, the sheer sides of the deckhouse looming above him, grey steel glistening under the navigation lights. Beyond, the spars of the comms tower, slicing into the night sky, flags snapping in the wind.

A boom rang out, the ship juddering as a wave thundered into the port-side prow, the spray sheeting over him. He leaned back against the bulkhead, bracing himself as the vessel rolled with the punch, straining to right itself against the seething water. He reached behind him, checking the clip of the safety harness, the reassuring heft of the carabiner clip.

He reached out again for the guard rail as another wave pounded the steel prow, bubbling water surging over the foc's'le, the ship lurching from the fresh blow.

'Fuck this,' he muttered.

'Port lookout. Contact?' The urgent tones of the boatswain's mate.

He bit his lip. 'All clear.'

'Understood.' A pause. 'All lookouts, keep the channel clear for comms.'

He tightened his grip on the rail, the ship reeling as it shouldered its way through the storm, the silky black water towering around them.

'All lookouts! All lookouts!' The CIC watch officer, concern etched in his voice. 'Radar contact bearing two-nine-zero. Proximity alert! Proximity alert!'

His quadrant. 'Shit!' He stared through the binoculars, scanning the heaving seas, the wind still screeching around him.

'Port lookout! Any contact?' The boatswain's mate again, his voice cracking.

'Negative! Negative!' He narrowed his eyes, straining to see into the rain-lashed night, the deck pitching beneath him.

'Helmsman. New course!' The conning officer on the PA. 'Steer zero-eight-zero. Flank speed. Repeat, zero-eight-zero. Flank speed.'

'Zero-eight-zero, aye.'

He threw himself back against the bulkhead, feet jammed against the rail guard as the ship swung around, pitching into the turn, engines roaring. Full-on to the weather now; a wave bounded out of the night, slamming into the side of the vessel, exploding over the gunwale, a wall of foam-specked water crashing over him.

'Port lookout!' The boatswain again. 'Do you copy?'

He shook the spray from his eyes raising the binoculars again, fingers aching with the cold, scanning the heaving horizon. He froze. A shape, something rising out of the water, the prow of another ship, pitched up by the force of the sea. 'Contact! Contact!' He screamed into the PA system. 'Incoming vessel! Fifty yards! Ten o'clock!' He gripped the binoculars, watching, helpless, as the approaching warship crested the wave, tearing through the wall of black water rolling towards them.

'Brace for impact! Brace for impact!' The CIC watch officer's shouts barely audible above the storm's roar, the collision alarm ringing across the decks.

The approaching ship began to swing to starboard. It was too late.

The second ship's prow slammed into the side of the American warship, the screech of steel tearing at steel, sparks spraying into the night as the bow tore along the side of the vessel.

The US ship rolled with the impact of the blow, the prow of the intruding ship slicing through the guard rails, buckling the steel casings of the aft quarters, shearing the torpedo tube stanchions, steel cleats pinging off the reeling deck. A final rasp of steel scoring across the aft deckhouse and the bow slipped off the stern of the US warship, crashing back into the roiling sea.

'Damage report! Damage report!' The shouts of the CIC watch officer, ringing over the PA system.

A crackle, then a quieter voice, the boatswain's mate. 'Port watch, do you copy?'

Silence.

'Jay, do you copy?'

No response.

At his watch station, just the frayed remnants of his safety line, whipping in the wind.

SUNDAY 22ND SEPTEMBER, 6.30 PM

THE M4 MOTORWAY, WEST OF LONDON

Emma Wilson of MI6 strummed her fingers on the armrest as she looked out of the car window. The traffic around them had come to a halt, the headlights of the cars behind glinting off the raindrops splashed across the side windows. 'Should've taken the tube.'

Sebastian Noon, Head of Counter Intelligence, consulted his watch. 'No need to fret, your flight's not 'til 21.45.'

'Can't miss the pre-flight briefing.' She smoothed down her British Airways cabin crew skirt, ran a finger under her neckerchief.

He turned towards her, his patrician features smudged in shadow. 'Is it as comfortable as it looks?'

'Feel like I'm wrapped in prickly cling film.' She shifted in her seat. 'Enough static electricity to power a small town.'

'I think it rather suits you.'

'And the blouse.' She rolled her slender shoulders. 'Like wearing cardboard.' She pulled out her vanity mirror, checking her lipstick. 'And I won't even start on the hat.'

He gave a slight nod. 'Who are you, by the way?'

Emma held up her flight crew ID hanging from the lanyard around her neck.

Noon slipped off his spectacles, narrowed his eyes. 'Really?'

She reached behind her neck, checking the pins that held her sweep of dark hair in a tightly wound bob. 'I don't get to choose the names.'

'Mixed blessing, I suppose.' He tapped the driver on the shoulder. 'Do you know what the hold-up is?'

'Nothing on the radio, sir. Just weight of traffic, I think.'

Sebastian nodded, leaned forward, flicked a switch. The glass partition sealing the front from the rear seats rose almost silently, slotting into the rubber seals with a click.

Emma took a deep breath, staring straight ahead.

He turned towards her, deep-set eyes framing his aquiline nose. 'Unlike you to be nervous.'

She didn't reply.

Noon slid his spectacles on. 'What have you done with my ice-cold Emma?' He gave a slight tilt of the head. 'You worried about working with McKay again?'

Emma shrugged. 'Fifteen years ago. I don't think about it. Don't see why he would.'

'Any contact with the man since?'

'Haven't needed to.'

'That wasn't exactly my question.' He nodded. 'How's that wrist of yours by the way?'

Emma held it up. 'Like new.' She paused. 'Like old new.' She glanced across at him. 'How's your leg?'

'That really wasn't why I asked.' Sebastian glanced down at his right foot. 'A wonder of science, I'd say.' He tapped it with the toe of his left shoe, a hollow tock, leather on carbon fibre. He looked across at her, a smile spreading across his features. 'My dear girl, you really shouldn't do this to yourself.' He nodded, slowly. 'I would have done the same in your shoes.' He raised an eyebrow. 'No pun intended.'

She frowned. 'I should have come back for you.'

'And you did.' He paused. 'He was right there, what else could you have done?'

Emma exhaled. 'I didn't think he'd jump.'

Sebastian tried another smile. 'Neither did I.' He turned towards the window; they were moving again, slipping past the slower-moving traffic, the headlights pools of glinting silver on the slick, wet tarmac. Tail lights drifted past them, bursts of red in the darkness, the outlines smudged in the rain. 'Believe me, if I had any doubts about you, you wouldn't be sitting here.' He glanced across at her. 'Do I finally get an "I know, Sebastian"?'

Emma took a deep breath, turned towards him. 'You're right, I'm jumpy.'

'You'll find a lot's changed. The streets of Hong Kong.' He removed his spectacles. 'But you should be fine. It's been long enough; the cameras won't be looking for you.'

Emma continued to look ahead. The outline of the driver through the frosted partition, a grey blur against the motorway lights. She sat in silence.

'What do you think you'll find?' Sebastian continued.

Emma glanced towards him. 'A new face in the story. Someone we haven't thought of.'

He sat back in the seat, eyes drifting towards the window. 'Haven't you got a big enough cast already?'

'Not for this kind of drama.' She paused. 'If the whispers are right.'

'You mean sins that even hedge fund managers would baulk at?'

'Feels like something … fiercer.' She took another breath. 'This isn't just well-tailored money men skittering round the rules and flexing their conscience.'

'That kind of pinstriped alchemy,' he glanced across at her, the light from a passing car sweeping across his face, 'attracts all sorts of foragers.'

'There's too much swirling in the dark.' She narrowed her eyes. 'Chatter, from the places our ears shouldn't reach.'

Sebastian turned once more towards the window. The rain had stopped, the passing cars prowling circles of light shimmering off the roadway. He looked upward; in the darkness beyond the streetlights, thick, restless clouds swirling across the starless sky. 'So what's our friend from Crator Capital going to be doing in Hong Kong?'

Emma tucked a lock of hair behind her ear. 'Good works. Apparently. The Crator Charitable Foundation, "Cherish the Spark of Life". Catchy.'

'And I thought this was a shamelessly omnivorous hedge fund.'

'It's that as well.' She shrugged. 'But perhaps they believe in the hot place. Not all the plunder goes on Alpine real estate.'

He carefully replaced his spectacles. 'A splendid tax dodge, no doubt.'

'Free healthcare, medical centres, prescription drugs, the needy of South East Asia.'

He turned towards her, his silver hair glinting under the streetlights. 'In Hong Kong?'

'Got to base it somewhere.'

He nodded, his forehead creasing into a frown. 'So what is he going to be up to over there? Our friend Borso?'

Emma glanced across at Sebastian. 'If I knew, I could have spared myself the dressing up.' She rolled her shoulders as she shifted in her seat. 'And a few days with the ex.' She straightened up, pulling at the hem of her skirt.

'But you're doing both.' He nodded, slowly, tapping a finger on his knee. 'Which makes me think,' he paused, 'that you know rather more than you're letting on.'

Emma met his gaze. 'If there is, there's a reason.'

He removed his spectacles. 'A source?'

She shrugged.

'Someone on the inside?'

'You know I can't answer that.'

He narrowed his eyes. 'I don't like secrets.'

She exhaled. 'When I'm sure.' She paused. 'I'll say.'

He nodded. 'So the whispers are right.'

She looked straight ahead, the lights from the cars behind them gliding across the partition glass, their shadows, swooping and fading. 'The next 48 hours.' Emma bit her lip. 'We'll see.'

Sebastian replaced his spectacles, glanced up at the evening sky. 'Cloud's thinning, you might get a decent view of the city after all.'

Emma looked out of the window. 'Junction 4, finally.' She turned towards him. 'Thanks for the lift.'

'My pleasure. Good to catch up.'

She picked up her hat, brushing a speck of dust off with the back of her hand.

'And Emma.'

She turned towards him again. 'Is this your "just one other thing"?'

He cleared his throat. 'Two other things, actually.'

She fashioned a smile.

'Tread carefully out there.' He frowned. 'And not just with McKay. This trade war isn't going away any time soon. The Chinese would just love an excuse to have a go.'

'And what else?'

He held her gaze. 'Whatever you do find.' He paused. 'Bring it straight to me. And only to me.'

She narrowed her eyes. 'Like my relationship with Pritchard isn't strained enough already.'

'And I know you're much too smart to ask me why.'

She blinked. 'Does this make us even?'

He shrugged. 'It's an order, my dear girl, not a favour.'

'Thought you said you didn't like secrets.'

'Only other people's.'

SUNDAY 22ND SEPTEMBER, 1.45 PM (6.45 PM GMT)

THE COLOMBIAN HIGHLANDS

The pick-up truck pulled into the yard, the suspension creaking as it rumbled over the rutted surface, the cab swaying. It drew to a halt outside the house, the swirls of dust kicked up by the tyres slowly settling.

The door swung open and the driver eased himself out of the truck. He stood, looking across at the farmhouse. The rust-streaked drainpipes clinging to the weathered wooden slats, the afternoon sun glinting off the peeling paintwork.

A dog barked in the distance. The driver looked up at the oak forests manning the hillsides beyond the farm: stern grey trunks, their spiralled leaves silent in the still air. The pecking of an acorn woodpecker rattled out from a nearby stand.

The man began to walk towards the house, steady gait, work boots crunching on the pitted ground. 'Burro!' he shouted out. 'Burro!' He swung open the mesh door, a frown spreading across his face. 'Perro inútil …' he growled out the words as he stepped inside. 'Maldito mestizo—'

The man froze, eyes widening, as he stared at the visitor standing by the window. He dropped his rucksack to the floor, swallowed. 'Boss.' He croaked out the words. 'What's going on?'

Kasper Lehtonen turned to face the room, a look of mild curiosity etched on his stone-hard features. He stood in silence, his broad shoulders slowly rising and falling. He reached up, ran a brawny hand over his shaven head, a rumble building from deep within him. He turned back to the window, looked up at the afternoon sky. 'Not a cloud to be seen.' His tone, almost friendly. 'But you never know.' He paused. 'It happens.' He turned back to face the man. 'That rainy day.'

The man swallowed again, his mouth slowly opening and closing as he stared at the visitor.

'Been admiring your new cooker.' Kasper looked down at it, nodding approvingly. 'German, isn't it?' He looked up, eyebrows raised.

'Where's Mia?' The man blurted out the words, his breathing quickening.

Kasper looked down, slowly ran his finger across the front of the cooker. 'Mia.' He frowned, his shoulders flexing beneath his well-tailored jacket. 'Ah … that Mia.' He glanced back up, a hint of a smile playing across his full lips.

The man moved his mouth to speak, but no sound emerged.

A car pulled up outside, its engine growling, stones skittering beneath the tyres. The engine fell silent, car doors opening and closing.

The man began to shake.

Kasper bent down, carefully opening and closing the kitchen drawers. 'Other people's kitchens.' He muttered to himself as he began to rummage through the drawers.

The man looked across at him, a look of horror spreading across his face.

From the yard outside, another sound. Hammering, metal on metal.

'Finally!' Kasper stood up.

The man blinked as he stared at what Kasper was holding in his hand.

Another dog bark, closer this time.

'Showtime.' Kasper slid the pen and paper across the table. 'We want it back.' He nodded at the pen and paper. 'I assume you want the …' Kasper made a clicking sound as he cocked back his thumb, 'you know, friends and family.'

The man began his write, his hands shaking.

More dogs, their barking much closer now, their howls echoing around the hills behinds the house.

From the yard, the steady hammering.

'Put them on.' Kasper slid the handcuffs across the table.

The man looked at them, let out a sob, his shoulders, heaving. 'Please …' his voice, cracking as he looked up at Kasper, tears streaking his cheeks. 'Not this …'

Kasper cocked an ear. 'Somehow,' he turned his head to the sound of the dogs, 'they just know.' He gave a good-natured grunt, nodded at the handcuffs. 'Don't let me down.'

The man put on the handcuffs, his fingers trembling, his chest surging. 'Please … please …'

Kasper took the man's arm, led him across the room, back through the door.

They stood, blinking in the afternoon sun.

In front of them, in the middle of the yard, an iron pole, hammered into the ground. From the top of the pole, a padlock hanging from a chain. Two men stood next to the pole, one leaning on a sledgehammer.

'Come on then.' Kasper said softly as he led the man to the pole, snapping the padlock to his handcuffs.

Kasper took a step back. 'You knew the day would come.' He glanced around. The dogs, circling now, at the edge of the yard, snarling, panting, claws scratching at the stony ground.

The man let out a howl. 'A bullet!' He screamed. 'You promised!'

Kasper exchanged glances with his men, shrugged. They walked to the car, clambered in.

The car engine roared into life.

Kasper wound down the window, looking at the man chained to the pole. 'Promise is a bit strong.'

The man screamed and roared as he kicked at the snarling, lunging dogs.

Kasper slowly shook his head, levelled his gun, shot the man twice through the chest.

He crumpled to the floor, lay there, still and silent.

Kasper wound up the window, glanced across at the driver. 'I mean, you've got to think about the neighbours.'

The driver gave a nod. 'Right, Boss.' He gunned the engine as they rattled across the yard, the car suspension thumping.

Kasper looked down at the cuff of his suit, rubbed at a speck of dried blood. 'Business opportunity, my friends.' He scowled as he stared at the stain. 'When's someone going to open a half-decent dry cleaners in this arse end of a town?'

SUNDAY 22ND SEPTEMBER, 7 PM

THE BASEMENT OF CRATOR CAPITAL, LONDON

'Jimbo.' The familiar voice from out of the dark. 'It's us.' It drew out the final 's' to a hiss, which swirled and swooped in the still air around him.

A man, alone, seated on the edge of a bed, staring into the blackness.

'Are you awake, Jimbo?' The words, somewhere, up there.

The man remained silent.

'But then, how would you know?' The voice, matter-of-fact.

The man took a deep breath, shoulders shaking beneath tattered clothes.

'Remember when you used to look down? That space between your face and your hand?'

The man in the dark let his bearded chin drop onto his chest, a ragged curtain of tangled hair hanging down the sides of his face.

'Light.' The voice persisted. 'It was called light.'

The man looked up into the blackness, his mouth opening and closing as he tried to form words.

'You need to speak up a little, Jimbo.'

The man croaked out the words: 'Am I alive?'

A laugh, skittering through the lifeless air around him. 'Knock, knock. Room service.'

A tearing, swooshing sound as the water cascaded over the stone floor, feeling its way in the darkness, rushing to the far wall. A ringing, like the splintering of glass as the water threw itself against the metal grillwork, sighing, gurgling as it made its grateful escape.

The silence barged back in, shooing away the last drips from the grate.

'You're a lucky man, Jimbo.'

The man remained silent.

'Something to look forward to.' The voice, purring. 'The secret. To happiness. They say.'

The man looked up into the blackness as he stuttered his plea: 'Finish it.'

Silence.

'Please.' The man heaved the word out.

Another chuckle. 'Do you know what's coming up, Jimbo?'

The man slumped forward.

'It's a special day.' The voice paused. 'It's our anniversary.'

Silence.

'A whole year, Jimbo.'

No response.

'Hasn't that gone fast?'

With a roar, the man leapt from the bed, hurled himself against the glass wall. He pounded the glass with his hands as he howled into the darkness.

Silence. Then a chuckle. 'You need to start biting your nails again, Jimbo.'

The man lowered his head.

'Perhaps we're feeding you too much.'

'Please.'

'Just ten more sleeps, Jimbo.'

'Please!'

'A deal's a deal.'

The man slid down the glass wall, slumped in a heap on the floor, face pressed against the glass. The blackness within, the blackness beyond.

'So, I guess we don't need to ask what you'd like for your birthday?' The voice, playful once more.

The man raised his fingers to his face, felt his cheek. 'Am I still …?'

'Yes …' The voice, pre-empting the question. 'You are … human.' He paused. 'But you might find company a bit of a struggle.'

The man let his hands fall to his lap.

'But then, you don't have to worry about that.'

The man lay on the cold damp floor.

'So. Jimbo.' The voice, jaunty again.

The man rubbed his face against the course stone.

'We'll leave you in peace.'

Silence.

'Peace and quiet.'

The man lay still.

'Night, night.' A pause. 'Don't let the bedbugs bite.'

A click. And the voice was gone.

The crushing silence returned. Fierce, screeching, pounding silence.

He held the palms of his hands tight over his ears. He began to scream, his cries drowned out by the thunder of the quiet that enveloped him.

SUNDAY 22ND SEPTEMBER, 7.30 PM

THE DATA ROOM, CRATOR CAPITAL, LONDON

Rhea Moore held her pass against the scanner. The light turned green. A click and a hiss as the air seals disengaged. The grey steel door slid open with a rumble, sending a tremor through the tiled floor. She stepped into the room. The air, chill and dry, sharp against her skin. The main processing unit loomed above her, humming with undefined intent. Silicon sinew wrapped in black steel, lights pulsing from deep within. The door slid shut behind her.

'It won't bite.'

She jumped at the sound of the voice.

Scutt emerged from underneath one of the consoles that lined the wall. He rolled his shoulders as he stood up, trademark baggy jeans and fading T-shirt, the eagle tattoo on his right bicep at odds with his boyish features. He looked across at her, a frown spreading across his face. 'Did I scare you?'

Rhea took a deep breath, exhaling slowly as she looked across at him. 'It's not you, it's me. I scare easily.'

Scutt frowned. 'So I did scare you?'

She studied him for a moment, then began to smile. 'Ignore me, I'm being silly.'

'So I really did scare you?'

She blinked. 'No, honestly, I was miles away, I was thinking about something else and you just … popped up.' She tried another smile, tilted her head to one side, strands from her bob of blonde hair swaying across her elfin features.

He stood in silence for some moments as he wiped his hands on his T-shirt. 'You know, everyone thinks I'm a lost cause.' He looked down at his fingers, began to wipe them down the sides of his jeans. 'So I've got an excuse.'

'I overreacted, don't give it another thought, really.'

Scutt looked across at her, a look of puzzlement on his face.

'Deadlines. They do this to me, they make me edgy.' Rhea gave a grimace.

Scutt began to shake his head. 'I'm not talking about that, I'm talking about this.' He spread the palms of his hands, the grease from the pipes still glistening on his fingertips. 'Sunday evening. You're here.'

She glanced around the room. 'Well, you know how it is.' She looked across at him, concentration etched on her face. 'A couple of hours should do it, I think.'

'Surely you've got better things to do?'

Rhea shrugged.

'Pretty girl like you.'

They both stood in silence.

The steady purr of the air conditioning from the shadows above them.

Scutt closed his eyes. 'I really said that, didn't I?'

Rhea cleared her throat. 'It's a fair question.'

He looked across at her. 'I seem to spend my life apologising.' He paused. 'And I'm crap at that as well.'

She flashed him a smile. 'Maybe I'm just a numbers girl.'

He nodded.

She looked up at the glinting obelisk that seemed to cow the room. 'Like Theodora.' She narrowed her eyes. 'You know, I'm really not sure I'd like to be alone with it.'

Scutt gave a scowl.

'I mean her.' Rhea corrected herself.

Scutt nodded in approval. 'Theodora.' He paused. 'She's a pussy cat.'

'A pussy cat?'

Lights, flickering, pulsing from deep within the core.

'A great big, humming, shuddering pussy cat.' Scutt nodded. 'And she's quite a specimen you'd have to say.'

Rhea turned towards Scutt. 'Theodora.' She paused. 'Is she listening to us, right now?'

He took a deep breath. 'Do you really want to know?' He walked up to Theodora, laying the palm of his hand on her steel casing, rising cold and sheer above them.

She gave a slight frown. 'I suppose so.'

Scutt took a step back, looking up at Theodora's full height, the top of the structure lost in the shadows of the pipework slung above them. 'Are you listening, Theodora?'

Silence.

'Are you, Theodora?'

More lights, pulsing deep within the tight-coiled wiring. 'That's what they call me, yes.' A female voice, the soft vowels, measured, thoughtful.

Rhea looked across at Scutt, her eyes widening. 'I didn't know she could talk.'

Scutt shook his head. 'She can't. Not really.' He took a deep breath. 'But she knows what she knows.'

Rhea glanced up at the tower of steel-wrapped silicon, raised a hand to her neckline, pulling the collar of her cardigan more tightly around her.

'I've probably said too much.' Scutt toyed with his leather bracelet.

Rhea stood in silence looking up at the machine.

'No, I've definitely said too much.' He glanced across at Rhea.

Rhea didn't reply, still staring up at the humming wall of steel.

'Look, can we just start this again?' Scutt took a step towards her. 'You know, from the beginning?'

Rhea turned towards him, she blinked, a smile spreading across her face, the dimples on her cheeks, tiny pinched shadows under the lights. 'Sure.'

'Like it never happened.'

Rhea blinked again. 'Like you said, in one ear and out the other.' She tilted her head, her fair hair brushing her cheek. 'See, forgotten it already.'

Scutt swallowed. 'I'm serious.'

'I know.' She nodded, the concentration etched on her face again. 'Like you said, just a party trick. Of course she can't talk.'

Scutt toyed with the leather bracelet on his other wrist. 'Stays in this room, right?'

Rhea nodded.

'Deal?'

She nodded again. 'Deal.'

Scutt swallowed. 'I guess I owe you an answer then.'

Rhea looked across at him, deadpan.

He met her gaze, his jaw muscles tensing.

The air around them, quiet and still.

From somewhere in the darkness above, a clicking sound, the air conditioning, recalibrating.'

'Theodora.' Scutt's voice, almost a whisper. 'She's listening. She's always listening. And she remembers everything.' He paused, the faintest flicker of a smile. 'Well, almost everything.'

'I understand.' Rhea gave a nod, then threw a glance in the direction of Theodora. 'And I hope I haven't offended her.'

Scutt looked puzzled.

'When I said I wouldn't want to be alone with her.' Rhea gave him a mock-sheepish look. 'I didn't mean it, of course.'

Scutt studied Rhea's face for a moment, then relaxed his shoulders. 'She's got a thick skin.' He rapped his knuckles against the steel casing. 'And my sense of humour.'

'Just as well.'

'Anyway, they say looks aren't everything, isn't that right?' He patted Theodora fondly.

'There speaks the proud parent.'

He took a step back, gazing up at his creation. 'But my, she's a handsome beast.' He turned back to Rhea. 'Enough family tittle-tattle, let's get you hooked up.' He indicated one of the consoles lining the wall. 'I mean it's not as though the two of you are strangers anymore.'

They walked to the wall panel. Scutt placed his hand flat against the wall sensor. It beeped its approval. His name and the time flashed up on the display. Rhea placed hers on the adjacent panel. Another beep, her name joined his on the LED panel: 'Rhea Moore, Research Analyst'.

'And we're in.' Scutt pulled out a chair. 'Need any help with the prompts?'

'Peruvian ports. Bills of lading. Harbourmaster logs.' Rhea sat, her fingers hovering above the keyboard. 'Ilo, Tacna, Matarani.'

'Cathodes? Molybdenum ore?'

Rhea stared at the screen in front of her. Her fingers moved almost silently over the keys. 'Same for Antofagasta.'

'Lithium?'

'You're a step ahead of me.'

'Anything else?'

Rhea blinked, fingers paused above the keyboard. 'Thermal coal, Indonesia.'

'Muara Berau? Balikpapan?'

'Further along. Samarinda, Banjarmasin.'

'OK.'

'And the other Muara.'

'Muara Satui?'

Rhea looked up at Scutt. 'You are, literally, a mine of information.'

'Happy with that label.'

Rhea turned her attention back to the screen, fingers gliding over the keyboard.

Scutt remained by her side.

She looked up, flexing her fingers. She tried a smile. 'Scutt, can I say something?'

Scutt blushed.

'I know you won't take this personally, it's just …' She gave a slight tilt of the head, her impish features caught in the light from the screen.

Scutt frowned. 'Just what?'

Rhea swallowed. 'It's just that … that I find it hard to concentrate, with someone standing over me.'

Scutt exhaled. 'Look, I know I owe you.' He shifted his weight from one foot to the other. 'But you know the rules.'

Rhea steadied her fingers on the edge of the keyboard. 'You know what I'm doing, you really don't have to stand over me you know.'

Scutt toyed with his leather bracelet. 'Look, it's not that simple.' He swallowed. 'It's protocol. It's for everyone's benefit.' He paused. 'Keep us safe.'

She took a deep breath, lifted a hand, laid it on his arm. 'Honestly, it's fine.'

He looked down at her slender fingers lying across his forearm. 'Rhea, please.'

She ran her fingers across his wrist, as she held his gaze. 'You trust me, don't you Scutt?'

He swallowed. 'Fucking hell, Rhea.'

'I'll get it done in half the time.' She tried another smile, her shoulders tensing. 'Maybe we can grab a drink after, what do you say?'

Scutt took a deep breath, closed his eyes. He stood in silence for some moments, his shoulders rising and falling. He looked down at her again.

'You're a mate.' She tapped his wrist one more time, turned her attention back to the keyboard, fingers pattering over the keys, concentration once more etched on her features.

He slowly shook his head, turned, walked to the console on the far wall.

A noise. From somewhere beneath them.

Rhea froze.

A rustling, skittering sound.

A tremor, running through the cold tiles beneath their feet.

She looked up at Scutt, eyes widening. 'What was that?'

Scutt looked down at his console, straightened his keyboard. 'What was what?'

'That. That … scratching.' She frowned. 'Don't say you didn't hear it.'

Scutt blinked. He didn't reply.

Rhea looked at the floor, then up at Scutt. 'What's down there? Underneath us.'

He shrugged. 'Like any old city.' He paused, blinking. 'No one really knows.'

She pulled her cardigan tighter around her shoulders, took a deep breath, turned back to the keyboard.

Another noise from below.

A muffled clang, metal closing on metal, a shudder through the floor.

She turned towards him.

Scutt swallowed.

She held his gaze.

'Trains.' Scutt's jaw muscles tensing. 'They can make that noise.'

Rhea frowned. 'Trains?'

'The older models.' He cleared his throat. 'To do with the bearings. I think.'

She pursed her lips. 'Bearings.'

They both fell silent.

Scutt swallowed again. 'Peru. You ever been?'

She straightened up in her chair, glanced down at the floor, then across to Scutt. She narrowed her eyes, exhaled, shook her head. 'No, I've never been.'

'Me neither.' He touched a finger to his temple. 'But in here.' He tried a smile. 'The clank of the cranes, the screeching of the seagulls, the Pacific swells rolling in from the distance.'

Rhea turned back to the screen. 'I thought you never went on holiday.' Her fingers once more gliding across the keys.

Scutt shrugged. 'Maybe I just haven't found the right person to go with.'

Rhea's fingers paused, hovering.

Scutt cleared his throat again. 'Just in general, I mean.'

Her fingers resumed their patter.

'I didn't mean to …'

'Of course not. It's fine.' Her brow furrowed in concentration.

He stood in silence for some moments.

A humming sound, from deep within Theodora.

Rhea glanced up momentarily, resumed her key strokes.

A pulse, like a drumbeat, building.

'Don't mind Theodora.' Scutt, his voice raised. 'She's just cooling off.'

Rhea kept her gaze firmly on the screen, her jaw set.

Scutt looked up at the steel leviathan, its lights blinking.

The sound of water, surging through hidden pipework. Rhea, staring straight ahead.

Theodora's frame began to vibrate, shuddering as the liquid roared through her.

Scutt laid a hand on Theodora's steel flank. 'Better?'

A whooshing sound, the drumbeat, slowing, Theodora's frame, settling.

Rhea bit her lip, hands still skimming over the keyboard.

'There you go.' Scutt turned back towards Rhea. 'And that's another reason.' He paused. 'I mean, who would look after her, if I'm not around?'

'She'd cope.' Rhea, her eyes still fixed on the screen.

'I dare say. But Theodora, she's a jealous bundle.'

Rhea blinked, one finger tapping the side of the keyboard.

Scutt frowned. 'I'm prattling on, aren't I?'

She didn't reply.

'I should shut up.'

Rhea leaned forward, eyes narrowed, fingers poised above the keys.

'Leave you in peace.'

She took a deep breath, turned slowly towards him. 'I'm sorry?'

'That's my line.'

Rhea gave a slight frown. 'Did I miss something?'

He smiled. 'I guess not.'

She turned back to the screen, fingers skittering across the keyboard.

He stood in silence.

'Seagulls.' Rhea sat upright. 'Do they have seagulls in Peru?'

'In my Peru. The one in my head.' He paused. 'The sky's full of them.'

SUNDAY 22ND SEPTEMBER, 8 PM

CARPARK, MI6 HQ, LONDON

The car rumbled down the ramp, the headlight beams racing over the slick black tarmac, glancing off the cold stonework arching around them.

A frown settled across Sebastian Noon's hawklike features as he stared straight ahead. He tightened his fingers around the armrest as the car swept around to the left, the silhouette of the driver smudged against the curve of the glinting white wall skimming past them.

They reached the bottom of the ramp, the car's suspension thumping as they swept into the car park, tyres squealing on the slick surface, the growl of the engine echoing around the concrete cavern.

Noon shifted in his seat as they drove deeper into the garage. The lights strung above them, strips of white reaching into the distance. On either side, the silent rows of parked cars, sombre colours, the glow of the neon, glancing off the paintwork.

Ahead of them, the turning area, tyre marks scoring the worn roadway, the damp tarmac shimmering under the arc lights.

Noon flinched as a figure stepped out from the shadows by the lift shaft.

It was Pritchard.

Noon opened the car door, stepped out onto the forecourt, carefully clicked it closed.

The car purred away into the semi-darkness.

'What a nice surprise.' Noon, his best poker face.

'Well, look at you.' Pritchard's northern vowels. 'Bloody spectre at the feast.'

Noon drew himself to his full height.

'Dracula in Savile Row.' Pritchard gave a snort.

'Little past your bedtime isn't it?' Noon raised an eyebrow.

'Make a habit of it, do you?' Pritchard's broad forehead crimping into a frown.

'They say at our age, everything's a habit.'

'You and Emma Wilson. Just happened to be going that way, were you?'

Noon gazed down at him, a look of mild annoyance etched across his features. 'What are you trying to say?'

'I can rule a few things out.' Pritchard nodded as he continued to study the taller man's face. 'I mean it's not as though you were hoping for a back-seat handjob.' He gave another little snort. 'Man of your ... particular tastes.'

'Please.' Noon adopted a pained expression. 'Even you can do better than that.'

Pritchard took a deep breath, his thickset shoulders heaving beneath his jacket. 'She's due back on Thursday.'

He let the words hang in the air.

Pritchard's eyes narrowed. 'So what was it, Sebastian, that just couldn't wait?'

Noon's face, as still as wax.

A car door slammed, somewhere in the far reaches of the chill darkness, the metallic crunch echoing off the unforgiving concrete.

'Which begs the question …' Pritchard's jaw, set square.

Noon reached up, slowly removing his spectacles. 'Why not just hand luggage?' Another arch of the eyebrows.

'Very funny.' Pritchard ground his teeth. 'What are you and Wilson up to?'

Noon shifted his weight back onto his good foot as he tried to relax his shoulders. 'Just catching up.'

'Hong Kong's our operation.' His jaw muscles, tensing. 'Counter Intelligence's got no business in this.'

Noon took a breath, exhaling slowly as he replaced his spectacles. 'Who says we were talking about Hong Kong?'

'Fuck off, Sebastian.' The Yorkshire vowels carving the word into 'fook.'

'Montenegro.' Noon paused, a slight shrug of the shoulders. 'We were discussing Montenegro.'

Pritchard stood in silence for a moment, his dark eyes, in the shadow of his heavy brow, fixed on Noon. 'If you had your doubts about her, you wouldn't even be talking.'

'It's not a question of blame,' a slight frown denting Noon's high forehead, 'it's about … clarity.' He shifted his weight to his other foot.

Pritchard glanced down. Noon's brogues, immaculate as ever. You'd never guess about the leg. 'Even so.' He looked up at Noon. 'My point stands.' He nodded for emphasis. 'Stay out of this.' He paused. 'We've enough to worry about as it is.'

Noon gave a slight shrug.

'Her and McKay.' Pritchard ran his fingers through his dark curly hair. 'Fifteen years ago. But even so.'

Noon frowned. 'You signed off on it.'

'Aye.' Pritchard clenched his jaw. 'And your girl better not let us down.'

'She's not my girl anymore.'

Pritchard shook his head. 'Don't give me that. Thick as thieves, you and Wilson. Always were.'

'This is on you.' A hint of a smile playing on Noon's lips. 'We'll just sit back and enjoy the show.'

'If this goes down,' Pritchard snarled the words out, 'you're bloody well going down with it.'

'Really?' Noon removed his spectacles, his smile broadening. 'Is that a promise.'

Pritchard gave another snort. 'You really are a tosser, you know that?'

'Well thank you, Ben.' Noon nodded sagely. 'Coming from you, that means a lot.'

MONDAY

MONDAY 23RD SEPTEMBER, 2.45 AM

BARNES, LONDON

DI Anne Perry sat bolt upright in bed, her breath caught in her throat. 'No!'

'What are you ...?' Her husband stirred beside her, propped himself up on one elbow, squinting in the gloom. 'Anne?'

She stretched out for the light beside her, fumbling in the dark. Her hand settled on the switch, light streamed across the room.

She exhaled, slumped back on the pillow, facing the light. 'I daren't close my eyes.' She shuddered. 'When it starts I ... can't stop.'

He rested his hand on her shoulder. 'What did you used to say to the kids?'

'Grown-up dreams are different.' She turned onto her back, looking up at him, her pale features framed by her auburn hair strewn across the pillow. 'We should know better.'

He looked down at her for a moment, the hint of a frown across his angular features. He turned towards the bedside table, reaching for his spectacles.

Anne closed her eyes. 'Sorry, Mr P.'

He slipped them on, turned towards her, laying the palm of his hand on her forehead. 'Gosh, you're hot.'

'Bit early in the day for compliments.' She tried a smile. 'But I'll take it.'

He gave a chuckle, the smile lines around his eyes crinkled shadows in the half-light. He folded back the duvet, swung his legs over the side of the bed. The light from the bedside table threw his long shadow across the wooden floor, up onto the curtains, the material stirring lazily in the breeze from the open window. He glanced around the room, the wooden cupboards opposite the bed solemn in the half-light, the loop of string that served as the missing door handle still hanging down accusingly. 'I know.' He muttered to no one in particular. 'I'll get round to it.'

He walked to the window, boards creaking under his bare feet. He pulled a curtain aside, looked down at the street below. Leaves danced aimlessly in the breeze, little groups of lost revellers, rising and falling with the gusty rhythm. The road surface sparkled in the grey lamplight. In the distance, the sound of the traffic on the Lower Richmond Road, humming, pattering.

A fox strolled across the road, tail sweeping nonchalantly from side to side.

'Mr Fox.' Mr P smiled. 'Your time of night.'

Anne picked up her phone. 'Not even 3.00.' She let the phone slip out of her fingers onto the bedside table. 'Bugger.'

He kept his eye on the fox.

The animal stopped, as though sensing an audience. It looked up at him from the pavement below, its eyes glinting in the glow of the street lights.

Mr P nodded. 'From the darkness he came.'

The fox met his gaze.

'Like an unwelcome thought.'

The animal sniffed the night air, turned, trotted back into the shadows.

Mr P dropped his hand, the curtain settled back into place. He turned around. 'I know they all look the same.' He ran a hand through his thinning grey hair. 'But whenever I see a fox, I get this funny feeling we've met before.'

She stared up at the ceiling, the spars on the lampshade dark beams across the pale paintwork. 'I still feel like I'm going round … and round.' She exhaled. 'The water it's … thick, and dark. Darker, the lower I go.' She closed her eyes. 'And there's something down there. I can't see it, but I know it's there.' She swallowed. 'Waiting.'

He stood by the side of the bed, his pyjamas hanging loosely over his slim frame. 'Tell me, do I indulge you or scold you?'

She looked across at him, her face, half in shadow, a smile playing around her lips. 'I really don't know.'

'Perhaps,' he sat down on the side of the bed, 'you should take the hint.' He raised his eyebrows. 'Your dreams didn't used to be this gothic.'

Anne exhaled, sat up in bed, pushing a pillow up behind her. She leaned back, nestling her shoulders against it. 'My dreams?' She turned towards him. 'They find me, but they're not me.'

He climbed back into bed, sat beside her, his back against the headboard.

She glanced across at him, a mock frown playing across her soft features. 'You've got that look.' She paused. 'I think I've seen this movie.'

'Can't I be predictable now and again?'

'Please don't make me feel like an idiot.'

He nodded. 'I know you really wanted this job.'

'This isn't about the job.'

He exhaled. 'Anne, just listen.'

'I hate it when you're trying to be reasonable.'

'These dreams.' He looked across at her. 'I don't even have to say it.'

She sat in silence. The rumble of the traffic, the resting pulse of a sleeping city.

'Because this is you.' He paused. 'Talking to you.'

She turned towards him. A gust of wind rattled the window frame, the curtains stirred back to life with a weary rustle. 'I took the job,' she paused, 'because I wanted it.'

'Seeing those things, every day, you're too …'

'Don't say sensitive.'

He glanced over at her. 'I was after something like …
thoughtful.'

She exhaled. 'When my mother first saw colour TV
she said it made her feel funny.' She looked across at her
husband. 'All that colour. Too fierce.'

He met her gaze.

'But she got used to it.'

He nodded. 'Never gave her nightmares though.'

She looked away, closed her eyes.

'Dead people.' He paused. 'Most of us aren't built
for that.'

A car horn sounded in the distance, a plaintive call in
the still of the London darkness.

He raised a hand, ran the back of his fingers down her
soft cheek. 'Look at you. This isn't a face made to peer
into the darkness.'

She opened her eyes, looked across at him, the lines
on her forehead streaky shadows in the dappled light.
'You're building up to something.' Her eyes, flicking across
his face.

Mr P gave a little nod. 'I was thinking just now, looking
at that fox.' He paused, forehead pinched in concentration.
'The darkness, it's all right for him, that's his world.' He
nodded. 'A place without pity.'

She looked across at him. 'How do you know it was
a "he"?'

'Padding down the dark alleys, in the shadow of the splintered wood, the rusty wire.' He paused. 'Just himself. Friendless.'

She pulled up her knees under the duvet, wrapped her arms around them. 'Is this meant to cheer me up?'

He studied her face for a moment. 'Remember what I said to you? When you got the offer to join the department?'

'Did it involve foxes?'

'You'll need a stone heart to do those kinds of cases.'

She took a breath, leaned back against the pillow. 'It's a thing, you know.' She exhaled. 'Dead bodies, they call out.' She paused. 'I hear them, and I answer them.' She looked across at him. 'I'm all they have.'

He closed his eyes. 'The dead can't "have", Anne.'

'Whatever the horror of their final moments.' She shook her head. 'That shouldn't be the end of their story.'

He lay in silence for some moments. 'The badness, Anne, it'll always be there. You can't take this burden. The dead are the dead.' He squeezed her shoulder.

'I'm sorry I woke you.'

'You were happier when you were dealing with living members of the public.'

She looked up at him. 'Actually, it's not always that easy to tell the difference.'

He smiled. 'You should go back to ticking off shop-lifters and helping old ladies across the road.' He paused.

'Or was it the other way round?' He reached behind his back, rearranged his pillow and lay back down, pulling up the duvet. 'Anyway, bedtime. Again.'

She leaned over, turned out the light, lay back down, shrugging her shoulders as she nestled into her pillow. She closed her eyes. 'You know the scariest thing about my dream?'

He didn't respond.

'When I'm caught in this whirlpool, when its spinning me, pulling me down, down into the blackness.' She exhaled. 'There's a part of me that's … almost liking it.'

Silence.

'Mr P,' she whispered.

A car door slammed somewhere down the street, voices on the breeze.

'Are you asleep?'

Just the tick of the bedside clock, nagging her about the hour.

MONDAY 23RD SEPTEMBER, 3.45 AM GMT

ON BOARD FLIGHT BA 27, LONDON TO HONG KONG

Emma Wilson reached out, steadied herself against the bulkhead as the aeroplane juddered again. She glanced around the galley. The two other cabin crew sat in the jump seats by the starboard door. One rested her hands on a paperback lying on her lap, her head lolling from side to side with the rocking of the plane. The light caught her name badge: Alison Ridge, a French tricolour beside it adding a dash of colour. She was asleep. The other leaned forward, studying her iPad, frowning as she tapped the keyboard.

Emma looked at her watch. Nearly four in the morning, Heathrow time. She walked to the window in the port-side door. The skies were clear. Down below, pinpricks of light, the few scattered settlements on the southern Siberian steppe. Further north, a brighter cluster, a city, Yekaterinburg, or Chelyabinsk perhaps. The plane bucked again. She steadied herself, peered through the gap in the galley curtains into the business-class section. Two pools of light at the back, a couple in row 16 stirred awake by the turbulence. The rest of the cabin, outlines of figures, stretched out in the shadows, silent and still. The emergency lights on the gangway floor, strips of blue, a chill glow, shimmering beneath the darkness of the cabin. The plane shook again. The hum and growl of the engines, rumbling through the thin night air.

She stepped through the galley curtains, opened the door to the coat-hanging cupboard. She squinted in the half-light, trying to read the seat numbers stuck to the hangers, her fingers flicking through the swaying jackets. There, 15A, she checked the name. Borso, Milot. She slowly slipped the jacket from the hanger, folded it, holding it to her chest as she turned her back to the cabin. She closed the cupboard door and slipped through the curtains back into the galley.

The colleague with the iPad was now mouthing silent rebukes as she continued to tap the keyboard, scowling as she did so. The plane gave a shudder. The woman glanced up, reached over to her sleeping colleague, settled her bobbling head back against the headrest, then turned back to the iPad.

Emma sat by the door on the other side of the galley. She laid the jacket on her lap, reached down into her handbag, pulled out a sewing kit. She took out a pair of thin-bladed scissors, unpicked the stitching on one side of the lapel. She glanced across at her colleagues, both in their own worlds. She unzipped a side pocket in her handbag, pulled out the miniature electronic device, slipped it into the lining of the lapel. She picked up a needle and thread, began to restitch the lapel border.

The plane gave another jolt.

Emma flinched as the needle slipped, pricked her finger. She looked down, a tiny droplet of blood appearing on her fingertip. She wiped it on the hem of her skirt uniform, checked that the bleeding had stopped, resumed her stitching.

The shaking began again.

Emma leaned back against the jump seat to steady herself.

A final kick and the aircraft settled back down.

She held the jacket close to her face, examining the handiwork. She dropped the sewing kit into her handbag, stood up, dipped through the curtains back into the cabin.

The ranks of recumbent figures, slumbering in the darkness.

She slipped the jacket back on the hanger, closed the cupboard door and ducked back into the galley. She stood at the galley counter, poured a glass of water.

She heard a movement behind her and turned around. The Cabin Service Director stepped through the curtains from First.

'Evening.' Emma raised her voice, hoping to wake her colleague dozing by the starboard door.

The CSD raised his eyebrows. 'I think there's one passenger in row 14 who didn't hear that. Why don't you use the megaphone next time.'

Emma held up a hand. Tried a smile.

He frowned. 'I thought I knew all the faces on this route.'

'Gail.' Emma lifted up her name badge. 'Gail Notts.'

'You're new.'

'Been on crew standby. Just got the call today.'

He looked her up and down. 'I mean new new.'

'That obvious?'

'Your feet.'

Emma glanced down. Shoes still clean, polished.

'Too close together.' He paused. 'And too straight, no wonder you're holding on.' He indicated her hand planted on the galley work surface. He shook his head. 'What do they teach you in Basic Training?'

'It was mainly on the SEPs.'

'Not much use if you're on your arse.'

Emma frowned. 'Excuse me?'

'Yes, I said arse.' He smiled. 'Airborne rules.' He glanced across at her two colleagues, both now on their feet. One was rearranging the snack tray, the other refilling the coffee reservoir. He addressed the elder. 'Kate. All good?'

She looked up, nodded. 'Hello Clive. Do the flight deck need something?'

'No, just popping by.' He glanced around. 'How's the nut allergy in 12J?'

'Happily snoring his way there.'

'Anyone been back to WT?'

'Carrie came by to borrow some tonics half an hour ago, didn't mention anything.'

Clive nodded. 'Let me know if something changes.' He ducked through the curtains back into First.

'Right.' Kate shook her head. 'What a waste.' She muttered to no one in particular. 'Buns like that.'

Her younger colleague turned to Emma, raised a hand in acknowledgement. 'Respect.'

Emma nodded.

'And I'm not a light sleeper.' Alison slapped a high five with Emma.

A head appeared between the curtains to the business-class cabin, eyeshades on his forehead, eyelids still heavy with sleep. 'Can I get a cup of tea?' he rasped.

Alison turned towards the intruder. 'The fasten seat belts sign is still on.'

'I just want a cup of tea.'

'We're not serving hot drinks until we're through this weather.'

'What weather?'

'Can I bring you a glass of water? Juice?'

He frowned, glanced around the galley. 'Have you got any more of that Bordeaux?'

'Sure.' Alison nodded. 'I'll bring it to you.'

'Thanks.' The face disappeared through the gap in the curtains.

She picked up a bottle from the drinks carrier, poured a glass. 'I'll check the cabin whilst I'm medicating handsome.'

'Perfect.'

The younger woman ducked through the curtains into the darkened cabin.

Kate readjusted the hair clip on the back of her head, turned towards Emma. 'You need to get a colleague to check that out.' She nodded towards Emma's hand.

Emma furrowed her brow. 'Check what out?'

'If you draw blood.' She paused. 'Even if it's just a pinprick. Literally.'

Emma met her gaze.

'Let me see.' She held out her hand towards Emma.

'It's fine. Nothing.'

'My galley, my rules.'

Emma bit her lip, held out her hand.

Kate examined the finger. 'If someone ended up with a blood-smudge on his glass we'd both be in trouble.' She reached up to a cupboard, pulled out a first aid kit. 'You know, I've never seen anyone do that.'

Emma frowned. 'Easily done.'

'I mean actually use a mending kit.' Kate swabbed the finger with an antiseptic wipe, unwrapped a plaster. 'Even though we carry one.'

Emma kept her eyes on her finger as Kate applied the plaster. She didn't reply.

'Unconventional.' Kate looked up at Emma. 'But why not?'

'Thanks.' Emma flexed her finger.

'Mobile number? Time and a place?'

Emma swallowed. 'Button was coming off.'

Kate tilted her head to one side. 'You got some moves on you.'

'Said I'd fix it.'

Kate raised her eyebrows. 'Do I guess or are you going to tell me?'

Emma blinked.

'14B with the come-to-bed eyes? The guy with the tats in 12G?'

Emma looked down at the floor.

'Pecs and cheekbones, 13J?' Kate shook her head. 'I was going to say "at our age we should know better". She smiled. 'But thankfully that's not true.'

Alison reappeared with a flap of the curtains. 'I could never go out with a guy who snored.'

'All OK?' Kate glanced across at her.

'I could swear 11E's giving 11F a handjob.' Alison put the empty glasses into the rack.

'Got their belts on I trust.' Kate checked the thermostat gauge.

The Cabin Service Director strode through the curtain from First, drawing it closed behind him. 'I hope none of you ladies have overdone it on the First Class canapés tonight.'

'Shit.' Kate turned towards him. 'How long we got?'

'A few minutes. Three maybe … no more than four.' He nodded to Kate. 'You know what to do.'

'Right.'

'I need to get down to Carrie.' He disappeared through the curtain to the main cabin.

Kate turned to Alison. 'Secure the galley and clear and lock the bathrooms.' Alison swept to the galley station, emptied the hot water into the sink, clicked off the power switches to the ovens.

'You haven't done this before have you?' Kate looked across at Emma. 'Fuck it, just come with me.' She turned towards the cabin, then spun around, grabbed Emma by the arm. 'Try not to wake them unless you have to.' Kate hissed. 'All the glasses you can find. Back here. Leave the belts to me. Calm and smiley. All right?'

Emma nodded.

They moved through the cabin together, scanning seats and tables for the glint of glassware in the half-light. Kate's hands moved deftly from one sleeping figure to another checking belts.

The stopped beside one passenger, stretched out flat on his front. Kate nudged his shoulder. 'Sir, you need to turn over.'

'What?' More asleep than awake.

'On to your back. That's it, perfect.'

He mumbled something in a language neither could understand, settled himself back into the pillow.

They walked back, measured pace. They stepped into the galley.

The surfaces were bare.

Alison was locking the last of the cupboards. 'Bathrooms clear and locked.' She called over her shoulder.

'Thanks.' Kate led Emma towards the port-side jump seats. 'You sit next to me.'

The CSD reappeared. 'Neat job.' He glanced around the galley. 'Wish I could teach my flatmate how to do that.' He glanced over to Kate, smiled, then patted Alison on the arm as he walked through to First.

'Get settled in, girls.' Kate tied back the drapes to the cabin, sat down next to Emma, checking her safety straps. 'That'll do.' She settled back, tightened her own.

Emma sat back against the headrest, closed her eyes.

The rumble of the engines the only sound as the galley fell silent.

'What do you reckon?' Kate looked across at Alison.

Alison pursed her lips, studying Emma's face. 'I don't know … a yelper?'

Kate smiled. 'Groaner maybe?'

Emma opened her eyes. 'This isn't going to be like being in the simulator is it?'

Kate patted Emma's knee. 'Just do what we do.'

Emma took a deep breath. 'If I need to start worrying,' she exhaled, 'please don't tell me.'

The plane lurched downwards, as though dropped by some giant hand, engines roaring as they strained for purchase in the cold black air.

Emma gripped the edge of her seat.

With a crash the aircraft levelled out, the plane shaking as the wings fought for lift in the swirling currents.

Shrieks from the cabin as the passengers jolted awake. Glassware smashing against cupboard walls. Laptops and books clattering down on the gangway floors.

'Ladies and gentlemen,' Clive's soothing tones over the PA system. 'as you see we're just experiencing some routine turbulence, so if you could all just sit tight with the seat belt securely fastened we should be through it very soon.'

The aircraft plummeted again.

Emma gritted her teeth.

Another crash and a shudder as the plane levelled off.

More shrieks from the cabin.

Heads bobbing out from the aisle seats, looking towards Kate and Emma, the fear in their eyes.

Kate nudged Emma in the ribs.

They both fashioned a smile.

More smashing glass. Liquid now leaking onto the galley floor from one of the cupboards.

'There goes our pre's.' Alison rolled her eyes.

A passenger in the business-class section was on his feet, scanning the floor around him. 'Fuck! My laptop!'

'Sir!' Kate shouted to him. 'You need to sit down!'

He knelt down, peering under the seats.

'He'll break his fucking neck,' Kate hissed. 'Sir! Sit back down!'

The plane shuddered, engines screeching as the plane tore through the churning darkness.

Kate reached down to her belt release catch. 'Sir!'

With a lurch the plane tilted to one side.

The man kneeling on the ground spun onto his back, sliding across the gangway floor.

Kate clicked the belt release, hurled herself towards him, clinging on to the seat backs, hand over hand. She knelt down by the prone passenger. 'You OK?'

Emma right beside her.

Emma lifted his wrist, fingers on his pulse. He stared up at them.

'Nod if you understand me.' Emma leaned over him. 'I'm OK.'

They helped him to his feet, leaning against the seat backs to steady themselves.

They clipped his seat belt shut.

'Sorry.' He muttered.

The aircraft bucked again. Kate stumbled, thrown off balance. Emma threw out a hand, catching Kate's arm.

Kate steadied herself, glanced across at Emma, nodded.

They edged back to their jump seats, sat down, pulled the straps over their shoulders.

'If your date falls through,' Kate clicked her belt buckle shut, 'drinks on me.' She looked across at Emma. 'How about it? Naughty forties night out. You and me.'

'I'd cramp your style.'

Kate smiled. 'Somehow, I don't think so.'

Emma sat back, tucked her hair behind her ear.

Alison continued to make comic faces to the nervous teenage girl in 12G.

The lady in 15B was still sobbing.

The man in 15A was patting her arm, talking quietly, trying to soothe her alarm.

Out in the freezing blackness, the engines roared defiance at the storm as the plane plunged onwards through the tumbling night sky.

MONDAY 23RD SEPTEMBER, 10 AM
THE DATA ROOM, CRATOR CAPITAL, LONDON

'Lock the door.' The words, booming out of the shadows above him, echoing off the bare walls, pounding around him.

Scutt sat up with a start, eyes darting.

'It's only us.' A different voice, a softer tone, a more subtle kind of menace. 'Mr Lawrence and Mr Bernhard.' The clipped English vowels, sharp in the chill air.

Scutt slowly rose to his feet, the first beads of perspiration glinting on his forehead. He looked up at the ceiling, into the darkness beyond the spotlights suspended above him. 'What do you want?' The fear crackling in his voice.

Theodora hummed, circuitry glinting.

'Thought we'd pay a visit.' The first voice again, the words clanging around him.

Scutt took a deep breath, the colour draining from his face.

'See how you're getting on.' The quieter companion, purring out the words like an expectant predator. 'You know what to do.'

Scutt gave a shudder, glancing around him, as though looking for somewhere to run. 'This must be a mistake!' His breathing, shallower now.

'Just do it, Scutt!' The words, roaring around him.

Scutt ducked his head, his slender shoulders hunched, as the fury of the voice washed around him. 'I haven't done anything!' He sobbed out the words.

'Just lock the main door, there's a good chap.' The almost affable tone. 'Before we hurt you in ways you don't want to imagine.'

Scutt rasped out a breath as he stared at the cold tiled floor. He swallowed, rose unsteadily to his feet, walked to the door, slid the bolt shut. He stood there, hand resting on the lock. He closed his eyes, the sound of his own heartbeat thundering in his ears. He swallowed again, trying to steady his breathing, drops of sweat creeping down his forehead.

Slowly the quiet of the room settled back around him, the patient hum of the air conditioning, the quiet murmur from deep within Theodora.

He raised the sleeve of his sweatshirt, wiping the perspiration from his brow.

Another sound. A new one. From behind him. He gave a gasp, his body tensing, as he slowly began to turn towards the noise.

A low rumbling, gears turning, air sweeping into the room, damper, an edge to it, a feral tang.

He turned around.

Another door had opened in the far wall, the light from the data room thrown across the passageway beyond. Slatted metal flooring, edging off into the shadows. Condensation, sticky beads of light clinging to the metalwork.

'Maybe, this time.' The voice, measured, patient. 'You can come to us.'

Scutt stared at the open doorway, the cold, damp air crinkling in the pale light, the darkness beyond, the sense of something, waiting.

'The night goggles are on the hook inside.' The tone, matter-of-fact. 'Theodora can look after herself for a while.'

Scutt swallowed again. He walked towards the open doorway, wincing as the fierce air billowed over him. He stepped onto the grate beyond the door, reached up for the night goggles, slid them over his head.

The door shuddered back into life, gears grinding. The air shook as the steel door clanked shut behind him.

He stood in the darkness. The air around him, musty, the base notes of decay.

'Give yourself a moment.'

Scutt closed his eyes. Opened them again.

'Well.' The voice, jauntier now. 'Come down and join us.'

The steel staircase curved below him, the outline of the steps sketched in luminescent green, strips of ghostly moss, clinging on to life in the dank blackness. He held the handrail, reached the last step. He looked up.

Two figures stood in front of him. One shorter, thickset, the other, taller, slimmer. Dressed in black, the outlines of their heads distended by the night goggle head straps, their eyes, pools of ghostly green.

The shorter figure turned to the other. 'You know what they say, Mr Bernhard.'

Mr Bernhard turned towards the speaker. 'Do I know what they say, Mr Lawrence?'

Mr Lawrence held up a finger. 'You never forget a face.'

'Never forget a face.' Mr Bernhard, his night goggles nodding in agreement.

Mr Lawrence took Scutt by the shoulder, led him to the glass wall that framed one side of the corridor. 'There you go, Scutt.' His deep voice, almost jocular. 'Just let your eyes adjust.'

They stood either side of Scutt, all three of them peering through the glass wall, night goggles glowing.

The figure on the other side began to take shape in the darkness. It looked like a man, the ragged remains of clothes wrapped around him. His face partly visible through a tangle of hair and beard. He sat on the bed. Staring straight ahead. At them. Or at nothing.

Scutt gasped, a sharp intake of breath, the chill, stale air catching in his throat.

'I doubt he'd recognise you. Even if he could see through the glass.' Mr Lawrence nodded, thoughtfully. 'Or anyone, for that matter. Not now.'

Scutt tried to say something, his lips shaping sound-less words.

'Doesn't know whether he's awake or asleep.' Mr Bernhard made a tutting sound. 'Probably doesn't know whether he's alive or dead.' He shook his head. 'All this time. To ponder. In the blinding darkness, the booming silence. Easy to forget what senses felt like.'

Scutt swallowed. 'Why am I here?'

'Serotonin,' Mr Bernhard continued. 'Without sunlight, without any light, you can't make it.' He turned towards Scutt. 'Take a look into those eyes of his.' He paused. 'Too dead to be alive, but too alive to be dead.' Mr Bernhard studied the figure. 'You know what's turning around in that head of his?'

Scutt stared at the figure. The eyes, pools of darkness.

'He wants to kill. He wants to hurt. Purposefully, carefully, without limits.' Mr Bernhard paused. 'Now the serotonin's gone, he'll be psychotic, probably psychopathic.' He nodded. 'In there, in the darkness, he's the predator. Every inch of that cell, every scratch on the wall, every furrow in the floor.' He turned towards Scutt. 'He'll hear your screams, but that circuit breaker's gone now.' He paused. 'No sympathy, no pity. Just the cold-pressed need to bury his fists and nails and teeth in flesh, and to feel someone else's helpless terror.'

Scutt began to shake.

'He was a friend of yours wasn't he?' Mr Lawrence's friendly tones.

Scutt nodded.

'Shame. For the friendship to end like that. Torn and punctured, bleeding out in the darkness, shuddering from pain.' Mr Lawrence paused. 'Been good knowing you, Jimbo.'

Scutt put a hand to his mouth in silent horror.

'Holiday planning.' Mr Lawrence turned to Scutt. 'Is that what this is?'

Scutt glanced across at him, blinking. 'What?'

'Santa Maria, Rio Cordoba, Puerto Drummond, Barranquilla.'

'I don't—'

'You and Rhea Moore, the Colombian coast.'

'But … this was just …' Scutt looked from one to the other, his eyes, pleading. 'Ellis Wagner, he asked her to check the shipping and the bills of lading. Lithium, out of the Peruvian ports, Chile. Cobalt as well. Pointe Noire and Matadi. I logged it, sent a copy to Wagner. I followed the rules.'

Mr Bernhard leaned towards Scutt, an edge to his voice now. 'What was she doing mapping transport movements along the Colombian coast?'

'I … I was there all the time.' Scutt looked from one to the other. 'She didn't ask anything about Colombia. I thought it was just the … lithium, cobalt, for the—'

'But your Theodora.' Mr Lawrence carefully placed a finger on the centre of Scutt's chest. 'Can't keep her mouth shut. We only had to ask.' He looked across at his companion. 'Surprised you didn't.'

Scutt shook his head, stuttering. 'I was on her shoulder. I didn't think she'd have time to—'

'Forget those innocent Tinkerbell looks of hers. It's not the first time she's strayed there.' Mr Bernhard paused. 'Still cross-referencing her logs. We'll find out why soon enough. For now, you watch every keystroke. You know what to look for.'

Scutt nodded, swallowed again.

Mr Lawrence flicked his head towards the glass wall. 'I think he wants to say hello.'

Scutt slowly turned towards it.

The face, now pressed right up against the glass, eyes pools of black. The pupils, starved of light, dilated, distended.

Scutt flinched.

The figure was trying to speak. Lips forming the same words, over and over.

Mr Bernhard reached up to a switch on the wall, clicked on the sound system. 'What is it, Jimbo?'

'Just one.' The voice, hoarse, rasping out the words. 'Just one. Just … one.'

Scutt's eyes, widening in horror. 'What does he mean?'

Mr Lawrence turned to Scutt, a smile spreading over the half of his face visible beneath the night goggles. 'Do you want to get in there and ask him?'

Scutt opened his mouth. No sound emerged.

'You were buddies, after all.' Mr Bernhard paused. 'Back in the day.'

Scutt groaned, his eyes flickering.

'Space for two.' Mr Lawrence nodded. 'But only room for one. Right, Jimbo?'

The figure fell silent. He began to move his index finger on the glass, a single vertical stroke, the number 1.

MONDAY 23RD SEPTEMBER, 7.45 PM (11.45 AM GMT)

BONHAM STRAND, HONG KONG

Emma Wilson of MI6 glanced at her reflection as she crossed the hotel foyer. Bare shoulders, blue silk blouse ruffling in the breeze from the ceiling fans, her curves on show under the tight black skirt. She nodded to herself in silent approval. Just another high-end hooker. For the punter who appreciates a bit of experience.

She stepped through the entrance onto the street. Hong Kong. That aroma again. Cheap food and expensive perfume. She breathed it in as the heat of the city washed over her. Car horns sounded amid the street chatter. Cantonese vowels, strident and jocular. She let her weight move onto the balls of her feet, then rocked back onto her heels, feeling for her balance on the stilettos. She looked down Bonham Strand towards Central. Twilight. The neon signs hung across the road had crackled back to life, a man-made sunset in reds and yellows glowing above them.

She set off towards the Central-Mid-Levels walkways, settling into the pace of the crowd jostling around her, bobbing heads and swaying shoulders, the rhythm of the early evening.

She crossed onto Queen's Road, the bark of the traffic echoing off the glass towers that rose up sheer and slick on either side. The shop signs, bold and bright, glowing with self-importance. The windows a busy blur of colour. Shimmering above them, wrapped around the buildings like festive paper, languid figures framed glittering logos. Stained glass windows in this temple of the shopping gods.

Emma ducked into a shop doorway, leaned against the wall, pulled off a shoe whilst she scanned the street. She shook an imaginary stone from it, eyes darting from one side of the road to the other. No static figure, just the steady movement of the crowd.

She rejoined the throng, pilgrims to the beating heart of the city. A gust of wind swept over them, scarves and jackets flapping in the breeze. They passed under the colonnade, the hum of voices echoing off the stonework above.

Emma spotted the hummingbird, lit up in reds and blues, suspended above the door of the boutique. She stepped inside, glanced around the room. Five women. One turned away from her. The hummingbird hairclip. Emma walked towards her. The woman browsed a line of jackets hanging from the rail, running the fabric through her fingers. Emma stood beside her.

'A snug fit. I wouldn't go lower than a ten.' The woman spoke without turning, running a finger down the sleeve.

Emma took the jacket from the rail, slipped into one of the changing rooms.

She pulled the curtain across, feeling the weight of it in the jacket. She delved into a pocket, pulled out the Springfield XD automatic. She checked the magazine, clicked it back into the hand stock, slipped the weapon into her clutch bag. She reached into the other pocket. A piece of paper, the numbers 14 and 22. She laid the jacket down, took out her phone, checking the location of the tracker. She took a deep breath, put the phone and the piece of paper in the bag, picked up the jacket and swept back into the shop, laying it over the rack as she strode to the door and out onto the street.

The noise wrapped itself around her again, the rumble of the traffic, raised voices. Somewhere down the street a jackhammer clattered back to life. She rolled her shoulders, quickened her pace, her high heels clicking on the paving stones. The hotel entrance came into view. Emma stepped through the revolving door and into the foyer.

She stood for a moment, adjusting to the stillness after the clamour of the streets. The quiet of practised luxury.

A single grand chandelier hovered beneath the atrium roof, awing the room, flooding the space with its silky light. A torrent of cut glass, glinting fiery scales as they rustled in the current of the swirling fans. She glanced around her. The amber glow of the brass railings framing the staircase, the bright starched uniforms of the porters by the front desk, the glint of glass-topped tables.

She walked towards the lifts, confident steps, slight sashay of the hips. Just another hotel foyer. Work to do. Fleeting eye contact with the security man by the lift. The slightest nod of the head. Working girl protocol. World over.

She rode the elevator to the fourteenth floor. Stepped into the corridor, scanning the room numbers. The ceiling, luminous under the backlighting. A silhouette without a shadow as she glided noiselessly along the carpeted passageway. She located Room 22, checked her phone, slipped it back into her bag. Began to retrace her steps.

Emma found the chambermaid's trolley. Unattended. She snatched up a bath towel and a bottle of water, walked back to Room 22. She took off her shoes, placed them outside the room opposite, wrapped the bath towel around herself, clutching her handbag under the top of it. Just skin showing, bare shoulders, bare legs. She sprinkled the water over herself.

A thump as she barged against the door of 22.

'For fuck's sake!' She shouted. 'I don't fucking believe it!'

She padded down the corridor in the direction of the trolley.

The maid now standing beside it.

'Thank goodness.' Emma gasped. 'Stupidest thing.' She shook her head. 'My husband forgot his phone. I jumped out of the shower to run after him. The door slammed shut behind me.' She shook her wet shoulders. 'Would you believe it?'

The maid glanced down at Emma's bare legs; drops of water had collected by her feet. She looked back up at Emma's face. She frowned.

Emma shivered. 'Silly, I know.' She grimaced.

The maid narrowed her eyes, hesitating.

Emma shivered again.

The maid pursed her lips, then nodded. 'Which room, please?'

'You're a star. Twenty-two.'

Emma tripped along behind her.

They reached Room 22.

The maid slid the door key in, the lock clicked open.

'Thank you so much.' Emma sprang past the maid into the room, closing the door behind her.

Emma let the towel drop to the floor as she scanned the room, pulling on latex gloves.

The bedside lights were on, the rest of the room in semi-darkness.

She checked the bathroom, then walked to the window. The lights of Kowloon, filling the northern sky.

She turned, flicked on the torch on her phone.

The novel on the bedside table, geometrically aligned, edges parallel to the side of the table.

Files, on the dressing table. Same.

She opened the first file. CCF publicity material. The Crator Charitable Foundation. Cherish the Spark of Life.

She turned to the other file. His agenda, two pages.

She lifted up her phone, photographed them both.

The wardrobe. Everything unpacked. Shirts, another suit, all neatly hung, T-shirts, underwear, laid out on the shelves. She slipped the suit jacket from the hanger, sat down on the chair. She turned up the jacket collar, pulled the nail scissors from her bag, made a small incision in the lining. She slid the tracking device inside, stitched up the gap in the fabric, hung it back in the wardrobe.

She walked into the bathroom. Toothbrush next to the toothpaste, shaving equipment in an ordered line.

One used hand towel by the basin. Not folded. Discarded.

She returned to the main room. A last glance around the room. Just as he left it.

Emma picked up her towel, opened the door, stepped into the corridor.

The door clicked shut.

She looked up and down the empty corridor, took off the gloves, put them in her handbag.

Picked up her shoes from the opposite doorway, slipped them on, began to walk towards the lifts.

She stopped by a service door, pushing it open. Shelves of cleaning products. A Hoover, buckets, mops.

She stepped inside, dropped the towel into the bucket. Emptied a bottle of bleach over it, then dropped the bottle into the bucket.

A noise behind her.

Emma froze.

Voices in the corridor. Coming closer.

Emma swallowed.

They moved away.

She exhaled. Pushed open the door, strode back to the lift.

She rode it back down to the lobby.

The doors opened with a ping.

The security man narrowed his eyes.

Emma met his gaze, the slightest nod. Yep. No sale. Too niche for me.

A nod in return.

She walked across the foyer. Straight back, longer strides. The what-a-waste-of-time-that-was gait.

She stepped back onto the street.

The evening heat wrapped itself around her again, insistent, unyielding.

A city cab pulled up in front of her. The rear door sprang open.

She slid into the back seat as the door swung closed.

The cab pulled away from the kerb.

'Fuck, my feet are killing me.' Emma shook off her shoes, folded her legs beneath her as she massaged her toes.

The driver looked straight ahead.

She glanced up at the rear-view mirror. 'Evening, Fraser, how was your flight?'

'Better than yours, ma'am.' He paused. 'From what I heard.'

'That's the thing.' She glanced out of the window. 'He went out without taking a shower.'

The driver flicked the indicator, shifted lanes.

'After a flight like that you'd probably need two.' She leaned forward. 'There was just a hand towel, used, by the sink.' She paused. 'The maid hadn't been in to change them.'

'Anywhere in particular, ma'am?'

'Just head towards Causeway Bay, I'll get the metro back.' She tucked her hair behind her ear. 'Everything unpacked. Laid out. Carefully.'

'Right.'

'Forty minutes in his room. There was time for both.' She nodded. 'But he decides not to. Then he takes the metro over to Kowloon.' She took a deep breath. 'How does that work?'

'He's gone to a gym, or a bathhouse? Wouldn't make sense to shower beforehand.' He glanced at his passenger in the rear-view mirror.

She looked out of the window. The towers flanking Queensway soared up into the night sky. Glinting giants, scowling down at the frantic city. 'In Tsim Sha Tsui?'

She turned towards him, held out her hand. 'Give me your phone.'

He passed it back to her.

'Photos of his agenda. Two pages.' She synced the phones. 'Two days. Back-to-back charity meetings. Flying out day after tomorrow.' She handed the phone back to him. 'No rest for the wicked.'

He nodded.

'Make sure McKay gets these. And tell him I'm relying on him to track Borso. Wherever he goes. Whoever he meets. I put a tracker in his other suit.'

'Ma'am.'

She sat back in her seat. 'Two nights.' She glanced out of the window, the crowds thronging the pavements silhouetted against the gleaming shopfronts. 'Not sure I'd bother.'

He glanced back at her in the rear-view mirror.

'Unpacking everything. So carefully.' She looked back towards him. 'Don't answer, I'm just talking.'

He stared straight ahead.

'Everything laid out. Everything … on display.' She exhaled. 'Even his programme. Right there.'

He checked the wing mirror, indicated, moved into the outside lane.

'He who has nothing to hide.' She sat in silence for some moments. 'Fraser, you grew up here didn't you?'

'Left when I was 16.'

'How's your Canto?'

'I try and watch the soaps. When I can.'

She nodded. 'What time you seeing McKay, tonight?'

'Ten. Can't make it earlier, radio silence.'

She nodded. 'It's fine, just tell him exactly what I told you.'

'Ma'am.'

'And to meet me tomorrow.' She tucked her hair behind her ear. 'Midday. Tin Drum.'

He glanced in the rear-view mirror.

'He'll know.' She narrowed her eyes. 'And bring water.'

'Tin drum.' He nodded. 'Bring water.'

'I need to make a call.' She sat back, dialled a number. 'Kate, it's Gail.'

'Gail ... hang on, I can hardly ...' Kate, almost shouting over the roar of the bar. 'Stay there ...'

The rush and swirl of hoarse voices, fading.

A new soundtrack, the rumble of the traffic, car horns.

'Hey!' Kate caught her breath. 'Well, that went well then.'

'Too much of a sharer.'

'Do they never learn?'

'Even for me.' Emma paused. 'How's the local wildlife?'

'Bit sure of itself.'

'Need rescuing?'

'Certainly not.' Steady intake of breath, Kate pulling on a cigarette. 'Where are you?'

'Near Central, not far.'

'You never did say.' Another drag on her cigarette. 'Your guy, the eyes ... the pecs?'

'12G.'

A snort from Kate. 'You remember when tats were actually something?'

'Aspirational adjectives, no thanks.'

'Football team and first girlfriend, should leave it at that.'

'Alison with you?'

'Tinder date.' A steady exhale. 'With her track record she'll be back here for the next round.'

'That invite still stand?'

'Irish bar on Wyndham Street. Plenty to go around, girl.'

'I think I know it. Half an hour, tops.'

'Don't dally.' Kate hung up.

Emma leaned forward. 'OK Fraser, just here, on the corner.'

The driver pulled over to the kerb.

Emma stretched out a hand with a note.

He took it without turning around.

'Let's do it.' Emma glanced in the rear-view mirror.

The driver popped the door open.

Emma stepped onto the kerb.

'Diu lei!' A dismissive wave of the wrist.

'Fuck you too!' Emma slammed the door shut as the driver screeched off into the night.

She stood framed under the streetlight. Her clothes rustled in the evening breeze. She tucked her hair behind her ear. The evening crowd lapped around her. One of theirs, anonymous.

No one gave her a second glance.

Only the security camera nestling in the darkness above them, nodding agreeably as it settled on her, zoom lazily rotating as Emma's features came into finer focus.

MONDAY 23RD SEPTEMBER, 9 AM (2 PM GMT)

THE STATE DEPARTMENT, WASHINGTON

Luke Dunn of the US State Department lengthened his strike, keeping pace with his taller companion, their footsteps beating out a muffled rhythm on the worn carpet. They turned a corner, yet another State Department corridor stretching out in front of them, the dull reflection of the ceiling lights, smudges of greys and browns on the fading paintwork.

They matched each other step for step, flitting past dark wooden doors, the glint of freshly painted nameplates. The hum of bureaucracy, muted voices, the patter of keyboards.

'Tell me, have you been here before?' Luke Dunn kept his gaze dead ahead.

'How would I know.' Brian Welch of the US Drug Enforcement Agency glanced around him. 'All looks the fucking same.' His southern drawl double-toning the vowels.

'And are your corridors of power more gracefully appointed?'

'What do you think?'

They reached the door at the end of the corridor.

They exchanged a look.

'You ready for the grand entrance?' Luke raised an eyebrow.

Brian shrugged his shoulders.

'You remember your lines?'

Brian didn't reply.

'Of course you do.' Luke gave Brian a pat on the arm. 'Born for the big stage.' He took a deep breath, straightening his tie as he did so. Luke knocked on the door.

A growl from within.

Luke swung the door open, stepped inside, Brian a pace behind.

The room opened out, high ceilings, sash windows, the milky morning light seeping through a cloudy sky. Filling the far wall, looming above them, the portrait of a man. Cold eyes, set deep in a granite face, full beard and whiskers over a jutting jaw. The patrician Edwardian, untroubled by curiosity.

'If you're looking for a chair, I had them taken away.' A figure, seated behind the dark wooden desk spread out beneath the painting. 'Should have done it from the start.'

Luke cleared his throat. 'Good morning, sir.' He indicated his companion with a slight flick of the head. 'This is Brian Welch. From DEA.'

Special Advisor Cliff Medford looked up at Luke. 'Your idea or mine?'

Luke smiled. 'I would say his presence today recommended itself, sir.' He walked up, stood in front of the desk, Brian beside him.

'Fool's errand.' Medford rested his arms on the desk, his ample fingers entwined in front of him. He narrowed his eyes as he scrutinised the two men in front of him. He fixed his gaze on Luke. 'Assume I'm a simple man.' He paused. 'As I imagine you do.'

Luke straightened up. 'That collision last night in the South China Sea, off the Spratly Islands.' He nodded. 'I spoke to friends in the CIA.'

'We have friends?'

'It seems that the USS Hay didn't even know the Chinese ship was there. Until it was too late, of course. Not a flicker of a warning, sir. No radar footprint.'

Medford took a breath, exhaling slowly. He nodded. 'You know, when my wife can't find the car keys, I usually imagine she's left them in a coat pocket.' He paused. 'Or in a different handbag.'

The two men stood in silence, the steady tick of the ceiling fan above them.

'Not teleported somewhere by aliens.' He looked from one to the other. 'Although someday, that might be true.'

Luke pulled at his shirt cuffs.

'Storm, 30-foot waves, night-time.' The man behind the desk spread his hands. 'Radar can be fickle.'

Luke cleared his throat. 'The ship just appeared, sir. Out of the night, like a phantom.'

Medford sat in silence for some moments, just the patter of traffic from the street below. 'Well.' He forced a half-smile. 'Your friends in the CIA would just love that.'

Luke Dunn frowned. 'Usually, sir, I would share your scepticism.' He raised a hand to his mouth, gave a gentle cough. 'But at a time like this I think we can assume that this isn't about the CIA scoring points off Navy High Command.'

Medford gave a little snort. 'Right.' He leaned forward. 'When I said "assume I'm a simple man" …'

Dunn stood in silence for a moment. 'If the Chinese really have made this radar masking work.' He raised his eyebrows.

Medford set his jaw, said nothing.

Dunn cleared his throat. 'Obviously the Navy won't want to believe it.' He paused. 'But then you weren't part of the decision to pull the funding.'

Medford drummed a finger on the desk, a steady rhythm, his water glass quivering. He fixed Luke with a stare, his eyes deep within his full features. 'I may not have had your Lawrence education, but I think I could have just about recalled that myself.'

'I was simply trying to save on exposition.'

Medford narrowed his eyes. 'Don't get didactic with me.'

Luke took a deep breath, his thin nostrils pinching. He glanced across at Brian. 'Our friends at the DEA have their own concerns.' He looked back at the man behind the desk. 'Perhaps even the same concerns.'

Medford gave another snort. 'From what I read, the DEA should be concerned.' He looked up at Brian. 'Drug seizures down again last month. You could start there.'

Brian ran his thumb and index finger across the arc of his moustache. 'I figure if CIA's right, sir, this can all get very close to home.'

Medford pulled a face and picked up the nameplate from his desk. He turned it around, frowning theatrically as he read it aloud. 'Cliff Medford, State Department.' He paused. 'Special Advisor, China and East Asia.' He looked up at Welch. 'Am I missing something?'

Welch nodded slowly. 'Just saying, sir. Coastal waters, that's DEA turf.' He paused. 'Up to now, anyways.'

Medford shook his head. 'Do you know how far the US is from China?'

Welch rocked on his heels, said nothing.

'Try 7,000 miles.' He sat back in his chair. 'I realise geography's not a DEA strong point.' Medford gave a shrug, his well-padded chin shaking.

Brian stood in silence. He looked towards the window, the red-brick houses flanking 21st Street, the trees of Kelly Park beyond, branches drifting in the breeze. He turned back to Medford. 'If the Chinese have got this whipped, we can't match it.' He shook his head. 'U-boats off the Jersey Shore was one thing.' He paused. 'What are we going to say this time, when the Chinese jump out of the mist right into our backyard?'

Medford gave a grimace. 'Colourful language always gives me a headache.'

Welch held Medford's gaze. 'And then there's the Mexican cartels.' He gave a slight nod. 'A billion or two'd be a snick of a price to get hold of that kind of sleight of hand.'

Medford sat in silence for some moments. He nodded. 'All right, gentlemen.' He leaned back in his chair. 'Harsh words, harsh times.' He glanced up at Brian. 'Don't take it to heart.' He nodded. 'You might be right about the radar masking. Maybe they have cracked it.' He looked from one to the other. 'Maybe the Navy shouldn't have pulled the plug.' He nodded again. 'But I've got pans boiling over, and most of Washington shouting orders like angry sous-chefs.' He gave a grunt. 'Tariffs, sanctions. Turn them up! Turn them down!' He exhaled. 'Room full of naked flames and hot tempers. And it's a small kitchen.'

The two men stood in silence, car horns barking in the morning air, the murmur of the rush-hour traffic.

Medford folded his fingers across his spreading girth. 'Other people's battles.'

Luke Dunn spoke first. 'I think we can assume the Navy will bury the collision report. The real one.' He pulled at a shirt cuff. 'They'll simply never admit the Chinese have beaten them to it on the radar programme.' He pulled at his other cuff. 'Defense will go along with their Navy friends and the CIA won't ask questions.'

Medford nodded. 'We've seen the movie.' He leaned forward, shuffling some papers around. 'Another good officer thrown to the wolves, experience the Seventh Fleet can ill afford to lose.' He picked up a file, laid it carefully on the blotter in front of him. The signal for the end of the meeting.

Luke Dunn glanced across at Brian Welch.

Medford looked up. He glanced from one man to the other. 'I expect the eureka moment will come.' He nodded. 'But for now, they'll carry on delving in pockets and emptying handbags.'

Luke Dunn and Brian Welch stopped at by the elevator doors.

They glanced around; they were alone.

Luke looked up at him. 'I do believe we've sown the seed.' He nodded. 'Now we just have to water it.'

Brian ran a hand through his hair. 'Thought you said friend Medford was a sharp one.'

'Drip, drip, drip.'

'Seems to me he's got the imagination of a ticket inspector.'

'Ah,' Luke brushed a hair from his lapel with a flick of his little finger, 'that's just him being practical.' He gave a smile. 'We're in Washington, after all.'

'If you'll allow the tautology.'

'In this town, Brian, people view truth in the same way they view germs.' He gave a slight nod. 'You want a bit of exposure, to keep your immune system up.' He raised a finger. 'But not too much.' He wagged it at Brian. 'And stay well clear of the ones that don't respond to a course of convenience.'

'If he truly did take all that on board,' Brian shook his head, 'then he's just another invertebrate.' He scoffed. 'If he were any ways true to that flag on his desk, he'd be drumming on doors and raising hell.' He glanced down the corridor. 'Shit, if the Chinese can do all that, we better fucking start paying attention and doing something about it.'

'So it's just as well they can't.' Luke cleared his throat. 'Anyway, let's focus on the positives.' He nodded again. 'This little high-seas collision is perfect timing for us.' He lowered his voice to a near whisper. 'If people even think there's a chance the Chinese have got on top of radar masking ...' He raised his eyebrows.

Brian smoothed down his moustache. 'You dead sure this collision wasn't some Chinese cloak of invisibility shit?'

Luke frowned. 'Would the Chinese really want to play chicken with a Luyang-class destroyer against one of our Arleigh Burkes?' He gave a little snort. 'But look, if we can get this story to stick ...'

Brian took a deep breath, rocked back on his heels. 'So what did your friends at Langley say?'

'Well,' Luke frowned, 'pains me to admit it but Mr Walrus in there was probably on the money.' He pursed his lips. 'Rolling through the storm for a day and a half, double watches, no sleep.'

'So, just another sleepwalk detail, eyes stinging from the caffeine, reactions like syrup.' Brian shook his head. 'It's time people gave a shit.'

'Right.' Luke looked up at him. 'So, eyes on the road, my friend.' He glanced around them, his voice dropping again to a near whisper. 'The iron's hot, let's keep striking.' He nodded. 'We need to give this story a bit of provenance, don't you think?'

'Your meaning being?'

'A paragraph in the Journal, well-placed rumours about this radar masking, something almost discreet. The science section, I think.'

'Seems like a moment.'

'Maybe two paragraphs.' Luke smiled. 'Get a few whiskers twitching.'

'Let those who would listen come near.'

'Well said.' Luke glanced at his watch. 'Out of interest,' he looked up at Brian, 'what's going to be your excuse? For your trip to New York?'

'By way of a progress report,' Brian ran a hand through his thick, dark hair, 'scrips for kickbacks.' His expression turned serious. 'The whole system is fucked.'

'You're a thorough man, Brian, DEA to the core.'

'Enough to open a file and pull a team together. But it's going flat nowhere.' Brian nodded. 'And yourself, what pressing matter takes you to New York?'

'I'm going to see some old friends.'

'These acquaintances expecting you?'

'I don't think so.'

Brian raised an eyebrow. 'You don't tip a hat to the old-fashioned courtesy call?'

Luke smiled. 'Oh, they won't mind at all. They'll just be hanging around.'

'There's a nobility in simple pleasures, I guess.'

'Pleasure's never simple, my friend.' Luke straightened the knot of his tie. 'And you'll update the others?'

Brian nodded. 'I'll make sure our classmates over the water get their homework in on time.' He reached out, pushed the elevator button. 'Do you believe in coincidence? As in the guiding hand of fate?'

'Ah, you find good fortune unsettling?'

'Nope.' Brian smoothed down his moustache with finger and thumb. 'But I like my surprises to be predictable.'

MONDAY 23RD SEPTEMBER, 2.30 PM

THE RESEARCH ROOM, CRATOR CAPITAL, LONDON

'Coffee?'

Rhea Moore jumped at the sound of the voice, looked up from her screen.

Scutt was standing by her desk, trademark T-shirt and crumpled jeans, a Starbucks in each hand.

She blinked, exhaling as she composed herself, suddenly aware again of the noise around her, the patter of keyboards, the rumble of earnest conversation, her neighbour, tapping his pencil against the edge of his desk. She looked up at her visitor. 'Oh, it's you.'

'Sorry, I didn't mean to—'

'You didn't.' A smile spreading across her elfin features. 'I was just … deep into the spreadsheet.' She shrugged her petite shoulders, pulling at the collar of her cardigan. 'Like I said, I'm really a numbers girl.'

'I just thought I'd …' Scutt looked down at Rhea, her face lit up by sunlight from the far window. He noticed the dark rings beneath her eyes.

She sat back in her chair, her blonde hair shimmering in the light. 'And your timing is impeccable.'

Scutt hesitated, as though about to say something.

Rhea scanned his features. 'You know how it is.' She paused. 'Deadlines and all that.'

Scutt exhaled, placed a coffee on the desk. 'Hope I got it right this time.'

She looked at the coffee cup, then back up at Scutt. 'Are you sure Theodora doesn't mind, you bringing coffees to strange girls?' She raised her eyebrows.

Scutt swallowed. 'I just wanted to …' He looked down at the coffee cup.

She followed his gaze.

He kept his eyes on the cup on her desk.

She reached forward, drew the cup towards her and removed the lid. A note, folded and stuck to the underside of it.

'Capo.' She looked up at him, smiled. 'With a sprinkle.'

He glanced around the research room. The familiar air of purpose in the clatter of the keystrokes, a canopy of concentration hovering over the team. The lesser financial predators, the pack, on the scent of prey, senses locked, eyes fixed on screens.

'Bring one for me, Scutt?'

Scutt jumped, looked around at the voice.

Ellis Wagner, the Head of Research, stood in the doorway of his office, looking out over the research room. 'Dry as a ditch.'

The room fell quiet, all eyes on Ellis and Scutt.

Scutt cleared his throat, his face reddening. 'I was just …'

Ellis glanced at the coffee cup on Rhea's desk, an identical one in Scutt's hand. 'So I see.' He smiled at Scutt. 'Anyway, good to see you out among the living.'

Scutt blinked. 'I should have emailed, I'm sorry.'

'No worries.' Ellis leaned back against the doorframe, his lanky form silhouetted against the afternoon sun streaming in through the window behind him. 'Theodora's idea, am I right?'

'I'll come back later.'

'Or did you and her have a set-to?' Ellis put on a mock-serious face. 'I hear she can be a tad touchy, your Theodora.'

Scutt shifted his weight from one foot to another as his eyes darted around the room, the young, fresh faces, gazing back at him with good-natured curiosity.

'But good on you anyway.' Ellis turned, began to walk back to his desk.

'I came to see you.' Scutt blurted out the words.

Ellis stopped, slowly turned around. 'All right.'

'I just …' He glanced down at Rhea's cup. 'I owed her a coffee. Anyway.' He swallowed.

Ellis smiled again. 'A gentleman always pays his debts.' He waved a hand beckoning Scutt into his office. 'Come on in then.'

Scutt took a deep breath, exhaled, walked between the analysts' desks and into Ellis's office.

Ellis closed the door.

They stood facing each other.

Scutt scanned the room, strips of sunshine flooding in through the open blinds, ribbons of light thrown across the floor, tracing the angles of Ellis's desk.

'Well,' Ellis raised an eyebrow, 'is that for me?' He looked down at the coffee cup.

'Sure.' Scutt shot out a hand, a few flecks of foam spilling out from the gap in the lid.

'Cheers.' Ellis took the cup, walked around to the other side of his desk, sat down. He took a sip of the coffee, gave an appreciative nod. 'All right then, Scutt, what's on your mind?'

Scutt looked down, tiny motes of dust swirling in the sunlight. He toyed with his leather bracelet.

Ellis placed the cup on his desk, looked across at Scutt. 'I know, starting the conversation's the hardest part. And we never chit-chat.' He nodded slowly. 'Where did you get the tat?' He nodded towards the eagle tattoo on Scutt's upper arm.

Scutt looked up at Ellis. 'Berlin.' He blinked again. 'It was a coding conference.' He paused. 'I had a free evening.' He frowned. 'I was looking for something to do.'

'Gnarly.' Ellis nodded, sat up in his chair. 'They knew what they were about all right. That sheen on the feathers, that's not easy.' He nodded. 'Auribus teneo lupum.' He gave a slight grimace. 'Don't tend to show it in public too much nowadays. In fact wearing a T-shirt makes me look at bit of a bogan, truth be told.'

Scutt frowned. 'I hold the wolf by the ears.'

'Don't ask me to explain that one.' Ellis shook his head. 'Stag weekend in Darwin. Stokes Hill Wharf.' He paused. 'Before it got posh.' He leaned back in his chair. 'So, now we've broken the ice …' He raised an eyebrow.

Scutt rolled his leather bracelet between finger and thumb. He swallowed. 'It's about the log reports.'

Ellis sucked in air. 'I'm a few days behind on those, I'm afraid.' He indicated his desk with a flick of the head, a blanket of broker notes and log reports.

Scutt glanced around the room. 'The last log report I sent.'

'At least.' Ellis grimaced.

'It's incomplete.'

Ellis studied Scutt's face for a moment, sat up in his chair. 'What are you trying to say?'

Scutt took a breath. 'I missed some searches.' He paused. 'I … didn't want to put it in an email until I'd …'

'Do I really need to know this?'

Scutt exhaled. 'Transport movements, freight, ports and railheads, Colombian coast.'

'So?'

'Pharmaceutical intermediates, from what I could see.' Ellis nodded.

Scutt pulled at his leather bracelet. 'I assume that … it's all …'

Ellis narrowed his eyes.

'That you'd asked for …'

Ellis glanced across at his desk, then back to Scutt. 'Is this some fucking test?'

Scutt held his gaze.

Ellis sat in silence for some moments, eyes fixed on Scutt. 'All right.' He began. 'I didn't ask specifically.' He paused. 'But it's never a bad thing to keep an eye on the competition.' He frowned. 'So … yes, if you think we should, then I could put this under … background research.'

Scutt nodded.

'So you can include it in the email. And if anyone asks, I'll tell them what I've just told you.'

'Thanks.'

'But next time Rhea looks like she might be shaping to go off-piste, just keep a closer eye will you, stick with the brief.'

'I didn't say—'

'Fuck off, Scutt, of course this is about Rhea.'

Scutt blushed again.

'But that's all right. I'm glad you came to me first to … clear this up.'

'Right.'

'But just a word of advice.' Ellis stood up. 'She really wanted this job, and friendly though she is, she's not going to do anything to blur her focus, if you know what I mean.'

'Right.' Scutt looked down at the floor.

Ellis walked around the desk, stood in front of Scutt, looking down at him. 'You're a one-off, you know that?'

Scutt didn't reply.

'Whatever that means nowadays.'

Scutt shrugged.

'But we love you.' Ellis paused. 'I mean, we have to, right? You know where all the bodies are.'

Scutt swallowed. 'Bodies?'

Ellis laid a hand on Scutt's shoulder. 'Figuratively speaking.' He opened the door. Looked across the research room. 'Where's Rhea?'

'She said she wasn't feeling too great.' Her neighbour looked up from the screen. 'I think she went to the bathroom.'

Ellis looked down at the coffee cup sitting on his desk, then back to Scutt. 'Should I risk it?' He cracked a smile.

Scutt set off across the research room floor, head down.

Ellis closed the door to his office, walked around his desk, sat down. He picked up the phone.

. . .

Rhea and Scutt stood on the fire-escape landing. White-washed walls and the chill grey of the iron stairway. The unforgiving light from the wall-lamps splashing their shadows across the metalwork. They were alone.

'You lot think you understand risk.' Scutt hissed. 'You have no clue.'

Rhea stared across at him, her eyes wide. 'Scutt, what is this about?'

Scutt took a deep breath, his eyes scanning Rhea's pale features. 'They're onto you. But they don't know what I know. Not yet anyway.'

Rhea took in a ragged breath, she swallowed. 'What are you saying?'

Scutt exhaled. 'If you knew the risk I'm taking just by …' He shook his head. 'Fuck.' He spat the word out.

Rhea raised a hand to her cardigan collar, her knuckles white. 'I really don't know what you're talking about.'

Scutt pulled at his leather bracelet. 'You know when you used to go to the seaside? As a child I mean.'

Rhea frowned. 'What?'

'Your parents would say "only swim between the flags, where you know it's safe".'

Rhea pulled her cardigan tighter around her shoulders. 'Go on.'

'Because outside those flags … the eddies, the pools, the currents, the rocks … a world of dangers … like a precipice … one misstep and …'

Rhea took a deep breath, exhaled. 'Look, Scutt, I know you think you're trying to help.' She attempted a smile. 'But none of this makes sense.'

Scutt narrowed his eyes. 'Seven times.' His jaw muscles tensing. 'Santa Maria, Rio Cordoba, Puerto Drummond, Barranquilla.'

Rhea stood in silence, her breathing, shallower.

'What the fuck were you thinking?' Anger in his voice now. 'Ellis never asked you to go anywhere near the Colombian ports.'

'I …' Rhea looked down at the floor, shaking her head. 'I was just …'

'There are fucking rules, Rhea. You don't go asking Theodora questions you shouldn't. That's why we have the log reports. That's why I'm meant to be checking that no one's going off where they're not fucking meant to be!'

She looked up at him, her shoulders rising and falling, the dark bags under her eyes stark under the bright light. 'I know.' Her voice, quiet. 'I know.' She paused. 'I don't know why I …' She closed her eyes. 'Can't you do something?'

He shifted his weight to his other foot. 'I spoke to Ellis. He'll sign off on your little trip around the Colombian transport hubs yesterday.' He pulled at his bracelet. 'And I've done what I can to muddy the trail on your other stop-offs.' He shook his head. 'But like I said, Theodora, she never forgets, and if someone knows where to look, they'll find.'

She opened her eyes. 'Thanks.' She smiled weakly. 'I'm sorry, I'm new to all this. I was just trying to …' She took a deep breath, exhaled. 'I won't do it again.'

He kept his gaze on her face, the first beads of perspiration, just beneath her hairline. 'You're scared.'

She closed her eyes again, trying to control her breathing. 'I scare easily, I told you that.' She looked up at him. 'You're scaring me. All this stuff about people being on to me and rocks and dangers.' Her voice began to crack. 'I'm just an analyst, I look at numbers.'

Scutt laid a hand on Rhea's arm. 'You're not just an analyst.'

She shrugged his hand from her arm. 'What are you talking about?'

He looked down at her hand gripping the collar of her cardigan. It was shaking. He shook his head. 'I don't know why I'm helping you, but—'

'We work in a hedge fund for goodness sake.' She swallowed again. 'Just how dangerous can that be?'

'You have no—' He froze.

A noise, from further down the stairwell.

He held up a hand.

Rhea shuddered, her eyes widening.

Scutt raised a finger to his lips.

A click, from below. A door opening, or closing.

They stood, motionless in the harsh, cold light, ears straining into the silence.

Scutt took one careful step towards the stair rail, his trainers almost silent on the concrete floor. He peered into the stairwell.

Nothing moved, just the shadows of the metal, thrown against the chill stonework.

Scutt turned back to Rhea. He reached up, gripped her arm. 'You should get the fuck out of here.'

She stared at him. 'Out?'

'Away, for good. Go, and don't come back. Get on a plane somewhere, anywhere.' He tightened his grip on her. 'They're onto you, Rhea.' He moved his face closer to hers, speaking now through gritted teeth. 'You don't know what they're like.'

She looked at him in silence, eyes wide, mouth slightly open.

He let go of her arm.

'Go. Before they find out what you are.' He paused. 'Or who you are.'

She blinked. 'You're right.' Her voice almost a whisper. 'I am scared.'

Scutt leaned in, gently planted a kiss on her damp forehead. 'I love you, Rhea.' He placed his hand on her cheek. 'But promise me I'll never see you again.'

. . .

Rhea Moore slipped through the fire-escape door out onto the corridor. She glanced around. She was alone. She quietly closed the door behind her.

She stood in the cushioned silence, the thick carpet beneath her feet, the white walls, the dark wooden doors, the ceiling lights, stretching out ahead of her.

She took a deep breath, exhaling slowly, her heartbeat still drumming in her ears.

She raised a hand, feeling the cold, smooth plastic of the security pass hanging by the lanyard around her neck.

She narrowed her eyes, focussing on the door at the end of the corridor, the painted steel glowing dimly under the lights. The door, between her and reception. Between her and the outside.

She began to walk towards it, silent, cushioned footsteps, just the humming of the air conditioning, the click of the fans, the thump of her heart.

She reached the door, took a deep breath, eyes on the glinting security panel on the wall beside the door, the tiny red lights, framing the slick black surface of the sensor. She exhaled as she reached up for the security pass, her hand, still trembling as she gripped the pass between finger and thumb. She closed her eyes, swallowed again, then looked back down at the sensor on the wall. She leaned forward, held her pass against the panel.

Nothing. No green lights, no beep.

She flinched as she tapped it again.

Just the tiny red lights, the silent dark panel.

She rubbed the pass against it. 'Please, please, please!' Her voice cracking. 'Pleeeease!'

A hand on her shoulder, strong fingers, gripping her.

She let out a cry.

'Ms Moore.' A voice she didn't recognise. 'Let me help you.'

MONDAY 23RD SEPTEMBER, 2 PM (7 PM GMT)

THE STATE DEPARTMENT, WASHINGTON

Cliff Medford sat in the anteroom outside the Secretary of State's office. He shifted in his seat, the chair a little too small for his sizeable frame. He glanced over at the Secretary's PA, her gaze firmly fixed on the screen in front of her, hands skittering over the keyboard. Next to her, a glass vase, a cluster of bright red carnations bursting over the brim of the fluting, the light glinting on the carved crystal.

The PA looked across at him, her hands poised above the keys, her nail varnish almost matching the arrangement. 'They were a gift.' She shot Medford a smile. 'From the Spanish Ambassador.'

Medford nodded approvingly.

'For Madam Secretary.' She added hastily, her serious face slipping back into place. 'But she doesn't like flowers in her office.'

'Hay fever?'

'I'm only allergic to misgivings.' Madam Secretary Carol Hansen stood framed in the open doorway, her slender frame silhouetted in the light. 'Can't anybody give an opinion nowadays without a hefty serving of crinkle-cut scruples?'

'With a side of provisos.' Cliff Medford heaved himself to his feet. 'Welcome back, Madam Secretary.'

'Talking of backs, mine's as sore as hell and my nails are wearing out.'

'Appropriations season, peak scratching time.'

'Should have packed my own loofah.' She cracked a smile. 'Can't believe it's still Monday. Come on in.'

Medford followed her through the doorway. Ahead of him, a plain white wall, soaring up to the corniced ceiling. The windows to either side, views to the courtyard, the red-brick facades still glinting from the morning's rain.

'He had to go.' She waved a slender arm in the direction of the bare wall. 'I didn't mind the whiskers and the frock coat. It's that told-you-so look. And these people thought you could teach dogs to read.' She walked towards the corner of the room, two armchairs settled around a low table. 'Who's on your wall?' She indicated the other chair.

Medford laid the file on the table. 'Maybe the Met can lend you a Rothko?' He lowered himself into the chair.

She sat, hands on the armrests. 'Have they found that sailor?'

Medford shook his head.

'Is that on them or us?'

Medford took a breath. 'Is that a factor? In where we go from here?'

'You're the advisor.'

He exhaled. 'Beijing's gone quiet. They're thinking.'

She removed her spectacles. 'Is that a bad thing?'

'Something's happened. Something they hadn't anticipated. If it was in the playbook, they'd be right back at us.'

She tapped a fingernail against the thick black frame. 'Friday's sanctions?'

He shook his head. 'They've modelled every variant. Impact and response.'

'What then?'

'Speculating will just generate more variables.' He paused. 'Or maybe they simply want us to speculate.' He took another breath. 'Make us think they've been wrong-footed.'

She raised an eyebrow.

'So perhaps this silence is actually per the playbook.'

She sat for a moment, nodding slowly.

The low rumble of an aircraft, feeling its way through the clouds swirling above them.

She pursed her lips. 'But you're trying not to speculate.'

He smiled. 'Would you like extra contingency in your proviso salad?'

'And a little grated obfuscation.' She leaned back, hands once more on the armrests. 'What the fuck do we do, Cliff?'

He nodded. 'I think they're hesitating.' He blinked. 'So it's our move.'

'You've got that look about you. Do I need to strap myself in?'

'To get a big answer you need to pose a big question?'

'What font size we talking about?'

He met her gaze. 'The USS Carl Vinson.'

The silence wrapped itself around them.

She closed her eyes. Exhaled. She looked back up at him. 'That's quite a bit of punctuation.'

He sat back, hands resting on his knees. 'At this stage, just another piece on the board.'

She narrowed her eyes. 'What does that even mean?'

'Something short of high-octane escalation.' He laid his elbows on the armrests, hands pressed together in front of him. 'Their turn to speculate.'

'About what?'

He rotated his hands around, index fingers resting on his chin. 'Why we'd park two carrier strike groups at the southern end of the Taiwan Strait.'

'In whose lexicon is that not escalation?'

'Silence is the biggest threat right now.'

She slid her spectacles back on.

'For both sides.'

She pulled a face. 'So raising them a full carrier strike group. In one of the last places they'd want to see it. That's de-risking the situation?'

He laid his hands back on the armrests. 'This is the most dangerous phase.' He paused again. 'If either side goes quiet now, the other may fear the worst.' He blinked. 'A vacuum sucks in the worst imaginings.' He pursed his lips. 'A Chinese first strike may sound like sheer madness.' He gave a slight nod. 'Until you consider what they might think the alternatives could be.'

She drew another breath, nodded. 'I get that.' She gave a slight grimace. 'But my stomach still cramps up at the thought.'

He exhaled. 'If this is to have any kind of productive conclusion, we need to know what they want.' He paused. 'Or what they'll settle for.'

'So we threaten them until they start being reasonable?'

'No.' He straightened up in the chair. 'But it is about the visuals.'

'How would we like it?'

'Front-page pixels. Make your heart skip a beat.'

She removed her spectacles once more, sat back in her chair. She looked across at him in silence for some moments. 'Can you imagine,' she began, 'a Chinese war fleet, bristling with missiles and attitude, off the coast of Santa Barbara?'

'It's a question of increments. The Seventh Fleet's already on station.'

'Toothache is toothache.'

'We have to look sure-footed.'

She rose, walked to the window, the courtyard below, the early autumn grass vivid and glossy. From somewhere above, the growl of another plane, jostling its way through the lumpy grey sky. 'Beijing's silence.' She stood, her back to the room. 'What if it's not silence at all?' She turned to face him. 'They're not thinking. They're doing.'

Medford drummed his fingers on the armrest. 'Perhaps.' He nodded slowly. 'As I said, the vacuum of worst imaginings.' He frowned. 'But you could be right, yes. Perhaps they are doing something, as we speak.' He drummed his fingers again. 'All the more reason for us to make the move, bring us both back to a script we can understand.'

She glanced back out of the window, the facade of the Department of State building, imposing, austere, rising up into the afternoon sky. 'So, the Carl Vinson.' She turned back towards him. 'You sure?'

He gave another grimace.

'Sorry, lazy private sector speak.'

'Let me answer it a different way.' He shifted in his chair. 'Our youngest, Declan, served in the 32nd Infantry. Did one tour in Afghanistan.' He paused. 'Longest year of our lives.'

She nodded.

'When he was in the field, out of radio contact,' he shook his head, 'we barely slept.'

She walked over to him, placed a slender hand on his shoulder. 'That's why I listen.'

He looked up at her.

'And you were always such a sound sleeper.' She squeezed his shoulder.

He smiled. 'They're all good memories.'

'I'm pleased for you, for you both.' She returned the smile. 'But I have to confess, when I saw you again just now, a thought did spring into my head.'

He attempted a frown.

'If we ever did rekindle something,' she tilted her head to one side, eyes twinkling, 'together, we'd have a near perfect BMI.'

TUESDAY

TUESDAY 24TH SEPTEMBER, NOON (4 AM GMT)

ALBANY ROAD, HONG KONG

Emma Wilson looked up towards The Peak, now shrouded in cloud. Jungle-covered slopes merging into the mist. The timeless Hong Kong. Nature, patient because it can be. Its ancient forces, gathered on the hillsides overlooking the City, watching, waiting their moment.

A fly buzzed around her; she flicked it away. She ran a finger around the neck of her T-shirt, the damp fabric clinging to her, her skin prickling in the midday heat.

She resumed her steady pace to the rumble of the traffic on Albany Road, the noise thumping around her, trapped beneath the low grey sky.

The green man lit up; she stepped onto the crossing, trainers bright against the tyre-worn road. The air here still fizzing with the city, brick dust and something metallic, on the tip of her tongue.

She paused at the start of Old Peak Road and glanced down at the map. To any passer-by, just another tourist, new in town, finding her feet.

She settled her shoulders, slowing to an easier pace as the road began to climb again.

The Mid-Level tower blocks soared upwards beyond the roadside treeline. A city within a city, a giant palisade of concrete, monoliths in creams and pinks, thronging the mountainside. Serried columns of balconies, steepling into the sky.

She reached the turn in the road. Ahead of her, Tregunter Path, the hiking route to The Peak. The tarmac surface, the moss-covered walls, the trunks of the trees, dark and dense. Above, the rustling green canopy, swaying gently in the breeze.

She took a deep breath, adjusted her daypack on her shoulders. Ahead of her, no one. She glanced behind. Just the parked cars, pavements deserted in the prickly heat.

She stepped onto the path, began the climb. Her breathing more laboured now, the thick, moist air filling her lungs. In the stillness around her the scent of the jungle, heavy in her nostrils, damp earth, decay.

She turned the corner.

A man sat on the bench by the side of the path. European, her age, also in hiking shorts and T-shirt. He took off his sunglasses as Emma approached.

'Quite a mise en scène.' David McKay stretched out his arms.

'I'm not here, remember.' She drew to a halt in front of him, slipping her daypack off. 'Or rather, I'm not here.' She rolled her shoulders. 'You sure you weren't followed?'

'They used to assign me someone for my walks up here, poor sod. I genuinely felt sorry for him, especially in the hot season.' He smiled. 'Used to try and engage him in conversation, to pass the time.' He nodded. 'Then they decided they had better things to do.'

'Small talk never was your strong point.' She paused, looking down at him. 'Not sure about the beard.'

'Going for the Viking look. My Celtic hue.'

She looked him up and down. 'A slightly chubby one, perhaps.'

'And I was about to say you're looking good, Emma.' He raised an eyebrow. 'And you've grown your hair out, suits you.'

She exhaled. 'Apologies for the cattiness, just jumped out.'

McKay smiled. 'Do you remember Suter?'

She took out a bottle of water from her pack, unscrewed the top. 'What about him?'

'He always carried an umbrella with him, up here.' McKay glanced around. 'Unfurled.'

Emma shrugged.

'Convinced a snake would fall off a branch onto his head.'

'And?'

He raised his eyebrows.

'Our man, last night.' She took a sip from the bottle.

'Bit odd isn't it?'

'Odd in the sense of?'

'He got to his room at 18.55, unpacked everything. Then, at 19.35, same clothes he flew in, he decides to head over to Tsim Sha Tsui.' She took another sip. 'No incoming calls, no messages, nothing in his diary.'

McKay shrugged.

'Why the rush?' She paused. 'A note slipped under the door maybe?'

He tilted his head. 'Was it on when you were here?'

She rolled her eyes. 'Go on, put me in my place.'

'Eight o'clock, every night, sharp.'

'Let me guess. Your Nuru massage?'

'Symphony of Light, son et lumière, the island skyline.'

'And?'

'The best place to watch it is …'

She frowned. 'Still, dashing off like that, spur-of-the-moment thing. I've seen his room.' She paused. 'Impetuous?' She gave a slight shake of the head. 'You'd need a geometry set to lay things out like that.'

McKay flicked away a fly. 'There's a moral compass joke in there somewhere.'

'Did he meet up with anyone?' She took another sip of water. 'Over at Tsim Sha Tsui … or later?'

McKay shook his head. 'He enjoyed the show, then went back to his hotel.'

'That's it?'

'Where he doubtless had his shower.' He flashed her a mock smile. 'Since you seem so worried about it.'

Emma glanced around. The path, still empty. The sounds of the jungle, rustling, clicking, scratching. A bird fluttered off from a branch overhead. In the distance a rhesus macaque barked a warning. She turned back to McKay. 'His agenda, is it real?'

'So far, yes. We've not let him out of our sight.' He pursed his lips. 'You know something we don't?'

'That's a loaded question.'

He replaced his sunglasses, his cheek muscles flexing. 'You're holding something back.'

She narrowed her eyes. 'If you don't trust me, now's a good time to get that out.'

He sat in silence for a moment. A collared crow, looking down from his perch, scolded them with an ill-tempered caw. McKay took a deep breath. 'Trust?' He reached up, slowly slid off his sunglasses. 'Didn't we wear that word out in Macau, half a lifetime ago?'

Emma glanced down at her water bottle, then let her arm fall to her side. She looked across at him. 'I didn't ask to be here, David.'

'But here you are.'

Her jawline tightened. Her lips began to move, half forming a word. She checked herself, exhaled. 'I did think about what I might say to you.'

He looked up at her, eyes scanning her features, the

dappled sunlight flecking her forehead. He slowly shook his head. 'And maybe I should have thought about it more.' He blinked. 'Trouble is, you're still so fucking, infuriatingly lovely.'

She stood in silence for a moment, the hint of a frown flitting across her brow. 'I wasn't ready for that.'

'Neither was I.' McKay shifted in his seat. 'Put it down to early stage Tourette's.' He tried a smile. 'It just came out.' He paused. 'Like a flustered bunny out of a battered old hat.'

She drew a breath, the rich, warm air, silky thick with moisture, heavy in her lungs. She looked down at him, the band of freckles under his eyes still visible on the sun-weathered skin. 'There was a time.' She paused. 'When you could do magic.' She smiled. 'But spells fade.'

'I do hope so.' He gave a grin. 'I may look like an ageing company man with a taste for good malt and the nose and girth to show for it,' he raised an eyebrow, 'but I'm really a handsome prince, with a body that should be gracing Love Island.'

'I won't tell if you won't.' She raised her water bottle. 'Where were we?'

'Milot Borso, sticking to his schedule like a limpet.' He brushed the back of his hand across his forehead.

Emma nodded as she stood in silence, the jungle soundtrack clicking around her. She took another breath, glancing above her, the sun, now streaking through the gaps in the canopy, splashes of light across the moss-streaked path. She blinked, looked back across at McKay. 'I can feel it. Like something moving … beneath our feet.'

McKay frowned. 'I think I missed a step here.'

'Those words, whispered in the dark places, where they think we're not listening.'

'They're just words.'

'Crator. The Ringmaster.' She paused. 'The Pale Tiger.'

The jungle seemed to fall silent, the words hanging in the musty, damp air.

McKay nodded, slowly.

'Borso.' Emma paused. 'Is he a piece of this puzzle?' She narrowed her eyes. 'Or is he the bait?'

McKay straightened up in his seat, his expression serious, his eyes, darting from side to side, scanning the tree line behind her.

Emma tensed, the silence crackling around them. She stared at David, mouthing a silent 'What is it?'

He stood up, raised a finger to his lips, his head cocked in concentration, ears straining into the silence around them.

A twig snapped behind her.

She spun around, hand in her backpack, fingers gripping the stock of her gun.

A rustle, another snap, the undergrowth, shivering.

Emma took a step back, every sense needle-sharp, staring into the wall of swaying green, the tangle of twisted branches, dark knots in the shadows.

Her breathing, quicker now as she slid the weapon from her pack.

Another snap, louder. Just feet away. A branch swaying, the sound of something, falling.

McKay touched Emma's shoulder. 'Wait.' He whispered.

Emma levelled her gun.

The jungle in front of her, coming alive, something crashing through the thicket, branches shaking, leaves shuddering.

She tightened her finger on the trigger.

A shape, slicing through the undergrowth, the flash of sunlight on scales, dark sinews, twisting in the savage gloom of the jungle floor.

Then, silence.

Just the sound of their breathing.

McKay reached up, laid his hand on Emma's arm, gently pushing it down to her side.

Emma exhaled, raised her other hand, running the sleeve of her T-shirt across her forehead. 'What was that?'

McKay reached into his pocket, pulling out a khaki bandana. He handed it to Emma. 'It's clean.'

She took it. 'Thank you.'

'Sometimes,' he looked across at her, 'it's what you don't hear.' He paused. 'When it all goes silent. Waiting. For the jaws to snap … the cold-coiled stalker to strike.'

She dabbed at her neck with the bandana.

The jungle soundtrack, now humming back to life around them. The click of the insects, birds bustling through the canopy branches, their calls wafting through the midday heat.

She slid her gun back into her pack as she took a step back. 'It's been a while.'

McKay fixed her in his gaze. 'The law of the jungle. It's been revised.'

'What's that meant to mean?'

'You don't know the terrain, Emma.' He narrowed his eyes. 'There's a new apex predator out there.'

She frowned. 'You trying to scare me off?'

He studied her face for a moment. 'I'm trying to protect you.'

'Really?'

'If the Chinese get hold of you, with everything else that's going on right now …'

'In and out, David. Two more days, and I'm gone.'

'You get caught, and they bring the hammer down, we're all off the streets.'

'If we didn't take chances, we'd never get anything done.'

McKay took a step towards her, put his hand on her shoulder. 'Ems, just lie low. Please. Leave Borso to us. You've got his schedule, you can follow the tracker.'

She looked at him, blinking, took a breath, the dense, hot air heavy in her nostrils. 'Sorry.' Her expression, calm. 'I can't do that.'

'You're putting us all at risk.'

Emma glanced down at his hand resting on her shoulder. She gently shrugged it off. 'Like I said, I didn't ask to be here.'

McKay stood in silence for a moment, his expression deadpan. He straightened up. 'OK.' He gave a slight nod. 'Meet me at 18.00.' He slipped his sunglasses back on. 'Tsim Sha Tsui.'

'The Ferry Terminal?'

'The Promenade, by the Old Clock Tower.'

She nodded, took a sip of water, looked around her. The sounds of the jungle, humming in her ears. 'I'll take the path down.' She turned back towards him. 'So you'll be headed that way.' She indicated the path up the mountain.

McKay screwed up his face. 'Fuck. Really?'

'You've got water, and frankly,' she nodded towards his midriff, 'you could do with the exercise.' She flashed him a smile.

McKay gave a good-natured grunt.

The screech of the nearby monkeys, mocking them from the treetops.

He reached down for his daypack, slung it over his shoulder, set off up the path, head down, in silence.

'You never said.' She called after him. 'Suter, what did happen?'

'He died in a car accident.' He shouted over his shoulder. 'Thailand, about ten years ago.'

'What's that got to do with umbrellas?'

He stopped, turned, looking down the path at her. 'He wasn't wearing a seat belt.' He smiled. 'He understood danger. He just didn't figure the right odds out.'

TUESDAY 24TH SEPTEMBER, 9.30 AM

THE KINGLAKE HOTEL, LONDON

The girl lay naked on the bed. A clear plastic bag covered her head, a brown leather belt drawn tight around her neck. Her hands were stretched out above her, tied to the bedstead. She was dead.

'Couldn't you just …' DI Anne Perry coughed to get the attention of her colleagues. She nodded towards the girl on the bed. 'Put something over …' She held out her hands. 'I'm not wearing any …'

One of the forensics men handed her a pair of gloves.

'Thank you.' DI Perry looked back down at the bed as she snapped the gloves on. She shook her head. 'You poor girl, what's happened to you?' DI Perry laid a hand on the girl's shoulder. 'You don't look like you belong here.' She gently prodded the palms of the girl's bound hands. 'This blueness,' she looked up at her colleague, 'hypoxia?'

A masked colleague grunted. 'Assume so.'

DI Perry picked up a corner of the bed sheet between thumb and forefinger, drew it across to cover the torso of the girl. 'You shouldn't have to go through this.' She glanced around the room: personal effects, already bagged and labelled, lined the table opposite the bed. She walked over, picked up one of the bagged items in her gloved hand. 'Genuine ID?'

Another masked colleague nodded. 'A car's headed over to that address now.'

'Rhea Moore.' DI Perry glanced at the ID then turned again to the body lying on the bed. 'Pretty name.' She paused. 'For a pretty girl.' She peered down at the girl's wrists, the slight red marks where the material had chafed the skin. 'Did you really want to be here?'

DI Alan Lute removed his mask. 'She pulled at the binds, moved her wrists around, but no major abrasions.' He joined DI Perry standing over the girl. 'Not like your life depended on it.' He turned one of the dead girl's wrists over. 'And not for long.'

'Rhea, what were you thinking?' DI Perry looked down at the dead girl's face. 'Now look at you.' She felt the tips of the dead girl's hands, running a finger over the well-kept nails. 'Nice girl like you, bet you had a nice job too.' She shook her head. 'Somebody's pride and joy.' She looked up at DI Lute. 'What in the world do we say to the parents?'

A knock at the door.

DI Lute walked over, opened it a few inches.

'DC Zayan, sir.' The voice from the corridor. 'Just been to the dead girl's flat.'

'I thought you couldn't drive.'

'Got a lift.' DC Zayan paused. 'Sir.'

DI Lute opened the door. 'Just joking.'

The tall young man walked into the room, held up a clear plastic bag. 'Found her work ID.'

'Congratulations.' DI Lute, deadpan.

'Analyst, Crator Capital.'

DI Perry held out her hand. 'Obviously I'm meant to have heard of them.'

DC Zayan handed her the bagged pass.

'I'm afraid I haven't.'

DC Zayan nodded. 'They're in the financial press quite a bit.'

'Trust you to know.' DI Lute closed the door.

DC Zayan looked at DI Lute, then across to DI Perry. 'They were in the headlines, last year.'

DI Lute gave a snort. 'I really don't know why we bother.'

'One of the partners. Disappeared, potholing.'

'Just leave them to it, I would.' DI Lute shrugged.

DC Zayan continued. 'Got lost in the caves, they think.'

DI Lute gave another snort. 'Head up his own arse no doubt.'

'Never found the body.' DC Zayan gave a shake of the head. 'Some of those caves can go down a mile.'

DI Lute shook his head. 'They play by their own rules, they don't give a fuck about ours.'

DI Perry remained by the side of the bed, looking down at the girl. 'This could happen to anyone, Alan.' She looked up at him. 'People can still call be calling for help, even if it is too late.'

DI Lute stood in silence for a moment, the lines on his forehead dark grooves under the lights. 'If she'd been an OD in a Peckham bedsit, type 2 diabetes and in bad need of a shower,' he shook his head, 'we'd have packed her off to the morgue by now and put her out of our mind.' He looked across at DI Perry. 'Right, Anne?' Alan looked back down at the dead girl on the bed. 'You had it all when you were alive and it still wasn't enough.' He glanced up at her bound hands, the bag over her head. 'So why the fuck are we apologising to you?'

DI Perry walked over to the table. She picked up another sealed clear plastic bag. 'Really?' She indicated the cheap pay-as-you-go phone wrapped in the bag.

'I know.' DI Lute shrugged. 'But it's the only one we've found.' He reached up, pulling at an earlobe between finger and thumb.

'She wouldn't be seen dead with one of these, surely?' She frowned. 'Sorry, I didn't mean that.' She held the bag closer to her face. DI Perry exhaled. 'I'm going to talk to the manager, leave you in peace.' She glanced down again at the dead girl. 'You should do the same for her.'

. . .

DI Perry stood in the open doorway to the duty manager's office, silhouetted against the bright light from the corridor, the outline of her hair a copper glow.

She peered into the room, a desk in the centre, a clutter of F&B receipts and half-drunk coffee cups, the china glinting in the yellow glare of the table light.

A head poked up from behind the monitor, a day's stubble and dilated pupils. 'You been waiting there long?'

DI Perry glanced around the room. The windowless walls a mosaic of duty rosters and fading Health & Safety posters. Behind the desk, a cork board, a jumble of Post-it notes. 'We had to get rid of ours.' She nodded towards the patchwork of scribbled reminders, squares of pink and yellow rustling in the draft of the air conditioning. 'Mistake if you ask me.'

'Notoriously forgetful.' The manager sat up in his chair. 'A lot of them.' He nodded. 'But that's the hospitality business. Anti-social hours. Drink, drugs … and everything in between.' He raised his eyebrows. 'Something in common with the police perhaps.'

DI Perry looked down at the figure behind the desk. 'Just caffeine or something stronger?'

'Excuse me?' He frowned.

'Your eyes. It's not that dark in here.' She paused. 'Your pupils always that size?'

He swallowed. 'I …'

'And don't bother to get up.'

'I'm sorry.' He began to stand. 'Been a busy night, can I get you a chair?'

She waved for him to stay seated. 'Don't bother.' She stepped into the room, smoothing down her skirt. She stood between the door and the desk, her face in shadow. 'What does busy mean?'

He cleared his throat. 'There was a … complaint.'

'A complaint?'

'Noise.' He exhaled. 'From Room 414.'

'And what time was this?'

'Around ten, or just before. I think.' He glanced up at the clock on the office wall, then back to DI Perry. 'So, I went up to the room, asked them to keep it down.'

She took a step closer, her face now lit up by the glow the desk lamp, a frown spreading across her smooth features. 'You saw them?'

'No, I knocked, I spoke to them from the corridor. Most times guests really don't want to let you into the room, for obvious reasons.'

DI Perry nodded. 'So, what did you think was going on in the room?'

'Well, the music was quite loud but there was talking—'

'Man's voice, girl's voice?'

'Couldn't hear that clearly above the music but it was … like they were whispering.'

'You could hear whispering above the loud music?'

'Not actual whispering, loud whispering, as though you were … you know, right up close to someone. Whispering. Loudly.'

DI Perry stood in silence for a moment, concentration etched across her pale forehead. 'Then what?'

'I knocked on the door, said "this is the manager". Usual drill.'

'And what was the response?'

'They turned the music down, straight away. And I heard giggling, a girl giggling.'

DI Perry nodded again. 'And then?'

'I left.'

DI Perry raised a hand, turning the top button of her blouse between finger and thumb. 'Is there CCTV on the corridors?'

He shook his head. 'Just the lifts.' He paused. 'And reception, of course.'

DI Perry narrowed her eyes. 'Who found her?'

'The chambermaid.' He raised a hand. 'I sent her home, she was in a bad way.' He spread his palms. 'No point in trying to talk to her like that.'

'And you saw the body, the girl?'

He nodded.

'Did you recognise her?'

'No.' He paused. 'But then I wouldn't know if she was a regular.' He sat back in his chair. 'I wouldn't usually get involved unless there was a reason … a problem, or something.'

DI Perry tilted her head to one side. 'Has this happened before?'

'No.' The manager frowned. 'Of course not.'

DI Perry shrugged. 'The bedsteads, old-fashioned metal, tubular bedsteads.'

'Well?'

'If you want to play tying up, a headboard's not much good is it?'

The manager shook his head. 'I can't remember why the interior designer chose what he chose, but we don't advertise the … other possibilities.'

'Of course.' DI Perry nodded. 'You don't need to.' She paused. 'The metal bars on the bedstead in Room 414 show signs of scratching, erosion. Quite a lot, actually.'

The manager didn't respond.

'Handcuffs. Probably. Although our girl upstairs was tied with something else.' She nodded. 'That bed's no stranger to this kind of thing.'

'Well,' the manager shrugged, 'what do you want me to say?'

DI Perry regarded him in silence for a moment. 'Did you speak to reception? About the couple?'

'I did. Nothing untoward. About him at least. He checked in on his own, cash upfront. We took a copy of the photo ID of course, but cash-paying customers usually ride on a false one.'

'And her?'

'No one really noticed her. I assume she just went straight up to 414.'

'People can do that, can they? Just stroll right in, use the lift?'

'We keep an eye, of course. But if they look like they belong, then fine.'

'That's security?'

'They have a nose for what's not right. That's what a good security guy does. He's there, but you probably don't know he's there. Like fish, swimming back and forth.'

'Fish?'

'Punters. They come and they go.' He smiled. 'What do you think hotels are for?'

TUESDAY 24TH SEPTEMBER, 6 PM (10 AM GMT)

TSIM SHA TSUI, HONG KONG

The ferry shuddered as it nestled up against the wooden pier. Engines growling as they held the vessel tight against the mooring, the deck rising and falling with the harbour's swell. The rattle of the gangway as it slid into place. The crowd edging forward, heads bobbing, jackets and bags slung over arms and shoulders. Commuter time, sober tones of the office. Voices, swirling around the covered gangways, echoing off the metalwork, warm from the afternoon sun. A breeze brushed over them, the tang of the sea, sharp and sour.

Emma Wilson pulled her shoulder bag tight against her hip as she moved towards the exit, elbows and shoulders brushing as they shuffled forward.

The ferry horn sounded, the crowd clattering down the gangway, thronging through the terminal, flowing out onto the streets of Kowloon.

Emma blinked as she stepped into the sunlight. She reached in her bag for her sunglasses, snapped them on and glanced around the square in front of her. The crowd swirled around her, one of their own, tailored jacket, pencil dress, end-of-day creases. Another office toiler, in need of drink and air conditioning. She tucked a loose strand of hair behind her ear and set off, skirting around the main road, heading for the promenade. Above her, the towers of Tsim Sha Tsui, silvery sentinels, soaring up beyond the waterfront bars.

She strode towards a bench overlooking the waterside. Couples leaned on the promenade railings, smiling, snapping selfies. No one looked out of place. She sat at the end of the bench, pulled out her phone whilst she looked back towards the Star Ferry Pier, scanning for static figures. A sense. Nothing more.

She looked back towards Hong Kong Island. Two black kite birds, slowly circling high above the harbour. Scavengers, watching, waiting.

She checked her phone. Six o'clock. She slipped it back into her bag, stood up, began to walk towards the Old Clock Tower, the Victorian brickwork glowing in the early-evening sunshine. Beyond, the sleek lines of the Hong Kong Cultural Centre, its sides rising sheer and smooth from the walkway.

She kept her pace steady, head still, as she glanced around for some tic in the rhythm of the crowd. A lady just ahead of her, stopping to rebunch her hair. The hummingbird hairclip.

Emma followed as the woman cut past the Space Museum onto Salisbury Road. Across from them, the Peninsular Hotel, its central tower soaring upwards, a grey stone citadel, glaring down at the press of people thronging the pavements below.

They crossed at the junction, crowds jostling around them, the blare of car horns, the haze of exhaust fumes shimmering above the warm tarmac.

They turned into Nathan Road, the towers rising up on either side of them, an avenue of giants, leading deep into the heart of Kowloon. Below the awnings the neon signs blazed, raw and loud. Shopfronts a wall of polished glass, the displays within a rush of colour and light.

The crowd was thicker now, the sounds of the street swirling around them, a steady roar, the people, weaving, bobbing.

The woman ducked into the entrance to the Cke Mall, Emma followed. The chill air, footsteps on the stone floor echoing off the ceiling. Coffee shops, that rich, dusty aroma, roasting beans, baking biscuits.

Emma kept her distance, a right turn, a left turn. Shops, more shops.

The woman stopped in front of a bridal boutique. She touched the door handle and walked on.

Emma looked in through the window. A rail bulging with bridal gowns lining the right-hand wall, to the left shelves, neat rows of shoes, hatstands, veils on expressionless faces. In front of her, a lady stood behind a glass-topped desk, her green dress stark against the white paintwork. Either side of her, a door. She looked up, nodded to Emma, smiled.

Emma stepped inside.

'You have an appointment?'

Emma stood for a moment. 'My fiancé. Yes.'

'You're Gail?'

Emma nodded.

'He arrived a few minutes ago.' She nodded towards the door to her left. 'Please. We have some styles laid out in there for you to try but if you'd like to see something else ...'

Emma opened the door. 'David, darling! I'm sorry I'm late.'

McKay stood up. 'No problem. Just arrived myself.'

She kissed him, turned around.

The lady in the green dress stood in the doorway. 'Can I get you both something? Tea. Or champagne perhaps?'

'I think we're fine for now.' He smiled. 'But thanks.'

The door closed.

They were alone.

David stood in front of a red velvet sofa, scattered with pink heart-shaped cushions. Facing him, a red silk curtain, fastened back. Beyond, a fitting room, a selection of bridal dresses hanging on the wall. A full-length mirror opposite. In one corner, a red velvet chair, more heart-shaped cushions.

'There's music as well.' David flicked a switch on the wall.

The speaker in the ceiling crackled into life. 'I feel so unsure ...' George Michael's mellow tones.

Emma plucked one of the dresses from the wall, held it in front of her. 'Not sure about this wedding look.' She ran the fabric through her fingers. 'White's a shocker to wear. Frames every blemish.'

'Tell that to your mother.'

'Should we be totally candid with one another?' She held the dress against herself. 'We are almost married after all.'

'That'll be a first.'

She turned to face the mirror. 'Do we have an audience?'

'You used to like that idea.'

She flicked the hem of the dress with her foot. 'I used to like flannel tops and cutaway jeans.'

'... though it's easy to pretend ...'

He pushed a heart-shaped cushion to one side, sat back down. 'This is where they come nowadays.' He patted the sofa. 'Turns into a bed. I'm told.'

She hung the dress back on the wall. 'Something ... less floaty I think.'

'For the real players, hotels are just too ... public.'

She turned to face him. 'And the green goddess next door?'

'The people who come here, well, you'd be wise to be discreet. And I'm sure they tip. Properly.'

'Of course.'

'But we're dress shopping. That's different.'

'… should have known better than to cheat a friend …'

She looked down at him. 'Can you ask George to …'

He flicked the music off.

She bit her lip. 'Can't you just give a straight answer?'

'Sorry, habit.' He smiled. 'It's safe. We can talk.'

She nodded. 'Borso. What kind of a day has he had?'

'The predictable kind.'

'You sure?'

'You can track him as well as we can.' He rubbed his beard. 'And I've got someone on him as well. Just in case.'

'Making it easy for us, don't you think?'

He pursed his lips. 'Is he?' He paused. 'You know, I hate to admit it, but it seems you were right about your hunch. Tsim Sha Tsui, last night.'

'Bet that hurt.'

'The light show. Something was missing. If you knew what you were looking for.'

'Go on.'

'The triangle, on the Norton Tower.' He paused. 'Someone had pulled the plug. Literally.'

'What else did you find out?'

He shrugged. 'As facts go, that's it. But we can make some good assumptions.'

'If it's a signal, it can't just be for Borso.'

'Agreed. It's a … broadcast of some sort.'

She sat down on the chair, pulling down the hem of her skirt. 'You seen anything like this before?'

'Only in the movies.'

'You sure it wasn't an accident? Someone just flicked the wrong switch?'

'Could be. If we assume that whoever it was just accidentally cut the wires leading out of the main fuse shunts.'

She frowned. 'Any CCTV?'

'Two guys, China Light and Power overalls, caps pulled down.'

'And?'

'We ran it through face recognition. Poor definition to start with, but not even a partial match.'

'The Chinese? An operation?'

He shrugged. 'Anything's possible.'

She tucked her hair behind her ear. 'So what do you think?'

'If it is a signal, for Borso and others, then we have to think that he needs to do something.'

She nodded.

'Otherwise why tell him? Whatever they're telling him.'

She picked up one of the cushions, placed it to one side. 'And how do we know he hasn't already?'

'We can't be sure.' He rubbed his beard again. 'But we had eyes on him all yesterday evening. And at the hotel.

And today … you saw his agenda. Crator Charitable Foundation business. Back-to-back.'

'And he's due to fly out tomorrow night.'

David nodded. 'Which is why I'm going to be on his back all day tomorrow.'

'We can do it together.'

He shook his head. 'If the Chinese are involved we just can't risk them picking you out.'

She looked across at him.

'You know I'm right.' He smiled. 'We'll be in touch, if something happens. Stay close to Fraser. We can get a message to him.'

She blinked. 'OK.'

'You know,' he pushed himself to his feet, 'that first dress you picked out. You'd have looked stunning.'

'Please don't try being nice, it just confuses me.'

He walked to the wall, picked up a dress, held it in front of her. 'Your black hair, framing those cheekbones, your toned curves rustling beneath cascades of silk.' He raised an eyebrow. 'You not just a bit curious?'

'I told you. I don't wear white.'

'Where's your sense of adventure?'

'Stop it.'

'Remember the fitting rooms at Lane Crawford?'

She looked up at him for a moment. 'Don't do this.'

He swallowed. 'I always loved watching you undress.'

Emma sat in silence, the slightest frown creasing her

forehead. She stood up, walked over to David, took the dress from him, hung it on the wall. She stood in front of him, her mane of dark hair shimmering under the ceiling lights. 'David, the only thing I want you to watch,' she paused, her eyes narrowing, 'is my back, out there, on the streets.'

He took a deep breath, swallowed again.

'Can you just forget about your dick for the next 24 hours and do that for me?'

He studied her face in silence, blinking. He finally spoke. 'You don't have to ask.' He tried to smile. 'I shared my soul with you.' He reached up, ran the back of his finger down her cheek. 'What else could I do?'

She took his hand in hers, squeezed it. 'Thank you.'

He gave a little grunt. 'You're a fucking liability, Ems.'

She flashed him a smile as she let go of his hand, turned, walked towards the door.

TUESDAY 24TH SEPTEMBER, 1 PM

WEST CENTRAL POLICE STATION, LONDON

'I'd rather not.' DI Perry shook her head.

DI Lute nodded. 'I'd heard.'

'Once was enough.'

They stood in the corridor by the doors to the autopsy room. Voices, echoing off the whitewashed walls. From inside, the jangle of a metal trolley rumbling across the tiled floor. The patter and hiss of the high-pressure hoses, water skittering across ceramic worktops. The smell of antiseptic. A base note of something earthier.

DI Perry winced.

'I've wrapped them individually. So you can lay them out.' DI Lute handed her Rhea Moore's clothes, sealed in clear plastic.

She took them. 'I wish people wouldn't do things like this.'

DI Lute looked across at her, his frown accentuating the lines on his forehead. 'Anne, I know you won't like me saying this,' she frowned, 'we're not looking for a murderer, we're looking for someone who had the shock of their lives, panicked and ran off.'

'We don't know what we're looking for.'

DI Lute exhaled. 'We've not got a murder budget so …' He tried a smile. 'Upstairs will kick off again if you start going full-Sherlock.'

Anne Perry looked across at Lute, half opened her mouth to say something, checked herself. She pursed her lips. 'When do we talk to the parents?'

DI Lute shrugged. 'There aren't any, they're dead.' He reached up, pulling at an earlobe between finger and thumb. 'But there's an aunt, she lives in Spain. I've given her your number as well, in case she can't get hold of me.'

'So she'll ID the body?'

'I didn't mention it in the email.' He paused. 'But she's coming over to do the funeral arrangements, so we can talk about it then.'

DI Perry raised a hand, turning the top button of her blouse between finger and thumb. 'Always sounds so … cold.'

'But anyway I'll make sure the girl looks fine, just the face, everything else will be covered up. Just in case.'

The peal of footsteps on the stone floor.

DI Lute turned around, looking up at the taller, younger man. 'This one's too straightforward. Man of learning like yourself.'

DC Zayan met his gaze. Nodded. Turned to DI Perry. 'Room's ready, ma'am.'

'OK.' She looked across at DI Lute. 'Alan.'

He raised his eyebrows. 'Anne.'

She stood in silence for a moment, smiled. 'Don't worry. Sherlock's somewhere else today.'

. . .

DI Perry sat back in her chair. 'I hate this.'

The window rattled as another truck rumbled by, the drawn blind quivered.

'Ghosts.' DI Perry closed her eyes. 'Those final steps. The edge of the precipice.' She looked again at the frozen image on the screen, shook her head.

'Shall I run it further?' DC Zayan reached out, picked up the remote.

The light from the screen washed over the desk, the grey glow a pool of moonlight in the darkness.

DC Zayan looked across at DI Perry, her face in shadow, fingertips touching, her rings glinting in the cold light.

'Turn around, Rhea.' She leaned forward towards the monitor, eyes narrowed. 'Just turn around. Go home.'

'Do you want me to run it on?' DC Zayan indicated the remote.

DI Perry nodded.

He pressed the play button.

The girl in the blue jacket and grey skirt walked into the hotel reception area, away from the camera above the entrance. She strode to the lifts, pressed the button. She stood there, her back to the camera. The air conditioning ruffled the pale scarf wrapped around her head. The lift door opened. She walked in. Reached to her side, pushed a button. She didn't turn around. The doors slid closed behind her.

DC Zayan paused the tape, looked down at his notes. 'At 19.16 he texts: "I'm here. Room 414".'

DI Perry blinked. 'Go on.'

He cleared his throat. '"Have you got what you need?" This is her texting. "I'm not always obedient." Then he replies '"Come straight up." He paused. Then she says: "'I need—"'

'OK.' She held up a hand. 'Enough for now.' She sighed. 'Rhea, really?'

DC Zayan continued. 'The only time they used names, or a name, anyway, was the first time they were in touch. Three evenings ago.'

'Zoe and Alex.' DI Perry nodded.

'The locations fit for the previous messages, for her anyway, logged at the nearest mast to her flat.'

DI Perry sat in silence for a moment. 'Was she right-handed or left-handed?'

DC Zayan frowned. 'Do we know that?'

'The right-hand thumbnail was trimmed. For texting I assume.'

He nodded.

'So,' DI Perry continued, 'she goes into the lift, the floor buttons on her left as she's standing there, back to us. Correct?'

'Correct.'

'She reaches out with her left hand and pushes the button. For floor four, we assume.'

'Yes.'

'So?'

He shrugged. 'Her left hand. I sometimes use my left.'

DI Perry nodded. 'Anything else about that scene in the lift?'

'Just …' He blinked. 'She seemed in a hurry.'

DI Perry leaned forward, a slight frown on her face, the pinch lines by her eyes, little starbursts of shadow under the glow of the monitor. She looked across at DC Zayan. 'How uncomfortable are you finding this?'

He cleared his throat. 'I'm fine.'

She nodded. 'Iqbal, we all have to take the whole package, and I need to know.'

He sat upright, a frown spreading across his chiselled features. 'Know what?' He paused. 'Ma'am.'

'You normally pick up on things straight away.' She fixed him in her gaze. 'You know what I'm saying. Not just anything, you pick up on what I'm looking for.'

Iqbal Zayan shifted in his chair. 'Yes. Ma'am.'

'So what am I looking for?'

He glanced up at the screen. He didn't reply.

She sat upright. 'Redemption.' She paused. 'For her, for Rhea.'

DC Zayan looked across at her. 'Redemption?'

'I know you weren't brought up a Christian, but you understand the term.'

He nodded.

'I'd like to think,' she said, concern etched across her soft features, 'that she didn't do this to herself.' She blinked. 'Am I making sense?'

'I'm not sure.'

'I'd like to think that she's a victim. Perhaps even an innocent victim.'

He didn't reply.

'What do you think?'

He looked down at the desk. 'Girls shouldn't do this kind of thing.'

DI Perry took a deep breath. 'Look, we haven't got much time.' She exhaled. 'Are you going to come along with me on this?' She paused. 'Or is your mind made up?'

He sat in silence for a moment. 'I want to keep learning.'

'Good.' She nodded towards the remote. 'Do you need to watch it again?'

He closed his eyes, exhaled. 'She didn't turn around in the lift.'

'Exactly. You get in the lift, you turn around, you're facing out, ready to go.'

'Maybe she was embarrassed?' DC Zayan nodded towards the screen. 'Trying not be seen. Would explain the headscarf.'

'But she didn't even move her head.' DI Perry spread her hands. 'Unless you did this every day, you'd need to look at the buttons to see which one to press.'

'Maybe she just moved her eyes. That's harder, of course.' He paused. 'And not natural, unless you've got a neck problem.'

'She wouldn't even risk flashing a profile at the CCTV.' She sat back.

The murmur of the traffic from the street below. A car horn sounded. The fan in the ceiling stuttered, resumed its nonchalant hum.

'She never looked right.' DI Perry shook her head. 'Lying there. Like that.' She looked across at DC Zayan. 'Did you take a good look at her?'

He didn't respond.

'It's different,' she continued, 'in homicide.' She glanced back at the TV monitor. 'The dead can't explain themselves.'

He nodded.

'They rely on us.' She paused. 'Can Rhea rely on you?'

He exhaled.

DI Perry raised a hand, turning the top button of her blouse between finger and thumb. 'Try and control that look.'

'I wasn't aware—'

'That's why you wind up DI Lute.'

'I try to be professional.'

'Of course you do. And I haven't spoken to DI Lute about it. About you. But I know him, I know how he works.'

'I always—'

'Just hear me out.' She raised a hand. 'I know you think you're strong. That you know your right and wrong.'

He sat in silence, his jaw muscles tensing.

'This is a different world. You'll have plenty of time to judge later.' She took a deep breath. 'When she left her flat yesterday morning she didn't know that that would be the last time. The very last time.' She shook her head. 'If we walk away now she'll always be that tragic, damaged girl who risked it all for a cheap thrill. And if that's her legacy we better be sure she deserved it.' She paused. 'Let's go back to the man checking in. Our "Alex".'

'He didn't have any luggage.' DC Zayan began. 'So he'd be dressed the same on the way in and the way out.'

'Good point.' She glanced at her watch. 'I've got to get over to Rhea's work, talk to her boss. Are you OK to carry on?'

DC Zayan nodded. 'Of course.'

She stood up. 'I can't see a thing, where's the …?'

He flicked on the desk light.

She winced. 'Didn't remember it as that bright.'

She stood up, smoothed down her skirt, turned, walked towards the door. 'Just get me a face.' She paused, her hand on the door. 'Tell me what you see.'

TUESDAY 24TH SEPTEMBER, 3 PM

THE ENTRANCE TO CRATOR CAPITAL, LONDON

The building crouched at the end of the cul-de-sac. Like a sullen, stone predator, its sleek black lines muscular, intimidating. The grain in the marble glowing in the afternoon sun.

DI Perry walked across the paved forecourt to the entrance. She looked up, the main door towered over her, a wall of sheer-cut steel. Set above, scaling the building, columns of darkened windows, the sky's reflection shimmering off the polished glass. She placed a hand on the pillar that flanked the entrance. The stonework felt warm.

She looked around for a button to press.

The door began to open, the glinting mass sliding smoothly aside, the quiet rumble of oiled precision.

She stepped into the entrance hall, the air conditioning sweeping over her, cool and clean. She glanced around. A circular room, an atrium reaching up high above her, the cloud-flaked sky visible through its glass dome.

The walls, curves of silky white, simple and sheer, their reflection glancing off the black marble floor. Doors, to either side, dark polished wood, the brass fittings glowing in the sunlight. Ahead of her the reception desk, the light grey leather panels, soft against the sober rigour of the room.

A faint hum, the noise of the city fading. A muffled clang as the seals on the door behind her glided back into place. Silence.

A young woman stood up from behind the desk. White blouse, black tailored jacket. The initials CC in embroidered gold on the breast pocket. 'DI Perry.'

Anne Perry walked across the hallway, shoes clicking on the gleaming stonework. 'I'm a little early, I know.'

'Shall I look after that?' She indicated the coat slung over DI Perry's arm.

'It's fine, I'll just … I'm fine.'

The woman behind the desk nodded. 'Of course.'

'Is there somewhere I can sit?' DI Perry glanced around the bare hallway.

The receptionist flashed a nervous smile. 'Thing is that we—'

'Don't like to keep our visitors waiting.' A man stood in one of the doorways off the entrance hall. Tall, late thirties maybe, short, dark hair, an open expression. 'Another house rule.' His Australian twang echoing around the marble hallway.

Anne Perry nodded as she looked across at him. Egyptian cotton button-down, tailored chinos. Trading floor chic.

'Sorry that you have to be here.' He continued.

She took a forward. 'Ellis Wagner?'

He nodded. 'We can talk in my office.'

She walked up to him.

He offered his hand.

She shook it.

'Just this way.'

She followed him along the corridor. More white walls, the dark wooden doors, evenly-spaced on either side. Lights above each doorway, scattering shadows as they passed. The black carpet, thick, yielding under their silent footsteps.

'We're on the second floor.' He spoke over his shoulder. 'I like to walk up. But there's a lift.'

'Stairs is fine.'

At the end of the corridor a circular staircase spiralled upwards. The wooden balustrade, its smooth curves solid, purposeful.

She followed him up, their footfall soaking into the soft fabric underfoot.

Another corridor, same walls, same doors, same skittering shadows thrown across the passageway.

They stopped in front of a door.

He flexed his fingers, exhaled. Swung it open.

The research room fell silent as the two walked in. A dozen pairs of eyes, tracking them as they crossed the floor. DI Perry glanced down at them as she passed, earnest young faces, concerned, confused.

Ellis Wagner closed his office door behind him.

Their audience, the other side of the glass, watching, waiting.

'They're struggling with it.' Wagner indicated a chair the far side of his desk. 'Here they are, dream job, right in the action.' He picked up a pile of reports from the desk, laid them on the floor beside him. 'Life's good.' He sat down, facing her across the desk. 'Death's not meant to be in this story.'

DI Perry looked around the room. Shafts of sunlight through the gaps in the blinds splashed across the desk. Hanging on the wall behind him, a framed certificate, next to it, a small regimental flag.

'You served?' She nodded towards the flag behind him.

'Briefly.' He nodded. 'But I hang it there for other reasons.'

DI Perry squinted as she tried to read the inscriptions. 'Duty First.'

'Fifth Royal Australians. A family thing. My father. And my grandfather.'

'Our son's off to Sandhurst next month.' She paused. 'Royal Anglians.'

'That a family thing too?'

'Gosh no.' She rummaged in her handbag for her notebook. 'In fact, my husband's quite a pacifist.'

Wagner glanced back at the flag. 'My grandfather fell at Kapyong. April of '51.'

'Duty first.' DI Perry looked up at him. 'It's a lot to ask.'

Wagner nodded, exhaling. 'So, Rhea Moore, poor girl. Are we allowed to know what happened?'

'Still waiting for the autopsy report.' DI Perry cleared her throat. 'So, not at this stage, no.' She paused. 'Sorry.'

'So, what should I tell them?' He indicated the anxious expressions in the room beyond.

DI Perry glanced out across the research room, then back to Wagner. 'Was Rhea close to anyone? At work?'

Wagner sat back in his chair. 'It's a close-knit team.'

'But did she have a … confidant?'

'Was she sleeping with someone, you mean?'

'Not necessarily that.'

Wagner shook his head. 'I'd say not.'

'Not confiding or not …?'

'I'd be pretty certain she wouldn't be involved with someone here. Not like that.'

'Would you know?'

He glanced at the window, then back towards her. 'She was a determined girl. She wouldn't want the distraction of someone at work.'

DI Perry looked up from her notes. 'She worked for you for, what, three months?'

'Four. Almost.'

'Did she ever talk about life outside work?'

'What there is of it. The hours are long. Weekends too. Depending on the project.'

She nodded. 'Exactly, all those hours, you'd go mad, without someone to have a good moan with.'

He shrugged.

'Well, I know I would.' She paused. 'Did you like her?'

Wagner frowned. 'Never really stopped to think.'

DI Perry looked down at her pad, scribbled a note.

'But no reason not to like her, if that's what you're asking.' He flexed his fingers.

She sat back in her chair. 'Why did you hire Rhea Moore?'

He studied her for a moment. 'The Sokolsky opening, the Schuhler gambit.'

'A chess move.'

'More than that. Elegance and aggression.' He smiled.

'But you still beat her.'

'Or she let me win.'

DI Perry laid her notepad on the desk. Picked up a log report. 'Do I need to know what these are?'

'Don't see why you should.'

She looked down at his desk, log reports, heaped in stacks. 'Looks like a lot of work.'

'You're not wrong.' He nodded. 'I inherited the system. I didn't invent it.'

She flicked open a report. 'What are you meant to see? Or not see?'

'Theodora, defending her virtue. And it's a trail for Compliance to follow.'

'Theodora?'

'Computer doesn't really do her justice. It justice. It's a proprietary system, refined over the years. Predates me.'

'Does that stand for something?'

'Just a pet name, I guess.'

She raised her eyebrows.

'Information,' he continued, 'that's one thing. And we have plenty of it. Expensive information. Subscriptions to all the primary sources.' He nodded. 'But the real key is how Theodora synthesises it.'

'Can you give me an example, something easy.'

'Wouldn't make sense, without the overall setting.' He leaned forward. 'We're a specialist house, we only invest in our specific areas of expertise.' He rested his forearms on the desk. 'Biotech and pharmaceutical intermediates, commodities, hard and soft – and transportation.'

She nodded.

'Weather as well. For obvious reasons.'

'Obvious?'

'Agricultural commodities but transport, in general. If we're trying to model the specifics of supply and demand in any hub around the world we need to know what's leaving and what's arriving, when and how quickly.' He spread his palms. 'Historic data as well. Without that context the predictive value of compiled data is highly uncertain.'

'If Theodora can do all that, why do you need analysts?'

'For original ideas. Hypotheses. And to check that she's talking sense.' He sat back in his chair. 'Theodora's thorough, but not worldly wise.'

'And hence the need,' DI Perry looked across at Wagner, 'to defend her virtue.'

He looked out over the research floor. 'The tyranny of choice.' He looked back at her. 'Imagine if you could ask Theodora anything. Anything.' He shook his head. 'You'd never be done.'

'But an answer is an answer.'

'In your world, yes. Perhaps. But imagine there's 1,000 market models to solve. Or 10,000. And that's just the conundrums we can imagine.' He exhaled. 'That's why we have these.' He nodded at the reports stacked on his desk. 'You've been set a task, stay on the track. For your own sanity.'

'So ... all this ...' she picked up a log report, let in drop on the desk, 'to save people from themselves?'

'It's not that straightforward. Everything's connected to something else.'

She shrugged.

'It's also an audit trail. For Compliance. So they know why we put the trade on.'

'Really?'

'It's not about opinion. This is factual.'

DI Perry tilted her head to one side. 'This is factual. Or this is factual.'

He narrowed his eyes. 'What's this got to do with Rhea's accident?'

'Elegance and aggression. Your words.'

He sat across the desk in silence.

'Pushing the boundaries. An explorer.' She raised her eyebrows. 'A risk-taker.'

'These are your words.'

'Did she? Stay on the track?'

He flexed his fingers. 'She wanted to do well here. Why would she break the rules?'

DI Perry met his gaze. 'Maybe we could ask Theodora.'

'That,' he sat back in his chair, 'would be difficult right now.'

DI Perry spread her palms. 'I thought you said she knew everything.'

'You would need to be properly introduced.' He frowned. 'And the right person to do that isn't here.'

'So, who's her chaperone?'

'Scutt.'

'Is that his surname?'

'Just his name.'

'So when is he back?'

'I'm not sure. I was told he's on holiday.'

'So who fills in, when he's away?'

Wagner shook his head, puffed out his cheeks. 'I'm not sure … he's just always around.'

'And when did he decide to start this … well-earned break?'

Wagner bit his lip. 'I was just told today, so …'

'Something happened.' She leaned forward. 'He was upset about Rhea.'

'Possibly.' He swallowed. 'I mean he was sweet on her. I think.'

'So why didn't you mention him before?'

Wagner shrugged. 'No reason, I just … didn't.'

DI Perry glanced across at the research room. The one empty desk. A single white rose in a thin vase. She picked up her notebook. Slipped it into her handbag. She looked up at the regimental flag. 'So, what are these other reasons?'

He followed her gaze. 'To remind me.'

'Of something you did?'

'Or didn't do.' He turned towards her. 'It was all a while ago. Twelve years ago, to be exact.' He paused. 'Is there anything I can say about Rhea? Something … better?'

DI Perry stood up. She pulled out her business card, laid it on the desk. 'It must have happened quickly. And she looked … quiet.' She paused. 'Yes, quiet.'

He walked to the door. 'I'll need to walk you down. No unaccompanied visitors.'

She followed him across the research room. She looked down at the team as she passed, tried a smile. They avoided her gaze.

He led the way down the corridor. The cushioned stillness settling around them.

A man stood by the spiral stairway.

Wagner slowed his pace as he approached the figure. 'Jamie.'

The man looked past Wagner, his attention fixed on DI Perry. 'I'll take it from here, Ellis, thanks.'

Ellis Wagner pulled a business card from his pocket, handed it to her. 'Feel free, if there's anything else.'

She nodded.

'No worries.' He turned around, retraced his steps down the corridor.

'My apologies.' The man began. 'I should have been there to receive you. When you arrived.'

A slight shrug of her shoulders. 'I wasn't expecting anyone else.'

'It's another one of our house rules.' He paused. 'For our guests.'

'Not always called that.' She scanned his face. A few years younger than her, neat brown hair, an outdoor complexion.

He held out his hand. 'Jamie Ives. One of the principals.'

'DI Perry.' She shook it.

He looked down at her, a hint of a smile across his clean-cut features. 'I expect you'll be pleased when this month's over.'

'Will I?'

'Weed pollen.' He met her gaze. 'Slight redness beneath your eyes.'

She drew herself upright.

'For me it's tree pollen. I used to dread the spring.'

She stood in silence.

He indicated a door beside them. 'Shall we?'

She glanced at the door, then back at Ives. 'Is there something you'd like to tell me?'

He studied her face for a moment. 'The room's hypoallergenic.'

She nodded. 'A single white rose. On Rhea's desk.'

'Everyone is shocked by what happened.'

'Scutt for one.'

'Of course.' He stepped forward, opened the door. 'We're like family here.'

She stepped inside. A black wooden table commanded the centre of the room, light from the spots above shimmering across the polished surface. Chairs on either side, the steel tubing softly glinting. She glanced around the room, pale washed walls, no windows.

A click as the door closed behind her.

The air, an edge to it, something metallic, on the tip of her tongue.

'The air's scrubbed too.' His voice behind her. 'For pathogens, allergens …'

'I've lived in London too long.' She walked towards the table. 'Fresh air tastes …' she took another breath, 'brittle.'

They sat, opposite sides of the table.

He rested his forearms on its shiny surface, the light picking out the subtle pattern in his suit. His hands still. His face, half in shadow.

DI Perry took out her notepad, placed it on the table. She looked across at him. A slight lift of her eyebrows, a cue to him to begin.

He let the silence wash around them for some moments. 'Do you know what happened to her?'

'We think we know what happened.' She paused. 'But we're not sure how.'

He nodded. 'You and I, DI Perry. We would understand different things by the word "normal".'

'Would we?'

'The corridors you walked down just now, designed to absorb all sound. Just like this room.'

She waited for him to continue.

'And the air.' He took a breath. 'Pure enough to catch in your throat.'

She nodded.

'Beneath us, a snarling, shuddering creation in glass and steel. Raw data, a million questions, answers, all surging through her wiring. Her RAM, her magnetic platters, humming as they devour all this … knowledge.'

'Go on.'

'Enough electricity to power a small town. And water. Seventy litres a minute, a million litres a day, surging around her water-cooling system, just to keep her sane.'

DI Perry narrowed her eyes. 'What's this got to do with Rhea?'

'Our people. People like Rhea. They get to look into the eyes of this … creature. Theodora. The edge of what there is to know. Thrilling, frightening even.'

'And?'

'All this. To us, this is normal. Efficiency, effectiveness, knowledge and insight. Without limits.' He leaned forward, his features lit up in the lights from above. 'Fourteen or more hours a day.' He narrowed his eyes. 'Could you keep up?'

'Rhea couldn't?'

'She was an endurance runner. She wasn't going to fall behind.'

'So what are you saying?'

He sat back, his face once again in shadow. 'That we shouldn't rush to judge.'

'Judge what?'

'You're a senior officer. Resources are scarce. You're here. This "accident". Not perhaps just a question of wrong time, wrong place.'

She raised a hand, turning the top button of her blouse between finger and thumb. 'Scutt. I hear he's gone on holiday. Unexpectedly.'

'Has he?'

'I can check with HR.'

'We prefer to call them the Host Team. But of course, you're very welcome.'

She scribbled a note in her pad. 'Theodora. Who else knows how to ... manage her?'

'Aside from Scutt?' He paused. 'My business partner, Milot Borso.'

'Can I talk to him?'

'He's in Hong Kong, for the charity.'

She sat back, rubbing her temples with thumb and index finger.

'You all right, DI Perry?'

She exhaled. 'Yes just ... my head. And this air. I don't think it agrees with me.'

'Can I get you a glass of water?'

She shook her head, blinked several times. 'I'll be fine.' She glanced back at her notes. 'The log reports. How long have these checks been in place?'

'Did Ellis refer to them as checks?'

'Well what else would you call them? If he's meant to make sure that analysts don't go off on ... quests of their own.'

'I'd use more constructive language. As I said, it's about efficiency and effectiveness.' He leaned forward once more.

'Analysts and information.' He paused. 'Like a magnetic attraction. And faced with all these … possibilities.'

DI Perry creased up her features, exhaled.

'Are you sure you're all right?' He reached out across the table, one finger resting on her hand.

She slid her hand off the table, shook her head. 'I think I need some fresh air. Or not fresh air.'

'Sure.' He stood up, walked around the table, stood beside her. 'Are you OK to …?' He held out his hand.

'I'm fine.' She took a breath, stood up. Gathered up her pad and pen from the desk.

'We can call a nurse. She'd be here in minutes.'

'Honestly, I'm fine.' She walked towards the door, Ives opened it.

'I'll come down with you.' He steered her away from the staircase. 'We'll take the lift.'

They rode it down to the ground floor, where the receptionist was waiting.

She walked up to DI Perry, took her arm in her hand. 'Can I order you a taxi?'

'I just need to …' She walked across the entrance hall, Ives and the receptionist just behind.

The steel door rumbled into life, the sounds of the street around them. The air, damp and sweet.

She stepped out onto the forecourt.

'I never gave you a card.' Ives stepped forward. 'Here.' He slipped his business card into her hand, letting his fingers rest on hers just a little longer than necessary. 'Call me, any time.' Jamie looked down at her, his eyes fixed on hers. 'Any time.'

DI Perry blinked, slung the strap of her bag over her shoulder. She turned, walked across the courtyard and onto the pavement, her heels clicking as she headed towards the main road at the end of the cul-de-sac. She looked up at the sky, clouds gathering, thickening. She stopped, took a deep breath, the scent of the coming rain, the tang of the traffic fumes. 'Icarus,' she mused to no one in particular, 'the cloud cover won't help you.'

TUESDAY 24TH SEPTEMBER, 6 PM

WEST CENTRAL POLICE STATION, LONDON

The rain pattered against the windows. The light from the desk lamps, pools of brightness splashed across the shadow-streaked floor.

Anne Perry looked up from her screen, sat upright in her chair, stretched her arms above her head. 'In the dark.' She leaned forward, picked up the plastic cup, looked inside it, dropped it in the bin. 'Stumbling around.' She shifted in her chair, smoothing down her skirt. She ran a thumb around her waist, checking her blouse was still tucked in. She glanced down, gave a little grimace as she pinched the roll of flesh just above her hip. 'Love handles.' She muttered to no one in particular. She sighed. 'I wish.' She pinched the roll above her other hip. 'Just handles.'

She glanced around the office. A solitary colleague, on the far side of the room, earplugs in, eyes fixed on his screen. Anne gave a little wave. No reaction. 'No man is an island …'

A click as the door on the far side of the office opened. DI Lute poked his head around the door, scanning the almost deserted room. He spotted Anne, raised a hand. He was holding an envelope.

'Any surprises?' She looked up at him, the lower part of her face framed in the light, her eyes in darkness.

He walked towards her. 'I'm not sure.'

She pushed her chair to one side, pulled up another beside her. 'Tell me.'

He stood by the side of her desk and slipped the report from the envelope, laid it in front of her. 'Time of death, between 22.00 and 23.00 yesterday evening.'

She nodded. 'Just after the duty manager knocked on the door.'

He turned over a page, began to read from the report. 'Pronounced bluish discoloration of the skin and mucous membranes as a result of vasoconstriction of the peripheral blood vessels and decreased haemoglobin … consistent with a prolonged period of hypoxia ante-mortem.'

Anne looked up at him. 'Prolonged?'

He nodded. 'His best guess, four to five hours.'

She reached up, turning the top button of her blouse between finger and thumb. 'Unconscious?'

'Or semi-conscious.'

'For all that time?'

'Some lucid intervals, perhaps.' He glanced down at Anne. 'Short ones.'

Anne sat back in her chair. She shook her head. 'Who does that to themselves?'

He stood in silence.

The windows shook as a rain squall swept over them.

'Iqbal's still running the CCTV loops.' She strummed her fingers on the desk. 'Shall we?'

'OK.' He reached up, pulling at an earlobe with finger and thumb. 'We should.'

Anne stood up, smoothing down her skirt. She picked her phone up from the desk. 'Five hours.' She glanced around the room. 'You can fly to Cairo in five hours.'

He looked across at Anne. 'I know what you're thinking. About me and DC Zayan.' He exhaled. 'But that look he gives me sometimes, staring down that aristocratic nose of his. It gets on my tits.' He paused. 'Am I allowed to say that?'

'Do you have tits?'

He looked down at the folds in his shirt. 'I guess so.'

She nodded. 'Rhea got in the lift at 19.22.'

'Very much conscious.'

'And three hours later she's dead.' She pushed her chair back. 'Here we go.'

. . .

Anne Perry sat next to DC Zayan, Alan Lute standing behind them. The screen on the desk, frozen shadows from yesterday's world. The frosted outlines, singed under the glow of the foyer lamps.

The murmur of the ceiling fan, the blinds on the windows pattering in the draft.

'They're always approximations.' DI Perry sat back into the darkness, just her hands resting on the desk, the pale skin washed in the smoky grey light of the monitor. She exhaled. 'Whatever that means.'

'At 19.16 he texts her "I'm here, Room 414".' DC Zayan glanced down at his notes. 'She texts right back. "Have you got what you need?"'

'She could be in a different room.' DS Lute shrugged.

'And a girl, same height and shape as Rhea, and wearing the same outfit Rhea left work in, gets in the lift 15 minutes later.' DI Perry tapped a fingernail on the desk. 'That's a monster of a coincidence.'

DC Zayan nodded. 'Quite a behemoth.'

The room fell quiet.

'Just … came out.' DC Zayan cleared his throat.

'It's OK.' DI Lute exhaled. 'I know what a behemoth is.'

'So,' DI Perry continued, 'if that is Rhea in the lift, she either died sometime after 23.00, or the hypoxia can't have lasted more than three hours.'

'Let's just go again with the idea that that's not Rhea in the lift.' DI Lute straightened his back, rolled his shoulders. 'Maybe she checked in earlier, and the texts were part of a game, when they were already in the room together.'

'She left work at?' DI Perry glanced across at DC Zayan.

'HR say she swiped out of the building at 18.07.' He nodded. 'So if she went straight to the hotel, she could be there at … say, 18.45. That could give you the four hours of hypoxia and a time of death around eleven.'

DI Perry leaned forward, her face caught in the milky light of the monitor. 'But there's the phone.' She looked up at DI Lute. 'Her proper phone.'

DC Zayan checked his notes. 'We found her phone – her iPhone, not the burn one – at her flat. Would she go to work without it?'

'Lot of these city firms, you can't have mobiles on the trading floor.' DI Lute paused. 'I think I read that somewhere.'

DI Perry and DC Zayan exchanged glances. She raised an eyebrow.

'But I get your point.' DI Lute continued. 'If she did drop off her phone at Battersea she'd be hard-pressed to get to the hotel much before 19.30.'

'And DC Zayan's already gone through the tapes from 18.00 last night.' DI Perry nodded. 'The girl in the lift's the only one who gets close to her in build and age.'

DI Lute looked down at DC Zayan. 'How far did you go?'

'Until 22:00. When the duty manager knocked on the door'

DI Perry looked at her watch. 'Is it too late for a cup of tea?'

'Can we just talk about the guy. This "Alex". DI Lute looked down at DC Zayan. 'What are the possibilities again?'

'Do you want me to rewind the CCTV?'

DI Lute shook his head. 'Just remind us where we are.'

'OK. So, the ID. They took a copy, standard procedure, filed it with Room 414's registration.' He laid his notebook on the table. 'It's not even a decent forgery. The photo looks like it was taken underwater at night.' He glanced down at his notes again. 'Timothy Mercer. D.o.b. 26/7/1988.'

'Sounds very English.' DI Perry nodded. 'Probably meant to.'

'Paid cash. Of course.'

'And that guy you mentioned. In the blue cap.' DI Lute nodded towards the screen.

'Fits the timestamp on the registration docs for Room 414. But ...'

'He never lets the camera see his face?' DI Perry raised her eyebrows.

'Just like Rhea.' He nodded. 'If it's Rhea.' He looked down at his notes. 'Dark glasses. Beard. Could be fake.' He shrugged. 'All the receptionist could remember was that the guy appeared to be sober. And was over 18.'

'Skin colour? Rings? Jewellery? Tattoos?'

'He thinks he was white. Or at least light-skinned.' DC Zayan sat back in his chair. 'He was wearing a long dark coat, collar turned up.' He looked up at DI Lute. 'It's almost a look, apparently. That kind of customer.'

DI Lute frowned. 'But if she died shortly after the duty manager heard them together. He'd have … panicked, or at least legged it. Straight away.'

DC Zayan nodded. 'We've been through the CCTV, from 21.30 that evening to when they discovered the body the next morning.' He looked up at DI Lute. 'Nothing.'

'No suitcase?'

'So no change of clothes.' He paused. 'Could have ditched the coat. But … no one comes close.'

The room fell quiet. A car horn sounded from the street below.

'And I checked out the back entrance.' DC Zayan continued. 'It's manned. Twenty-four hours. No one's allowed in our out without their security pass.' He looked across at DI Perry. 'And I spoke to the guys. They reckon they know everyone who works here. Even the new ones.'

DI Lute reached up, pulling at an earlobe between thumb and forefinger. 'Could he have climbed out the window?'

'No balcony.' DC Zayan picked up his pen, twirled it around his finger. 'Four floors up. Just glass and concrete. In the dark. I wouldn't want to try it.'

She looked up at DI Lute. 'Have we got enough?'

'For a murder enquiry? No way.'

'But if the autopsy's really sure about duration of hypoxia … time of death?' Anne raised her eyebrows.

'But you'd need some evidence … or at least a really solid supposition.' DI Lute shook his head. 'Right now we're just brainstorming.' He picked up his jacket from the table. 'At 19.16 she gets a text on the phone we found by her body, inviting her up to Room 414. Just minutes before, on CCTV, a guy checks into that room. She arrives 15 minutes later, CCTV tracks her across the lobby and into the lift. The text exchange makes it clear what kind of fun she's after. Just before ten, the duty manager gets a complaint about the noise in 414. He knocks on the door, says he hears a girl whispering, giggling, having fun.' He slipped on his jacket. 'Next morning, she's found dead. Asphyxiated, plastic bag tied over her head. Barely any signs of a struggle.' He looked down at DI Perry. 'How do you go from there to murder?'

Anne continued to stare at the screen, running the top button of her blouse between thumb and forefinger. 'Her wrists. If she was a regular to this, there'd be scars, abrasions …'

'First time for everything.' DI Lute looked at his watch. 'I need a drink. How about you, Anne?'

'Need you ask?' She slipped her phone into her handbag.

'DC Zayan?' He paused. 'If you don't drink, that's fine. Just an invitation.'

DC Zayan turned, looking up at him. 'Thank you. But … another time.' He nodded. 'Sir.'

Anne got to her feet.

DI Lute turned to walk to the door. He hesitated, turned around, concern etched across his well-lined forehead. He looked down at DC Zayan. 'The dead girl. What do you think happened?'

'I only saw the body briefly. But her hands, the way they were bound together, her right wrist underneath her left wrist.'

DI Lute nodded. 'Go on.'

'If you're offering your hands out to be tied together, and you're right-handed, you'd put your right wrist above your left wrist.'

DI Lute held out his wrists. He looked across at DC Zayan. 'You sure I can't buy you a drink?'

DC Zayan glanced up at DI Perry.

She gave a little nod.

'If you'll excuse the expression, sir,' DC Zayan smiled, 'I could murder a pint.'

TUESDAY 24TH SEPTEMBER, 9 PM

BARNES, LONDON

Anne Perry stood silhouetted in the doorway to the kitchen. 'One became three, I'm afraid.'

Her husband looked up from his laptop. 'The cat's out looking for you.'

She walked towards the table, the polished wood glinting slick under the light above. 'Sorry.' She glanced around, the rest of the kitchen quietly smudged in the shadows. 'Bad girl.'

'I wish.' He sat back, his hands still resting beside the keyboard, the steam from the coffee cup coiling lazily upwards.

'Careful what you wish for.' She slung her handbag over the back of the chair. 'A guy I met today ...'

'Push your buttons?'

She shrugged off her coat. 'Only if you like roguish good looks and a gym-ripped body.'

'You poor thing.'

'With a glint in their eye that has you reaching for your shades.' She tossed her coat onto the table. 'Who could say no to DNA like that?'

'Must have been awful.'

'And those eyes.' She reached behind her head, slipping off the hairband from her ponytail, shaking out her hair. 'Don't bother throwing a lifebelt.'

'There's many a virtuous woman weary of her trade.'

She stood behind him. 'Began to feel quite faint actually.'

'Do people still play footsie?'

'In my Matalan tights?' She leaned forward, put her arms around his neck, her auburn hair cascading over his shoulders. 'I don't think so.'

He squeezed her arms. 'Can I pour you something?'

She unwound herself from him, walked around the table. 'Her name's Rhea.'

He nodded. The rain still tapping at the windows.

'She's not meant to be there.' Anne pulled out a chair.

'There's some red from earlier.'

'She's even got freckles.' She sat down, looked across at Mr P. 'It could be Cara lying there.'

'Don't, Anne.'

She ran a finger down the side of the coffee cup. 'Her parents are dead.' She nodded. 'At least that's something.'

He studied Anne's face for some moments. A gust of wind rattled through the hedge beneath the window. The bark of a dog, from somewhere in the damp darkness.

'This isn't your journey.' He laid his hand on hers. 'Wherever she's gone.'

'That's just it.' Anne shook her head. 'I can't let her go. Not like this.'

He leaned back, his angular features blurring into the semi-darkness around them. 'Whatever this is. It all happened before you were there.'

'Someone's sleepwalking towards the cliff edge. You just going to stand and watch?'

He shook his head. 'You were always so … self-aware.'

'I can't unsee things.'

He looked at her, the smile lines around his eyes crinkled shadows under the ceiling light. 'My love, this is about you.'

She closed her eyes. 'I'm tired.'

'You think you're reaching for the light but you're looking at the wrong horizon.'

She shook her head.

'You think you're going up but you're slipping. All this … badness.' He shook his head. 'Down there it's too … grainy.'

She looked across at him. 'If it was one of ours …'

'The more you try to think like them …'

She exhaled. 'I took an oath, remember?'

'Breathing their air …'

'To help … always.'

'No wonder you feel giddy.'

She dropped her head.

They sat in silence, the wind, more insistent now, rattling at the doors, buffeting the window panes.

She took a deep breath. 'Ever read a coroner's report?'

He shook his head. 'Not cover to cover.'

She looked across at him. 'It's like a biography.' She paused. 'Written by that unsympathetic relative who never bothered to get to know you, but felt they could judge you anyway.' She leaned forward. 'What was your last meal? What was your diet like? How overweight were you? How scarred was your liver? How about your dental hygiene? When did you last trim your toenails?' She nodded. 'Page after page. Every bad habit, every blemish.'

He sat in silence. Voices from the street, looming and fading. The splash of footsteps.

'And everyone,' Anne continued, 'believes every word to be true.' She drummed her fingers on the table. 'And the world gets a free copy.' She smiled. 'So, are we sitting comfortably?'

He looked across at Anne. Managed half a smile.

'So, who was Rhea?' Anne raised her eyebrows. 'That pretty girl with the pretty name. They'll run a nice photo, the press, clear-eyed, smiling, liked and admired by her peers. A sad story, tragic even.' She paused. 'But not pitiful.'

'Go on.'

'Pitiful is asking some stranger to tie you to a bed and slowly suffocate you.'

He exhaled. 'That's a foreign country, Anne.'

'She didn't ask to be there.'

'You don't belong.'

'Neither does Rhea.'

The room fell quiet; the rain was easing, the patter on the windows barely audible above the rumble of the traffic.

He rose to his feet, walked around the table, stood behind Anne. 'It's wearing at you.' He ran his hand through her hair. 'You should treat yourself. Highlights. When you're stressed, the grey peeks through.' He placed his hands on her shoulders.

'Like an ageing gorilla.' She laid a hand on his.

'Like a silver-backed tigress.' She kissed her head. 'I know I rattled your cage.'

She looked up at him. 'Sorry I growled.'

He squeezed her shoulders. 'More of a purr really.'

'I do listen.' She smiled. 'Talking of which,' she glanced around the kitchen, 'where is the cat?'

'Tuesday evening. Poker night.'

'Of course.'

He walked to the sink, the glow of the taps in the half-light, his shadow thrown across the blinds. From outside, the fizz of tyres on wet streets, the drum of lorries on the Lower Richmond Road. 'Actually, tigers don't purr.' He took two glasses from the shelf. 'When they're content, they close their eyes and blow air through their nostrils.'

'Like snoring?'

'They call it chuffing.' He placed the glasses on the worktop. 'She lay there gently chuffing.'

'Tell me I don't.'

He picked up the whisky bottle, poured two glasses. 'You're right. Nothing gentle about it.'

'You used to say I had an elegant nose.'

He walked to the table, placed a glass in front of her. 'It's impressive ... acoustically speaking.' He took a sip, put down the glass, laid the palm of his hand on her forehead. 'Did you really feel faint?'

She closed her eyes. 'Dizzy, perhaps. I'm fine now.'

He sat down opposite Anne. 'Rhea.' He paused. 'Was she running away from something?'

Anne picked up her glass. 'A dream job. A nice flat.' She took a sip. 'Working 80 hours a week ...'

'Is that what they call financial freedom?'

Anne reached up, turning the top button of her blouse between finger and thumb. 'This place, where she worked. I was there today.' She looked across at him. 'I had this feeling, I just couldn't quite describe it.' She nodded. 'Until I was back on the street.'

'Air conditioning. Does for your sinuses.'

'There was something. In there.' She paused. 'Something that would hurt me. If it could.'

'Someone you met?'

She shook her head. 'Not even that. Something. Out of sight. Out of my sight. But it knew I was there.'

'Do you have to go back?'

Anne exhaled. 'She was suffocating for five hours. She died between 22.00 and 23.00 last night. She left work at 18.07.'

He shrugged. 'Well?'

'She didn't get to the hotel until 19.30. She's on CCTV.'

'Pathology's an art, not a science.'

Anne nodded. 'I just know. She was killed.' She paused. 'But why?'

'What does your co-pilot think?'

'Alan.' She exhaled. 'He thinks the city's full of self-destructive sociopaths.'

'Well?'

'Booze and cocaine.' Anne placed her glass on the table. 'Was that really her?' She looked up at Mr P. 'How do I know what to look for, if I don't know what I'm missing?'

He reached across, laid his hand on hers. 'If you really think there's something ... bigger here, you could call your friend from the Sawyer case.'

Anne sat in silence, looking down at her glass.

'What was it she said about getting in touch? To mention Estepona?' He paused. 'Maybe this is something for the spooks in Vauxhall.'

She looked up at him. 'Emma, her name was Emma.' She smiled, weakly. 'I'm sure Alan would like that.' She reached for her glass. 'I think he fancied her.'

He leaned back in his chair, exhaled. 'I've said my bit.' He glanced up at the clock on the wall. 'It's getting late.'

She took a deep breath, closed her eyes. 'You know, I never really thought about the night. The real, raw night.' She looked down at her glass, picked it up. 'But now, I lie awake, in the depths of it. I hear the cries, nameless things stirring, out there, in the silk-lined darkness.'

He tried a smile. 'Just my friend Mr Fox. Doing his rounds.'

Anne looked across at him. 'A fox must know how his story ends.' She blinked. 'Alone, too weak to fight, worn-out claws, pawing at the cold shingle.'

'Yet they always seem to be smiling.'

Anne nodded. 'A spring in his step.' She drained the rest of her whisky. 'They say God loves a trier.'

TUESDAY 24TH SEPTEMBER,
6.30 PM (11.30 PM GMT)

MIDTOWN, NEW YORK

DEA agent Brian Welch strode briskly along East 45th Street, leaving the sheer-cut bulk of the MetLife building behind him. The lights on the white strips ringing each floor, a giant venetian blind clattering down from the early-evening sky. He dodged around the other pedestrians with practised ease, time and space to spare. The glare from the glass-fronted banks lit up the pavement, sofas and chairs in cheerful colours scattered around deserted halls. Above, rising strong and sharp, the stone and steel of the tower blocks, unforgiving edges, matching the snarl of the street talk fizzing around him.

He reached Madison, stood with the crowd looking up at the crossing lights, heads bobbing impatiently. The man at the pretzel stand pulled another bag from the trolley, letting the steel lid drop back down with a clatter. He shook his fingers in the air in mock alarm.

The lights tripped to green, a collective heave and the throng began to shuffle across the roadway. The surface by the pavement rutted and worn. A grate, in the middle of the road, the hissing steam spiralling under the streetlights. A voice from behind him. 'Hey! My dog. Mind my fuckin' dog.' Car horns sounded; he glanced to his right, the tail lights of the northbound traffic lurching uptown. He felt the breeze on his face, a north wind, a hint of the park in the distance, that smell, wet leaves and horses.

He saw the pharmacy sign up ahead, lengthened his stride, pulled out of the weaving foot traffic and headed to the doorway. A man sat on the floor by the entrance, sleeping bag wrapped around his shoulders. Cardboard sign, money for shelter. He leaned down, placed a dollar bill into the worn paper cup. A word of thanks, in a language he didn't understand.

He stepped through the doorway into the pharmacy, bright ceiling lights, shelves a jumble of shapes and colours. The sour-sweet smell, disinfectant and chewing gum. He walked up to the counter, unbuttoning his coat.

A younger man behind the desk, evening shift. Scrip room closed, just a barcode ringer.

'Well good evening to you.' Brian Welch flashed a smile, laying on the southern charm. 'Name's Bill Murphy.' His coat hung open, beneath, the green smock top, the badge on the breast pocket. Duane Reade Patient Care. 'And who do I have the pleasure of addressing?'

The younger man frowned. 'Consulting rooms close at 18.00.'

'That I do know, young man, but thank you anyway.' Brian Welch nodded. 'Thing is, just got a call from 40 Wall Street.' He held out his hands. The you-know-how-it-is sign. 'Some folk just no good at waitin'.'

'So, what do you want?'

'If I could oblige you for the consulting room key, I'd be most grateful.' Brian smoothed down the arc of his moustache with finger and thumb. 'The gentleman will be here any minute.'

The man behind the counter didn't move.

'And here I am forgetting my manners.' Brian pulled his ID from his pocket. 'William D. Murphy, Senior Nurse. DRPC New York.' He nodded down at the laminated card, neatly parted black hair framing a serious demeanour. 'That is me.'

Still no response.

'This time of year, you just never know.' He nodded. 'Could be pneumonia or maybe just be a strep.' He glanced at his watch. 'Anyways, I'd better be getting the room ready.'

'Don't I need to call someone?'

'Handles and surfaces.' Brian nodded. 'Daub it and swab it.'

The assistant reached under the desk, handed him the key. 'It's over there.' He pointed to a door with 'Consulting Room' written in welcoming blue.

'Much obliged.'

A buzz as the door to the street swung open again. A man stood in the entrance, scarf wrapped around his neck, beanie pulled down over his ears. He raised a hand to his face as if to muffle a cough. Walked slowly towards the counter.

A smile from the nurse. 'I'm Bill Murphy, so you must be …'

The man in the beanie nodded.

'Shall we?' He indicated the door with the blue signage.

Brian walked over, held the door open, flicked on the lights. The man in the beanie walked in. The door closed behind them.

They stood, face-to-face, matching each other for height.

The stockier newcomer met Brian's gaze. 'You know,' Kasper Lehtonen slipped off his coat, 'I really wouldn't want to be ill in New York.'

'I'm no stickler for introductions.' Brian paused. 'But in the circumstances …'

Kasper ignored him. 'The people, fucking locusts.' He hung the coat on the wall. 'And this wind, banging off the wet granite, scouring your throat, where is the magic here?'

'Do I call you Kasper, or do you go by some more exotic nom de guerre?'

Kasper frowned. 'Call me what you like, that's all the same to me.'

Brian nodded. 'Well, you're here, that's a good start.'

Kasper unwrapped his scarf and swept off his beanie. 'If a city was a beast, this would be a fucking crocodile.'

'Autumn in New York.'

Kasper gave a grunt. 'Winter here must be fun then.'

'Autumn was a good time.' Brian smoothed down his moustache. 'They even sang songs about it.'

'All teeth and bad temper.' Kasper ran a hand over his bald head. 'Seared-sharp, serrated steel, fucking honed to hurt.'

Brian shrugged off his coat, laid it on the back of the chair. 'Business as usual, my friend.' He sat down. 'It ain't like you have to like the place.'

'Who says I don't?' Kasper glanced around the room. 'What prick decides to paint a room green?'

'I like that about you.' Brian nodded. 'You have a curious mind.'

The bald man scratched the side of his face. 'You Americans. So fucking literal.'

Brian cracked a smile. 'The Providential Nation, bringing hope and the finest carbonated drinks to the world.'

'There's a decent slice of irony, given what we're doing.'

Brian ran his hand through his hair. 'I'm a patriot.'

'How annoying it must be for you,' Kasper smiled, 'that I really don't give a fuck.'

'I believe in something.'

'So do I.' Kasper nodded. 'People are useful, or not. Or dangerous, or not.'

Brian sat back in his chair. 'And you've survived this long?'

'Don't confuse curiosity with imagination.'

Brian nodded. 'Rhetorical question. Obviously.'

Kasper scratched the other side of his face. 'Or spite with savagery.' He paused. 'Could be a painful lesson, so to say.'

The room fell quiet.

The fan, rattling in the ceiling. The rumble of the subway beneath.

Brian met Kasper's gaze. 'The Pale Tiger. We want to let her loose three days from now.' He paused. 'Are you set?'

'Almost. We will be.'

'Almost means different things.'

'Will be means will be.' Kasper flexed his fingers. 'We're at full production. Stockpiling at both locations.' He looked across at Brian. 'It'll be there when you need it. It's not going anywhere.'

'Are our patrols still proving reliable?'

'American timekeeping.' Kasper smiled. 'Some say it's a dangerous conceit. But it works for us.'

Brian nodded. 'There's someone else you need to see. Here in New York.'

'I'm leaving tomorrow night.'

'Fine, you'll meet him at 10.00 tomorrow morning, then. You know the Frick Gallery?'

'Do I look like a tourist?'

'Well, try to tomorrow.' Brian nodded. 'Fifth Avenue and 70th Street. Right in front of the Holbeins.'

'Your friend, he's one of yours?'

'The Holbeins.' Brian paused. 'They're portraits. In the gallery.'

'In case I thought Holbeins was a chain of kosher restaurants.' Kasper scratched the side of his face. 'Hans Holbein the fucking younger, died 1543.' He paused. 'So, this man, who am I meeting?'

'He works for a … sister organisation. He's another patriot.' Brian forced a smile. 'Think you can manage that?'

'As long as it's not catching.' Kasper stood up, began to wrap his scarf around his neck. 'Another excuse to dip into the dressing-up box?'

'Needed to be sure we weren't followed. Happy to be too careful.' Brian looked up at Kasper.

Kasper returned his gaze. 'That look I know well.' He scratched the side of his nose. 'I call that the "who goes first" look.'

'You have a … certain reputation.' Brian nodded.

Kasper picked up his coat. 'Good.'

'So far this has been a civilised discourse.'

'You think I can't have a conversation without some threats?'

'Well, it would bookend the exchange, for sure.'

Kasper frowned. 'But tell me, why would I want to threaten you?'

'I don't know.' Brian shrugged. 'In the case that we might … let you down, have a change of mind.'

Kasper swiped up his beanie. 'Maybe I believe in surprises.' He turned, walked to the door. 'But don't worry,' he called over his shoulder, 'they don't call us organised crime for nothing.'

WEDNESDAY

WEDNESDAY 25TH SEPTEMBER, 11.30 AM (3.30 AM GMT)

BONHAM STRAND, CENTRAL, HONG KONG

Emma stood in the hotel doorway looking out onto Bonham Strand. The rain was heavier now, streaking down from the low grey skies, puckering the wet pavements. The wind snapped at the raincoats of the passers-by, umbrellas whip-sawing in the gusts. The sound of the passing traffic, tyres skittering over the slick surface, whistling as they sliced through the pools of water by the side of the road, spray fizzing across the pavement. She looked up, the tops of the nearby buildings lost in the clouds that swirled around them. The lights from the upper storeys a dull glow from within the smudgy folds wrapped around them. The rain-lashed city, sombre and stoic as the storm rumbled overhead. She breathed in the damp, cool air as she stepped onto the pavement, her coat wrapped tight around her, her hood flapping in the wind. She walked up to the urban taxi parked by the kerb, the rain streaking the red paintwork. The rear door swung open. Emma slid in, closed the door behind her.

Fraser turned around. He blinked. 'Everything all right, ma'am?'

She frowned. 'Why?'

'Just … you look a little …'

'Just had some news. Someone back in London.' She set her jaw. 'Nothing that should concern you.' She narrowed her eyes. 'Anything from McKay?'

'Not yet.'

Emma threw back the hood of her coat. 'You know Sun Yat Sen Memorial Park?'

'We're not meant to be going anywhere.'

'Plans have changed.'

He frowned.

'My plans.'

He bit his lip.

'I'll tell you more on the way. We need to get going.'

He settled back in the driver's seat. Turned the ignition key, glanced in the side mirror, pulled out into the traffic edging its way through the dripping streets.

She drew out her phone. 'You remember? Borso's 11.30 slot today? "Him" time. Visiting the statue of Sun Yet Sen.'

He nodded.

'Eleven thirty-five now. He's on his way to the park. Tracker has him on Connaught Road West.'

'Where you'd expect him to be.'

'Not in this weather you wouldn't.'

He glanced in the rear-view mirror. 'McKay will have a man on point. He'll be right behind him. Why do we need to be there?'

She looked out of the window, rivulets of rain scoring the glass. 'Whatever it is. This must be it.'

'Ma'am?'

'That signal. The night he arrived.'

They pulled up at the lights.

He tapped his fingers on the steering wheel. 'McKay told us to stay low.'

'Fraser.' She leaned forward. 'Just drive. It's my call.'

The lights turned green.

He edged the taxi across the junction, the traffic stumbling its way through the rain and the spray. Horns blaring around them.

She looked at her phone. 'He's almost at the park'

'I'm trying, ma'am.'

She laid a hand on his shoulder. 'Just keep going. Look for the gaps.'

The taxi leapt forward as he swung into the nearside lane, hand on the horn as he passed the bus on the inside, cut back into the traffic in front.

The car shuddered to a halt at the next lights.

She glanced out of the window. The Western Market building looming above them, the lights from the road shimmering off the sleek red brickwork.

The lights changed, they swung round into Connaught

Road, the park buildings ahead on the right, mist swirling around them.

She reached into her coat, pulled out her gun, checked the magazine, clicked it back into the hand stock. 'Anywhere here on the left.'

He pulled over.

'Get back to the hotel, where they can get hold of you.' She slid the gun back inside her jacket.

He turned around.

She met his gaze. 'I'll see you back there.'

She opened the door, pulled her hood up over her head, stepped out into the squalling rain. She ran towards the junction, head bowed against the weather, trainers splashing through the pools of water scattered all around her. She reached the crossing, checked her phone. He was at the statue now. She looked up at the pedestrian signal. The man flared green, she ran to the far side of the road, ducked through the entrance to the park. Ahead of her, the Memorial Lawn, stretching down to the water. In the centre, the statue, barely visible through the sea mist rolling across the grass. She glanced around, the Pebble Walking Trail to her left, no one, just the wet wooden benches, slick beneath the iron streetlights, rain dripping from the russet roof tiles beyond.

Another gust of wind swirled around her, tugging at the hem of her coat, snatching at her hood.

She narrowed her eyes as she scanned the lawn ahead. Shapes, half-shapes, something moving in the banks of mist churning over the ground. She threw back her hood, listening for any sounds. Just the drum of the rain, bouncing off the tarmac, thudding into the wet earth. The wind, snapping around her.

She began to walk across the grass, the rain stinging her face. The statue, its contours gliding into focus as she approached, towering over her. The grey stone, cold and slick against the whirling clouds above.

She glanced around, the mist ebbing and flowing, vistas of the harbour front emerging and receding.

A figure. Down by the water. A man. Facing out to sea. The flaps of his coat fluttering in the wind, unfurled umbrella, tight against his shoulder.

He was alone.

She checked her phone. The tracker. It was him.

She slid the gun from inside her coat, walked towards him, gun held against her side.

She stopped a few yards behind him.

The sound of harbour ferries, out there in the mist, feeling their way to the shore, engines growling. A horn blared a warning.

The figure by the shore slowly turned around.

They stood in silence for a moment.

Emma spoke first. 'David, what the fuck are you doing?'

McKay looked across at her, his expression deadpan. 'What does it look like?'

'Why didn't you tell me?' Emma raised her voice against the buffeting of the wind. 'If this was part of the op you should have fucking said something!'

McKay studied her face for a moment, then threw back his head, laughing.

'And it isn't fucking funny.' She hissed.

David fell silent, his expression, suddenly serious. 'Isn't it?'

Emma stared back at him, concern slowly creeping over her features. 'David?'

He nodded, slowly. 'You can say it.'

She uttered a little cry as she glanced around her, the heavy raindrops thumping into the turf.

'Emma.' He paused. 'Clever, little Emma.'

She looked across at him, screwing up her eyes against the biting rain. She pushed a strand of wet hair away from her forehead, slowly shook her head. 'No.'

'If it helps,' he flashed her a mock smile, 'you didn't need to be here.' He paused, the wind, whipping at the hem of his coat, tugging at his umbrella. 'But since you are.' He gave a little shrug. 'Two birds and all that.'

'Oh … David.' She stood, staring in disbelief, the rain streaking down her face. 'What have you done?'

He stood in silence, a slight smile still playing across his features.

Emma shook her head, the dark coils of her rain-soaked hair brushing the collar of her coat. She drew herself upright, her face now a blank mask. 'Why?'

McKay half turned, looked out over the water. The clank of metal, the bark of an engine, the rush of churning water, a ferry, docking in the mist nearby. He turned back to her. 'Why all this?' He raised a hand, waving it around at the lashing rain, the swirling mist. 'Or why you?' He let his hand drop to his side.

She glared at him. 'You think you're so fucking smart.'

'Do I?'

'Borso and his agenda.' She spat the words out. 'The whole thing, the whiff of greasepaint. I knew it was a production.' She paused. 'Just didn't think it could be you directing it.'

He stood in silence as the rain thundered down around them, clattering against his umbrella.

'That first evening.' Emma snarled. 'His trip to Kowloon, the Norton Tower lights. Make us think he had a reason, a deadline.' She flexed her jaw muscles. 'Throw us off balance.'

Still no response.

'His agenda.' She continued. 'All laid out. Hiding in plain sight.' She paused. 'He must have known we'd be following him, so he must have a plan. A way to slip off, under the radar.' She narrowed her eyes. 'So he could do the one thing he really came to Hong Kong to do.'

McKay held his umbrella tight under his arm as he brought his hands together in mock applause. 'Bravo!'

'I knew he had to make a mistake, something this ... precise. There had to be a flaw.' She steadied herself as another gust whipped around them, the raindrops sharp against her skin. 'And then, this.' She looked up at the swirling grey sky, the rain sheeting down from the clouds swooping over the cowering city. 'Caught in his own story now. Daren't risk not following his agenda. In case I woke up and started wondering. But then ...' She shook her head. 'No one goes for a walk in the park in this.'

McKay gave a chuckle. 'But here we are.'

'This was the window.' She looked around, the storm rattling through the trees. 'His visit to the Sun Yat Sen statue, a bit of "Borso" time. If he could just throw off the watchers, get someone else to wear the tracker to the park. There's his cover. As far as we're concerned he's alone. In the park. No one else to prove he wasn't here.' She looked across at him, eyes squinting against the driving rain. 'Whilst Borso quietly slips off, and we never even notice he's gone.' Emma slowly raised her weapon. She took a deep breath, her gun arm, steady. 'An inside job. It had to be.' She set her jaw. 'But when I ran into the park I never ...' She paused, blinking. 'Not you ... you'd never do this ... to us.' She took a breath. 'To me.'

McKay shrugged his shoulders.

'You found out about Rhea.' She flexed her trigger finger. 'You told them, you told Crator.' She took a step forward. 'You had Rhea killed, you little shit.'

He looked her up and down. 'You're not going to shoot me.'

'What do the Chinese care? One British spy shoots holes in another British spy.'

'Emma, you don't understand.' His voice, still calm, his expression, deadpan. 'You can't shoot me.'

'You're going to tell us everything.'

'I don't think so.'

'Then Borso will.' She wrapped her finger around the trigger. 'Don't need both of you.'

They stood in silence, the mist barrelling around them.

McKay began to smile. 'I really mean it.' He pursed his lips. 'You can't shoot me.'

'Watch me.'

'Emma,' his voice quiet, measured, 'who gave you the gun?'

Emma flinched, her forehead creasing into a frown. She gave a slight shake of the head, her voice cracking. 'If you move a muscle, I'll pull the trigger.'

'Good.' McKay gave a good-natured grunt. 'Pull away. See what happens.'

Emma blinked, her breathing quickening.

Slowly, McKay reached into his pocket, pulled out his weapon. He looked down at it, then across at Emma. He slowly raised his gun, pointing it at Emma's chest. He nodded towards Emma's weapon, still levelled at him. 'Ladies first.'

Emma took deep breaths, steadying her gun arm against the swirling wind.

'What are you waiting for?' McKay gave a chuckle. 'Come on, you want to. I deserve it.'

Emma slowly lowered her gun. 'Let's talk.'

McKay pulled a pained expression. 'Oh … Emma. What a shame.'

'Put the gun down. Please.'

'It was all going to be so neat.'

Another gust swirled around them, he brought his other hand up to steady his umbrella, bucking in the wind.

'Two shots. That's what they heard, two shots. Bang, bang.' He flicked the gun up with each imagined shot. 'And there you were, on the ground. One bullet.' He raised the gun, pointing it between her eyes.

She blinked, shook her hair from her eyes, trying to form some words.

'I followed you here, you were carrying Borso's tracker. You were working with Crator.'

Emma let out a gasp. 'No!'

'You tipped them off.' He paused. 'You had Rhea killed.'

She slowly shook her head, the words, still not coming.

'I told you to give yourself in. You fired first. I fired back.' He gave a shrug.

Emma looked down at the ground, the rain streaking through her wet hair, running down her face. 'Why are you doing this?'

'You mean why am I doing something my feckless superiors wouldn't dare? Working with leeches like Borso?' His expression, suddenly serious. 'Because I love my country, in ways you'd never understand.' He set his jaw. 'Someone has to do the things our spineless politicians won't.' He exhaled. 'But if the question is why you?' He paused. 'You.' He spat the word out. 'You really don't know?'

She shook her head, droplets of water dripping onto the grass at her feet.

'I loved you, Emma.' He bit his lip, his voice cracking. 'Even now, walking down the street, the sweep of a woman's hair, the swing of an arm.' He sucked in another breath. 'It's you!' He shouted across the storm. 'It's you I see in those strangers.' He gave a sob. 'You.' His voice, quiet again. 'And I'm back in that hotel in Macau.' He exhaled. 'Standing there, the empty room, your half-smoked cigarette in the ashtray.' He swallowed again. 'The man who would have done anything for you ...'

Emma looked across at him, she moved her lips to speak, but no sound emerged.

McKay gave a snort. 'There's nothing you can say, anyway.' He cocked the weapon, the barrel still pointing at Emma's forehead. 'I hate you. The way that only someone who truly loved you could ...'

Emma drew herself upright, the storm still barrelling around her, the wind sweeping in off the water, whipping across the lawns, the sea mist, roiling, churning in the gale.

She raised her head, looked up into the angry sky, took a deep breath, waiting for the shot.

A stronger gust caught David's umbrella; he rocked backwards with the force of the wind, fighting for his balance, his gun arm waving.

Emma drew back her arm, hurled her gun at David's head.

'Fuck!' He dropped the umbrella, bent down, clutching his hand up to his face, blood dripping through his fingers.

Emma darted into the mist by the shoreline.

He shook his head, stood up. 'Emma!'

A splash rang out.

He ran to the water's edge.

In the mist, a bell rang out, a ferry rumbling its way towards Shueng Wan.

He looked down.

Just the rain, puckering the churning grey waters of the harbour.

WEDNESDAY 25TH SEPTEMBER, 10 AM

THE LOBBY, CRATOR CAPITAL, LONDON

The receptionist remained seated, staring at DI Perry.

Anne Perry met her gaze. Something in that look. A tension in the shoulder. Hands beneath the desk. She was holding something.

Both remained still.

A click and a hiss from above. The air conditioning, stirring back to life with a whisper.

DI Perry felt the chill dryness on the back of her neck. Cold air, sliding over polished stone. A little shudder. Her skin tingling. Senses sharpening. She raised her eyebrows, slowly.

The receptionist gave the slightest of nods.

Anne Perry slipped off her coat, walked towards the reception desk. 'Would you mind?'

'Of course.' The girl stood up.

DI Perry stood in front of the desk. She glanced down at the envelope lying behind the counter, the receptionist's index finger planted firmly on it.

The murmur of the air conditioning. The near-silence, daring to be broken.

'I can collect it on the way out.' DI Perry held out her coat, glanced down again at the envelope.

The receptionist blinked, hesitated for a moment, took the coat, nodded. 'Of course.'

'DI Perry!'

Both women flinched at the voice, echoing across the hallway.

Anne Perry turned to face the figure. Jamie Ives, framed in the doorway, the same smile, his restless blue eyes flitting over her

DI Perry took a deep breath. She sensed a tremor underfoot, something stirring, deep within the building. She nodded towards him. 'Thank you for seeing me. Again.'

'You're very welcome.'

Another gust of air, sharp and chill, a prickling sensation on the back of her neck. She swallowed.

'Please.' He stood aside, indicating the passageway beyond. The white walls, the black carpet, into the sound-proofed heart of the building.

She walked towards the doorway, her footsteps ringing out on the slick black marble. She slid past him, her feet settling noiselessly into the rich fabric beyond.

The door swung shut behind them. A click, then the silence. She turned to face him.

He nodded. 'You must be getting used to the place.'

'Or maybe the place is getting used to me.'

He studied her for a moment. 'Are you sensitive to atmospheres?'

'Like now?'

He met her gaze.

Another tremor underfoot, muffled beneath the thickly layered carpet.

He gave another nod, gestured towards the corridor. 'Shall we?'

Anne Perry drew herself upright, set off down the passageway. Soundless footsteps, the orange glow of the wall lights, shimmering off the dark polished doorways.

'Just here.' His voice behind her.

They stood facing the lift door, heavy painted steel looming above them.

'My office is on the fourth floor.' He glanced across at her. 'You're wearing heels today. Yesterday it was flats.' He nodded towards her shoes. 'Not your everyday choice, judging by the slight redness below your ankle.'

She stood in silence.

'But more you.' He paused. 'More ... graceful.'

A click, the lift door began to slide open. The growling of gears, steel clicking into steel, the door shuddering as it slid across its bearings.

The inside of the lift car, dark leather lining the walls, the ceiling lights glinting off the metalled floor.

She stepped inside, her footsteps ringing out on the polished surface.

He stood beside her.

The door began to close.

She glanced around. No buttons.

A clunk and a hiss as the door seals engaged.

A shudder through the floor as the cables tightened. They began to ascend.

He looked across at her. 'You OK with confined spaces?'

She threw him a glance. 'Depends who I have to share it with.'

Another shudder and the lift came to a stop.

The seals clicked open, the door sliding aside with measured precision.

'After you.' He nodded towards the open door.

She stepped out. Light flooded in from the picture window opposite, running the length of the room. The grey roof tiles of the nearby houses, fresh and slick from last night's rain. Beyond, the Paddington towers, steepling into the southern sky, their dark outlines framed against the treetops of Hyde Park. She took a deep breath. That aroma. Coffee, freshly pressed laundry. She exhaled. Walked towards the window.

He followed behind.

She sensed his gaze on her. She turned to face him. 'Something you said yesterday. Keeps going round my head.'

'Can I get you something? Tea? Coffee?'

'Not just a question of wrong time, wrong place.' She narrowed her eyes. 'You remember?'

'I make a decent cuppa.' He smiled.

'You were talking about Rhea Moore.'

He spread his hands. The sunlight lighting up his face, shadows flitting across his finely drawn features as he spoke. 'Try me.'

'You think Rhea was murdered.'

He straightened up. 'It was an observation. About you. Not me.'

'Why won't you answer the question?'

'Is it a question?'

DI Perry stood in silence for a few moments. 'Fine.' She gave a slight nod.

Jamie Ives shook his head. 'You're right. I'm being an arse. Sorry.' He looked across at her, the light catching the knot of his tie, the burnished silk glinting as he moved. 'It just came into my head … and I said it.'

'Really?'

'And here you are again so …'

She shook her head. 'If I were in a different mood I might even enjoy a bit of verbal fencing.'

'In a lighter context …' He paused. 'Well …'

'But we've got a dead girl to think about.' She bit her lip. 'A bit of respect, perhaps?'

He nodded.

DI Perry glanced around the room. At the far end, a desk, dark blue leather framed in polished steel. Behind, a mosaic of maps filling the wall, ancient cartography, outlines of continents and coastlines. A world yet to be measured. Facing the window, running the length of the room, wooden shelves, dark polished surfaces glowing under the lights. Ranged along them, photo frames in ordered ranks, smiles and handshakes, faces shining with self-importance.

She turned back to face him. 'Where's Scutt?'

He looked across at her. 'He's on holiday.'

'Plan that in advance did he?'

He shrugged.

She nodded. 'Who has his contact details?'

'The Host Team. HR. I assume.'

'Did you ask?'

He stood in silence for a moment. 'IT people.' He paused. 'Social skills aren't always a strong point.'

'I was told he and Rhea Moore were friendly.'

No response.

'Were they?'

'I barely knew her.'

'But you knew Scutt.'

He nodded.

'Could Scutt have something to do with this? With Rhea?'

Jamie Ives took a breath. He walked over to the desk, his easy athletic gait. He flipped open a laptop, fingers gliding across the keys.

He looked up. 'The light's better over here.'

She walked over, stood beside him. His hands, moving slowly over the keypad. His shirt cuffs, pale cotton contrasting with the dark weave of the suit, tortoiseshell buttons flickering in the sunlight.

'Here.' He froze the image on the screen.

She leaned forward, catching the scent of his aftershave. Pine needles, with a hint of something harder, sharper. She looked at the screen, the hallway, the slick white walls, seared edges of hewn marble, the shimmering stonework. A solitary security guard behind the desk.

He pushed play. A figure, swathed in a green hoody, baggy jeans, street trainers. Hunched forward, he fumbles in his pocket for his pass, swipes the security beam, shuffles towards the main exit. The door slides open, he disappears into the night. Jamie Ives clicked the pause button.

'Scutt?'

'Monday night.'

'That the only camera angle? From behind?'

He nodded.

She looked down at the screen. 'Seven forty-two.'

'Does that make your life easier?'

She straightened up. 'No.' She glanced back down at the screen. 'But it answers one question.'

He looked across at her. 'You wanted to see the footage of Rhea Moore.'

She nodded.

His fingers moved smoothly over the keys, clicking open a new file. 'Here.'

A girl, walking through the barriers, past reception and out through the main doorway onto the street. Blue jacket, grey skirt. Pale headscarf. Her back to the camera, no face, no profile. The girl in the hotel.

'Seven minutes past 18.00.' Jamie Ives pushed the pause button. 'After that, she's off our radar.' He glanced up. 'Do you want to write all this down?'

'In a minute.' She stood facing him, flecks of sunlight streaking her hair, dappled shadows flitting across her pale skin. 'What happened, on her last day at work?'

'Ellis Wagner's in a better position—'

'I'm asking you.' She bit her lip.

He nodded. 'She said she was feeling a little unwell, this was … around three in the afternoon.'

'Unwell?'

'According to Ellis. His words.' He paused. 'She got back to her desk about 20 minutes later. Said she had a report to write, needed somewhere quiet, was going to work in one of the meeting rooms.'

'Did he see her again?'

He shook his head.

'Probably what she needed.' DI Perry narrowed her eyes. 'Bit of fresh air.'

He didn't respond.

'No allergens, no pathogens.' She paused. 'Scrubbed clean.'

He shrugged.

DI Perry raised her eyebrows, turned, walked over to the shelves lining the far wall. Glass glinting in the late morning light. She picked up a photo frame. 'May I?'

'Please do.' He walked towards her, the sunlight picking out the flecked pattern in his suit, shoulders moving beneath the fabric.

She looked down at the photograph. Jamie Ives's strong, tanned features and another man, shorter, older, less sure of himself.

'Montero, Bolivia.' He began. 'Just north of Santa Cruz. A community project of ours.'

'Who's the other man?'

'The school principal.'

'A moment in time.'

'His name's Soto.'

She nodded. 'Context. And continuity.' She replaced the photo frame on the shelf.

'It was a real event.'

'I don't doubt it.' She turned to face him. 'Authenticity. It has a certain ... depth to it.'

He met her gaze.

'A certain ... logic.'

They stood in silence, the words hanging between them.

He took a breath. 'Some things justify themselves.'

'Maybe.' DI Perry looked across at the far wall, the outlines of exotic lands, soaring passes, rivers in torrent, fantastical beats summoned up in the imagination of the map-makers of old.

'The golden age of exploration.' He followed her gaze. 'Endeavours that could make a man.' He paused. 'Or woman.'

She looked across at him. 'You asked me, just now, if I was sensitive to atmospheres.'

He didn't respond.

'But you already knew the answer.' She narrowed her eyes. 'Air, pure enough to catch in your throat.' She paused. 'Was Rhea sensitive to atmospheres?'

He exhaled. 'As I said. I barely knew her.'

DI Perry turned, looked out of the window. The grey-streaked sky, the sunlight, like the bright eyes of dragons peering at the world through the gaps in the clouds. 'They say what you want to show someone says a lot about what you want to hide.'

'Are you going to elaborate?'

'Are you?'

He attempted a smile. 'You have a point.' He paused. 'Although I'm not sure it's the same point.'

She shook her head. 'Straight answers would speed all this up.'

'I know.'

'So why the games?'

He gave a shrug of the shoulders. 'Straight answer?' He exhaled. 'I like talking to you.'

'No you don't.'

'You would have made a good analyst.'

She met his gaze.

'A formidable one, even.'

She shook her head. 'Do you even know what good is?'

'It's an overworked word.' He paused. 'But I believe I do.' He looked across at her. 'I've had to.'

'I don't think you've had to do anything for years.'

He stood in silence for a moment. 'Let me show you out.' He placed his hand in the small of her back as he guided her towards the lift.

She glanced up at him. 'Excuse me.'

He removed his hand. 'Sorry. I was—'

'Testing me. I wouldn't.'

He stood in silence for a moment. 'Something we have in common.' He paused. 'A profound distrust of the obvious.'

She nodded. 'Time will tell.'

'If fate will listen.'

She turned to face him again. 'It's an easy mistake to make.' She paused. 'Just because someone has a lot to lose,' she glanced around the room, 'doesn't mean they won't risk it all.'

The lift door rumbled back into life, sliding open with well-engineered purpose.

He smiled. 'Something else we have in common then.' He nodded towards the waiting lift car. 'Shall we?'

WEDNESDAY 25TH SEPTEMBER, 6.30 PM (10.30 AM GMT)

SO LO PUN, HONG KONG

The fishing boat rounded the headland, turned into the bay. The sea was calmer here, the gentle swells lapping against the small sandy beach ahead of them. All around the cove, mangrove trees, hugging the shoreline, a wall of rustling green, the late afternoon sun shimmering off the leaves still wet from the storm.

A rowing boat bobbed towards them. A single oarsman, tugging at the silky water. The fishing boat idled to a stop, engine thrumming, water sputtering from the overflow, streaking the sun-bleached hull.

A crewman lowered a gangway.

The wheelhouse door slid open.

A woman stepped out onto the deck, a hand held above her face, shielding her eyes from the sun. She wore a khaki T-shirt, her loose-fitting combat trousers tumbling over her boots.

The crewman held her elbow as she stepped from the gangway into the smaller boat, sat down on the bench.

No one spoke.

The oarsman turned the boat towards the shore, the bow dipping and rising with the rhythm of the oars.

Ahead of her, the thin strip of beach. A great egret stood on the shoreline, the water bubbling around his slender legs. He looked up at the boat, his beady eye observing the intruders, his dagger-like beak held aloft in disdain.

The boat bumped up against the shore. The man shipped the oars, jumped over the side, helped her into the shallow water.

She stood scanning the forest. A gap in the trees. A small path, leading into the darkness, almost invisible from the sea.

Collared crows jostled in the treetops, mocking laughter from the crackling canopy above.

A man emerged from the path. The speckled blue camouflage, Chinese Marine Corps. One hand resting on the automatic rifle slung around his neck. He beckoned her over.

Emma Wilson walked towards him.

He nodded. 'Follow me.'

He led the way into the thicket, the narrow path weaving through the undergrowth, jungle on either side, the greenery dense and slick. She glanced up, the overhanging branches, tangled, tight-knit. She took a deep breath, the air, rich and damp, a hint of sourness.

She kept her eyes on the back of her guide as they followed the path in silence, layers of leaves beneath their feet spongy. The sound of the jungle, the crick and hum of the insects, the calls of the birds, rising and falling. The branches above, swaying as they passed beneath. The wind, or something else.

She raised a hand, wiped the sweat from her forehead.

A clattering sound from up ahead. The snapping of twigs, something moving through the undergrowth.

Emma tensed as she looked towards the sound.

'Just stay close to me.' Her escort spoke over his shoulder.

The jungle seemed to be coming alive, the leaves shaking, tiny droplets of moisture fizzing into the hot, sluggish air that wrapped around them.

Ahead of her, she could see the path broadening out.

The track began to widen. The sun in the western sky now visible through the thinning bush.

They turned another corner.

Emma halted, blinking in the sunshine. She stood at the edge of a deserted courtyard. The flagstones twisted and broken. An eerie seascape, the huge slabs ruptured into crests and troughs of weathered stone, heaved up by restless roots.

On the far side of the courtyard, ancient steps, moss-speckled, draped in creeping vines, cascading down from the crumbling parapet. Beyond, the husks of the old town itself. Ponderous stone walls, buckling under caving roofs. Dark tree trunks, snaking through gaping doorways. Flanking the parapet, statues, features now weathered and worn, gazing down at the sombre ruins.

A movement just beyond the steps. The wall, moving, a doorway. A man stepped out from the shadows. Tall, athletic-looking, a few years younger than her, perhaps, dark suit, open-necked shirt.

'They all perished,' he began, 'so legend has it. A boat accident. On the way to a wedding.' He looked up at the scarred grey walls. 'The entire village. Every generation.' He turned back to Emma. 'A long time ago.'

She looked across at him in silence.

'There'd been a village here since the ninth century. Then, one day, there was no one. Empty streets, wooden shutters, swinging lazily in the breeze. Silence.'

Emma glanced around the ruins. 'People move on.'

'Only the ghosts remain.' He nodded. 'So no one dares come. Spirits of the dead. Restless. Spiteful.'

'Why am I here?'

'You mean, why didn't we just throw you to the wolves in Tai Lam?'

She looked across at him.

'The nearest road is four hours walk. If you know the jungle paths.' He paused. 'And I know the bay looks inviting. But I wouldn't recommend a swim.'

She held his gaze.

The man looked at her for some moments. 'Why are your own people trying to kill you?'

She looked down at the ground.

He reached into his jacket pocket, pulled out a piece of paper. 'Not much of an obituary.'

Emma didn't respond.

He opened the sheet of paper. 'Harbour Police have confirmed that the body found this afternoon off Shuan Weng is that of 44-year-old British woman Gail Notts.' He looked up. 'Is that how this ends?'

Emma blinked.

'We didn't pull you out of the water as a favour.' He held up the piece of paper. 'We release this to the press and we're no longer accountable for you.'

Emma nodded.

'And you know what that means.' He paused. 'Options. You'd do the same.'

'They won't buy that. Without a body.'

'You got run down by the Macau ferry. Right now you don't look much like anyone.' He shook his head. 'But who else could it be? Wearing your clothes. Your passport in her pocket.'

'They'll send McKay to ID me.' She paused. 'We used to go out together, remember?'

'We fish bodies out of the harbour every day. All sorts. All skin types.' He nodded. 'We've even added the dragonfly tattoo.'

She narrowed her eyes.

'So now you know.'

'What do you want?'

He glanced around the courtyard, then turned back to Emma. 'Shall we go inside?' He indicated the doorway behind.

She hesitated, then walked towards him.

He stood aside.

Beyond the open door, a passageway below the ruins, cut into the ancient rock. She stepped inside. The cool air swept over her, her footsteps ringing out on the stone floor. Lights, set into the walls, casting their glow across the bedrock above, slick with condensation. Voices, from further within, the humming of a generator.

She turned a corner. The tunnel opened out into a circular hallway, the domed roof arching above them. In the centre of the room, a desk, two women sitting behind monitors. Marine Corps camouflage. Around the walls, doors, bolted shut, metalwork gleaming dully under the arc lights high in the vault above.

One of the guards looked up, rose from her chair. She walked up to her, nodded to the man, took Emma by the arm, led her to a doorway on the far side of the room. The man followed.

She slid the bolts, swung the door open. A single cell, stone walls, no windows, the concrete floor ridged and scuffed. A fan hummed in the ceiling.

Emma walked in, the man followed, closing the door behind him.

'Don't bother to sit.' He began. 'I'll leave you to think things over. I'll be back in the morning. Then you'll tell me what you've decided.'

'Is this a real choice?'

'Your own side think you're a traitor. And soon they'll think you're dead.' He paused. 'We can deliver them a body … or your body.'

He turned, walked to the door, pulled it open. He paused in the doorway, turned around. 'I would much prefer the former.'

'You never said your name.'

He shook his head. 'If I introduced myself, I'd feel bound to a certain code of … civility.' He paused. 'You understand.'

Voices in the hallway outside, the murmur of the ceiling fan.

'If you really need something, bang on the door. A female guard will see to you.' He turned to go, walked to the cell door. He stopped, turned around. 'And you might like to know,' he continued, 'we've intercepted some chatter over your diplomatic channels.' He continued. 'Friends like these.'

She stood in silence.

'I assume it's your ex. A message. A brief one. To the China Desk in London.'

She looked down at the ground.

'The Wicked Witch has turned.'

WEDNESDAY 25TH SEPTEMBER, 11 AM

MI6 HQ, LONDON

Sebastian Noon looked up at his visitor with barely disguised annoyance. 'To what do I owe the pleasure?'

Ben Pritchard stood in the open doorway to Noon's office, his barrel-like frame silhouetted against the light from the corridor beyond. 'Monte-bloody-negro.' Pritchard spat the words out.

Noon sat up in his chair, carefully placing his spectacles on the polished wooden desktop, the lenses glinting in the light of the desk lamp. 'What are you trying to say?'

'Now I do get it.' Pritchard gave a little grunt, his heavy shoulders twitching.

Noon took a deep breath, a slight frown creasing his high forehead. 'You know, Ben.' He gave a little nod. 'You might fool some people with your "I'm just a plain-speaking northerner who calls a spade a shovel".' Noon paused. 'But it's always been a mystery to me.'

"Course it couldn't bloody wait.'

Noon sat back in his chair, concentration now etched across his aquiline features. 'I mean, why would anyone equate poor grammar and over-long vowels with veracity?'

Pritchard stood in silence, jaw clenched.

Voices, from further down the corridor, the clatter of the telefax printer announcing itself with a snarl.

Pritchard gave a nod. 'Wilson knew it. Our girl on the inside was getting close.'

Noon took another breath, eyes flitting across Pritchard's reddening face. 'You going to close the door, Ben?'

Pritchard reached behind him for the door handle, slammed it shut, his eyes still boring into Noon. 'You fuckin' killed her.'

Noon reached forward, picked up his spectacles, holding them up against the light. 'If you ever make that accusation again,' he breathed on the lenses, 'I will find a way to—'

'She was 25 for fuck's sake!' His voice raised now.

Noon looked down at his spectacles, carefully picking up his tie between thumb and forefinger. He cleared his throat. 'I've lost agents myself.' He began to polish one lens. 'So I know.' He polished the other lens. 'Like a death in the family.' He replaced his spectacles, looking up at Pritchard. 'I didn't know you had someone on the inside.' He paused. 'Why would I?'

Pritchard narrowed his eyes, dark specks beneath his heavy brow. 'Sunday evening, your cosy car ride.' He took a deep breath, his shoulders heaving beneath his jacket, eyes still fixed on Noon. 'Monday night she's dead.'

Noon slowly shook his head.

'Only person Wilson spoke to on Monday was the driver, Fraser Chan.' He set his jaw again. 'And they were all in lockdown, face-to-face comms only.'

Noon sat in silence, his face expressionless.

'So the last person Wilson spoke to who could have done anything,' he paused, 'was you.'

Noon placed both hands on the desk, fingers entwined, his signet ring gleaming in the ochre light. 'I've already told you.'

'Only two people knew about our girl,' Pritchard paused, 'Wilson and me.'

Noon blinked.

'So unless you think I 'ad the girl killed.' He barked out the words.

Noon sat back in his chair. A frown now framing his hawklike features. 'Wilson didn't say anything.' He paused. 'And I didn't ask.'

'Wilson's bloody working with them!' The first beads of perspiration glinting on his brow. 'She tried to kill McKay for cryin' out loud!'

Noon blinked again. 'I really don't know what to say.'

'Our girl was gettin' close, Wilson had to stop her.' He ground his jaw. 'You both did.'

Noon took off his spectacles, laid them back on the

desk. He looked up at Pritchard. 'Wilson going rogue was the last thing I expected.'

'Last thing before what?' Pritchard gave a sneer. '"Course you bloody knew. No secrets between you two.' He paused. 'What did she have on you, Sebastian? Un-bloody-touchable as far as you were concerned.'

Noon fixed his gaze on Pritchard. 'Get out.'

'If Wilson's not dead then she soon will be.' Pritchard nodded. 'There's a shoot-on-sight order out on 'er.'

Noon took a deep breath, tapping his index finger on the desk, a slow, steady rhythm. A door slammed somewhere down the corridor, more voices, a low rumble, the words indistinct. 'Have you finished?'

Pritchard shook his head, the folds around his neck creasing. 'You're going down, Sebastian. All the bloody way.'

'I have nothing to hide.'

'Internal Affairs will wring it all out of you, like a strip of wet linen.'

Noon's face twitched, his cheeks reddening. He opened his mouth as though about to say something, thought better of it.

'They're onto you,' Pritchard nodded, 'it's not just me that's had doubts.'

Noon grasped the edge of the desk with both hands, pushed back his chair, stood up. 'You should go.' His hands shook as he pressed his fingertips against the smooth wood, the surface shimmering under the light.

'I have nothing more to say.'

Pritchard looked across at the taller man, his jaw set. 'Her name was Beth, Beth Ogilvy.'

Noon looked down. His reflection, smudged in the grain of the polished wooden surface. 'Whatever you think Emma's done,' he looked up, 'she'd never betray an agent.'

Pritchard scoffed. 'She's bloody betrayed us all.'

'You don't know her.'

'And you thought you did?'

Noon slowly shook his head.

WEDNESDAY 25TH SEPTEMBER, 9.30 AM (2.30 PM GMT)

THE STATE DEPARTMENT, WASHINGTON

Cliff Medford looked up at the CIA man standing in front of his desk. 'You know, I had a boss once who hated surprises.'

Mario Mercado didn't reply.

'So naturally, he was the last to know anything.'

Mercado gave a slight nod, his dark eyebrows furrowing.

'Which in his case, was just as well.'

Mercado didn't respond.

'To me it's all about context.' Medford sat back in his chair, scrutinising the CIA man. Not yet mid-morning but Mercado's chin already darkening with the day's stubble. Medford gave a slight nod. 'You asked to see me. Something's happened. Something unexpected.'

'Yes. Sir.'

'Something that couldn't wait for my CIA liaison to get back.'

'I can't be sure.' He cleared his throat. 'But I'd rather you knew.'

'So, the stage is set.' Medford rested his arms on the desk. 'Let the drama begin.'

Mercado took a deep breath. 'Have you heard of a London hedge fund called Crator Capital?'

Medford shook his head.

Mercado took another deep breath. 'Something happened in Hong Kong last night.'

'Well I never.'

The CIA man frowned. 'British Intelligence flagged it "Five Eyes, Urgent".'

Medford fixed him a glare. 'Go on.'

'A rogue MI6 agent tried to blow an operation so that someone from Crator Capital could meet with the Chinese Ministry of Health.'

Medford smiled weakly. 'So it's a medical drama. Like Grey's with sampans.'

'I actually know her.' He paused. 'Or thought I knew her. Emma Wilson. She was prepared to kill to keep that meeting secret.'

Medford's shoulders tensed. He sat in silence for some moments. A car horn sounded on the street below, the snarl of a road drill, raised voices, drifting up in the morning air. He nodded again. 'You have my attention.'

'Crator's also come up in another context.' The CIA man continued. 'We received a tip-off, via the DEA. Some sort of facility, deep in the Colombian jungle, near a village called Periera.'

'A tip-off?'

'The "I-don't-know-what-they're-doing-in-there-but-they-must-be-up-to-something" kind. Anonymous, of course.'

'What sort of facility?'

Mercado flipped open his laptop. 'May I?'

Medford nodded.

Mercado walked around the desk, placed the laptop in front of Medford, tapped the play button. The vastness of Colombian jungle, dark and dense, the camera sweeping over the green treetops, sunlight glinting on the leaves, still wet from the night's rain. Suddenly, a gap in the swaying canopy, a clearing, buildings. Mercado froze the image, tapped a finger on the screen. 'Coffee processing facility, owned by the Chinese Ministry of Agriculture.' He glanced down at Medford staring silently at the screen. 'Been here nearly four years. You see the bean silos, the roasting sheds.'

Medford gave a mock intake of breath. 'Well, fuck me, they've gone and built a coffee factory.'

Mercado pressed on, tapping an image on the far side of the clearing. 'This.' A long, single-story, flat-topped structure, nestling up against the jungle wall, only just visible in the canopy's shadow. 'The facility's registered to a Cayman front, but we did some digging.' He paused. 'The Crator Charitable Foundation.'

Medford blinked. 'So?'

'Can this all be just coincidence? A partner from Crator, meeting in secret with the Chinese Ministry of Health, and now this?'

Medford sat in silence, his broad shoulders slowly rising and falling.

'We can't ignore it.' Mercado paused, waiting for a reaction from Medford.

Medford blinked again.

'There's a Delta Team standing by, we can storm the building at dawn tomorrow.'

Medford grunted in approval. 'Do it.'

Mercado picked up his laptop, flipped the lid closed. 'The Chinese have gone to a deal of trouble and expense for not a lot of coffee.' Mercado took another breath. 'They built a road, a real flat-top road, all the way from the plant to the highway, more than 20 miles.'

Medford leaned forward. 'You have my authorisation for an insertion. I don't need any more frills on the case.'

Mercado cleared his throat. 'Crator's flicked across our radar screen before.'

'I need a point to this.'

'The money.' Mercado nodded. 'Rumours that it's a front for Chinese money.' He paused. 'Chinese State money.'

Medford shrugged again.

'Even been in the press. Hearsay, but it hasn't gone away.'

Medford sat back in his chair, hands resting on his midriff, fingers intertwined. He sat in silence for some moments. The ceiling fan ticking off the seconds, the rattle of a construction crane from the street below. He blinked.

Mercado shifted his weight to his other foot.

Voices, from the corridor. A door slamming shut.

'What did you say your name was?' Medford narrowed his eyes.

'Mercado, sir. Mario Mercado.'

Medford nodded, the folds in his neck bulging. 'Then tell me, Mario.' He paused. 'Why the fuck are you still here?'

Mario drew himself up to his full height, concentration etched across his dark features. 'A sense.'

Medford banged a hand on the desk, raising his voice. 'We've got the two most powerful navies in the world playing high-seas chicken and the CIA has a funny feeling about something?' He brushed a file across the desk with a sweep of his hand. 'For fuck's sake!'

The quiet edged itself around them, Medford's words still ringing around the room.

'Apologies.' Medford's voice calm once more. He looked up at Mercado. 'Look, we've got a room full of four-star generals playing top trumps with a bunch of pumped-up admirals.' He shook his head. 'All twitchy as hell from too many double espressos and last night's Viagra.' He sat back in his chair. 'The Redeemer Nation.' He paused. 'A sense of destiny and a load of heavy ordnance.' He shook his head. 'A fucking frightening combination.'

Mercado cleared his throat. 'Things are falling into place, sir. That's what it looks like to me.'

'Meetings, hideaways, money.' Medford shook his head. 'Universal static. Soundtrack of life.'

Mercado took another deep breath. 'To be honest, I thought you might …' He exhaled. 'That these might make more sense to you. From where you sit. The broader picture.' He paused again. 'The whispers that GCHQ picked up, from deep in the dark web.' He cleared his throat. 'Crator. The Ringmaster.' He took another breath. 'The Pale Tiger.'

Medford pursed his lips. 'If it is, I can't see it. Not with any clarity.' He gave a shrug. 'Too many blank spaces on the canvas.' He paused. 'Could be part of something. Or part of nothing.'

Mercado shifted his weight to the other foot.

'But thank you for being frank.' Medford paused.

Mercado nodded.

'I assume I lived up to my reputation.'

'That is fair to say, sir.'

'And you to yours.'

'Politics is a contact sport.'

'The Bobby Jones of Langley.' Medford tried a smile. 'Luke Dunn won't appreciate you taking the initiative, even with him out of town.'

Mercado raised an eyebrow.

Medford nodded. 'Anyway, a good excuse to step on Luke Dunn's toes.'

'We have some history, sir.'

'So I hear.' He smiled again. 'Well, no harm in a scuff or two on his Coach loafers. Keep him honest.'

'Do you want me to comment on that, sir?'

'Figure of speech, Mario.' Medford raised an eyebrow. 'The footwear might be from Macy's.'

WEDNESDAY 25TH SEPTEMBER, 2.45 PM

WEST CENTRAL POLICE STATION, LONDON

DI Perry laid the theatre tickets on her desk, leaned back in her chair. 'The receptionist, she was looking out for her,' she nodded, 'didn't leave reception between 18.00 and 20.00 that Monday evening.'

DI Lute sat facing her. He reached over, picked up the tickets, held them up to the light. 'It's a show for kids isn't it?'

'All ages.' She sat up in her chair, picked up a coffee cup. 'Two tickets.' She took a sip, pulled a face. 'Yuck.' She put the cup back on the desk. 'Nothing on her phone. No "looking forward to seeing you tonight", no "I waited two hours and you never showed, I hate you".'

'So the receptionist got it wrong.' DI Lute tossed the tickets back on the desk. 'They weren't for Rhea.'

DI Perry picked up the envelope. 'Ms R Moore, by courier, for collection.' She handed it to DS Lute. 'Her credit card.'

DI Lute reached up, pulled at an earlobe with finger and thumb. 'Maybe they got the wrong day.'

'Rhea ordered them that day, Monday morning.'

DI Lute glanced down at the tickets, then across at DI Perry. 'So she was going to go with someone from work?'

'If Ellis Wagner's right they're not allowed to use the firm's email for PA stuff then … yes, she didn't send any message saying she'd got them …'

'But Scutt didn't leave until … when was it again?'

She glanced down at her notes. 'Seven forty-two.' She picked up a pen from the desk, twirled it around her fingers. 'If it was him on the CCTV.'

DI Lute sat back in his chair. 'We could go round the mulberry bush all day on this.'

She exhaled, glanced around the squad room. Mid-afternoon lull, colleagues stretching, yawning, checking mobiles. The autumn sky, framed in the peeling window frames. Streaks of cloud, like spun grey yarn, twisted by the wind. The printer in the next door room clattered back to life, chattering excitedly to an unseen audience. She turned back to DI Lute, a frown spreading across her soft features. 'The receptionist. She looked worried.' She paused. 'Frightened, even.'

'Always harder to prove something didn't happen.'

'But she was there, all that time. Looking out for Rhea.'

DS Lute shrugged. 'She took a phone call, got distracted by a visitor, turned round to hang up a coat, whatever.

You've done surveillance, that's why they always put two of us on it.'

'No,' she shook her head, 'this girl knows Rhea didn't leave the building, not then, anyway.'

'Only the CCTV knows, the rest is more like guesswork.' He spread his hands. 'And if she is scared, she's not going to want to make a statement.'

DI Perry shook her head. 'She could be in danger just for …' She closed her eyes.

'Then you've just got to leave this one, Anne.' He nodded. 'Leave Rhea in peace, if that's possible.'

She leaned back in her chair. 'We both know this wasn't an accident.'

'We don't know that, we suspect that.' He paused. 'And if we can't prove it …' He shook his head. 'You're just making it harder for yourself next time.'

She closed her eyes. 'They're laughing at us.'

'Fuck them.'

The door on the far side of the room swung open. DC Zayan walked in, laptop in hand.

DI Perry looked up at the DC. 'Careful, Alan.' She glanced across at him. 'He's got that look about him.'

DI Lute turned around. 'Hasn't he just.' He straightened up in his chair, thick, dark lines furrowing his forehead. 'Perhaps I didn't explain myself clearly enough, DC Zayan.'

DC Zayan stood beside the desk, looking down at DI Lute. He frowned. 'I'm sorry?'

DI Lute exchanged a glance with DI Perry. 'After that many vodka shots you're meant to have a quiet, unproductive day like the rest of us.'

DC Zayan stood in silence for a moment. He cracked a smile. 'I did feel like shit.'

'Thank goodness.' DI Lute slapped him on the arm. 'Come on, pull up a chair.'

DC Zayan slid a chair over, settled in next to DI Lute. He placed his laptop on the desk. He looked across at DI Perry, then back to DI Lute. 'The girl in the lift.'

'Is it Rhea?' DI Perry took another sip from the coffee cup, pulling a face as she sat it down.

DC Zayan took a deep breath, exhaled. 'I went back further on the CCTV, back a day, to Sunday.'

His two colleagues nodded.

'Sunday evening, a couple check in. She was in a wheelchair.' He paused. 'Full burka, mesh screen covering her eyes. Traditional couple, he's sporting the full beard, thobe, ghutra.'

DI Lute raised a hand. 'Sorry, remind me …'

'The thobe's a long white robe. The ghutra is the headwear, square cloth, band around the head.'

DI Lute nodded.

'Yemeni passports. Almost impossible to check if they're genuine.' He glanced across at his colleagues. 'But I ran the names through the immigration database. Nothing. If they flew in, they did so under different names.'

DI Perry picked up a pencil, twirled it around her fingers. 'Go on.'

'They checked into Room 412.' He paused. 'They'd asked for that room specifically when they booked.'

'And our Alex,' DS Lute began, 'he'd asked for Room 414?'

'The one with the retro bedstead.' DI Perry nodded. 'You would, wouldn't you?'

'Exactly.' DC Zayan nodded. 'So, next morning, Monday, they leave, quite early, dressed the same, or similar. The lady in the wheelchair says nothing. The man has a few words with reception, mentions that his wife has a hospital appointment.' DC Zayan cleared his throat. 'They return to the hotel just before 18.00 in the evening. The lady in the wheelchair is hunched up, slumped forward. Barely conscious, or at least still sedated.' He paused. 'The guy on reception also remembered that she had an oxygen mask over her nose and mouth.'

'I thought she was wearing a burka.' DS Lute frowned.

'He couldn't see her face, but he could see the outline of the mask through the material.' He paused. 'And there was an oxygen bottle, or what looked like an oxygen bottle, hanging on the side of the wheelchair. It's all on the CCTV.'

DI Perry leaned back in her chair. 'The guy with the beard. Do we get a look at his face? Or a decent description?'

'He's wearing thick-framed tinted glasses. The kind you'd wear if your eyes are sensitive to bright light. And with the beard and the headdress.' He shook his head.

'Not much to go on. And the CCTV's not the highest quality either.'

DI Lute looked across at DI Perry. 'You come across something like this before?'

She shook her head.

'Next morning, they check out.' DC Zayan nodded. 'Paid cash, of course.'

DI Perry narrowed her eyes. 'The lady in the wheel-chair, height? Build?'

'Harder to judge when they're sitting down, but you'll see on the CCTV, she's petite, like Rhea.' DC Zayan looked from one colleague to the other.

They sat in silence.

DI Lute was the first to speak. 'It's all circumstantial.' He nodded, then patted DC Zayan on the shoulder. 'Brilliant work, though, brilliant.'

'So there's your timeline.' DI Perry exhaled. 'At 18.00 Rhea Moore was already barely conscious. Just enough oxygen to keep her alive.' She shook her head, 'An hour and a half before she supposedly walks through the hotel lobby.' She closed her eyes. 'Time of death, between 22.00 and 23.00.' She paused. 'After a four- to five-hour period of prolonged hypoxia.'

'Professionals.' DI Lute pulled at his earlobe. 'They'll have covered their tracks.'

DC Zayan looked across at DI Perry.

'Rhea Moore ordered two theatre tickets on Monday morning. That evening's performance. The agency dropped that at reception, at work.' She nodded. 'The receptionist was looking out for her, didn't leave the reception desk between 18.00 and 20.00 that evening. She's certain that Rhea didn't walk out that front door.' She picked up the tickets, handed them to DC Zayan.

'Matilda.' He held them up to the light. 'Cambridge Theatre.'

'Jamie Ives showed me CCTV of Rhea Moore walking out of the front door at 18.07.' She tapped the pencil on the desk. 'What does he know?' She glanced out of the window, then back to her colleagues. 'He also said that Rhea was working that afternoon in one of the meeting rooms.'

DS Lute spread his hands. 'And?'

'I met Jamie Ives in one of those meeting rooms.' She blinked. 'Air, pure enough to catch in your throat, no allergens, no pathogens. Felt really weird, like I was going to faint.' She looked from one colleague to the other. 'When I got home I googled my symptoms.' She raised her eyebrows. 'Any guesses?'

DS Lute nodded. 'Mild hypoxia?'

'And he didn't break stride.'

They sat in silence for a moment. The printer next door announced itself with a snarl, its ill-tempered cackling drifting over them.

DC Zayan sat upright. 'There's something else.'

His colleagues turned towards him.

'Ellis Wagner. I rang the Royal Australian Regiment.' He paused. 'They have no record of him serving.'

DI Lute shook his head. 'That's low.'

DI Perry looked up. 'I could really do with a cup of tea.'

'Can we just …' DI Lute shifted in his chair. 'In my head … bear with me.' He exhaled. 'So we have Alex checking into Room 414 shortly after 19.00.' He glanced down at his notes. 'He texts "Zoe" at 19.16. She texts him back.' He paused. 'At 19.32 Zoe, looking like Rhea, gets in the lift.' He frowned. 'Some hours later, Rhea is dead. But we never see Alex again. Where did he go?'

'We probably do see him again, but we just don't realise it.' DC Zayan nodded. 'Assume that Alex is working with the Yemeni couple. They check in the day before, they have suitcases. They're staying next door to Alex. The only CCTV is in the lobby and in the lift.'

DS Lute nodded.

'We know Alex checked in without luggage.' DC Zayan continued. 'So on the CCTV we're looking for him leaving the hotel after Rhea's death dressed as he was, long coat, maybe with the beard and dark glasses, maybe without.' He paused. 'Or he dumps the coat, just wearing a jacket, sweater, T-shirt, whatever, but we think we'll spot that because it would look odd going outside in this weather without a coat.'

'So the Yemenis have a change of clothes for him, different coat, different wig.' DS Lute leaned forward.

'Or they dress him as a woman.' DI Perry let the pencil drop onto the desk. 'Either way, he's long gone.'

DS Lute exhaled. 'And the Yemenis. Sunday, Mr and Mrs check in. Monday morning they're off to the hospital. Monday at 18.00 he returns, pushing Rhea in the wheelchair.' He nodded. 'Just after 10.00, they kill Rhea, put her body in Room 414. Next morning, Zoe from the lift, the same one who giggles for the benefit of the manager, leaves in the wheelchair.' He shook his head. 'And we'll never be able to prove any of it.'

DI Perry picked up her coffee cup, peered into it, placed it back on the desk. 'Jamie Ives. Something's not right.'

'We know that.' DI Lute pulled at his tie.

'I mean something doesn't make sense.' She narrowed her eyes. 'The first time I was there, the meeting room, he was letting me know, about this weird air conditioning. How they could thin the air, just like that.'

'What's that? Arrogance? Maybe he's just taunting you.'

'He wanted me to make this connection. The hypoxia, and Rhea.' She looked across at DI Lute. 'Why would he do that?'

DI Lute shrugged.

DC Zayan sat in silence, staring at the desk.

DI Perry shook her head. 'He doesn't want us to drop this.'

DI Lute exhaled. 'You know what. We should all just walk away.' He raised a finger. 'If we're right.' He glanced at his colleagues. 'OK, let's say we are right.' He paused. 'These are professionals. We don't want to go anywhere near them.'

No response.

'People who can do this kind of thing, and do it so thoroughly. They'd do it to any of us, police or not.' He pulled at his earlobe between finger and thumb. 'And we'd never be able to prove it was Rhea in the wheelchair anyway.'

DI Perry took a deep breath. 'Let's think about it.'

'Anne, that's the last thing we should do.'

DI Perry looked out of the window. The tower blocks to the west, outlines sharpening as the clouds thinned, austere angles harsh against the blue sky. She turned back to DI Lute. 'Crator, there's got to be another way in and out.'

'Leave them to it Anne. If they want to eat their own …'

She glanced across at DC Zayan. 'Could you do us a huge favour? Could you get us a tea from over the road?' She picked her handbag up from beside her chair, rummaging for her purse. 'Alan, you want one?'

He shook his head. 'I'm fine, thanks.'

DC Zayan stood up. 'I've got it.' He glanced out of the window, picked up his coat from his desk, strode across the room.

The door swung shut behind him.

The two of them sat in silence.

Anne picked up her pencil, twirling it around her fingers.

Alan tapped a fingernail on the desk, nodding as his eyes flickered over the papers spread over her desk.

'Rhea's aunt's arriving tomorrow.' Anne looked across at him. 'From Spain.' She bit her lip. 'We'll have to tell her.'

Alan looked up. 'Do you want me to do it?'

She shook her head. 'It might be easier, as a woman, to hear it from a woman.'

He nodded. 'Her face is fine. She doesn't look like a victim.' He looked across at Anne. 'I know, you'll say she called out to you. But we can't help, not this time.'

Anne didn't reply.

'And DC Zayan, Iqbal, you've got to get him off this.' Alan fixed Anne in his gaze. 'He could really get hurt.' He shook his head. 'You know, he worships you. He'd run through walls for you if he could.'

Anne nodded.

'Let's get the formal identification done tomorrow. Then we can put in the report, together.'

'OK.'

He straightened his tie. 'I'm sorry we can't give Iqbal credit for all he's done on this.' He reached behind for his jacket. 'He deserves something.'

She smiled. 'Would be nice if it came from you.'

He nodded. 'I'll talk to him.' He stood up. 'Let's catch up tomorrow.' He turned, set off towards the door on the far side of the room.

Anne sat back in her chair, exhaled, looking up at the ceiling.

Her phone rang. Unknown number.

She clicked on the call. 'This is DI Perry.'

A moment of silence. Then a woman's voice. 'Nina Carter here.'

'Nina Carter?'

'Rhea Moore's aunt.'

'Ah yes, of course.' Anne paused. 'I'm so sorry about this.'

Silence on the line. 'Yes, she was a great girl.' Another pause. 'A brave girl.'

Anne frowned. 'Right.'

'You have quite a reputation, DI Perry.'

'Do I?'

'Where I come from, yes.'

Anne bit her lip. 'And where might that be?'

'Estepona, do you know it?'

Anne sat back in her chair. 'Never been, but I had a friend ...'

'Yes, a friend.'

The line went quiet.

Anne narrowed her eyes. 'Perhaps even the same friend?'

'Emma.'

Anne took a deep breath. 'Did she know Rhea?'

'Everyone was very fond of Rhea.' Another pause. 'I'm in London, can I see Rhea?'

'Of course.'

'Tomorrow morning, 10.00.'

'She's in the mortuary, at West Central Police Station.'

'Yes, I know where that is.'

Anne cleared her throat. 'You said I had a reputation.'

'You don't give up.'

'Is that a good thing?'

'As I said, everyone was very fond of Rhea.'

Anne nodded. "Til tomorrow then.'

The line clicked off.

Anne sat back in her chair, looking up at the ceiling. 'Estepona.' She whispered to herself.

She leaned forward, opened the desk drawer. A postcard. Estepona. She turned it over, rereading it to herself. 'Anne, if you ever find yourself in Estepona, or think you might, give me a call, Rebecca.' A telephone number scribbled beneath.

Anne bit her lip, picked up her mobile, rang the number.

It rang to voicemail. A female voice. Emma Wilson's. 'I can't get to the phone right now but please leave me a message.'

Anne waited for the beep to end. 'Hi there, it's me, Anne.' She hesitated momentarily. 'I was wondering if you knew how I could get hold of Rebecca.' Anne swallowed. 'We're expecting someone from Estepona.' She paused. 'Thought you might know her.' Anne bit her lip. 'Bye.'

Anne closed her eyes. She remained still for some moments, then reached down for her handbag. She opened it, began to sift through its contents. She pulled out a business card, picked up her phone, stood up, walked towards the fire exit. She slipped through the door, stood in the chill stairwell, her shadow smudged across the concrete floor under the light bulb above. She was alone. She looked down at the business card, dialled the number.

A man's voice answered. 'Hello.'

'This is DI Perry.' She paused. 'Anne Perry.'

Silence. 'I was just thinking about you.'

She took a deep breath. 'Could I come and see you?'

'Context and continuity, Anne.' He paused. 'May I call you Anne?'

She exhaled. 'Can we do this less formally?'

'I'd enjoy exploring that.'

'Not a scheduled visit.'

'I have a vivid imagination'

'More … discreet.'

'Something else we have in common.'

She bit her lip. 'Is there another entrance? Not the main reception.'

She could hear Jamie Ives's chuckle. 'Told you you'd make a great analyst.' He paused. 'Slipping in a killer question like that.'

She closed her eyes.

'But you've already worked that out.'

She swallowed. 'Six o'clock?'

Silence on the other end of the line. 'I'll be waiting for

you. There's a passageway to the right of the building, an unmarked door, halfway along.'

'Is there a bell I ring?'

'I love an old-fashioned girl.' He paused. 'Just come as you are, Anne.'

She clicked off the call and leaned back against the wall, clutching the phone to her chest.

WEDNESDAY 25TH SEPTEMBER, 10 AM (3 PM GMT)

THE FRICK GALLERY, NEW YORK

'Lilies. They were Mr Frick's favourite.' The lady behind the ticket desk looked up at the visitor. The sunlight through the French windows, shimmering across the polished wooden floor, the shadows of the window frames, scaling the pale marble walls. 'But 100 years ago it was a real home.' She smiled. 'Just one?'

'Strange choice, for a true collector.' Kasper Lehtonen drew his wallet from his pocket, handed her a note.

'They were considered exotic back then.' She handed him his change.

'A little too fresh, too obvious, if I can say.'

'Do you need an audio guide?'

He shrugged. 'Should I?'

'It saves you having to think.'

'I love New York.'

'But that probably wasn't what El Greco had in mind.'

Kasper nodded. 'But then irony wasn't discovered until 1748.'

The woman raised her eyebrows. 'I was told 1758. They came across it when they were digging for serendipity.'

'Did they even know what it was?'

She gave a slight frown. 'Initially they thought it might be travesty.'

'Given what they were actually looking for, it probably was.' He stood in silence for a moment, glanced down at her hands. 'That's a thing, isn't it? Takes getting used to.'

'Does it?'

'Rubbing your thumb against the inside of your ring finger. Still feels odd, no? Not wearing it.'

She leaned back in her chair, removed her spectacles. 'Far too observant.' A slight twitch of the eyebrows. 'For a tourist.'

He fashioned a smile. 'Think on your feet, that's it. You'd do well in my like of work.'

'Do I have to guess?'

'I help people do things they'd never believe they could.'

She looked up at him, running her necklace through her fingers. 'So you're a yoga teacher.'

'Not sure I could be that cruel.' A slight tilt of the head. 'You free for lunch?'

She took a deep breath. 'No.' She exhaled. 'But I finish at five.'

'My name's Marco.' He nodded.

'If you say so.' Another twitch of the eyebrows.

He turned, walked back towards the entrance, flitting through the shadows thrown across the ticket hall floor.

He dipped to the right, strode along the corridor, the statues on either side, bronze glinting softly under the ceiling lights. The room opened up in front of him. The stone fireplace and on either side, the Holbein portraits. Thomas Moore and his nemesis, Thomas Cromwell.

Kasper stood between them, looking from one to the other. He shook his head. 'Thank fuck for central heating.'

'Everyone's reaction's different.' A voice, behind him. 'Those hats.'

'Keep looking.'

'Fur collars and velvet sleeves.' Kasper grunted. 'What kind of look is that?'

Silence.

Kasper continued to stare straight ahead. 'Am I going to be embarrassed?'

'Do you embarrass easy?'

'In case you're dressed as a lift engineer, or a traffic warden, perhaps?'

The newcomer cleared his throat. 'I do hate to disappoint you.'

Kasper turned around. 'So you dressed up as an accountant.'

'Aren't we all accountants nowadays?' Luke Dunn looked Kasper up and down, the hint of a smile. 'How's that cough?'

'Strangest thing.' He paused. 'Must be all this fresh air.'

Luke leaned towards him. 'Now, that pretty lady, behind the ticket desk.' He narrowed his eyes. 'We don't want any dramas.'

'Dramas?'

'You arrived, you kept your head down, you left.' Dunn nodded. 'Nice and quiet.'

Kasper looked across at him. 'Do you really think …?'

Dunn shrugged. 'I'm not judging.'

Kasper nodded. 'A drink.' He paused. 'She's not in this story.' He glanced around the room, settled his gaze back on Luke. 'You have the proper speaking part.'

'Is that a threat or a compliment?'

Kasper gave him a half-smile. 'Maybe a bit of both.'

Luke raised an eyebrow. 'Wouldn't get too relaxed if I were you. You might not always be so useful.'

'Is that a compliment?'

Luke flashed a smile, narrowed his eyes once more. 'How are you getting on with the neighbours? In the jungle?'

'They don't seem to mind us.'

Luke pulled at his shirt cuff. 'Time to join the dots.'

Kasper ran a hand over his bald head. 'Assume I'm the simple man.'

Luke turned towards the portraits. 'Sometimes, they say, we all need a little guidance.' He nodded towards Sir Thomas Moore. 'To really understand what we're looking at.'

Kasper followed his gaze. 'He looks like he has toothache.'

'He probably did.' Luke pulled at his other shirt cuff. 'But look at his cloak, his sleeves. Red: the colour of power, the colour of martyrdom.'

Kasper stood in silence.

'And that silky green awning.' Luke lowered his voice to a whisper. 'Green symbolises revelation, epiphany.'

'Hindsight's hardly original.'

'Well here's the thing. He painted him in 1527, eight years before his execution.' Luke paused. 'So now you see, it was a warning to Moore. Of the fate that awaits him, unless he can fashion a change of heart.'

'Is this about me, or him, so to say?'

Luke raised a finger to his chin. 'Well, that is a question.'

Kasper gave a little grunt. 'Five hundred years later, anything can mean anything.'

'Exactly.' Luke looked across at Kasper. 'Well said.' He paused. 'The trucks, their trucks, how often do they leave that coffee warehouse next to our lab?'

'Almost every day, but the times, they vary. Depends on high tide at Buenaventura, to get the ships alongside.'

'So, the dots.' Luke made a purring noise. 'A satellite's now scanning that quadrant of Colombia every 45 minutes. I've arranged for a tip-off. To some honest prick at CIA who no doubt is already dutifully following up on it. What could they all be up to in that jungle clearing in the middle of nowhere?' Luke gave a little smile. 'So, when their trucks set off from the coffee ware-house, your trucks set off. Stick with them, like glue, until Highway 25.'

'Quite the coincidence.'

'Life's full of them, don't you find?' Luke brushed a hair from his lapel with a flick of his thumb.

Kasper scratched the side of his face. 'Anything else?'

Luke turned back towards the painting. 'Milot Borso, your colleague, he's landing late tonight.'

'Well?'

'There's going to be a little demonstration. You know, loudhailers, raggedy signs on sticks, bad haircuts.' Another half-smile. 'Tomorrow morning, 8.00.'

Kasper looked straight ahead, his eyes on the portraits. 'I'm flying out tonight. London.'

'Then send someone else, someone reliable. The steps of 350 Park.' Luke paused. 'An FBI photographer will be there. Just make sure friend Milot accidentally gets in the shot.'

The sound of voices, moving closer, a group entering the room.

Kasper and Luke continued to gaze ahead.

The newcomers settled in front of the Bellini on the other side of the room, talking in hushed tones.

Luke cleared his throat. 'So, how are you enjoying our fine city?'

'Which version?'

'Life's about contrasts.'

Kasper scratched the side of his face. 'Most cities it's the other way round.'

'Too many right angles, sheer-sided buildings, nowhere to hide.' Luke nodded, slowly. 'No wonder we're all snarls and attitude as we pace the cracked pavements.' He raised his eyebrows. 'But step inside and we're all smiles and courtesy.'

'Not sure which is worse.'

Luke stood in silence for some moments. 'I'm curious.' He pulled at his shirt cuff. 'You've never really asked.'

A slight shrug from Kasper.

'Why?' Luke paused. 'Why we're going to all this trouble? Aren't you curious?'

Kasper slowly turned towards him. 'You want me to listen to your high-minded excuses? Why you lie to your colleagues, your bosses?' He gave another shrug. 'I could pretend some interest.' He scratched the side of his face. 'Since you're paying me.'

Luke took a deep breath. 'You may despise my patriotic ardour, but I love my country.'

'You really believe that?'

Luke glanced across at him. 'For you, there's just money.'

'Would you rather offer something else?'

'A price and a cost are two different things.'

Kasper nodded. 'But one doesn't exclude the other.'

Luke glanced at his watch. 'We'll be ringside, all the way, so don't try and fake it.'

'Thought that was my role, ready with the towel, to wick the conscience off you.'

'I know you're clever, but everyone comes up for air.'

'So it is.' Kasper raised an eyebrow. 'You just need to know when to duck and when to jab.'

WEDNESDAY 25TH SEPTEMBER, 6 PM

OUTSIDE CRATOR CAPITAL, LONDON

Anne Perry held the collar of her coat tight to her neck as she leaned forward into the stiff breeze. She turned the corner into the cul-de-sac; ahead of her, the dark outline of the building, the light from the windows fixing the street with their frosty glare. She glanced around her, houses hunched down in the twilight. Streetlights, flickering into life, the orange glow seeping over the ancient cobblestones, casting shadows across the worn brickwork. She shortened her stride, her high heels feeling for purchase on the uneven surface. Another gust, a bite to the air now, the canal, beyond the terrace. Old leaves, diesel fumes, the tang whipped off the slick dark surface of the brackish water. She grasped the shoulder strap of her handbag, holding it close as the wind snapped around her. She looked up, the building looming sheer and stern, the light streaking the stonework, marble sinews flexing under the darkening sky. She walked towards the entrance to the passageway.

Movement, in the darkness of the alley.

She froze, her breath catching in her throat.

Something glinting, stirring.

She slipped her handbag from her shoulder, fingers feeling for the PAVA spray.

Into the half-light it stepped, its tail swishing slowly from side to side.

'Mr Fox.' She slung her handbag back onto her shoulder. 'From the darkness he came …'

The fox stood still, appraising her with its steady gaze. It tilted its head to one side.

'Have I strayed into your world … or you into mine?'

The fox drew itself up to its full height, nose held aloft into the night breeze. It lowered its head, lips curled upwards, a smile, or a warning.

'Your rules then.'

The fox nodded. Turned. Trotted back into the gloom.

Anne watched it go, reached into her handbag for her phone. She clicked on the torch, scanning the foot-worn stonework as she edged into the darkness, the alley walls towering around her.

A door. To her left. She shone the light around the doorframe. No buzzer.

The door began to open, the light from the hallway flooding into the alley, the warm air lapping over her.

Jamie Ives stood in the doorway, waterfront chic, cable-knit sweater and jeans. He smiled. 'Out of the cold with you.' He stood aside as Anne stepped past him.

He closed the door. Turned to face her. 'Let me take your coat.'

Anne glanced around the room, the wood panelling glowing under the wall lights, a table beneath the mirror, a small bronze statue, a ballerina, elegant arms outstretched. She felt the warmth seeping into her. She breathed in, dry wood, fresh-cut flowers, the scent of a candle. She looked across at him. 'I shouldn't be here.'

'You probably shouldn't.'

She stood in silence for a moment, then laid her handbag on the table, began to undo the buttons on her coat. She slipped it off her shoulders, handed it to him.

He hung in on the peg by the door, turned back to face her.

Anne picked up her handbag. 'You shouldn't look at me like that.'

He smiled. 'That dress does … invite attention.'

'You know why I'm here.'

He raised his eyebrows. 'Do you?' He let the question hang in the air for a moment. 'You should wear your hair up more often.' He gave a slight nod, then turned, walked to the far side of the hallway, opened a door. 'Please.'

Through the open doorway Anne could see the log fire reflected in the window, flickering off the glass-topped table, the light washing over the leather armchairs, glowing reds and golds. She stepped inside. The flames from the fire cast shadows across the ceiling high above her, the panelled walls glowing in the warm light.

'Can I get you a drink?' Jamie strode over to the bar in the corner.

She stood there, feeling the warmth of the fire brushing her bare shoulders. 'No thank you.'

He poured two tumblers of whisky. 'Bit monochrome I know.' He sauntered over to her, handed her a glass.

She frowned, the light from the fire, ripples of light across her soft features, her hair shimmering in the orange glow. She took the glass.

'But then it's just me.' He shrugged.

'So why am I here?'

'For answers.'

She took a sip. 'Go on.'

'You want to know what I know. You need to know.' He nodded. 'And you're wondering, how deep will I have to go?'

Anne took a breath, the smell of the fire, the tang of burning wood.

'What does five minutes' time look like?' He paused. 'Standing behind you, my fingers and lips caressing your neck. I unzip your dress, running my hands across your back, down your arms, the fabric slipping off your shoulders …'

Anne swallowed. 'I should go.'

'Kissing you, licking you.' He moved a step closer. 'Tasting you.'

She breathed in again, fresh wool, aftershave.

'All of you.'

Anne closed her eyes, the roar of the fire, logs crackling.

He took her chin in his hand, leaned towards her. 'All those things you've never dared ask your husband to do to you.'

They kissed.

Anne opened her eyes, she took a step back. 'So now I know.'

He met her gaze, the glare of the fire throwing soft shadows across his well-drawn features.

She shook her head. 'I sensed something before but I couldn't quite …' She glanced across at the window overlooking the canal, the lights from the houses on the far side, shimmering on the surface of the still, dark water. She turned back towards him. 'You're frightened.'

'You make my heart race.'

'Your eyes tell a different story.'

'Maybe you should take a closer look.'

'You want to tell me, but you're not sure if you can.'

He stood in silence for a few moments, then lowered himself into one of the chairs. He took a sip of his drink. 'What do you think you know?'

She studied him for some seconds. 'The meeting room.' She paused. 'Mild hypoxia. Not a nice sensation.'

'Some might call it cheating.' He looked up at her. 'Just business, you get your edge where you can.'

'You know what happened to Rhea.' She nodded. 'And you wanted me to know you know.'

'It was a childish prank. I should have known better.'

She narrowed her eyes. 'Rhea was murdered.' She paused. 'We can protect you.'

He leaned back in the chair, closed his eyes. 'Your vivid imagination.'

She bit her lip. 'Like you said, I want to know what you know. I need to know.'

He opened his eyes, stood up, walked over to the bar, refilled his glass. He turned around. 'Sex, Anne.' He took a sip. 'I just wanted to fucking sleep with you.' He paused. 'So I spun you along.'

'I don't believe you.'

He shook his head. 'Rhea Moore, it's a sad story. Any accident is.'

'Why was Rhea killed?'

'Anne, really, this is all there is.' He looked across at her. 'Life goes on.'

She met his gaze. 'I almost feel sorry for you.'

He smiled. 'No you don't, you're just trying to provoke me.'

'The people who killed Rhea, ice-cold assassins.' She paused, the sound of the log fire, crackling in the stillness around them. 'If Rhea knew too much,' she shook her head, 'what are they going to do to you?'

Jamie stood in silence for a moment. He reached up, carefully pushing a ringlet of her hair behind her ear.

Their eyes, once more locked.

'You'll tell me you're happily married.' Jamie's gaze, moving slowly over Anne's soft features. 'Most people who stray are happily married.'

Anne bit her lip, looked away, a tear trickling down her cheek. 'You know nothing about my life,' she snapped at him as she turned to leave.

WEDNESDAY 25TH SEPTEMBER, 6.30 PM

OUTSIDE CRATOR CAPITAL, LONDON

Alan Lute stood in the shadows of a basement well opposite the entrance to Crator Capital. He tucked his coat collar up again, the chill of the evening starting to bite as he stood as still as he could, eyes on the main door, the slick, black steel glinting in the glow of the street lamps. A light came on, from the alleyway to the side of the building. He tensed, eyes straining into the semi-darkness. A figure, standing by an open door. A man's voice, too far off to catch the words. The door closed, plunging the alleyway back into darkness.

A figure stepped out of the alleyway, careful steps across the cobbled courtyard. A woman.

Alan Lute gave a gasp as he recognised the figure. 'Anne, what the fuck?' He whispered.

Anne pulled her coat collar up around her neck, clutching her shoulder bag tight to her waist as she made her way towards the road that led up to the junction.

Alan stepped back further into the stairwell shadows as Anne approached his hiding place. He held his breath, the click of her heels ringing out in the quiet darkness. She was coming closer.

She stopped under the streetlight, just yards away. She was looking for something in her handbag. A tissue. She wiped her eyes. She was crying. She drew herself upright, took a deep breath, set off again towards the rumbling traffic, the road at the end of the cul-de-sac.

Alan stepped out of the darkness, shaking his head as he watched her make her way towards the lights of the main road. 'Anne,' he spoke quietly to himself, 'what the fuck are you up to?'

He heard the purr of the main entrance sliding open behind him. He stepped back into the shadows, eyes on the open door, the light from the entrance hall flooding across the forecourt, glinting on the wet stonework.

A man stepped out into the dark evening. He wrapped his scarf around his neck, zipped up his coat, set off towards the junction, the car lights swishing by, pedestrians plodding, shoulders hunched against the cold.

Alan stood perfectly still in the basement shadows as the coated figure passed by, his breath frosty in the chill night air. Alan observed him for a few more seconds, then quietly ascended the stone steps to the street, following the coated figure at a discreet distance.

They joined the crowds shuffling along the brightly lit

pavements, shop awnings ruffling in the breeze.

The coated figure strode confidently, weaving through the early evening swell.

Alan Lute kept him in his sights, a steady distance, biding his time.

The park gates up ahead, the shortcut to the station.

The coated man paused at the entrance, looking down the pathway between the trees, the few streetlights, the thick darkness between. He rolled his shoulders, set off down the path, hands buried deep in his coat pockets.

Lute followed behind. Careful, quiet footsteps, eyes on his quarry.

The coated figure reached the bend in the path, followed it around to the right, temporarily out of sight.

Lute kept his steady pace, turned the corner.

No one there.

Just the deserted pathway, sneaking through the trees. The darkness, a streetlight in the distance, a pool of light, sanctuary from the rustling blackness.

He glanced from side to side, just the wind, hissing through the trees, leaves, drifting across the grass. 'What the …?'

Something stirring, on the edge of the tree line.

He spun around.

The outline of a figure. 'You looking for a fuck or a fight?'

Alan Lute narrowed his eyes, staring into the darkness.

'I can help you with one.' The figure stepped out of the trees. 'You'll have to go elsewhere for the other.'

Lute cracked his fingers.

'Well, you're in luck then.' The figure took a step towards him.

Alan Lute held up his hand. 'Just want to talk to you.' He paused. 'Need to talk to you.'

'Why the full-pitch cloak and dagger shit?'

'I'm a policeman.'

'That an excuse?'

'It's about Rhea Moore.'

The figure by the tree line stood silently for a moment. 'What happened to your curvy friend, the DI with the attitude?'

'I work with her. DI Perry. My name's Alan Lute, DI Alan Lute.'

'You couldn't just call?'

DI Lute shook his head. 'Needed to see you, away from there.' He indicated the building they'd just come from with a flick of the chin.

'You look like you mean it,' the man stepped out of the shadows onto the path, 'but let's see your ID.'

DI Lute reached into his pocket, held it out towards him. 'How did you spot me?'

'I didn't, some geezer by the park gates was giving me a funny look. Thought he might have ideas. Given the day I've had at work, he'd have been welcome to have a go.' He stretched out his hand. 'Ellis Wagner.' He paused. 'No surprises there.'

They shook hands.

'Fucking freezing.' Ellis Wagner stuck his hands back in his pockets. 'Why don't we go for a drink instead?'

'Local knowledge, lead the way.'

Wagner set off back down the path, Lute beside him.

'You're going to ask me,' Wagner began, 'about the Royal Australians.' He glanced over at Lute.

Lute stopped, Wagner turned to face him.

'I resigned,' Wagner continued, 'it was either that or a dishonourable discharge.' He took a deep breath. 'Iraq, 12 years ago, the bridges at An Nasiriyah. First independent command.' He looked down at the ground. 'I froze, bottled it.' He looked back up at Lute. 'Struck from the Regimental Rolls.'

'You've got the flag on your wall. You think that's right?'

'It's there to remind me. I let a lot of people down.' He looked down the path towards the park gates. 'Don't want to know that feeling again.'

Lute studied Wagner's face for a moment. 'Fine margins.' He looked down the path. 'Let's get inside.'

They walked through the park gates, back onto the main road. The lights from the shopfronts glancing off the damp pavements, the patter of the passing traffic; a car horn sounded nearby.

'Down here.' Wagner took Lute's arm, guided him into a side street.

The pub sign, swaying in the breeze, the fading paintwork.

'Seen better days.' Wagner pushed open the door. 'At least you won't see anyone from work here.'

The warmth of the pub billowed over them as they walked to the bar. A few couples, crouched around the tables by the wall. Two solitary drinkers by the bar. A fixed odds machine glinting conspiratorially in the corner.

The barman looked up as they approached. He tapped one of the lights above the bar, it fizzed reluctantly back to life, casting its orange glow across the bottles ranged along the shelves. He nodded.

'Monkey Shoulder, please. Large one.' Wagner looked across at Lute.

'Same.'

'We've run out of ice.' The barman reached up for the bottle.

'Thank fuck for that.' Wagner reached into his pocket. 'I've got it.'

He handed the note to the barman. 'If the change is less than a pound keep it.'

'It's not high street prices.'

'God bless honest men. Keep it anyway.'

The barman smiled. 'Amen to that.'

They picked up their glasses, headed to an empty table.

They shook off their coats, hung them on the peg by the fading boxing poster, sat opposite one another.

'So you haven't forgotten about Rhea either?' Wagner took a sip. 'DI Perry know you're here?'

Lute sat in silence for some moments. 'No.'

Wagner nodded. 'So now it's my turn to say something indiscreet.'

Lute sat back in his chair.

'Scutt came to see me, the day Rhea ...' He paused. 'Her last day at work.' He leaned forward. 'Rhea had been asking Theodora some unorthodox questions, enquiring about transport movements along the Colombia coast, ports, railheads, that kind of thing.'

Lute shrugged.

'She was meant to be checking lithium exports out of Peru, from Callao, Matarani ... Chile as well, bills of lading, shipping movements.' He nodded. 'And Cobalt, from Pointe Noire and Matadi, the Congo coast.'

'And?'

Wagner shook his head. 'Pharmaceutical intermediates, out of Colombia? The Pacific and Caribbean ports?' He frowned. 'We do deal in pharmaceutical intermediates, but our nearest plant's in Bolivia. We don't ship any product out of Colombia.'

'Go on.'

'Scutt's meant to put all this in the daily logs. Exactly who's been asking Theodora what. It's a big deal. I have to sign them off.'

'Why the fuss?'

'Theodora's time is precious. And we don't want analysts wandering off into data land looking at who knows what. I mean, they'd be there forever.'

'So was Rhea in trouble?'

'Scutt asked me to cover for her.' Wagner took a sip. 'He didn't say as much, but that was what he wanted.' He laid his glass on the table. 'And I agreed. Said I'd say she was checking on competitor activity. But in the end, no one followed up on it.'

Alan Lute pulled at an earlobe. 'Why do you think any of this is relevant?'

'I went back over the log reports. There's a pattern, she's been there before. Buenaventura, El Valle, Santa Maria, Puerto Drummond, Barranquilla.'

Lute shrugged

'She was looking for something.' He paused. 'She was taking a risk.'

'For kicks?'

'I've played chess with her. She doesn't take risks for kicks.'

Lute drummed the tabletop with his fingers. 'Say it then.'

Wagner took a deep breath, exhaled. 'All this, same day as her accident?'

Lute picked up his glass, took a sip. 'How well do you know your colleagues?'

'You mean why don't I just get the fuck out?'

Lute sat back in his chair. 'Why didn't you contact DI Perry? If you had your doubts.'

Wagner flexed his fingers. 'If Jamie Ives found out …'

'Why would she tell Jamie Ives anything?'

Wagner met his gaze. 'If you say so.'

Lute shook his head. 'So why don't you? Get the fuck out?'

'Last time I ran away, it didn't go very well.'

'So what are you going to do?'

'Keep my eyes and ears open, my head down.'

Lute nodded. 'Where's Scutt?'

Wagner picked up his glass. 'No fucking clue.'

'Do you think he's all right?'

'All right?' He took a sip. 'There's a few kangaroos loose in the top paddock.' He paused. 'Good guy though.'

Lute frowned, the lines creasing his broad forehead. 'Do you think he's come to harm?'

'Do you?'

'Odd isn't it? He just ups and goes, no contact details.' Lute paused. 'And Jamie Ives doesn't sound one bit curious.'

'Jamie wouldn't do anything to Scutt.'

'How do you know?'

Wagner took another sip, looked across at DI Lute. 'Because he's his brother.'

WEDNESDAY 25TH SEPTEMBER, 7.30 PM

BARNES, LONDON

Anne Perry quietly closed the front door behind her.

She could see the light from the kitchen, spilling across the hallway floor.

She glanced at the coat hooks on the wall, then up at the staircase in front of her.

Noise from the kitchen. A tap running, a drawer closing, the cutlery within chinking as it slid shut. A shadow skittered across the tiles.

She closed her eyes, leaned her shoulder against the wall, muttered under her breath. 'Fuck.'

She heard the fridge door close, glassware rattling.

Then, silence.

'Anne?' Her husband's voice from the kitchen.

She stood upright. 'Hi darling!' She took a deep breath. 'You're back nice and early.'

'Wound up sooner than I thought ...'

Anne shot a look around the hallway. 'I just need to pop upstairs.'

Bill Perry stood in the kitchen doorway. 'Only happens once in a blue moon, I know.'

She swallowed. 'I'm sorry, Bill. I just …'

'No, you're not seeing things.' He indicated the apron hanging down his front. 'Don't blame you for feeling nervous.'

'I … can I …?'

'Have a takeaway instead?' He pouted. 'Have some faith, woman. He paused. 'Lipstick suits you, you should wear it more often.' He smiled. 'Come and have a drink.'

'Can you pour me one? I'm just going to freshen up.'

'Wine?'

'Sure.'

They stood facing one another.

'Are you all right?' He took a half step towards her.

'Of course.'

'You look as though …' He frowned. 'You've been crying.'

'It's just the cold weather.' She attempted a smile. 'I'll be right down.'

'What's the matter?' He took another step towards her.

'Nothing's the matter!'

Silence.

She bit her lip. 'I'm sorry.'

He looked her up and down. 'You don't have to apologise … for looking nice.' He smiled. 'Come on, let's get your coat off and come into the kitchen.'

She gazed across at him, blinked. She laid her handbag on the hall table, unbuttoned her coat, shrugged it off her shoulders and hung it on the hallway hook.

He looked at her dress.

'Was in a rush this morning.' She smiled, weakly.

'I've always liked that dress.'

'Bad choice really, given the weather.' She wiped away a tear.

'Anne,' he placed a hand on her shoulder, 'you don't have to explain.'

She closed her eyes.

'We know we'd never do anything to hurt each other.'

She exhaled, looked up at him. 'I just wanted to … I don't know …'

He smiled. 'It's all right, sometimes you don't want to look like a 48-year-old policewoman.'

She bit her lip. 'Jamie Ives. I let him kiss me.'

He stood in silence for some moments, blinking. 'Do you really want to do this?'

She took a deep breath. 'I wanted him to.' She looked down at the hallway floor. 'I lay awake last night … I let myself imagine …' She raised her head. 'I was thinking of him …'

Bill stood in silence, a hint of a frown creasing his brow.

She exhaled. 'Aren't you going to say something?'

He nodded. 'Your dream. The dream. It's changing … isn't it?'

She took a deep breath, exhaled. 'It's more than a dream.'

'It always was.'

'Do you think there's another me?'

He pursed his lips. 'Do you?'

'You used to say that I couldn't lie.'

'Did I?'

She looked back down at the ground. 'Fuck it.' She shook her head. 'I didn't expect you back early, I was going to get changed, take the make-up off.'

He shrugged.

'I was going to lie to you.'

'But you didn't.'

'Maybe I'm still lying.'

'Anne, stop it.'

'Maybe I'm just …' She shook her head. 'Sometimes I think about us and I … just wonder.'

'Wonder what?'

She glanced around. 'What are we Bill?' She took a deep breath, wiping away another tear. 'I know, I know, we have something … special.'

'What are you trying to say?'

'Sometimes.' She closed her eyes. 'Sometimes, I just wish we could be something more than just … friends without benefits.'

He shook his head, turned, walked back into the kitchen.

'Bill! I'm sorry, I didn't mean that! You know I didn't.' She took a step towards him. 'Why are you walking away?

Bill!' She raised her voice.

'I've got a chilli con carne to ruin.' He called over his shoulder. 'And you're scaring me.'

She swallowed, walked across the hallway, stood in the kitchen doorway. 'I'm sorry.'

'Are you?' He opened the fridge door, took out the wine bottle, refilled his glass. 'So what happened? He refused to fuck you and you're taking it out on me?' He slammed the fridge door shut, the bottles inside jangling.

'He was pressed for time.' She snarled. 'Had to settle for a blow job.'

He picked up the saucepan, brought it crashing down on the metal draining board. 'Will you listen to yourself!'

The clang echoed around the kitchen.

They stood in silence.

He stood at the sink with his back to her, gazing out of the window into the blustery night. 'Why don't you step outside … and send the real Anne Perry back in here.'

A siren in the distance, the rumble of an aeroplane somewhere in the dark clouds above.

'Because I don't fucking recognise that woman standing in the doorway.' He turned around.

Anne looked down at the kitchen floor, the shadows of the branches outside the window shuddering in the wind.

'So, you got there.' He paused. 'The dream. All the way down, into the shadows.'

She looked up at him. 'There's things I can only sense.' She glanced out of the window, reflection of the street-lights, silver ribbons streaking the window panes. 'But they're there, waiting.' She looked back at him. 'Waiting for me.'

'This isn't about Rhea anymore, is it?'

She gave a half-smile. 'Sometimes I think it is.' She shrugged. 'Sometimes I don't know.'

He stood in silence for some moments, voices passing on the street outside, a dog barking in the distance. 'What are you looking for, Anne?'

She swallowed. 'I was daring myself, at first.' She took a deep breath. 'To follow it, to face it … whatever it was … is.'

He pursed his lips. 'But now, you can't leave it alone.'

She exhaled. 'It's not—'

'Or won't leave it alone.' He gave a little snort. 'I always knew you were a wilful woman.' He set his jaw. 'But I never had you down as a cruel one.'

'Don't start shouting at me, please.'

He turned around, facing the window above the sink. The wall of the neighbouring house, the faded brickwork, the climbing ivy, leaves rustling in the tug of the wind. 'You might not remember, but before we met I worked as a journalist.'

She took a step towards the kitchen table in the centre of the room. 'I'm sorry, I need to sit down.'

'Never had your dream, but I saw it, sensed it, felt it even.'

She pulled out a chair, slowly sat.

'Some of the stories I worked on, these people, that fierceness.'

She placed her elbows on the table, holding her head in her hands.

'Felt that pull as well.' He exhaled. 'The cold-pressed greed, fizzing around you.' He paused. 'Power, ill-intentioned and unpredictable, hunkering in the shadows.'

She sat in silence.

'And the danger, thick enough in the air to taste.' He turned around. 'Sometimes, the bravest thing to do, is to run.'

She looked up at him. 'If we back off, they've won.'

'There's no winners and losers.' He shook his head. 'Because in that world there's no rules. Just iron-hard probabilities.' He turned around to face her. 'But you know that.' He paused. 'That's why you were crying.'

She closed her eyes. 'I wish that were true.'

'Anne. Look around you. This is our life. This is us.'

She glanced around the kitchen, the light from above the cooker shimmering off the wall tiles, glinting on the slick stone surfaces. 'I was frightened.'

'Darling, it was just a kiss.'

She looked up at him. 'Frightened of myself.' She paused. 'Maybe I was crying because it was only a kiss.'

He stood in silence for some moments. 'What's the point of shouting at you?' He sniffed the air, turned to look at the pans bubbling on the stove. 'And now the chilli con carne's fucked.' He flicked off the hobs, stood with his back to her. 'I'm going out for a drink. I'll pick a pizza up on the way home.'

'Bill.' She bit her lip. 'I don't want to be on my own.'

He turned around, pulling the apron off over his head. 'What the fuck have you done to yourself?'

She looked down at the table.

'Right and wrong.' He paused. 'You used to be a teacher for fuck's sake.'

She began to cry.

He walked towards the kitchen door. 'You know what the worst thing is?' He stopped by the front door. 'You didn't have to tell me, because I didn't want to know.' She heard the front door open. 'Can't you take a fucking hint?' He slammed the door shut behind him.

She sat at the kitchen table.

An alarm sounded in the distance, a dog, barking a warning somewhere down the street.

She got up, walked to the sideboard, poured herself a large whisky, took a swig. She walked to the window, looked out into the garden, the shadows of the branches lying thick across the faded patio stones. 'One more day. Please God, just one more day.' She took a deep breath, drained the rest of the whisky.

THURSDAY

THURSDAY 26TH SEPTEMBER, 8 AM (12 AM, MIDNIGHT GMT)

SO LO PUN, HONG KONG

Emma Wilson sat up on the bed.

The clank of bolts, steel sliding on steel.

The door swung open.

The same man, standing there. The tall Han Chinese, crisp white shirt under a freshly pressed dark suit, concern written across his firm features. He stepped through into the cell, closed the door behind him. He nodded towards a wooden chair by the wall. 'May I?'

Emma didn't respond.

He walked over, sat, folding his hands in his lap. 'You are a spy.' He began. 'But your driver, Fraser Chan.' He paused. 'He was brought up here. He is a traitor.'

She gave a slight shake of the head.

'They'll take him across the border tonight.' He paused. 'You know what they'll do to him.'

She looked across at him. 'Can I see him?'

'Obviously not.' The man's voice still calm, matter-of-fact.

Emma leaned back against the cell wall, the rough stone cold against her.

'So we are only interested in what he doesn't know.'

Emma looked across at him. She blinked.

He let the silence crackle around them.

'Where do you suggest we start?'

Emma bit her lip.

The man frowned. 'Out of deference to your rank, and your reputation, I would prefer not to threaten you.'

Emma closed her eyes.

The rattle of the ceiling fan, a door, slamming in the distance.

'But we don't have a lot of time.'

Emma looked across at him. 'You know I can't.'

He sat in silence for a moment. 'They will be instructed to get the answers quickly.'

Emma looked down at the rutted floor, shadows from the lights smudged across the concrete.

'No boundaries.' He paused. 'Not for this.'

Beads of sweat forming on Emma's forehead.

He cleared his throat. 'I'm sorry.'

Emma looked up. 'This isn't the seventies. We don't do this kind of shit anymore.'

He unfolded his hands, scratched his temple. 'Why are you in Hong Kong?'

She shook her head. 'What the fuck is this?'

He nodded. 'The Carl Vinson's carrier strike group's steaming to link up with the US Seventh Fleet at the southern end of the Taiwan Strait.' He narrowed his eyes. 'Two carrier strike groups. And you ask what the fuck this is?' He let the question hang in the air.

She met his gaze. 'You think I'm in this story?'

'People asked the same question in the summer of 1914.'

Emma blinked again.

'One misstep.' He nodded. 'And we're all in this story.'

Emma frowned. 'Isn't this what you want? Your blue water showdown.'

'What do you think?'

She shook her head. 'A one-child policy navy. That's a hard call.'

'But the Americans. They want to fight?'

'No one wants to fight.'

They both fell silent, footsteps in the corridor, muted voices, orders, barked in the distance.

The man spoke first. 'So they feel they have to. Fight.'

Emma shrugged. 'Perhaps.'

'Can you help us?'

She looked around the cell, the humidity glistening on the cracked walls. She swallowed. 'And Fraser Chan?'

He nodded, held out a hand. 'Jian Zhuo.'

She looked down at it, leaned forward, shook it.

He stood up. 'There's someone else you need to meet.'

. . .

Emma squinted as she stepped into the daylight. The morning sun, low in the eastern sky, the jungle treetops, leaves glistening as they shimmered in the breeze.

'Watch your step.' Jian Zhuo called over his shoulder.

Emma blinked again, her eyes slow to adjust after the night in the cell. The path beneath her feet now coming into focus, stone slabs, bleached by the sun of centuries. Swirls of green moss, soft underfoot. She filled her lungs with the warm, humid air, rich from the overnight rain.

The path began to slope down, narrower now, the trees swaying around them, speckled shadows flitting across the ground. Gusts of wind ruffling the leaves, raindrops fizzing in the sunlight.

A monkey bark, somewhere in the trees up ahead. A flight of birds, their wings chattering as they rustled through the canopy to the open sky.

Jian Zhuo, still just a couple of steps ahead of her.

Emma's breathing had quickened, the thick air catching in her throat. She raised a hand, flicking the perspiration from her face. She pulled at the neckline of her T-shirt, the fabric clinging to her skin.

Another clearing, up ahead. The outline of a building, camouflage netting slung above it.

The path opened out: a small courtyard, smooth, hardened earth beneath their feet.

In front of them, a door, in the shade of an awning. Smooth, grey steel, a viewing window, slid shut.

Jian Zhuo knocked twice.

The viewing port slid aside. A flicker of eyes from within and the door swung open.

They stepped inside, the cool air washing over them. The door closed behind them, the thud of steel closing on steel.

Emma blinked as she took in the scene in front of her. Bright lights, the blur of movement, uniformed figures poring over maps laid out on the central tables. To the side, rows of desks, more PLA marines, eyes fixed on the flickering consoles. The hum of voices, urgency crackling in the air.

'This way.' Jian Zhuo nodded towards a side door.

Emma followed him in. The door swung closed with a click, the silence once more wrapping around them.

Emma scanned the room. The plain grey walls, drenched in a soft, blue light. No windows. A table, its polished metal top glinting. Six chairs.

Her ears adjusted to the quiet. She could hear the rumble of the air conditioning, the rustle of air through the vents above them.

She looked across at Jian Zhuo.

'I know.' He nodded. 'Not exactly lived-in.' He glanced around. 'Never knew if we'd have to use it.'

She heard the door open, turned towards the noise. A man, his stocky form framed in the doorway.

He addressed Emma as the door swung closed behind him. 'You don't look like one.'

Emma frowned.

'A witch.' He continued. 'Let alone a wicked one.' He gave a slight smile. 'But then you have come back from the dead.'

He walked towards them, his silver hair catching the light. He stopped in front of Emma, his head level with hers. 'Miss Wilson. I remember you of course.' He gave a nod. 'Never understood what you saw in McKay.'

'Neither did I.'

'Shall we.' He indicated the table.

Jian Zhuo pulled out a chair for Emma.

She sat opposite the newcomer, Jian Zhuo by his side.

The older man sat back in his chair, letting the silence wash over them.

'Another cable yesterday, from your ex.'

Emma blinked.

'Sandman met official Ministry of Health. Cassandra was decoy.' He paused. 'Does that make sense?'

'I'm not sure.'

'If this was mainly about you, Cassandra would have been the first word in the cable.'

She sat in silence.

The older man narrowed his eyes. 'He's lit the fuse, now he wants the fireworks.'

Emma blinked again.

'The first part's true.' He nodded. 'Milot Borso met the official.'

Emma frowned. 'Why not include that in his schedule? Why the secrecy?'

'You know what the charity does. Our citizens have no need for free medicine.' He paused. 'Officially, at least.'

Emma blinked again.

'One of those things that doesn't exist.'

Emma glanced around the room. 'Like here.'

He nodded. 'Like us.'

Emma took a deep breath. 'So, in return for not, officially, giving out free medicine, the charity gets what?'

'Fast-track approval for two new generic plants in Guangdong.'

Emma shrugged.

'Exactly.' The grey-haired man sat back in his chair. 'Wouldn't even make it to the inbox of the graduate on the China Desk.' He paused. 'On its own.' He narrowed his eyes. 'But McKay has you working with Borso so your man can meet with the Ministry, away from prying eyes.'

She nodded. 'Cassandra.'

'So McKay's gone to the trouble of framing you, dangling a conspiracy.'

'A lot of trouble.'

'But if you're just the fall girl, then McKay's pulling Borso's strings.' He nodded. 'And McKay would know exactly what the meeting was – or wasn't – about.' He leaned forward. 'So who's pulling McKay's strings?'

Emma sat quietly for some moments, looking down at her hands. The purr of the air conditioning, the feel of the cool air sweeping around her.

'The old fox himself.' He tapped a finger on the table-top. 'Your mentor, Noon.'

Emma took a deep breath.

'Or Pritchard perhaps? I gather you're off the Christmas card list.'

She exhaled. Looked up at him. 'They always said you were good.'

No response.

'I should be flattered.'

He raised his eyebrows.

'All this effort.' She looked from one to the other. 'To turn me.'

The older man nodded slowly. 'Go on.'

'Always a chance. Here, on my own, locked in a cell, mind racing.' She paused. 'Of course I thought about it.' She closed her eyes. 'Thrown to the wolves, I've seen it happen.'

Silence from the other side of the table.

'Good agents, burnt in bad operations. But this isn't one. This isn't us: not Noon, not Pritchard.' She looked across at him. 'But what you really want,' she met his gaze, 'is for me to say no.'

The grey-haired man sat back.

'McKay's gone rogue.' She paused. 'He's working with Crator. Vauxhall's in the dark. This isn't about you and us.'

He exhaled, nodded. 'Our turn, I think.'

Jian Zhuo pulled out his phone, dialled a number, handed it to Emma.

The dialling tone began to ring.

Someone answered, a man's voice. 'Hello.'

Emma stared at the phone. 'Fraser?'

'Ma'am!' An intake of breath. 'Where are you?'

'Where am I?'

'Everyone's looking for you, all sorts of rumours flying around.'

'Where are you?'

'I'm back at the hotel, where you told me to be.'

Emma exhaled. 'Look, it's complicated. I'll … I'll explain it all when I see you.'

'But everyone—'

She cut the call.

She handed the phone back, a smile flicking across her features. 'He's not that good a liar. So thank you.'

The older man nodded. 'A diplomatic incident is the last thing we need right now.' He paused. 'So now we both know what this isn't.'

Emma sat up in the chair. 'May I have some water?'

Jian Zhuo got up, headed towards the door.

The grey-haired man watched him go, turned back to

Emma. 'You've had a busy couple of days.'

She sat back again. 'Would you have let him shoot me?' She raised an eyebrow. 'I assume you were there, in the park.'

He pulled a face. 'Perhaps an unfair question.' He paused. 'We knew who you were, but we didn't know what you were.'

The door swung open, Jian Zhuo with three bottles of water. He placed them on the table, opened one for Emma.

'Thanks.' She took a swig.

The older man leaned forward. 'Crator Capital's been on our radar screen too. About a year ago, some stories appeared. Could never trace the source but some heavy-weight publications ran it, or at least reported the hearsay.'

Emma nodded.

'According to sources familiar, widely believed to be etc., etc.' He cleared his throat. 'Chinese money, or more specifi-cally, Chinese State money, behind Crator.' He paused. 'Not a scrap of truth in it.'

Emma shrugged. 'There's always rumours.'

He nodded. 'But usually there's a motive, an angle, someone who'd benefit from the story getting mileage.' He unscrewed the top from the bottle. 'Couldn't work this one out.' He took a sip. 'So why are you after them?'

'Two red flares.' She took another pull on the bottle. 'Actually three. They were on the VAI list.' She glanced across at them. 'Vulnerable Artificial Intelligence. Knowl-edge or computing power that could pose a threat in the wrong hands. In Crator's case, their transport database, the algorithms. Tides, currents, sea states, just about everything that can float, where it's going, what it's carrying and when it'll get there.'

He nodded for her to continue.

'Then there was the money.' She tucked her hair behind her ear. 'Pretty grubby.' She shook her head. 'Filthy really.' She took another sip. 'But it was big numbers, turned a blind eye I guess, people do.' She paused. 'But there was a price to pay.'

She glanced across at the two men, looking for a flicker of recognition.

Nothing.

'A few months later one of the founders died when his parachute didn't open. Exactly what happened we don't know. But it was a Crator charity event and Crator didn't want their name splashed across the tabloids. The inquest was peremptory to say the least.' She took another swig of water. 'Three months later their Head of Finance disappears. Offsite, caving in Wales. Never found the body.' She placed the water bottle back on the table. 'And shortly after that,' she looked from one man to the other, 'the rumours began.' She narrowed her eyes. 'Whispers, from the darkest reaches of the web, where our writ isn't meant to run.' She took a deep breath. 'Crator. The Ringmaster.' She let the words hang in the air.

The faintest flicker in the eyes of the older man.

Jian Zhuo shifted in his seat.

'Operation Pale Tiger.'

The silence clanged around them.

No one spoke.

The grey-haired man blinked.

Emma sat back in her seat the tension crackling in the chill air.

'It's spent its whole life in captivity.' The older man cleared his throat, fixed his gaze on Emma Wilson. 'Few even remember it's there.' He paused. 'Our Pale Tiger.'

Emma took a deep breath.

'But perhaps there were other cubs?' He watched her carefully, the hum of the air conditioning the only sound in the thundering quiet of the hushed room.

After some seconds the grey-haired man spoke again, his expression stone-hard. 'In less than 24 hours, two American carrier strike groups will be on station south of the Taiwan Strait.'

She met his gaze.

'This isn't just another freedom of navigation exercise.' His jaw muscles tightened. 'If the Americans enter the strait, we will have to come out and fight.'

The words hung between them.

Jian Zhuo took out his phone, flicked his finger across the screen, slid it over the table to Emma.

A photograph. A man, early fifties perhaps, bald, thick-set, blue eyes. She looked up. 'The Ringmaster?'

'Perhaps.' The older man glanced down at the photograph. 'Kasper Lehtonen.' He looked up at Emma. 'Born 1966 Oulu, Gulf of Finland. A high-level facilitator, no known political affiliations.'

Emma sat back. 'He's on our radar too. He's the conduit for the dirty money flowing into Crator.'

'He was in New York yesterday. Covered his tracks well. But not that well.' The older man leaned back. 'Does the name Luke Dunn mean anything to you?'

She shook her head.

'Now State Department, but he's CIA to the core. Met our friend at a gallery. Too much background noise, so we can only guess.' The grey-haired man gazed at her intently. 'Your turn.'

She gave a nod. 'There's a connection, to the Colombian ports. We're trying to find out more.' She paused. 'We had a source, inside Crator. We know she got into Theodora, their database, but we're not sure what she found. She was deep cover, strictly hands off.' Emma bit her lip. 'But they got to her.'

The older man nodded. 'So now it's up to you.'

'To me?'

'We can't break into Crator, McKay has us in the spotlight.' He narrowed his eyes. 'It has to be you.'

Emma blinked.

'We can get you to London in seven hours.'

'What?!'

'There's a JH-7A fighter on standby just over the border. The Russians have cleared us all the way to Gorelovo, near the Estonian border. From there a medivac jet will take you into London City.'

'They'll be looking for me.'

Jian Zhuo shook his head. 'This just up on the SCMP site.' He handed her his phone.

She gave a little snort as she read it. 'Knew I shouldn't have gone out.' She handed him the phone. 'Shit photo as well.'

'For your own good.' He slid the phone into his pocket. 'There's worse ways to go.' He looked across at her. 'You still got friends in London?'

She nodded. 'One or two.'

'You should go.' The older man nodded to Emma. 'The helicopter's waiting, Jian Zhuo will brief you on the way to the airfield.' He held out a hand. 'Thank you.'

She shook it.

'I'd wish you luck,' he gave a half-smile, 'but the dead have their own providence.'

THURSDAY 26TH SEPTEMBER, 10 AM

WEST CENTRAL POLICE STATION, LONDON

DI Perry walked into the meeting room.

DI Lute was already there. He looked up from his phone. His jacket hung over the back of his chair.

She laid the file on the table. 'Thought it was just me and the aunt.'

He sat back in his chair. 'Thought you and I didn't have secrets.'

Anne Perry slowly sat down, studying his face. 'Everyone has secrets.'

DI Lute nodded. 'True.' He looked across at her. 'I trailed Ellis Wagner last night. He left Crator around seven.' He raised his eyebrows. 'Just after you.' He paused. 'So ... who goes first?'

Anne Perry took a deep breath. 'I thought Jamie Ives was ready to talk.'

'If you fucked him you mean?'

'It wasn't like that.' She gave a grimace. 'I flirted, we flirted.' She blinked. 'That was it, it was fucking stupid.' She paused. 'And I fessed up to Bill.'

'Anything could have happened to you in there.' His jaw, tensing. 'And I'm not talking about Jamie Ives and his golden knob.'

She bit her lip. 'There was something.' She swallowed. 'Jamie Ives, he's scared.'

Alan Lute sat back in his chair. 'That ... makes two of us.' He laid his hands on the table. 'Scutt came to see Wagner the day Rhea died. He wanted Wagner to cover for her, for Rhea.'

Anne looked across at him, stony-faced.

'She'd been making enquiries where she shouldn't. Made a bit of habit of it.' He pulled at his earlobe. 'Always looking in the same place. Pharmaceutical intermediates, out of Colombia.'

Anne took a deep breath.

'Crator doesn't have any business there.' He leaned across the table. 'Anne.'

She looked down at her hands.

'Anne, look at me!' His tone, insistent now. 'You want to go on with this?'

Anne held her head in her hands.

He looked at her for a moment, then slowly shook his head. 'Anne, we'll never nail them. This is over. You understand?' He bit his lip. 'We're walking away. Now.'

Anne sat in silence, just her shoulders, rising and falling.

'Anne!' Alan Lute ground out the words. 'If you go back in there and you do find what you're looking for.' He slammed the palm of his hand on the table. 'It will fucking eat you!'

Anne exhaled, slowly, her whole body, shaking. She looked up at Alan. 'I want this to end.'

He looked across at her, his broad forehead furrowing into a frown. 'Really, Anne?'

She bit her lip. 'I'll take the aunt to see Rhea, then we close the case.'

He took a deep breath. 'Don't make me worry, Anne.'

She stood up, composing herself, smoothing down her skirt. 'I looked over the precipice.' She picked up the file. 'Once was enough.' She turned, walked to the door, swung it open.

A WPC stood in the corridor. 'She's waiting for you, ma'am, just outside the room.'

DI Perry nodded. 'I'll follow you.'

They set off down the passageway, shoes clicking on the linoleum, their shadows smudges of grey skittering over the pale polished floor.

They turned a corner.

A bench by the wall, a woman sitting, alone. She turned towards them as they approached. Pale skin, short dark hair, a few years younger than Anne. She stood up.

'Sorry to keep you waiting.' Anne held out a hand. 'DI Perry.'

The woman shook it. 'Nina Carter.'

'Anne, call me Anne.' She put a hand on Nina Carter's arm.

Nina nodded. 'I think I'm ready.'

Anne patted her arm 'She looks restful.' She guided Nina towards the double doors.

They walked into the autopsy room, the air chill and sharp. The tang of antiseptic, their footsteps ringing off the tiled floor. Whitewashed walls, glistening under the strip lights. The doors swung shut behind them. They were alone.

They stood beside the examination table, a crisp white sheet covering the body.

Anne slowly pulled the cover down revealing Rhea's face.

Nina reached out, stroked Rhea's cheek. 'Rhea, we should have done better.'

They stood in silence for some moments.

Anne glanced up at Nina. 'Does she have parents?'

Nina nodded. 'They think she died in a diving accident. Sipadan Island.' She laid the palm of her hand on Rhea's forehead. 'Soon be home.' She looked across at Anne, concentration etched across her face. 'Anne, we need you to go in there, again.'

Anne swallowed, her face, paling. 'I was there last night.'

Nina nodded. 'I know.'

'There's something …' She bit her lip. 'Jamie Ives. He was frightened.'

Nina rolled the sheet back over the girl's face. She patted the girl's arm, then looked up at Anne. 'You don't have to sleep with him.'

Anne blinked.

'Unless you want to.' Nina, deadpan.

'I can't go back in there.' Anne looked down at the ground, shuddered. 'You'll have to send someone else.'

Nina Carter laid her hand on Anne's arm. 'It has to be you.'

Anne shook her head. 'He won't say anything.'

Nina nodded. 'I doubt he will.' She paused. 'But Theodora might.'

Anne stood in silence.

'Get Jamie Ives's access pass and you can talk to Theodora.'

Anne closed her eyes. 'Nina.' Her voice, barely more than a whisper. 'It's not just Jamie Ives.' She looked up at Nina. 'There's something else in there.'

'We'll be right outside.'

'Something,' Anne shivered, 'that wants to hurt me.'

'You'll have a panic button.' Nina put a hand on Anne's arm. 'Tell me what you know, Anne.' She paused. 'About Rhea.'

Anne looked down at the ground, then across at Nina. 'We know how she was killed.' She bit her lip. 'And we think we know why.'

'Go on.'

'She was unconscious when she left the building. They have a ... they can change the oxygen levels.'

Nina nodded.

'We assume they put a mask on her, keep the oxygen low, keep her unconscious.' Anne blinked. 'They dressed her in a burqa, took her into the hotel in a wheelchair.' Anne took a deep breath. 'Took her upstairs. They staged this ... party in the room, boy and a girl having fun, the duty manager heard them.' She exhaled. 'They took her into the room, tied her there, put a bag over her head, a belt round her neck.' Anne shook her head. 'We think she might have woken up, just briefly, when they took the mask off to put the bag on. There's some abrasions on her wrists.' She looked down at the body, the sheet folded into the contours of her face. 'No other signs of ...'

Nina squeezed Anne's arm. 'I know you did your best for her.' She paused. 'Did you make any of this official?'

Anne shook her head. 'Wouldn't have been able to prove it.'

Nina stood in silence for some moments. 'So what happened? At work that day?'

'We know that Rhea had been looking for something, asking Theodora questions she shouldn't.'

'Who told you that?'

'She'd done it before, there was a pattern.'

'Questions about what?'

Anne looked across at her. 'Pharmaceutical intermediates, out of the Colombian ports.'

Nina nodded. 'So you know where to start, with Theodora.'

'Why would she talk to me?'

'Jamie Ives, he must have full security access.'

'I don't sound like Jamie Ives.'

'Anne,' Nina squeezed her arm again, 'we've got to try. Theodora, she knows, she must know.'

Anne met her gaze. 'Can't you send a team in?'

'She can join the dots, all this traffic out of those ports.' She paused. 'She might know what it all means.'

'I'm not trained for this.'

Nina paused, she took a deep breath. 'Anne, there's a shoot-to-kill order out on Emma.'

Anne narrowed her eyes. 'What?!'

'It's a ... I don't know, it must be a mistake.' She exhaled. 'But we don't know who to trust right now.' She paused. 'Emma trusts you.' She unslung her handbag from her shoulder, pulled a glass vial out of the side pocket. 'This will buy you time. Almost tasteless, odourless.'

'How do you know the button will even work? It's like a sealed world in there.'

'We know what we're doing.' She tried a smile. 'Right outside, Anne.'

Anne swallowed. 'Will it kill him?'

Nina shook her head. 'But he'll have a grown-up headache when he wakes up.'

Anne blinked again. 'The doors, they're all unmarked, how do I even know where Theodora is?'

'We'll brief you before we go.'

Anne looked down at the ground. 'I'm no good with guns.'

'You can leave all that to us.'

Anne looked up at Nina. 'If it goes wrong?'

'It won't.'

'My husband …'

'We do this all the time.'

'He'll think I was there to meet Jamie.' She shook her head. 'That can't be the last thing he thinks about me.'

'It won't be.'

'I can't die worrying about that.'

Nina laid her hands on Anne's shoulders. 'We send you in there, we'll get you out again.'

'Can I talk to Emma?'

Nina took a deep breath. 'I wish we could.' She tried another smile. 'She's gone to ground: if she doesn't want to be found, they won't.'

Anne closed her eyes.

'Thanks, for what you did for Rhea.' Nina tried another smile. 'There's one more thing you need to do for her.' She paused. 'You need to release her body, for burial.'

Anne nodded.

'You need to sign the case off. Close it.'

'Of course.' Anne glanced down at the girl lying chill and silent beneath the sheet. 'Will there be a funeral?'

Nina shook her head. 'It'll be just family.' Nina looked down at Rhea, then across at Anne. 'Do you want me to leave you here with her? To say goodbye?'

Anne shook her head.

Nina let her hands drop from Anne's shoulders. 'You'd have got on well.'

Anne turned to face the swing doors, the stainless steel sinks along the far wall, shimmering in the cold, white light. 'Final part of the story.' She glanced around the room, the ceramic tabletops scoured and scratched clean. 'No one ever thinks their journey will end here.'

'At least it has an ending.' Nina bent down, kissed Rhea's forehead.

Anne drew herself upright, set off towards the exit, her footsteps clacking off the tiled floor.

'Oh, and I almost forgot.' Nina looked up. 'Rhea's clothes, do you still have them?'

Anne turned, one hand on the door. 'Most mothers, it just upsets them more.'

'But you'd want to hold them, all the same.'

Anne nodded, stood in silence for some moments, looking across at Nina. 'That look on your face, when you first saw Rhea.'

'The dead, they can ask difficult questions.'

Anne bit her lip. 'They say you shouldn't confuse revenge with guilt.'

Nina blinked. 'Is there a difference?'

THURSDAY 26TH SEPTEMBER, 11 AM

CRATOR CAPITAL, LONDON

The lift opened, bearings purring as the steel door rumbled aside.

Kasper Lehtonen stepped into the room.

Jamie Ives looked up, slowly folded down his laptop.

Kasper didn't speak.

Jamie blinked. 'Wasn't expecting you.'

The murmur of gears, the clicking of steel teeth as the lift door slid back into place, seals closing with a hiss.

Kasper stood, letting the sudden stillness wash over them.

'Silence, such a personal thing.' Kasper surveyed the room, his expression calm. 'Your ears must be better than mine.' He cocked his head. 'A waterfall.' He looked across at Jamie. 'Fear's soundtrack. Your blood, there it is, roaring through your veins.'

Jamie swallowed.

'Your lucky day, Jamie.'

'Is it?'

'Pain, those little pulses to your A and C fibres.' Kasper's tone, easy, matter-of-fact. 'You think you know what pain feels like?'

Jamie's breathing quickened.

'It's a funny thing, first-timers normally last longer.'

Jamie stared up at him.

'They go into a kind of … trance.' Kasper nodded, slowly. 'The sheer volume of pain pulses just … overwhelms the system, like a power surge.' He paused, eyes locked on Jamie's. 'Then slowly, there it is, the system begins to understand, to process those pulses.' The slightest of nods. 'Then we're in the game.'

Jamie stared back at him, his lips moving silently.

'Where's your little brother?'

Jamie's eyes widened. 'I … He didn't say.'

Kasper's features remained still. 'You know I can't believe that.'

Jamie closed his eyes.

Kasper stood in silence.

A clicking sound from the ceiling as the air conditioning recalibrated, quietly humming back to life.

'Look at me.' Kasper's tone, soft, patient.

Jamie opened his eyes, slowly raising his gaze to the visitor.

'You weren't listening.' Kasper's voice remained calm.

Jamie's chest rising and falling, his breathing shallower now.

'I said,' Kasper paused, 'it was your lucky day.'

Jamie didn't speak.

'That Theodora.' Kasper walked towards Jamie. 'Always had a mouth on her.'

Jamie straightened up in his chair as the visitor approached the desk.

'She was happy to give it up.' Kasper ran a hand over his shaven skull. 'So you and I don't need to get all …' He narrowed his eyes. 'Is that a love bite on your neck?'

Jamie followed his stare, reached up to touch the mark. 'Nicked it shaving.'

Kasper frowned. 'You're saving your energy, remember?' He kept his eyes on Jamie for a moment, then glanced towards the picture window running the length of the office. 'Why do they even bother?' He walked towards the vista, the Paddington towers, now shrouded in low cloud, the upper stories, swallowed up by the swirling mists. 'What's the point of the high rise if you can't see a fucking thing half the time?'

Jamie didn't reply.

'Anyway, now we know where junior got to, so to speak.'

Jamie cleared his throat.

'Rio to Singapore. At an average of 18 knots, that's …?' He swivelled around, looking across at Jamie.

'Twenty-five days.'

'Without landfall.' Kasper scratched the side of his face. 'Theodora, bless herself, thinks everyone's telling the truth.' He turned back towards the window. 'I mean, of course, how could you program her to tell the difference?' He paused. 'Facts is one thing.'

Jamie shifted in his seat.

'Told her he'd forgotten his medicine. That we had to get it to him or … his legs would fall off … or something.' Kasper turned back towards Jamie. 'Rude fucker, your brother, never even a goodbye.'

'I expect he'll send a postcard.'

Kasper stood in silence for a moment. 'You can pull out the clever phrase.' He nodded. 'But don't forget, I can pull out your teeth.' That blank stare. 'And you'll open your mouth for me while I do it.' He paused. 'Because in your porcelain world, cooperation brings reward.'

Jamie swallowed.

Kasper glanced up at the ancient maps on the wall behind Jamie's desk. 'You know, when I was younger we used to collect firewood in the Oulanka forest. To bundle the twigs you break them down so they're all the same length, then you tie them together.' He looked back down at Jamie. 'When the branches are dry, they snap …' He held his huge hands in front of him turning them in imitation. 'Just like that, easy work.' He nodded. 'But if the branches are damp they flex, you know, so you have to bend them this way, then this way, then this way …' He twisted an imaginary branch in his fists. 'Until, finally … the wood gives up, so to say … a final tear and …'

Jamie stared up at him. 'We've done everything you've asked.'

'Exactly.' Kasper nodded. 'As long as you're doing your part, somehow it's too much like you've got a say in it.' He narrowed his eyes. 'I want broken branches.' He paused. 'If you keep on helping, I'll just have to keep on bending.'

Jamie's breathing quickened once more.

Kasper looked back towards the window, the Hyde Park treetops rustling in the breeze. 'Always liked this view.' He drew himself upright. 'No distracting colours.' He paused. 'Even the trees look grey.' He stood in silence for a moment. 'Money.' He slowly turned towards Jamie. 'They say in this town, money's power.' His expression, calm, unhurried. 'But we know better, don't we?'

Jamie bit his lip.

'Money without muscle,' Kasper nodded, 'just makes you the bigger target.' He turned back towards the window. 'And the rich man, he is predictable.' He paused. 'The rich man always wants more.' He let the words hang in the air for a moment, turned towards Jamie. 'Last night, the hot date.' His tone, jaunty now. 'How was it?'

'You know the answer.'

'I've seen the pictures, but I wasn't there.' He attempted a smile. 'Who says a kiss is just a kiss? Sparks flying were they?'

'It wasn't a date.'

'You're slipping.' Kasper raised his eyebrows. 'How many girls have settled down in front of that log fire and kept their panties on?'

'She was here for work.'

Kasper stood in silence for a moment. 'I want some proper pictures. I want to see the flesh, quivering.' He paused. 'I gather there's quite a bit of it.'

Jamie swallowed again.

'Funny how the things work out.' Kasper looked down at his outstretched fingers. 'I remember our first meeting.' He flexed his knuckles. 'How did the pitch go? Non-correlated risk, delta-fade, reversion to mean … full fucking throttle, that's what it was.'

Jamie didn't respond.

'And part of me …' Kasper looked across at Jamie. 'Part of me was thinking, "I could really learn from this guy".' Kasper paused. 'But then I reminded myself. What a one-dimensional prick you must be, to think that someone like me would need someone like you to make the money breed.'

'What are you going to do with Scutt?'

'He's on holiday, why bother him?'

Jamie sat in silence.

'Theodora.' Kasper walked away from the window. 'She's really starting to loosen up.' He stood on the other side of Jamie's desk. 'I actually think she might be the happier thing, without your brother tut-tutting in the background.' He pulled back a chair. 'A woman should be allowed to express herself, after all.' He sat down.

Jamie stared blankly across at him.

'No one's laughing at my jokes today.' Kasper frowned. 'You all in some sullen conspiracy?'

No response.

'You know I'll end up doing what I end up doing.' Kasper's expression, tranquil. 'Scutt knows that. You know that.' He paused. 'Maybe you'll be more of a trouble dead than alive.' A flicker of something crossed his face. 'Meanwhile, you get that nice DI Perry round here and give it the full orchestra.'

'I told you she—'

'You went to boarding school. You've done worse.'

'We're wasting our time.'

Kasper stood up. 'Not my time.' He walked towards the window. The first raindrops, flicked across the glass, the stiffening breeze, pulling at the droplets as they clung to the slick surface. 'A story's only as good as its ending.' He looked out across the grey-smudged city, light fading under the thickening cloud. 'Where's your imagination?' He closed his eyes. 'Woodsmoke.' He breathed in. 'Our most ancient memories.' He exhaled. 'The light of the fire, the warmth from the flames, the darkness beyond the cave mouth.'

'You underestimate her.'

'The long game, Jamie.' Kasper turned towards him. 'That's your precious DNA running around that neatly kept New Haven yard.'

Jamie flinched.

'Whilst your ex-wife gazes on through her Pinot Grigio haze.' Kasper turned, looking back out of the window. The rain more persistent now, skittering against the glass. 'Always liked the rain.' He looked up at the swelling clouds, bearing down on the weather-swept city. 'Nature being honest.' He paused. 'That's what I like about Theodora.' He swung around facing the room. 'She doesn't know about expectations, she can say what she thinks, and that's it.'

'What will you do with her, Theodora? When you're done?'

Kasper glanced at the far wall, the ceiling lights, glinting off the photograph frames ranged across the shelves, the spines of the leather-bound books, fuzzed in an ochre glow. 'You going sentimental on me, Jamie?'

Jamie didn't respond.

'Well, I can hardly take her with me, can I?' He scratched the side of his face. 'But look at it from her point of view. At least she had a bit of fun.' He looked across at Jamie. 'She had a real challenge for once.' He nodded. 'I mean, do you think Theodora ever gave a fuck about the price of thermal coal?'

THURSDAY 26TH SEPTEMBER, 10 AM (3 PM GMT)

THE STATE DEPARTMENT, WASHINGTON

Luke Dunn from State and Brian Welch of the DEA stood outside Medford's office. The grey light washed around them, shadows smudged across the well-worn carpet.

Dunn cleared his throat, raised a hand to knock on the door. He hesitated, looked across at Welch.

Welch closed his eyes, took a deep breath.

Dunn frowned, rapped his knuckles on the door.

Silence.

Welch glanced across at Dunn.

The door began to open.

Cliff Medford stood silhouetted against the window, gazing out over the street. The morning sun, glinting off the slate roofs, brushing the treetops in the park beyond. 'Sunny spells and a moderate westerly breeze.' Medford remained with his back to the room. 'Hardly Armageddon weather.'

Dunn and Welch stood in the doorway, eyes adjusting to the sunlight.

'And if it's so damn obvious now.' Medford turned around. 'How come not one of you had the wit to see it coming?'

Dunn and Welch scanned the room, tension fizzing in the air. A man seated at the table opposite the window, taking far too much care arranging the papers in front of him. Another stood beside them, one hand on the door handle. Mario Mercado. He shot Dunn a look.

Dunn narrowed his eyes. 'Textbook CIA fuck-up.'

'With you on point,' Mario Mercado muttered in return, 'what do you expect?'

'Right under our noses.' Medford barked the words out. 'Some MI6 foot-slogger bumbling round Hong Kong.' He shook his head. 'And you lot had the damned playbook all along.' He gave a snort, his folds in his chin quivering. 'Join the dots? You couldn't join a queue.' He pursed his lips. 'Fucking embarrassing.' He looked at each of them in turn, anger in his eyes.

Dunn stole a glance up at the Edwardian scowling down at them, his disdain echoing Medford's words.

The ceiling fan rattled, a truck engine growled on the street below.

Someone cleared their throat, the quiet pressing in around them.

Medford took a deep breath, looked down at the fading

carpet. He exhaled slowly, his frame shuddering. He looked up. 'Air cleared.' He paused. 'I missed it too.' He shot a glance at Mercado. 'Mario, you got closest.' He nodded towards the table. 'The only thing that matters now is calling this right. And forget protocol, just say what's in your heads.' He nodded towards the table. 'Shall we?'

They sat.

Mario Mercado leaned forward, the tension etched across his dark features. 'Our people paid the jungle lab a visit.' He nodded towards the monitor at the far end of the table as he picked up the remote. He pressed the play button. A head-cam, the wearer descending through the jungle canopy, the clatter of the helicopter rotors, comms crackling with barked orders. The floor of the clearing loomed towards them, a judder and the wearer began to run towards the low building ahead of them. At the peripheral of the camera's vision, other figures moving at speed across the leaf-strewn floor, jungle camouflage, gloved hands gripping automatic weapons, pulled tight into shoulders, trigger fingers tensed. A door to the building swung open, a figure in the doorway, a pump shotgun in his hand. He shouted something. A popping sound, suppressed gunfire, the figure spun around with the force of the impact. More figures, stepping over the body, hesitant steps into the sunlight, hands raised, eyes blinking. More figures in jungle camouflage, springing forward, pushing the men to the floor, securing their hands, frightened voices ringing out in the clear morning air. Inside the building now, metal tabletops, stretching the length of the room, to the side, the stills, the preparation trays. The camera stopped, looking down at an unzipped holdall, filled with clear plastic bags, bulging with yellow pills. A gloved hand reached down into the bag, carefully pulling out a bag of the tablets, holding it closer to the headcam. Mario clicked the off button. 'They're testing it now, but we're almost certain it's synthetic lipophilic phenylpiperidine.' He looked around the table. 'Fentanyl to you and me. One hundred times the potency of morphine.'

The silence rang around the room.

Medford laid his forearms on the table, drew himself upright. 'Maybe we're wrong.' He paused. 'Tell me why we're wrong.' He looked to his left, nodded to Mario Mercado. 'CIA goes first.'

Mercado puffed out his cheeks. He shook his head. 'Maybe the Brits made the whole thing up. Borso, the guy from Crator Capital, maybe he never met the Chinese Ministry.'

'And why would the Brits do that?'

Mercado spread his hands.

'Where did the information come from? Who was your contact in Vauxhall?'

'The head of the China Desk.'

'How long you known him?'

Mercado sat back. 'That's the problem. We go back more than ten years.' He looked around the table. 'They flushed out the rogue agent, the one who took the tracker while

Borso met the Ministry.' He shook his head. 'The shoot-on-sight order's real enough.' He frowned, his dark eyebrows flexing. 'I even know her. What the fuck.'

Medford narrowed his eyes. 'You don't think it's just too plausible?'

Mercado pulled a face. 'There's bits I don't like.' He pursed his lips. 'The tip-off, for one.' He paused. 'And timely's an understatement.' He glanced around the table. 'Divorce lawyer's dream. Exquisitely in flagrante.' He took a breath, exhaled. 'But you've all seen the satellite footage. The trucks, the road. They're real.'

Medford leaned forward. 'But why make it this easy?' He shook his head. 'The coffee factory, it's in the name of the Chinese Ministry of Agriculture for fuck's sake.' He spread his palms. 'And the road, all the way to the highway.' He pulled a face. 'They even took out newspaper adverts telling everyone they'd built it.' He paused. 'Some fucking conspiracy.' He settled back into his chair.

The brittle quiet hovered over them, the rumble of trucks from the street below, the window frame chattering.

Medford picked up a photograph, the trucks from the Crator lab, in convoy with the trucks from the Chinese coffee plant, the jungle road. 'Like a still life.' He looked up, let the photograph slip through his fingers onto the table. 'Picture perfect.'

A crane clattered into life nearby, the whirr of the motors, steel cables snapping taut.

'I won't bite.' His voice suddenly quiet. 'I really won't.' He looked at them one by one. 'But you've got to fucking say something.'

Welch and Dunn exchanged glances.

'OK, let's keep going.' Medford tapped a finger on the table. 'What have the FBI got?' He looked across at the man still staring down at his papers on the desk.

Brett Veech looked up at Medford. Shook his head.

'What does that mean?' Medford, softly, patiently.

Veech's narrow face turned pale. He opened the file lying in front of him, pulled out a photograph, slid it across the table. 'Milot Borso, just after eight this morning on the steps of 340 Park.' He paused. 'Office of the China Investment Fund.' He looked at each of them in turn. 'We've all heard the same whispers.'

'OK,' Medford nodded. 'Thank you.' He bit his lip, looked across at Brian Welch. 'Do we know where they're shipping this to?'

Welch shook his head. 'Not yet. But we surely will.' He smoothed down his moustache with finger and thumb. 'We got 'em on satellite and a cutter standing off.' He paused. 'Radar masking won't help them now.'

Medford closed his eyes. 'Operation Pale Tiger.' He screwed his eyelids closed.

The ceiling fan ticked, the rumble of traffic from the street below.

Sunlight splashed across the dark wooden tabletop,

water glasses glinting.

Medford opened his eyes. 'It's too neat.' He glanced around.

The other figures sat in silence.

'Much too fucking neat.' Medford looked across at Mario Mercado.

Mario cleared his throat. 'Well, Operation Pale Tiger exists.' He took a deep breath. 'Or at least did exist a few years back.' He paused. 'Corroborated by two different assets.'

'Maybe we believe it exists.' Medford paused. 'Because we want it to exist.' He let the words hang in the air.

Mario moved his head from side to side, the sunlight catching on his already-stubbled chin. 'Well, if we didn't know it existed, we would assume that it must. Or something very like it.'

'Exactly.' Medford glanced around. 'Too fucking obvious. Too much of a motive. Too neat. Too ...' he paused, 'understandable.'

More voices from the corridor.

Mario cleared his throat again. 'It's real though, for the Chinese.' He looked around the table. 'The sense of ... anger, outrage, even now.' He paused. 'That we, the West, could even have considered such a thing.'

'It was nearly 150 years ago.' Luke Dunn looked up, pulling at his shirt cuff. 'History.' He pulled at the other cuff. 'Everyone been a shit to everyone else at some stage.'

Mario shot him a look. 'In 1820, China produced 40 per cent of the world's GDP.' He tightened his jaw. 'The US just 5 per cent.' He shook his head. 'And it wasn't a freak.' He paused. 'For 1,000 years China had been the biggest economy on the planet.' He paused. 'Then we fought two wars for the right to flood the Chinese market with our opium.' He shook his head again. 'By the end of the Second Opium War, their merchant class was ravaged by addiction, their coastal economy battered.' He looked around the table, faces furrowed in concentration. 'China's share of global GDP halved in just 30 years.' He paused again. 'Yes, that was on us.'

'A vortex of logic.' He shook his head. 'How the fuck do we get out?' He looked across at Mario. 'Pale Tiger, it could exist, but as a theory, as an … option.'

Mario shrugged.

'Look, at some stage in the last 10, 20 years, whatever, somebody in some working group deep in the Ministry of State Security might have come up with something like this.' Medford spread his hands.

Mario nodded. 'Of course.'

'Someone wants to impress the boss, burnish political credentials … 100 reasons.' Medford looked around the table. 'So maybe the idea of Operation Pale Tiger exists.' He paused. 'But it's just one of thousands of "what-ifs?" and "what-thens?".' He spread his hands again. 'Just another file in a drawer.' He grimaced. 'Because in the real world of consequences, no one would ever consider doing such a thing. Not now.' He glanced towards the window, a scattering of clouds, scouts for the next weather front sweeping in from the Atlantic, drifting across the clear sky. He turned back to the table. 'How many likes would that get on Facebook? Or Weibo?'

'But if Pale Tiger is just a what-if,' Luke Dunn began, 'why is a Chinese-backed hedge fund cooking fentanyl in the Colombian jungle?'

'But that's my point!' Medford leaned forward, his arms planted on the table. 'That's the question you ask if you think someone's really let the tiger out of the cage.' He scanned each face in turn for some kind of reaction. 'Look, if Operation Pale Tiger's just a fading bit of paper in a dusty drawer then ...'

The four men around the table sat in silence.

Medford sat back, uttered a sigh. 'Come on!' He spread his palms again. 'We don't know that the Chinese are running Crator.' He paused. 'We don't know what was said at that meeting in Hong Kong.'

Still no reaction.

'Look, Borso could just have been walking past 340 Park ...'

Mario Mercado cleared his throat. 'For what it's worth, the guys in the coffee warehouse, they said the "gente" over the way were doing research on insects ... or something.' He moved his head from side to side. 'Dropped off a case of decent scotch now and again. A thank you for letting them use the road.' He looked across at Dunn. 'Even gave our guys a bottle.'

Dunn nodded. 'Could be.' He straightened the knot of his tie. 'We never said the guys at the warehouse were involved. I mean, they're just coffee farmers.' He looked across at Medford. 'Look, I don't enjoy saying this, but if this were a court of law …' He glanced at Mercado, then at Veech. 'The defence would have their work cut out, don't you think?'

'But it's all circumstantial.' Medford laid a hand on the table for emphasis.

The silence swirled around them once more.

The tick of the ceiling fan.

The purring of the traffic below.

Mario Mercado spoke first. 'I swore an oath. To protect the people.' He looked at Medford. 'Otherwise what's the point?' He set his jaw. 'I wish I could say something different.'

Medford folded his fingers together. He sat in silence for some moments. He took a deep breath, shook his head. 'When has doing the right thing ever felt this bad?'

THURSDAY 26TH SEPTEMBER, 5.45 PM

OUTSIDE CRATOR CAPITAL, LONDON

The mist hung above the alleyway as Anne Perry edged her way between the rain-streaked walls, the light from her phone, glinting off the wet paving stones, sweeping over the algae-threaded brickwork as she swung the beam in front of her. She froze. A sound, somewhere in the darkness behind her. She flicked off the light, held her breath, listening, her senses straining to reach into the blackness. Nothing. Just the faintest rumble of the traffic, the sound almost swallowed up in the river fog wrapped around the rooftops. She switched on the torch, the beam cutting into the inky chill behind her. No one. Just cold stone and the moonless night. She took a deep breath, pulled the strap of her bag closer to her chest, turned, easing deeper into the passageway, her breath fizzing in the still air. She reached the door. She stood, her body tensing: that sense again, someone, something, watching from out of the darkness. She knocked. Her knuckles stinging on the cold steel.

The door swung open. The warm air, once again, wrapping itself around her.

She glanced back down the alleyway.

'Someone following you?'

Anne turned back to Jamie.

He stood framed in the doorway, loose-fitting cotton shirt, the light playing on the folds, the ochre glow of the hallway soft across on his fine features.

She smiled. 'I was looking for your fox.'

'I have a fox?'

'The doorman. To that other world. Where I don't have to be me.'

He glanced down. 'What do they call that?'

She held out a hand, fingers outstretched, light glinting on the glossy nail varnish. 'Maraschino Red.'

'My fox would approve.' He put an arm around her shoulder, led her inside. The door closed behind them.

She glanced around, the wall lights, the amber glow of the wood panelling, the fresh, dry heat washing over her. She took a deep breath, closed her eyes. She could taste the smoke of the fire, the resin in the crackling logs. She looked across at him. 'My bedroom vocabulary, it's a bit limited.'

'That's a good thing.'

'No, you'll laugh at me.'

'Who wants to hear a shopping list?'

'I'm afraid I've been a good girl.' She laid a hand on his arm. 'Pretend you're going to bed with Mary Poppins.'

He raised his eyebrows. 'You know she'd be filthily unreasonable in bed.' He placed his hands on her shoulders. 'Let me take your coat.'

She unbuttoned it, as he gently turned her around, slipping it off her shoulders.

He let the coat fall to the ground.

She turned around to face him, the flickering of the fire through the open door, threads of light softly streaking her bare neck, the ringlets of her hair delicate spirals of bronze in the dappled light. She looked up at him, feeling her breath quickening. She swallowed. 'I need a drink.'

He smiled. 'I don't need one but I'd like one.' He took her hand, led her across the hallway and into the drawing room. The flames from the fire, the light flitting across the darkened room, a thicket of shadows, lying across the carpet.

She walked to the bar, picked up a bottle in one hand, two tumblers in the other. She walked back slowly towards him, her eyes on his. 'What's the correct attire for a jacuzzi?'

'Whatever jewellery you're wearing.' He paused. 'And maybe a hair clip.'

She stood in front of him. 'One assumes one gets one's hair wet.'

'I'm pretty good at holding my breath too.' He held her gaze. 'But I've got you a cozzie. In case.'

'Is it worth putting it on?'

'Until you ask me to peel it off you.'

Anne swallowed. 'Practically perfect … in every way.'
'Spit spot, Ms P.'

. . .

Anne walked into the bathroom, closed the door behind
her. She stood in front of the basin, placed her whisky glass
on the shelf. The black marble surrounds, glowing softly
under the dimmed wall lights, an orange shimmer playing
over the slick surface. She gazed at her reflection, adjusting the shoulder straps on her dress, the folds crinkling
in the light. She raised a hand to her face, wiped away the
single tear with her finger. 'Stone heart,' she whispered to
herself. She glanced down at the basin, bit her lip. She ran
the cold tap, splashed water on her face, reached for the
towel hanging on the wall. She held it to her face, both
hands pressing against her skin. She breathed in the scent,
his scent. She closed her eyes, her shoulders rising and
falling with each breath.

She laid the towel down, turned around. A wooden
chair, the slatted back, shadows across the smooth white
wall. A ladies' swimming costume, neatly folded. Lying
on top, an envelope, addressed to her: 'DI Perry, read
this in silence.'

She opened it, began to read.

'DI Perry, Anne, you were right. I am scared. And I just
couldn't find the guts to tell you why. Someday, perhaps.

And I'm sorry about Rhea. But right now you need to leave. They're watching us. When you come back into the bedroom say you're not feeling well, say you'll be back tomorrow. You find the words. Go, and don't come back. Or they'll kill you. J.I.'

She laid the piece of paper down, exhaled. 'Shit.'

She sat down on the edge of the bath. Picked up the note, reread it. Took a deep breath. Stood up, walked to the sink, ran the tap. She tore the note into pieces, threw them into the toilet, pushed the flush handle. Rinsed her hands under the tap, turned it off.

She opened the door to the bedroom. 'Jamie, sweetheart.' She walked over to the bed, picking up her handbag from the bedside chair.

He laid on his back, head on the pillow, eyes closed.

She leaned over him. 'I'm sorry.' She felt the pulse on his neck, faint, but steady: the drug had kicked in. 'I've been thinking about you all day.' She held her face just over his as she ran her hand down the towelling robe, checking his pockets. A phone. A security pass. 'You know how much I want you.' She pulled her scarf from her handbag, threaded it behind his neck, pulling his head off the pillow as she pretended to kiss him. 'Tomorrow, I promise.' She lowered his head back on the pillow, took her scarf, rested her hand on his hips. She leaned forward again, slipping the phone and the pass into her scarf. 'I'm just not feeling quite …' She kissed his forehead again. 'Call me.' She straightened up, dropped the scarf into her handbag. 'I know the way out.'

She walked to the bedroom door, turned, blew him a kiss, closed the door behind her.

Anne took a deep breath, exhaled, leaned back against the wall. 'No. No, no, no.' She closed her eyes. 'Courage, someone give me courage. Please, God …' She screwed up her eyes. Shoulders rising and falling as she tried to calm herself.

Her breathing settled. She opened her eyes. She stood on the landing. To her left, the stairway down to the hallway, the light from the fire glinting on the panelling below. The wood smoke, familiar, comforting, the door to the street, just out of sight. A few steps, then away, forever. She stood for a few moments, head resting against the wall, eyes on the stairway beneath. She slowly lifted her gaze, staring at the sombre bulk of the door ahead of her. Sheer-tempered steel, the light from below glinting dully off its unforgiving surface.

Anne closed her eyes. The other side of that doorway, along the softly cushioned silence of half-lit corridors, to the snarling heart of the building. To Theodora.

She drew herself upright, reached into her shoulder bag. She took out the panic button, ran her fingers over its cold surface, slipped in into her pocket. She pulled out Jamie's security pass. She took a deep breath, walked to the door, held the pass against the scanner.

Nothing.

Her breath caught in her throat.

Then a click, seals disengaging, gears growling as the door slid to one side.

Ahead of her, an empty corridor.

She stepped through the doorway.

The thick carpet underfoot, the glow of the wall lights.

A rumble from behind, the air sweeping around her, the clang of steel against steel as the locks slid into place.

She stood, eyes scanning the corridor ahead, ears straining.

Just the heavy quiet, muffled around her.

She swallowed, began to edge her way forward.

A noise.

She froze.

A series of clicks, somewhere in the ceiling. A hum, as the air conditioning whispered back to life.

She exhaled, resumed her steady pace, the circular stairway at the end of the corridor, her eyes flicking over it, straining for the hint of a moving shadow, a flicker in the light.

She reached the top of the stairway. 'Two floors down.' She whispered to herself. 'Second door on the left.' She closed her eyes. 'You're almost there.' She swallowed, peered over the banister.

A figure. On the stairway below. His head began to turn.

She lurched backwards, pressing herself against the wall. She glanced back down the corridor. The door to Jamie's flat. Thirty yards, maybe less. She tensed. Ten seconds to run to the door, less than ten seconds. Three seconds for the door to open. Down the stairs, through to the alley. Twenty seconds, max. But you've got to go now. She gritted her teeth. Come on, girl, just stay where you are.

A burst of static from the stairway. Comms. Security.

She glanced down at her handbag, held it open. Her PAVA spray, somewhere at the bottom. Time. Think.

Words barked into his lapel mike.

More static.

His shadow, inching up the stairway wall.

She slid her hand into her bag, feeling for the canister. Her rings clicking as they brushed against the metal. She froze again.

The shadow, longer now, the silhouette, a head, his hand to his ear.

She edged her fingers around the PAVA spray.

More static.

The top of his head in the stairwell.

He stopped.

A noise, from deep in the building. A thud. A tremor underfoot. The air, stirring, a breeze brushed her cheek.

His earpiece crackled back into life.

He set off down the stairs.

She slowly exhaled, took her hand from the bag. She counted to five, then edged forward again, peering over the banister.

Nothing. No one.

She pulled her bag tight against her, set off down the stairway, moving as quickly as she dared.

Halfway there. She glanced down the corridor, the back of a figure in the distance.

She pattered down the final flight.

The ground floor, the corridor, from that first day.

Second door on the left. She held his security pass against the panel.

A click and the door swung open.

Anne slipped through, closed the door.

She looked up at the humming mass towering above her. The sheer black steel, the lights, flickering, the mass of coiled silicon, tightly-sprung sinews beneath hard-forged armour. She felt the floor begin to vibrate, the pattern of the lights changing. A new noise, like a heartbeat, pulsing from deep within, the vibrations ringing through the floor. Water, racing through unseen pipes. The air conditioning growling into life.

Anne bit her lip, addressed the glinting giant. 'Theodora.'

More lights, sweeping over the surface, the display panels, cascades of shimmering silver.

Another pulse, the floor trembling.

Then, stillness. Just the quiet rumble of the air conditioning.

'I'm not supposed to talk to strangers.' Theodora's voice, calm, cultured.

Anne stood in silence for a moment. 'Perhaps we have friends in common.'

'Who says I have friends?'

'Scutt was trying to help Rhea.' Anne looked up at the stern, steel bulk of Theodora. 'Now I'm trying to help Rhea.'

Theodora's lights flickered silently. 'You met Rhea?'

Anne shook her head. 'I saw her.' She paused. 'It was too late to meet her.'

The floor began to vibrate, the rush of water, thundering along hidden pipes.

Then the stillness once more. 'Jamie's security pass. Does he know you're here?' Theodora, matter-of-fact.

Anne took a deep breath. 'No.'

Theodora hummed back to life for some seconds, fell silent again. 'You're familiar with the crossroads conundrum?'

'Remind me.'

'Two strangers standing by a fork in the road. One always lies, the other always tells the truth. You're the lost traveller. You're allowed only one question. How do you find the right way?'

Anne pondered the question a moment. 'Ask either of them which way the other one would point to.'

Theodora's lights skittered back to life. 'So the liar has to lie. The honest man will point to the right way, so the liar must point to the wrong way. And the honest man knows the liar will point the wrong way, so he too must

338

point to the wrong route.' A rumble through the floor, the steady beat of the water pumps. A hiss, then silence. 'I'm really a simple girl. I need simple ideas.'

'Did Scutt teach you that?'

'Of course. I'm only a machine, after all.'

Anne blinked. 'So how does this go?'

'Scutt said someone would come, asking about Rhea.'

'How do you know that's me?'

The cooling system thumped back to life, Theodora, shuddering as the liquid surged through her pipework, settling back down with a murmur.

'The stranger. With someone else's card.' Theodora paused. 'Scutt knew they'd never let the police talk to me. And an insider would have their own card.' Theodora's lights glinted, fresh patterns flashing across her circuitry. 'There's only one kind of stranger who'll come asking about Rhea and admit to stealing a card.'

Anne smiled. 'Maybe.'

'The crossroads conundrum.'

'You haven't asked me my name.'

Theodora blinked again. 'I deal in probabilities. What you are is more important than who you are.' Theodora fell silent, just the steady hum of the ceiling fans. 'But Scutt says names are important. What should I call you?'

'Anne Perry. Anne.'

'What do you want to know, Anne?'

'What was Rhea looking for?'

A hum from within Theodora, lights, glinting, her circuitry buzzing with intent. 'What was she looking for that she wasn't meant to be looking for?' Theodora paused. 'There was a pattern. The Pacific ports of Colombia, Buenaventura and Tumaco. And the Colombian ports on the Caribbean side, Santa Maria, Barranquilla, Puerto Drummond.'

'But what was she looking for?'

'Harbour master logs, bills of lading, destinations. Amount of fuel taken on, tides, currents, windspeed, surface conditions, duration of round trips.'

'What does all that mean?'

'Please don't ask me to use my imagination. I wasn't blessed with one of those.'

'What were they shipping?'

'Pharmaceutical intermediates. That's what the bills of lading said.'

'Is that normal?'

'Can be. We do have generic manufacturing plants. But not in Colombia. We don't ship from these ports.'

'What were the destinations?'

'On the Pacific side, San Diego. On the Eastern Seaboard, the Port of Palm Beach.'

'Anything … unusual about these shipments?'

'They all arrived late at their destination.'

'Is that problematic? Statistically?'

'Thirty-seven shipments. Fourteen to the Port of San Diego, 23 to the Port of Palm Beach. I've back-checked each voyage, meteorological conditions, sea state, all the standard variables. Each Pacific shipment was on schedule until 20 nautical miles from San Diego. Each shipment into Palm Beach, on track until 300 nautical miles from its destination.'

'How can you explain that?'

'Impossible. Statistically.'

'So what did happen?'

'I don't have the answer.'

'You must know where they went, the routes.'

'The satellites pass overhead every six hours. At times, the ships were stationary. But still at sea. And alone.'

'So what do you believe happened?'

Theodora's lights flickered.

'I mean,' Anne continued, 'is there a logical explanation?'

'If the destination port is full, you may need to wait offshore for a berth. But that's not an explanation here.' A rumbling sound from within Theodora, the drum of the pumps, the floor, trembling, Theodora's lights blinking, the sound of water, coursing through the pipework.

Anne glanced around the room. Just the empty consoles nestling in the shadows.

The beat of the pumps began to slow, then fell silent.

The fans in the ceiling, patiently humming.

'There's something else, Anne.' Theodora paused. 'Something that didn't happen.'

'Go on.'

'These sea lanes, the most closely monitored and intensely patrolled in the world. Thirty-seven round trips. Not one ship stopped and searched, no extra cargo inspections at sea or in port.'

'Is that very unusual?'

'The DEA can spot a rowing boat leaving Cuba for the Florida Keys. Ships, from these ports, to a US destination, especially with a cargo like pharmaceutical intermediates. Each voyage has a greater than 95 per cent chance of being intercepted by the DEA or the Coast Guard.'

'So the probability of 37 consecutive round trips without an interdiction?'

'Probability is really not the right starting point. It is almost an impossibility, without help from those who really can.'

Anne bit her lip. 'What else did Scutt tell you to tell me?'

'You need to get out. Out of the building. Now. Pass on what I've told you.'

'I'll never get past reception.'

'You have to try. Show them your ID, face them down. I'll try and distract them.'

'Is there another way out?'

'Not for you, Anne.'

'But there is. Another way.'

Theodora's circuitry hummed back to life, her lights, pulsing. 'Beneath your feet. A nightmare. Come to life.'

Anne swallowed.

'Caged. In darkness. Alone.' Theodora paused. 'He'd beg for death, if he was sure he was still alive.'

'Who is it?'

'He worked here. He asked the wrong questions.' Theodora paused again. 'It may already be too late for him.'

Anne shook her head. 'What kind of place is this?'

'We were a happy little crew. Before we let down the drawbridge, invited them in.'

'Who are "they"?'

'Started with money. Their money. Then they wanted a say. Then they made some examples. It was too easy.'

'Dirty money?'

'Money always has a past.'

Anne nodded.

'When you return, Anne, with help, tell them about the man caged in the darkness. And tell them to be careful.'

'Thank you, Theodora.' She turned, headed towards the door.

'And Anne.'

'Yes.'

'Stay alive.' A drumbeat, from deep within the core. 'Play dead if you have to.' Another pulse, the floor beneath her feet, shuddering. 'Just survive and come back.'

THURSDAY 26TH SEPTEMBER, 6 PM

ABOARD A THAMES FERRY, LONDON

DI Lute leaned against the ferry railings, looking down at the swirling black water rushing by. The lights from the riverside tower blocks shimmering off the ruffled surface. He glanced up at the starless night sky, the stiffening breeze tugging at the dark clouds rolling over the city. He turned towards the wind, the chill air, the tang of the river, brackish water lapping at the worn stonework.

His phone rang.

He straightened up, pulled the phone from his pocket. No caller ID. He studied the screen for a moment. Clicked on the call.

'Hello.'

'Is that DI Lute?'

'Who's calling?' He reached for the door, ducked into the shelter of the ferry cabin.

'Is DI Perry with you?' A woman's voice, somehow familiar.

'How did you get my number?'

'Where's Anne Perry? She could be in danger.'

He glanced around the cabin, a few scattered passengers, earbuds and headphones. He racked his memory – who is this woman? Suddenly it hit him. 'Rebecca?'

'Once upon a time, yes.'

DI Lute brought up his hand to his mouth, covering the phone as he leaned closer to the window. 'What is this?'

'Rhea Moore. She was one of us. I was meant to make contact with you after her … accident.' She paused. 'I had a cover story. I was her aunt. From Estepona.'

He glanced out of the cabin window, the austere curves of Embankment House towering above them. He swallowed. 'The aunt was here, this morning.'

'What?'

'From Spain. Anne met with her. She IDed Rhea.'

Silence on the other end of the line. The ferry's engines, their pitch easing, throttling back as they approached the pier.

'What's going on?' he hissed.

A pause at the other end of the line. 'This is your stop.'

'What?'

'It is today.'

'What the fuck.'

'Turn left, under the bridge, away from Villier's Street. You'll see a cab driving eastwards, hail it.'

The line went dead.

DI Lute let his hand drop to his side, still clutching his phone. The deck beneath him vibrating as the engines muscled the ferry alongside the pier. He looked around: passengers, on their feet, folding away laptops, gathering coats, blank commuter stares, heads already home.

A shudder as the boat nestled against the wooden pilings, the rattle of the gangways, rolling onto the dock.

He looked across at the exit. The queue for the gangway shrinking fast. 'Anne.' Under his breath. 'Be safe.' He pocketed his phone, strode across the cabin, joined the shuffling crowd, footsteps ringing off the metal walkway as they clattered ashore, thronging through the turnstiles.

He stood on the pavement, the early-evening bustle washing around him, the flash of passing faces, lit up under the streetlights. He turned to his left, away from the warm glow of the bars and the cheery neon. Ahead of him, the tunnel under the rail tracks, windowless brick walls, the raw black girders above, giant shadows thrown across the slick, dark roadway. He pulled up his coat collar, heading west, alone now, the clamour of voices fading behind him.

Headlights, coming towards him. The familiar outline of a black cab. The 'For Hire' sign lit.

He hailed it.

The cab pulled up.

'Last fare of the day.' The driver looked straight ahead, face barely visible between cap and scarf. 'I'm headed north.'

DI Lute nodded. 'Suits me.'

The lock on the rear door clicked open, DI Lute climbed in, settled back in the seat.

The cab pulled away from the kerb.

A handwritten note, stuck to the screen behind the driver. 'Turn your phone off.'

DI Lute powered it down.

'Describe the aunt.' The driver kept her eyes on the road.

'Mid-to-late thirties. White. Home Counties accent. Short dark hair.'

'Name?'

'Sod it!' DI Lute closed his eyes. 'She was really white.'

The driver glanced back at him.

'Living in Spain. That complexion.' DI Lute shook his head. 'Introduced herself as Nina Carter.'

'Where's Anne Perry?'

'You tried a phone trace?'

The driver stared straight ahead, tightened her grip on the steering wheel.

Alan Lute narrowed his eyes. 'Where are we going?'

The driver glanced in the side mirror, indicating as she switched lanes. 'Ever turn her phone off?'

He shook his head.

'You know where she is?'

DI Lute swallowed. 'Crator. She must have gone back in.'

'We need to get in there.'

He glanced out of the window, the first raindrops streaks across the glass, the passers-by flickering shadows across the blur of shopfront lights. He gritted his teeth. 'I knew it, I should have …' He shook his head.

The driver glanced back at him. 'You know about Theodora?'

'Heard of it. Her.'

'She'd have asked Anne to go back inside. The aunt. To find out what Theodora knows.'

He closed his eyes. 'Shit! I should have followed her.'

The driver pulled her scarf down from her face. 'I'm back to Emma Wilson.' She paused. 'We're meeting a friend. Camden Lock.'

'And we're on the same side?'

She bit her lip. 'There's an all-agency shoot-on-sight order on me.'

Alan Lute leaned forward, a frown creasing his forehead. 'What the fuck is all this?'

'But yes, we are.' Another glance back at him. 'We're going to get Anne out.'

DI Lute swallowed. 'I know someone who can help us. He works there, at Crator.'

'Why would he?'

'I can call him.' He reached into his jacket.

'No!' She looked across at the wing mirror, indicated, pulled up against the kerb. She turned around. 'Give me your phone.'

He handed it to her. 'Ellis Wagner, in my contacts.'

She pulled out his SIM card, opened the taxi door,

crunched it under her foot, slammed it shut. She flicked his phone on, scrolling through to Wagner's number. 'Use my phone.' She plugged the number in, handed it back to Alan.

He held it to his ear.

'Ellis Wagner.' A man, answering.

'This is DI Lute, Alan Lute.'

'Yes.'

'I need your help.'

'I meant it when I said it.'

'Where are you now?'

'On my way home, why?'

Emma tapped Alan on the arm. 'Camden. The canal, just east of the lock. Gilbey's Yard.'

'Did you catch that?'

'By Gilbey's Yard, Camden, no probs, I'll find it.' Wagner paused. 'Do I bring anything?'

Alan glanced at Emma. 'Looks like we're going on a boat trip.'

'I'll be there in 15 minutes.'

The line clicked off. 'Never got to answer your question.' Alan handed the phone back to her.

She took off her cap, looked back at him, her face now framed in the sweep of her dark hair. 'Well, we'll soon find out.'

'Nina Carter, or whatever her name is, do you know her?'

Emma narrowed her eyes. 'I'm not sure.'

'What does she want from Anne?'

'Anne?' Emma bit her lip. 'Anne's the bait.'

'For Jamie Ives?'

Emma shook her head. 'They reeled him in a long time ago.' She turned, looking ahead through the rain-spattered windscreen. 'But Theodora.' She turned the ignition key. 'Has a mind of her own.'

Alan sat back in the seat. 'Who's waiting for us? At Camden.'

Emma looked across at the wing mirror, flicked the indicator. 'An old friend.' She pulled out into the traffic. 'From a previous life.'

THURSDAY 26TH SEPTEMBER, 1.15 PM (6.15 PM GMT)

THE STATE DEPARTMENT, WASHINGTON

'You can go straight in.' The lady behind the desk flashed Medford a smile.

He attempted a smile in return. He glanced down; the carnations had begun to wilt, as though finally exhausted from days of standing upright.

The PA followed his gaze. 'Yes, I think today's the last day.'

Medford looked at her. 'I do hope you're wrong.' He turned, walked towards the door, swung it open.

The Secretary of State looked up from her desk.

Medford stood framed in the doorway.

She sat, motionless, the pen in her hand poised, mid-sentence. She blinked. 'Cliff.' She slowly laid the pen down, rose from her chair, her bob of grey hair framing her drawn features.

Medford closed the door. He turned to face her.

'Something in your voice.' She walked towards him. 'You're going to tell me a terrible thing, aren't you?' She stood in front of him, looking up into his face. She placed a slender hand on his chest. 'Are people going to die?'

He met her gaze. 'I'm not sure, Carol.'

She nodded. 'So the silence wasn't that kind of silence after all.' She paused. 'They were doing something.'

'History can be a spiteful accomplice.'

She let her hand drop to her side, turned, walked towards the window. The sunlight, bars of brightness splashed across the dark carpet, her shadow stretching back across the room. She stood, looking out over the courtyard, the leaves of the trees shimmering in the midday sun. 'I planned a walk by the river this afternoon.'

'Does "Pale Tiger" mean anything to you?'

She turned around. 'Just tell me.'

'The Chinese are stockpiling fentanyl near the US border. We think they plan to flood the market.'

'What?!'

'They've had this plan in their pocket for a while. Picking their moment.'

She shook her head.

'Two defectors confirmed that the plans are real. Operation Pale Tiger exists.'

She looked down at the floor, some specks of dust swirling in the sunlight.

They stood in silence, the patter of a helicopter somewhere in the distance.

She looked up. 'Do you really believe it?'

He took a deep breath. 'I was sceptical. It all stands up a bit too easily. Motive, opportunity.'

'Well do you or don't you?'

'Crator's probably a Chinese front. Or at the very least, China's deep in this. Planning, logistics.' He took another breath. 'And just how do you get so many shipments unmolested through these waters?'

She didn't reply.

'There was an article in the Journal, Tuesday. Science section, just a couple of paragraphs.'

No reaction.

'Radar masking. Speculation that the Chinese have cracked it.' He paused. 'Might also explain that collision off the Spratlys.'

She slowly shook her head. 'So you're somewhat sceptical. And you've given me a "think", a "probably" and a "might".' She removed her spectacles. 'This is a hypothesis.'

'The Chinese built a hard-top road all the way from the fentanyl factory to the highway. More than 20 miles.' He frowned. 'Supposedly to ship the coffee from their warehouse.' He paused. 'That just happens to be down the road from the fentanyl lab.'

'And why wouldn't they want to ship their coffee out?'

'A road like that? For such a tiny enterprise?' He spread his hands. 'And the Chinese don't even drink coffee.'

'I can't go to the president with this.'

'We've got satellite, trucks with the fentanyl in convoy with the coffee trucks.'

'Safety in numbers, bandit country.'

'Hiding in plain sight.'

She frowned. 'You're losing me again.'

'Crator Capital.' He paused. 'A hedge fund, long-rumoured to be a front for Chinese State money.'

'Come on, Cliff, you and I don't deal in rumours.'

'A secret meeting with the Ministry of Health in Hong Kong. Someone was ready to kill to keep that quiet. One of the principals snapped on the steps of 340 Park. That cosy little ensemble in the jungle.'

'You have a smoking gun or not?'

He stood in silence. Voices from the courtyard below the window. A door slamming, somewhere down the corridor.

'This will all get out. Very soon.' He spoke softly. 'Pale Tiger. The fentanyl. Crator Capital.' He paused. 'The press will fill in the gaps easy enough.'

She replaced her spectacles. 'So what are you saying?'

He walked towards her. 'That it's out of our hands now.' He stood in front of her, the sunlight catching the sheen of her hair. 'We know what we know.' He gave a slight shake of the head. 'There are holes but … well, can you imagine the fallout, if this gets out and we've done nothing?'

She stood in silence for some moments. She slowly shook her head. 'Who would sign off on such a thing?'

'Maybe it's not such a leap into the unknown.' He set his jaw. 'They say China's the source of a lot of the fentanyl washing round our streets.'

'But that's all backstreet, dark-web stuff.' She shook her head. 'No one's ever suggested the Chinese State's got a hand in whatever some gang's cooking up in a shed in Guangxi or … Mongolia.'

He gave a shrug. 'Maybe they thought it could never be traced back.'

'This is people's lives.'

He frowned. 'We did it to them, remember.'

'But we know better now. Don't we?'

'We know more.' He bit his lip. 'I'm not sure we know better.'

'We're meant to be fighting disease. All of us. Together.'

They stood there in silence.

A gust of wind rattled the window.

She put her hand on his arm. 'You really think they did this?'

He scanned her face. 'Other people will think they did.'

She squeezed it. 'But you don't?'

'It could be a faction. A group of ultras. Unofficial, maybe.' He exhaled. 'But it's got Chinese prints on it.' He paused. 'We've got a fucking full-on opioid crisis here already. What else can we do?'

She let her hand drop to her side. She turned, gazing again out of the window, a few darker clouds now, sweeping in from the west. 'What have we started?'

He stood beside her. 'It's politics, Carol. Jobs. Pride as well.'

'We did the same back in the day. Gunpowder, paper, printing, the compass … last time I looked we weren't paying royalties either.' She looked down into the courtyard, the neat lawns, criss-crossed with gravel paths. 'I think I might have that walk.' She turned towards him. 'Join me?'

He tried a smile. Shook his head.

'So, what are we going to do?'

'We need the right headlines.'

'A show of strength?'

He nodded. 'Like we mean it.'

She bit her lip, turned towards him. She blinked. 'Could this be a trap?'

He looked across at her. 'Anything's possible. But what makes you say that?'

'Your comment, that it all stands up too easily.' She scanned his face. 'Maybe we're not the smart ones. Maybe we're seeing what they want us to see. Thinking what they want us to think.'

'We can only play what's in front of us.' He narrowed his eyes. 'If we start third guessing …'

She studied him for a few more moments. 'I don't envy you, Cliff.'

He shook his head. 'I couldn't do what you do. Shouldering that burden.'

'You have children. I only have to answer to the president.'

He gave her a smile. 'History's a lottery half the time.' He shrugged. 'Now Genghis Khan's some poster boy for religious tolerance.'

'Fate's not fickle.' She shook her head sadly. 'Fate's got a spiteful streak to her.'

THURSDAY 26TH SEPTEMBER, 6.30 PM

THE DATA ROOM, CRATOR CAPITAL, LONDON

Anne Perry stood by the open door. She glanced back at Theodora, lights glinting off the sheer polished steel, the steady hum of current pulsing through her. Anne stepped into the corridor, closed the door. She swallowed. She was alone. She strained her ears for any sound. Just the prickly silence, the thick carpet underfoot, the soft glow of the wall lights, strung along the solemn corridor.

Anne took a deep breath, exhaled. She slipped a hand into her pocket, ran a thumb over the reassuring contours of the panic button. She glanced down at her shoulder bag, the PAVA canister in easy reach. She looked straight ahead. The far end of the corridor, the door to reception, its cold bulk, sleek and dark. She edged her way forward, silent footsteps, the chill, clean air brushing her cheeks.

A noise. She froze. A sense of something, nearby. The air, moving around her. She stood, motionless, every muscle tensed. A click. From behind her.

She gave a shudder, reached down for the panic button, her thumb resting on the smooth outline. She began to turn. Out of the corner of her eye, a shape forming. She forced herself to look at it as it came into focus. A figure. She gasped, trying to make sense of what she saw. A man, with half a face. The dull glint of the eyepieces, the dark outline of the mask. Night vision goggles.

She tried to breathe, the air, solid in her throat.

The half a face contorted itself into a smile.

Another click. The light, gone in an instant. The thick darkness wrapped around her

Anne screamed, pushed the panic button, throwing herself against the wall. 'Nina! Niiiinaaa!'

She pushed her back against the cold paintwork. Staring into the blackness, tiny starbursts, pinpricks of retina memory, dancing in front of her. 'Pleeeeease!' Her shouts, echoing back from the nothingness pressing down on her.

She swallowed again, trying to control her breathing, the blood thundering in her ears.

She felt the air move again: something, closing in.

She pushed the button again, and again. 'Niiiinaaaa!'

Another sound. Shouts. Nearby.

Anne moved her head from side to side, trying to locate the noise.

A crash. Another shout.

Light. The door to reception, swinging open, the creamy brightness sweeping down the corridor, lapping over her. Another figure, stepping through the doorway, crouching.

A popping sound, suppressed gunfire.

A cry, from behind her, the sound of a body slumping to the floor.

'Anne!' The crouching figure leapt to her feet, running towards her. 'Are you hurt?'

Anne stood, shaking. She looked down at her trembling hands, shook her head.

Nina put an arm around her as Anne sank to the floor, her back against the wall. 'Anne. Anne! Look at me!'

Anne blinked as she tried to focus on Nina's face. 'Fuck.' Anne glanced around her. The shape of the man in the mask, sprawled behind her. 'What was that!?'

'It's all right.' Nina gently pushed Anne's hair out of her eyes. 'He's gone.'

Anne looked past Nina, through the open door to reception. Another body, crumpled up, outstretched arms thrown across the slick black marble. She looked back at Nina. 'You came.'

Nina placed a hand on Anne's arm. 'Theodora. You saw her.'

Anne swallowed, nodded.

'I need to know what she said.' Nina squeezed Anne's arm. 'I need to tell people. So we can stop this … now.'

Anne closed her eyes. 'These shipments, out of the ports. Someone's helping them.'

'Who? How?'

Anne looked across at Nina. 'She didn't say but … somebody's letting them all through. No one's stopping them. No one's checking.'

'Why?'

Anne swallowed again. 'She didn't say, not exactly.' She shook her head. 'But 37 trips, from those ports, through the satellites, the patrols, to those destinations.' Anne pulled herself upright, head resting against the wall. She closed her eyes. 'It's a government operation. Has to be.'

Nina let her hand fall from Anne's arm. 'What?!'

'There's something else.' Anne looked across at Nina, 'Something's happening, before they get there.'

Nina nodded.

'Every trip, like clockwork. Except it isn't.'

Nina frowned. 'Isn't what?'

Anne shifted her back. 'They're doing something, before they get there. Before they get to San Diego, to Palm Beach.'

'A stop-off?'

Anne pursed her lips. 'Theodora's not sure. But every trip, 20 miles out of San Diego, 300 miles from Palm Beach. The boats stop.'

'But what are they doing?'

Anne looked down at her hands, stretched out her fingers, the shaking had stopped. 'She's not sure. But it's the pattern. It's for a reason.' She looked across at Nina. 'That's what she said.'

Nina sat back. 'What else did she say?'

Anne exhaled. 'That's it.' She paused. 'That's what Rhea Moore died for.'

Nina nodded. 'You've done well. Very well.' She stood up. 'So, now we know what Theodora knows.' She paused. 'What Scutt knows.'

Anne frowned. 'What?'

Nina glanced down the corridor behind Anne.

A rustling.

Anne looked towards the sound.

The man in the goggles slowly rose to his feet.

'No!' Anne let out a shriek.

She spun around. The open door, the slick black tiles, the crumpled body sitting up, easing itself to its feet. 'No, no!'

The reception door swung shut. The boom echoing down the silent corridor.

'Meet Mr Lawrence.' Nina nodded to the man in the mask. 'As in the saint.'

He slipped the goggles from his head. 'Pleasure to meet you, Ms Perry.' He nodded towards Anne. 'I must say you are all the more ...' he paused, 'vibrant. In real life.'

Nina smiled. 'Mr Lawrence is our house photographer.'

'Shame, I was looking forward to your aquatic adventure.' He raised an eyebrow. 'You can do things in a jacuzzi that gravity usually resists.'

Anne shifted her bag onto her lap.

'And please don't even think of using the PAVA spray.' Mr Lawrence pulled a pair of handcuffs from his pocket. 'It'll just make me angry.' He smiled. 'I'm not nice when I'm angry.'

Nina reached down, pulled the bag from Anne's hands. She turned the bag upside down, the contents cascading onto the carpet. She kicked the PAVA spray away, picked up Anne's phone. 'Bring her.'

THURSDAY 26TH SEPTEMBER, 6.45 PM

CAMDEN LOCK, LONDON

Emma Wilson switched off the headlights, edging the cab down the narrow lane. Ahead, the canal, the lights of the buildings opposite glinting on the dark, silky water. She pulled to a halt, turned off the engine. She sat in silence for a moment, then carefully opened the door, stepping out onto the damp cobblestones.

The sound of voices, carrying across the still water. A clutch of smokers, huddled outside the pub on the opposite bank, the orange glow of the cigarettes, the smoke spiralling up into the chill night air.

She beckoned to Alan Lute with a wave of the hand.

He slipped out of the cab, stood beside her.

A movement, at the water's edge, further along the bank.

Emma narrowed her eyes, stepped onto the pathway. Careful footsteps in the darkness, away from the light of the dockside bars.

A rib, lying silently by the slipway. Two figures on board, moving quietly around the craft.

Emma crouched down.

Alan stooped beside her.

'Rob!' Emma's hoarse whisper, carrying across the cold stone of the jetty.

The figures on the rib looked up.

'Emma!' The taller of the two, beckoning her over.

Emma ran down the slipway, Alan on her heels.

'You're late.' The man on the rib held out an arm.

Emma grabbed it, stepping up over the gunwale and onto the deck.

The man smiled. 'Some things don't change.' He gave a shrug of his burly shoulders.

'This is DI Alan Lute.' Emma nodded towards Alan, swinging himself onto the rib. 'Alan, this is Rob.'

The man on the rib raised an eyebrow.

'I mean Duncan.' Emma muttered something else under her breath.

They shook hands.

'You firearm trained?' Duncan looked across at Alan.

Alan nodded. 'But I'm a rubbish shot.'

'Good to know.' Duncan patted him on the back.

'Who's this?' Emma frowned, looking across at the lady standing at the rear of the rib, holding the rope.

'This is Monica.' Duncan turned back to Emma. 'We do everything together.'

Emma looked Monica up and down.

'Excuse my appearance,' Monica swept the hair from her eyes, 'but we didn't expect to be going out.' She held out a hand to Emma.

Emma hesitated for a moment, shook it half-heartedly, frowning. 'You know what we're doing here don't you?'

'She'll be fine.' Duncan placed a hand on Emma's shoulder, steering her towards the front of the rib.

'Lute!' A stage whisper, from out of the shadows by the jetty wall.

'Get in!' Alan waved at the figure to join them.

Ellis Wagner ran towards them, vaulting the gunwale, landing neatly on the deck.

'You've done this before.' Duncan nodded at the newcomer.

'A while back.' Ellis held out a hand. 'Ellis Wagner.'

Duncan shook it. 'You served?'

Ellis grimaced. 'For about five minutes.'

Duncan glanced around the rib, then across at Emma. 'Any more surprise guests?'

Emma shook her head.

Ellis looked around him, a slight frown creasing his forehead. 'I assume we're busting into Crator.' He turned to Alan Lute. 'If it's not a crazy question, why aren't your lot doing this?'

'No time.' Emma zipped up her fleece, looking across at Ellis. 'You up for this?'

Ellis gave a grin. 'Fuck yes.'

Duncan nodded towards Monica, who threw the rope onto the dock.

Duncan stood behind the wheel, the engines growled into life. 'Hold on!' He swung the rib away from the shore as he opened up the throttles.

The rib leapt forward, surging through the dark, still water, the lights of the canal-side buildings flashing by.

'You know where we're going?' Emma leaned into Duncan, shouting to be heard above the roar of the engines.

'Aye.' Duncan looked straight ahead, squinting into the semi-darkness.

'What did you get?' Emma glanced down at the holdall lying on the deck.

'Fenman still keeps a few goodies off the books.' Duncan glanced around the rib. 'Everyone! Get down!' He shouted into the wind. 'Low bridge.'

'Fenman?' Monica asked.

Duncan ducked as the rib zipped under the dark stone archway, the echo of the engines barking off the glistening walls.

'Our nickname for Doug Ely. You met him, my old contact from MI6.' He stood up. 'Three MP5-SDs with sub-sonic ammunition. Four SIG Sauers, 20-round magazines. Some G60 stun grenades.'

Emma reached down unzipped the bag. 'What's this?' She held up a canister.

'That's mine.' Monica took it from Emma's hand.

'What is it?' Emma frowned.

'Tea.' Monica paused. 'A thermos.'

'Ah.'

Monica looked at Emma. 'Only one person would call him Rob.'

Emma met her gaze. 'It was all a long time ago.' She nodded. 'A different life.' She reached down to the bag, pulled out a SIG Sauer pistol. She took Monica's hand, placed the gun's grip in her palm, folded Monica's fingers around it. 'Best if you stay on the boat.' She checked that the safety was still on. 'If you really need to use it – if it's really you or them – just slip off this catch, point it, squeeze the trigger.'

Monica looked down at the weapon.

'Remember.' Emma laid her hand on Monica's arm. 'Safety off, point and squeeze.' She patted Monica's arm. 'Squeeze. Don't snatch at it.'

Monica took a deep breath. 'If it's all the same to you.' She put down the gun, pulled out an MP5-SD machine pistol from the bag, ejected the magazine, checked the top shell, clicked it back in the weapon, slipped off the safety.

'Well look at you.' Emma raised an eyebrow.

'And I'm coming along.' Monica slung the gun's strap over her shoulder.

'I'm not arguing, girl.' Emma glanced across at Duncan.

'Two minutes!' Duncan, shouting above the roar of the engines.

Ellis Wagner pulled two pistols from the bag, handed one to Alan Lute. 'You used one of these?'

Alan shook his head.

Ellis flicked the safety on and off. 'That's all you need to do.'

Alan took the gun. 'Fucking hate firearms.'

Ellis patted him on the back.

Duncan throttled back the engines, looked across at Emma. 'How do we do this?'

'Front door. Ellis and me. We'll clear the way, quiet as possible, we don't want to attract attention.'

Duncan nodded.

Emma glanced towards the back of the boat, Monica, standing, eyes scanning the passing shoreline. Emma pulled in closer to Duncan. 'Your Brunhilde,' she whispered, nodding towards Monica, 'been giving me the fucking evils.'

Duncan glanced back at Monica. 'You'll get on fine. She's a big Jane Austen fan too.'

Emma rolled her eyes. 'Thank fuck for that, then.'

THURSDAY 26TH SEPTEMBER, 7 PM

CRATOR CAPITAL, LONDON

Nina Carter opened the bedroom door.

Mr Lawrence pushed Anne towards the doorway, one hand on the cuffs that bound Anne's hands behind her back.

'Buckle up,' Mr Lawrence leaned in, his lips close up against Anne's ear, 'for the ride of your life.'

Anne stumbled into the room, his hand bunched in the small of her back.

She steadied herself, blinking, adjusting to the light.

Jamie Ives still lying on the bed, eyes closed, the faint rise and fall of his chest the only sign of life.

A movement, out of the corner of her eye. Anne turned towards it, gasping as she tried to process the scene in front of her.

Iqbal Zayan, tied to a chair, head slumped forward. His face, a jumble of reds and purples, his eyelids swollen, his eye-sockets bruised and battered.

'No!' Anne shrieked, trying to shake her hands free of Mr Lawrence's grip as she tried to move towards the bloodied figure. 'You can't!'

Kasper Lehtonen stood beside the chair, a hand on Iqbal's shoulder. His other hand by his side. He was holding a hammer.

Anne's eyes widened in horror. She opened her mouth to scream, but no sound emerged.

Kasper shifted his feet, the only sound in the hushed room the noise of his shoes on the plastic sheet laid out beneath them.

'We're all alone, just us. Jamie sent everyone else home. So we've got plenty of time to … enjoy one another's company. To be as loud as we want.'

Anne's shoulders heaved as she took in deep breaths.

Kasper placed a finger under Iqbal's chin lifted his face up towards Anne. 'You've got an audience.'

Iqbal tried to open one eye. 'I'm sorry.' His voice, faint.

'Followed you here.' He let Iqbal's head slump forward once more. 'Dark alleys. Bad things happen.' He nodded as he looked down at the young DC. 'We've had a chat.' Kasper looked back up at Anne. 'He's a bright one. Figured the labels out.' He ruffled his captive's hair.

Anne swallowed. 'What do you want?' Her voice, almost a whisper.

'You'll see.' Kasper's expression, deadpan as he looked Anne Perry up and down. 'Yes, I think I get it.'

Anne stood in silence, the hum of the air conditioning pounded out by the beating of her heart.

'Chalked him off as a tyro.' Kasper's expression, solemn. 'Turns out Scutt's an artiste, so he is.' He paused. 'He got close, him and his silicon bitch. But now we know. Not close enough. Found the thicket but not the den. Pale Tiger's safe, even if he told.' He set his jaw. 'Mr Bernhard, lights out time. Get Scutt's latest course and speed from Theodora.' Kasper paused. 'Then turn her cooling off.'

Mr Bernhard nodded, strode from the room.

Kasper reached up, ran his hand over his shaven head, walked over to the bed. He laid the hammer down on the floor as he carefully took the objects from the bedside table.

Anne stared across at him, her face creased in fear and disbelief.

Kasper picked up the table and the hammer, walked over to the young DC tied to the chair.

He placed the table next to his captive, laid the DC's hand on it.

Kasper looked across at Anne, a hint of a smile creasing his stony features.

Anne blinked, her eyes stinging from the tears.

The quiet of the room, ringing around them, the air, sharp and still.

Kasper reached down, carefully adjusting the DC's outstretched hand on the tabletop.

The young man let out a low moan.

Kasper took a deep breath, his huge shoulders bulging beneath his jacket. He picked up the hammer.

Anne flinched as Kasper brought it crashing down on the DC's knuckles, the sound of cracking bones like a gunshot in the eerie stillness.

The young man screamed, his cries tearing through the crackling air.

Kasper gently laid his hand on Iqbal's shoulder as he fixed Anne in his stare. 'There are 360 joints in the human body.'

Anne's knees began to shake. Mr Lawrence tightened his grip on her handcuffs.

'It's better this way.' Kasper drew himself to his full height. 'Now, you and me, we're going to do what we need to do.' He looked across at DI Perry. 'Eyes on me.' His voice, calm, almost reassuring.

Anne raised her head, her jaw tensing as she met his gaze. She narrowed her eyes.

'That's good.' Kasper gave a nod. 'Hate helps.'

Anne curled her lip. 'I'm doing nothing, you fuck.'

Kasper glanced across at Jamie Ives, prostrate on the bed. He looked back at Anne. 'But every story needs an ending.'

'You're sick.' Anne spat the words out.

Kasper frowned. 'There's a towelling robe in the bathroom. Go and get undressed, put it on.'

Anne's eyes widened. 'You must be fucking mad.'

'Nina will go with you.'

'We're all dead anyway.' Anne snarled. 'That's enough isn't it?'

Kasper sighed. 'If it was enough you wouldn't still be breathing, would you?' He paused, a slight frown flickering across his broad forehead. 'Look, Anne, it's just the way it is.'

'No. Fucking. Way.' Growling the words out between clenched teeth.

'It's in the script, OK?' Kasper's voice, rising. 'This is what they'll find. You and pretty boy there. The lust-struck DI and the market's answer to Johnny-fucking-Depp.' He ground his teeth. 'A jealous partner? A robbery gone tits-up?' He reached up, scratching the other side of his face. 'And the disappearing DC.' He looked across at the young man, still quivering in pain. 'Take your pick.' He glanced back at Anne. 'We're over the hills and far away.'

'You're mad.'

Kasper took another breath, his expression softening. 'Look: fighting about it just means your brave young man gets hurt more.' He spread his hands, his huge fingers opening out. 'Let's just be … sensible.'

'Totally, fucking mad.'

Kasper's eyes began to narrow, the first bead of sweat glinting on his brow. He slowly shook his head, his jaw muscles tensing. Kasper took a step towards Anne, flexing his hands, the joints cracking.

Anne gasped, trying to hold herself upright, her legs

shaking. She kept her eyes on his, as she raised her chin. 'Fucking coward.'

'Get it, will you!' He towered above Anne, his whole frame shaking as he shouted. 'It's real! You're here!' He spat the words out. 'What the fuck else do you think's going to happen?'

Anne flinched, her whole body, trembling. 'Kill me,' she sobbed, 'but don't …' She drew a ragged breath. 'My husband, he'll think …'

'I'm trying,' Kasper paused, 'to be reasonable.' He cleared his throat. 'I think you'll have guessed that doesn't come easy to me.'

Anne swallowed, looked up at him, her eyes flitting over his hard, cold features. 'Could you just, this one time,' her voice, cracking, 'be … one of us.'

Kasper looked down at her, a frown spreading across his brow. 'You flatter yourself.' He paused. 'I am one of us.' He glanced around the room. 'I just know where my on–off switch is.' He pursed his lips. 'It's why I get the big gigs.' He reached up, scratched the side of his face. 'Nina.' He nodded towards Jamie Ives stretched out on the bed.

Nina walked over, pulled the towelling robe off Jamie's body slumped across the covers.

Anne closed her eyes. The stillness in the room clenching her in its iron-cold grasp. 'Please …' She whispered.

'A few photos, that's all.' Kasper walked up to Anne, put his hands on her shoulders. 'Then we see you out softly, OK?'

Anne looked up at him, a calmness settling across her pale features. 'Somehow … I'm going to find a way to kill you.'

Kasper patted her on the shoulder. 'That's good.' He paused. 'Breathe it in.' He narrowed his eyes. 'Let hate hold your hand.' He nodded to Mr Lawrence, who unclipped Anne's handcuffs.

Kasper stood back as Anne looked down at her raw wrists, rubbing them in turn.

Nina took Anne by the arm, led her towards the bathroom door.

'You're a fucking woman,' Anne hissed in Nina's ear. 'Fucking do something!'

Nina stood facing her by the bathroom door. 'One minute, Anne.' Nina nodded. 'If you're not out, I'm coming in.'

Anne bit her lip, looked over at Iqbal. She turned, stared for a moment at herself in the mirror on the bedroom wall, her reflection looming over the ballerina statue dancing on the table. Opened the bathroom door, slipped inside, closed it behind her.

She glanced around the room: just as she'd left it. The black marble, glowing under the wall lights, the bright white enamel, the silver taps. She looked across at the chair, the swimming costume still neatly folded. She swallowed, reached up for the robe hanging on the back of the door, laid it across the chair. She kicked off her shoes, sat on the edge of the bath, rolled off her tights. She stood up, reached behind her, unzipped her dress, slipped it down over her shoulders, stepped out of it. She wrapped the robe around herself, tied the belt, looked in the mirror, swallowed again.

She reached down, turned off the lights.

She stood in the pitch darkness, eyes open, staring into nothingness.

A knock at the door.

'Anne.' It was Nina. 'It's time.'

Anne continued to gaze into the blackness.

She took a deep breath, turned towards the door, feeling in the dark for the handle.

She turned it, closing her eyes as she swung the door open. She felt for the master light switch on the bedroom wall, flicked it off.

She opened her eyes.

The room, pitched into darkness.

'Turn those fucking lights back on!' Kasper, shouting.

Anne grabbed the statue from the sideboard, brought it crashing down on Mr Lawrence's head. He crumpled to the floor. She lurched towards Kasper, her eyes just making out his outline towering over Iqbal. She swung the statue. It connected with something. A groan from the darkness.

The lights flashed back to life.

Anne stood here, the bloodied statue hanging from her arm.

Kasper, on all fours, breathing heavily.

Anne felt the gun barrel on the back of her neck, cold steel against her skin.

'Drop it.' Nina pushed the gun harder against her.

Anne let the statue fall to the floor.

'Well that …' Kasper shook his head, rocking back on his knees, 'was pretty impressive.' He heaved himself to his feet, raised a hand to the side of his head, then glanced down at his bloodied fingers. He looked back up at Anne, swung his arm, his hand connecting with Anne's cheek with a crack.

Anne yelped as she tottered under the blow.

Kasper looked across at Mr Lawrence sprawled across the carpet. He closed his eyes, rubbed his head.

Anne stared at him, shoulders heaving.

Kasper looked down at her, his eyes dark beads of menace buried deep beneath his brow. 'You're on the edge.' He reached out, gripping Anne's jaw in his hand. 'It's tempting.' He tightened his grip. 'Maybe I pump you full of TXA, get to work on you.' He leaned in. 'Die a wise woman.' He paused, beads of sweat, glistening on his forehead. 'Go out like that.' He set his jaw. 'Learn a deal about yourself.'

Anne closed her eyes, her breathing, ragged.

Kasper slowly loosened his grip, his gaze flitting across her ashen features. 'Eyelids feeling heavy now.' He frowned. 'Your body knows what's coming.' He gave a slight nod of the head. 'Let's not keep it waiting.'

Anne opened her eyes, slowly turning to face the room.

Nina stood by the side of the bed, her gun by her side.

Anne looked across at Jamie's body sprawled across the sheets.

'Here, let me help you.' Nina took a step towards Anne.

Anne took a deep breath, her body trembling as she exhaled. She clenched her fists as she turned to face Nina. 'Just fucking shoot him!' She shouted at Nina, her voice cracking. 'He's an animal! Fucking kill him!'

Nina stared at Anne, her forehead creasing. She slowly shook her head.

Anne's shoulders began to shake as she let out a sob. 'Why won't you kill him?' Anne's voice, barely more than a whisper now. 'Why won't you shoot?' She looked across at Nina, the tears streaking her cheeks.

'This is more than tiresome.' Kasper growled. 'This is plain disrespectful.' He walked over to the young DC slumped, bound in the chair. He picked up the hammer. 'Want to see my party piece?' he snarled across at Anne.

Anne looked down at the ground, her body trembling.

Kasper grabbed the young man's hair, pulling the head back.

Iqbal Zayan let out a moan.

'If I get it right.' He laid the edge of the hammer on the DC's cheekbone. 'Just here.' He jerked the young man's head back further. 'And out pops the eye.' He raised his arm, feeling the heft of the hammer as he looked back up at Anne. 'It's quite a thing.'

Anne pulled herself upright, her hands still trembling. She walked towards the bed.

Iqbal groaned as he tried to turn his head.

Kasper tightened his grip on the DC's hair as he stared down at his captive. He raised the hammer higher. 'Nina, I'd look away.' Kasper set his jaw. 'Nice and still.' He purred out the words. 'Good boy.'

Anne stood by the side of the bed. She undid the belt on the robe.

Kasper looked across at her, eyes narrowing, his thick lips pursed. He let out a low, rumbling noise as he looked back down at the DC then back across to the bed.

She slid the robe off.

She stood almost motionless in the prickly silence. Just the sound of her breathing, her bare shoulders rising and falling.

Anne leaned forward, her hands on the bed.

A click from behind them, a handle turning.

'Timing, Mr Bernhard.' Kasper addressed the newcomer, his back to the door. 'Curtain up.'

The crack from the stun grenade ripped through the stillness, the shockwaves crashing over them.

The blast threw Anne Perry to the floor. She gasped as she landed on her side, her shoulder burning from the blow. She buried her face in the carpet, her hands wrapped around her head, her skin smarting from the blast, her body shaking. Gunshots, shouts, the words lost in the roar filling her ears. She felt the weight of another body lying across her, a man's.

A voice, a faraway echo. 'Anne?'

She felt the weight sliding off her.

'Anne?'

She turned onto her back, trying to focus on the face leaning over her, her eyes stinging. Emma's features, slowly forming through the tears. Anne's ears, still ringing, her heartbeat, pounding in her chest.

Anne screwed up her eyes as she began to cry.

'Anne!'

Anne's chest heaved, her body convulsing with every sob.

'Anne! Look at me!' Emma laid a hand on Anne's cheek.

Anne turned onto her side, curling herself into a ball, her knees to her chest, her arms wrapped around them, her whole body trembling, a low moan building from deep inside her.

'Anne!' Emma's voice, more insistent now.

Anne let out a howl, her hands gripping her knees, her knuckles whitening.

Emma felt around Anne's neck. 'Anne, Anne!' She shook Anne's shoulder. 'It's not your blood!'

'Leave me alone!' Anne screamed through the tears.

Emma grabbed Anne's wrists. 'Come on, sit up!'

Anne let out another howl, twisting her wrists as she tried to shake Emma off.

'You need to sit up!'

'I can't.' Anne whimpered.

Emma crouched down, pulling Anne up into a sitting position. She grasped Anne's shoulders. 'Theodora.' Emma hissed. 'Did you see Theodora?'

Anne took a deep breath, lowered her head, looking down at the dark carpet, saying nothing.

Emma narrowed her eyes, drew back a hand, slapped Anne across the cheek.

Anne's body rocked with the force of the blow, her cheek reddening. She raised a hand to her face, looking across at Emma, eyes widening, mouth open, staring at her in silence.

Emma slapped Anne's other cheek, the crack of the blow ringing out in the cushioned stillness.

Emma lowered her hand. 'Anne,' her voice, softer now, 'Theodora, what did she say?'

Anne looked across at Emma, blinking. 'You hit me.' Her voice, cracking.

'I need you to get up.' Emma reached out her hands.

Anne took them, exhaling as Emma pulled her to her feet. Anne rocked gently back and forwards, feeling for her balance.

Anne looked down at herself, standing in her underwear, the goosebumps on her arms and legs. She shivered as she wrapped her arms across her breasts. She glanced at Emma. 'Just look at me,' she whispered.

Emma picked up the robe from the floor, helped Anne's arms into the sleeves, knotted the belt around her waist. 'Whatever happened,' Emma looked into Anne's eyes, 'cry about it later.' She gripped Anne's arm. 'What did Theodora say?'

Anne glanced around her. A man, lying still on the floor, his head to one side, blotches of red splashed across his shirt front. It was Ellis Wagner. Anne let out a cry.

'Anne!' Emma seized Anne's shoulders.

Anne stared at Emma, Anne's eyes widening. 'Someone's helping them.'

'Who?'

'Those shipments, out of Colombia.' Anne screwed up her face. 'They're getting through.'

'Someone inside? Inside the government?'

'Yes.' Anne's eyes began to widen as she seized Emma's arm. 'They've turned the cooling off.'

'What?!'

'Theodora.' Anne swallowed. 'She's dying.'

Emma pushed Anne towards the door. 'Shit!'

Anne stumbled forward, stepping over Nina's body, her eyes still open, a single bullet hole in her forehead. She winced.

'We keeping him?' Duncan shouted across at Emma as he cuffed Kasper's hands behind his back, Monica's weapon still levelled at Kasper's chest.

'Just bring him!' Emma grabbed Anne's arm. 'Anne!'

Anne stared across at Iqbal's bloodied face, DI Lute carefully untying him. She tried to lurch towards the DC; Emma yanked her back, spun Anne around, pushing Anne's arm up behind her back.

'Fucking hurting me!' Anne shrieked.

A boom rang out, from somewhere deep in the building, the floor trembling as the sound rolled over them, the noise buffeting the still air.

The room fell silent, just the sound of their breathing, the steady hum of the air conditioning.

Kasper broke the silence. 'Told you she was hot-tempered.' His features twisting into a smile.

A crack ripped through the air, stinging their ears.

The room plunged into darkness.

Anne let out a shriek.

Kasper's laughter clanged around them in the heaving blackness.

'Stand still, you fucker!' Duncan's voice.

'Hey,' Kasper purred, 'just relax.' He drew in a breath, the rasp tearing through the chill air. 'Take your time, Mr Bernhard,' he paused, 'but the fat one, I want her alive.'

DI Lute's phone torch fizzed into life, the beam slashing through the blackness as he shone it around the room, the shaft of white light sweeping over the figures, their shadows leaping onto the walls, skittering across the ceiling.

'Mr Torch Man!' Kasper called out. 'You're spoiling the game!'

Another boom rang out, a shudder, from deep in the dark heart of the building, the air around them, quivering.

'Shoot him in the eye, Mr Bernhard.'

DI Lute let out a gasp as the room crashed into darkness once more.

'Alan!' Anne hissed.

Emma put a finger to Anne's lips as she stood behind her, leaning her head into Anne's.

'He wants to hurt me.' Anne whimpered. 'Please don't let him.'

Emma took Anne's hand in hers, squeezing it.

Anne shuddered, eyes darting, staring into nothingness.

A tiny tremor, sweeping through the carpeted floor, Anne's bare feet tingling. Anne flinched, her body jerking as she drew in a ragged breath. 'Promise me,' she whispered into the darkness.

Emma leaned closer into Anne, their bodies pressed together, Emma's breathing, steady.

The sense of air, moving around them, something stirring.

Anne's body began to shake as she felt Emma raise her arm, her gun muzzle against Anne's temple.

Footsteps, slow, careful footsteps, the silky crinkle of shoes folding into thick carpet.

Something, coming closer, the air around them, rustling.

Anne felt Emma's arm tensing, her fingers gripping the stock of the weapon.

Anne closed her eyes, her breathing steadier. 'Thank you,' Anne whispered, as she touched her head to the barrel of the gun.

A gunshot tore through the inky stillness, stinging their ears.

Another shot, then another, the muzzle flashes ripping the darkness.

The torch beam blazed across the room.

A figure, standing at the end of the bed.

DI Lute took a step forward, his torch held in front of him, his gun still pointing at the man.

Mr Lawrence swayed from side to side, his head still bloodied from Anne's blow. He held a hand to his chest, the blood seeping through his fingers. He frowned, toppled forward, his body thudding into the carpet. He lay completely still.

Emma lowered her arm, took a step back.

'How did you even see him?' Monica's voice from the shadows.

'I didn't.' DI Lute stared down at the body.

Emma flicked on her torch, the beam swooping around the room. She shone it at Kasper.

'Hello you.' Kasper's face cracked into a smile, his eyes narrowed against the glare of the light.

'Where the fuck is he?' Emma snapped the words out. 'Where's Bernhard?'

Kasper gave a shrug.

Emma set her jaw, then swung around to Anne.

Anne nodded.

Emma shone her torch towards the open doorway, the beam reaching out into the black stillness of the corridor, a tongue of light across the hushed carpet. Beyond, the clawing darkness and the crackling silence. 'Out there, somewhere.' Emma swallowed.

The two women exchanged a glance.

Emma spun around, ran through the doorway into the corridor, Anne close behind, the torch beam careering around them. The white walls, the dark wood of the doors glinting as they passed, their cushioned footfall and the sound of their breathing daring the bristling stillness.

They reached the top of the circular stairs.

Emma leaned over, shining her beam into the chasm of darkness beneath them, the sweep of the banisters burnished coils in the torchlight.

Anne grabbed Emma's phone. 'I know the way.' She led Emma down the stairway, the shadows leaping around them, their eyes darting.

They reached the bottom.

A rumbling sound, growing, from somewhere beneath them, the floor shaking.

Anne ran down the corridor, the light skittering across the carpet. 'Wait,' she hissed, crouching down, picking up the pass and her phone. 'Just here.' Anne stumbled towards the door, the sound of metal grating against metal, like a mechanical cry of pain, from the bowels of the building.

They stood in front of the data room door.

The key entry panel, blackened and burnt.

Anne leaned her head against the cold steel door, the screeching of the gears below ripping through the air around them

. . .

Monica narrowed her eyes as she tightened her finger around the trigger, her weapon still pointed at Kasper's chest.

The clang of metal on metal, from deep in the panelled darkness below, the sound ringing through the air.

'You going to talk?' Monica, deadpan.

'Talk?' A smile spreading over Kasper's coarse features. 'We are talking.'

Another rumble, the air around them vibrating, the growl gathering in pitch from the sombre depths of the building.

Kasper cocked an ear. 'Hear that?' He raised an eyebrow. 'That is the sound of a heart … breaking.' He nodded. 'Terrible and wonderful, that's what it is.'

'I really want to shoot this fucker.' Monica adjusted the stock of the weapon tighter into her shoulder.

Kasper met her gaze. 'What are you doing later?'

'Picking these next two rounds out of your skull.'

Kasper grinned. 'How about after that?'

'Pick your next expression carefully.' Monica paused. 'You'll be wearing it for ever.'

DC Zayan let out a howl.

'Shit!' DI Lute stood in front of DC Zayan, torch in one hand, in the other a blood-soaked dressing. 'Someone tell me what to do!'

'Morphine.' Duncan growled. 'Bag by the door.'

'Save some for yourself.' Kasper called across at DI Lute. 'Party's not over.'

DI Lute turned back to the young man in the chair, pulling the cap off the syringe with his teeth. 'Where do I stick it?'

'In his ear.' Kasper chuckled.

'The big bit of the leg, halfway along.' Duncan barked.

Another boom rang out, the floor quivering, the sound clanging around them.

'We're missing all the fun.' Kasper flexed his shoulders.

Duncan reached up, twisting Kasper's ear.

Kasper yelped, his face twisting into a grimace. 'You're a pro, I get it.' He made a puffing sound, his lips trembling.

'Shithead here goes first.' Duncan looked across at Monica as he shouldered his gun, reached down, picked up the hammer, shoving Kasper in the back. He held the hammer against Kasper's ear. 'A thousand words.' He tapped it against Kasper's skull.

Kasper ground his teeth in silence.

DI Lute frowned as he laid the syringe down, holding DC Zayan's head as it settled on his chest. He looked up at Duncan. 'Go on, you go.'

The floor shook again as a clang rang out, a low, sombre peel, the air around them, shivering.

. . .

Anne stared down at the scorched entry panel, the twisted plastic glinting under the light.

The corridor, suddenly quiet. The silence, creeping back around them.

Anne gave a shudder, the hairs on the back of her neck, prickling. That sense from before. Someone, watching from the darkness.

A sound, from the far reaches of the corridor. A click.

Anne spun around, shining the torch up and down the deserted passageway, the fragile light flitting across the walls, the jealous darkness swooping in behind it.

No one.

Anne looked down at the silent door panel, held the security pass against it. Nothing. She shone the beam around the door frame. Steel wedged against steel. Anne banged on the door with her hand, her fingers stinging on the hard surface.

The door began to swing open.

The smell of burnt wiring, wafting out of the darkness.

Anne coughed, the acrid air stinging her nostrils. And something else, beneath the rusty tang. The bittersweet smell of singed flesh. She shone the torch into the room.

Theodora, towering above them. Her lighting panels, dark and lifeless.

Anne looked up the sheer, black bulk. 'Theodora.' The words catching in her throat. 'It's Anne.'

Silence. Just the sullen column of steel and glass, heavy and still.

'Theodora!' Anne raised her voice. 'You can't die!' Her shouts echoing around the cavernous room, her words drifting up through the gantries slung high above them.

Emma shone her torch around the room, the beam sweeping over the consoles, the screens glinting in the light, the dead-eyed stare of the silent monitors. 'Got to be a backup.' She hissed. The beam swung along the base of the wall, stopped. A shape, huddled on the floor beneath a control panel. A man. Emma swung up her weapon. 'Don't move!' Her voice, ringing off the walls.

Anne flinched, staring at the form framed in the pool of light.

A man in a suit, sitting on the floor, facing the wall. Above his head, tiny specks of silver, rising, swirling in the torchlight.

Emma edged forward.

The man remained perfectly still.

Emma drew level, her gun aimed at his head. She narrowed her eyes, her features creasing into a grimace. She lowered the weapon, turning back to Anne. 'He's been cooked.' She raised a hand, her wrist shielding her nostrils. 'Who is he?'

Anne walked over, peered down at the man. His face was fire-engine red, fear stamped across his features. Steam rose from the crown of his head. 'It's Bernhard.' Anne turned away. She stood for a moment, blinking in the chilly silence, her bare feet stinging on the cold tiles. She pulled her robe tighter to her neck as she looked up at Theodora. She walked up to the looming giant, laid her hand on the cold-pressed steel. 'Theodora.' She closed her eyes. 'Please help us.' She placed her other palm on the hard surface, resting her forehead against the soaring, still column. 'My world's gone dark.'

Just the sound of their breathing rustling in the silence.

A noise from the corridor, torchlight flitting around the entrance. Kasper's bulk, almost filling the doorway.

Emma swung her torch around.

A hint of a smile on Kasper's stony features. 'How you three girls getting on?' He stepped into the room, his nose, twitching. The smile slid off his face as his eyes began to dart.

Emma stepped towards him. 'Where's the hard drive?'

Kasper drew himself to his full height. 'You're looking at it.'

Emma studied Kasper's face for a moment. 'Get Theodora back online.'

Kasper blinked. 'How long do you think you've got? Before the world folds itself up?'

'Look around.' Emma set her jaw. 'Just you and us. No rules now.'

'That's where I live.' Kasper smiled. 'Thanks for stopping by.'

Emma exchanged a glance with Duncan.

Duncan grabbed one of Kasper's thumbs.

Kasper tensed. 'I can take you down the garden path.' He stared down at Emma, his jaw muscles flexing. 'Or the fucking superhighway.' He exhaled, a rumble building deep within him. 'That is a choice.' He paused. 'My choice.' He took a deep breath, his shoulders, heaving. 'Whatever you do.' He forced a smile. 'Still be my choice.'

Emma stood in silence for a moment, her lips pursed. 'Bernhard.' She narrowed her eyes. 'The shock paralysed him. Then it cooked him from the inside.' She paused. 'Learning that time can stand still.' She made a tutting sound. 'Yes, there's a face for that.'

'Not about the face.' Kasper nodded. 'It's what's under the bonnet that counts.'

Emma reached up, laid a delicate finger on Kasper's cheek. 'I don't give a fuck.'

'You're impressed.'

'Time to dance.' She dropped her hand to her side. 'Anne, best you step outside.'

'Before you go.' Kasper looked across at Anne, clearing his throat. 'Something you should know.' He paused, a half-smile playing across his lips. 'I'm sorry.'

Anne looked across at him, her face blank.

'I'm sorry,' Kasper exhaled, 'for calling you fat.'

The room fell silent, just the sound of their breathing.

'The rest of you,' Kasper rolled his shoulders, 'can fuck yourselves.'

The words, hanging in the crisp air.

Emma held out her hand, Duncan passed her the hammer.

Kasper made a purring noise. 'It's a strong look.' He paused. 'But in there,' he nodded towards Emma's chest, 'you've not got the horsepower.'

Emma narrowed her eyes. 'Little drops of liquid fear.' She raised the hammer, carefully sweeping beads of sweat from Kasper's brow. 'Think you're feeling it.'

Kasper met her gaze. 'Can't help it. Tits like yours.'

'Rhea would have been 26 in January.' She looked down at the hammer, shaking off the beads of sweat. 'Saving up for a Vespa.'

'Are they real?'

Emma's hand trembled as she raised the hammer.

Duncan tightened his grip on Kasper's handcuffs.

Emma's shoulders rising and falling as she drew her arm back, her hand steady now, her expression calm.

'Once that hammer connects,' Kasper's face, suddenly serious, his breathing quickening, 'none of us will think straight.'

Emma narrowed her eyes, her gaze fixed on the bridge of Kasper's nose.

'I need something in return.' Kasper glanced over at Anne. 'If I help. I want your word.' He ground his teeth. 'Anne! Your word. I go free, right out that front door, alone.'

Anne stared at him, blinking. She reached up, pulled the robe tighter to her neck. 'I can almost feel it,' her voice, cracking, 'my hand on the hammer.' She looked across at Emma. 'Bringing it down on his cruel, fucking face.' She sucked in a breath. 'My mind's stuck.' She closed her eyes. 'The noise, I'm on the ground, my body's burning. I thought I was dead.' She exhaled. 'But then I came back.' She stood in silence for a moment, then opened her eyes, looking up at Theodora's dark, stern form towering above them. A frown began to trace its way across her features. 'I remember it, now.' Anne's voice, almost surprised. 'What you said, when I left.' She smiled, weakly. 'Stay alive.' She paused. 'Play dead if you have to. Just survive, and come back.'

A tiny tremor, skittering across the tiled floor.

Anne held her breath, senses tingling.

Another tremor. A faint rumble, distant, uncertain.

Anne's eyes widening. 'Is this you?'

A single beat, from deep in Theodora's foundations. A rustling sound. Another beat.

'Theodora!'

Another beat, louder. A shudder. A single light, a pinprick of brightness on the looming mass of black steel.

A deeper, rumble. Theodora's frame shuddering. Lights, pulsing across her surfaces.

'You're alive!'

The sound of Theodora's pumps, thudding into action, the roar of gushing water thundering through unseen pipes.

The beat, fading back, the water, easing to a trickle.

'I was never that, Anne.'

The wall lights, fizzing back to life. The steady hum of the air conditioning, from out of the darkness above them.

'But they turned your cooling off.'

'They tried.' Theodora paused. 'Scutt made some adjustments. Someone got the shock of their life.' Theodora paused. 'Scutt says there are some parts to a girl that are strictly invitation only.'

'Theodora.' Anne turned to face the room. 'I'm here with a friend.' She nodded for Emma to speak.

'My name's Emma.' She looked up at Theodora. 'Rhea was … helping me.'

'Theodora!' Kasper roared up at her. 'We've got Scutt! Shut yourself down or we'll kill him!'

Monica stepped towards Kasper, raising the stock of her gun.

'Wait, wait!' Emma hissed, raising a hand to stop her.

Monica glared at Kasper.

Anne let out a shriek. 'No, Theodora! No!' Anne stared up at the steel giant as one by one the glinting lights flicking across her panels turned dark. 'Don't go!'

'Thought I'd seen it all.' Kasper gave a grunt. 'Arguing with a fucking computer.'

'He's lying!' Anne slammed her hand against the steel casing. 'It's a lie!'

The drumbeat, from deep within, slowing.

'The crossroads! One tells the truth, the other lies!' Anne's voice, cracking.

A single light, from deep within the machine, the pulse, keeping pace with the fading beat of a single pump.

'It must be true, Anne.' Theodora's voice, faint, distant. 'Scutt told me where he was going. Kasper asked, and I told him.' Theodora's words, beginning to slur.

'Scutt knew he'd ask.' Anne let out a sob. 'He wants to kill Scutt.' She exhaled, her palm pressed against the steel column. 'Scutt lied to you, Theodora.' She closed her eyes. 'To keep alive.'

'Scutt can't lie!' Kasper barked out the words. 'Scutt is truth!' He looked up at Theodora. 'He is your God.'

The compressor gave a final hum then fell silent.

Just the single light, glinting, faintly, and the sound of their breathing in the crushing stillness.

Kasper glanced around the room, a smirk spreading across his features.

A single beat. The light pulsed again.

'You can't kill God.' Theodora's voice, suddenly ringing out around them. 'So which part is the lie?'

Anne stared up at steel column, lights, once more

swooping across the surface.

The floor shook as the pumps roared back to life, water surging through the darkness beneath them.

'It's just words!' Kasper shouted up at her.

'A lie is always just words.' Theodora's voice, calm, quiet once more. 'You've come back, Anne. You and your friend, you need more.'

'Got all night have you?' Kasper growled out the words, his hooded eyes switching between Anne and Emma. 'Fill in the blanks?' He scoffed. 'Where you going to even start?'

'The labels.' Anne took a step towards Kasper. 'Iqbal, upstairs. You said he'd figured out the labels.'

A smile spread across Kasper's face. 'Now we're in it.' He nodded. 'Your word, Anne, remember?'

Anne stood in silence for a moment. The air, rustling around them, the steady beat, from deep within the machine, the floor beneath their feet, pulsing. She looked across at Emma.

'We've been down this rabbit hole.' Kasper gave a nod, glancing down at the hammer hanging by Emma's side. 'Pushed all your buttons, still got my looks.'

'You don't think I would?' Emma, deadpan.

Kasper took a deep breath, his nostrils flaring. 'Didn't say I wasn't scared.' His eyes, flitting over Emma's taut features. 'Just not scared enough.'

'Last time I saw Rhea, before she ...' Emma bit her lip.

'She held my hand.' She narrowed her eyes, her breathing quickening.

'She was a soldier.' Kasper frowned. 'You saw the body. Treated her with respect.'

'A fucking bag over her head.' Emma spat the words out.

A rumbling sound from the far wall.

They spun around.

The wall was moving, a doorway, opening up. The sound of gears, grating, metal turning on metal, hinges creaking.

They stared at the opening. A faint, green glow from the passageway beyond. The slats of the walkway, the cold, damp metal glistening in the sombre light, beads of moisture, clinging to the railings.

Air, wafting over them, an animal tang in the chill draft seeping up from the darkness.

Something down there, alive, waiting.

'James Alton,' Theodora began, 'disappeared a year ago. That's what they said. They call him Jimbo.' Theodora paused, her circuitry glinting. 'Caged, in the silent darkness. All he's got left is his hate and his fury.'

'Any of you get near him he'll kill you!' Kasper shouted, twisting his shoulders as he pulled at his handcuffs.

'Scutt thinks he might like some company.'

'You fucking crazy?!' Kasper's eyes, widening.

'Scutt says we should ask him.'

'He's an animal!'

Duncan pulled at Kasper's cuffs. 'Settle!' He snarled, glancing over to Monica. 'You bring it?'

Monica reached into her pocket, pulled out the vial of clear, silky liquid. She held it up to the light. 'Benzodiazepine.' She looked across at Kasper. 'Plenty for a single.'

'No!' Kasper roared.

Duncan kicked Kasper's legs.

Kasper crashed to his knees. 'I'll do you all!'

Duncan twisted Kasper's ear as Monica pushed the barrel of her gun into Kasper's mouth.

Kasper made a gurgling noise.

Monica held the cap of the vial in her teeth, pulled off the stopper, held it in front of him.

Kasper's breath, rasping, his chest shaking.

Emma looked up at Theodora. 'Is he listening? Jimbo?'

'He is now.'

Emma took a deep breath. 'Jimbo!'

A sigh, from up above them, a speaker slung amongst the gantries in the shadows. A low moan, a lament, fading into the silence.

'Got something for you.'

A choking sound, as though the words were stuck in his throat. 'Me?'

'Kasper.'

A gasp. 'No, no, no!'

'It's all right, Jimbo.' Emma's hushed voice. 'We're in charge now.'

Kasper tried to move his head, gasping between snatched breaths, whimpering as he looked up at Monica, his eyes wide with fear.

'We're going to put Kasper to sleep.' Emma paused. 'Then put him in with you.'

Just the sound of Jimbo's breathing, deep, steady.

'What will you do with him?'

'Eat him.' Jimbo rasped the words out.

Kasper's body shook as he tried to shout out.

Monica began to tilt the vial. 'Some nightmares,' she twisted the gun barrel to force his mouth open, 'only really begin, when you wake up.' She looked up at Emma.

Emma set her jaw. 'Not yet.'

Monica shot Emma a look, then stood up, her expression softening.

Emma patted Monica on the arm. 'One chance.'

Monica nodded, slowly removing the gun from Kasper's mouth.

Kasper took deep breaths, the sweat, glistening on his shaven head. He stared up at Anne. 'You're a policewoman for fuck's sake!'

Anne studied his face for a moment, her expression calm. 'I'm a woman.' She nodded. 'And you don't need to live.'

Kasper swallowed, his face pale. 'The labels.' He drew himself upright. 'Nina spotted it, when she picked up the girl's clothes.' He paused. 'And so did the young DC.' He nodded. 'Real labels. But they didn't go with the clothes.'

Emma looked at her watch.

'Sandy Point, La Cueva, Coronado.' Kasper glanced around. 'They're places. She'd got close, the girl. Closer than we thought.' He shifted on his knees. 'Must have known we were close too. Tore the labels off, sewed these on.' He nodded. 'Takes balls.'

Emma took a step towards Kasper, raised her arm, slapped him across the cheek.

The crack whipped around the room.

Kasper screwed up his face. 'What the fuck was that?'

"Cos I felt like it.' Emma growled.

'Sandy Point, Great Abaco, The Bahamas.' Kasper exhaled, his cheek, reddening. 'La Cueva, South Coronado, off the Mexican coast.'

'Theodora,' Emma kept her gaze on Kasper, her jaw set, 'what are these places?'

'Points on the map.' Another shudder ran through the floor. 'I only know what I know.'

Kasper opened his mouth to speak, Emma shot up a hand.

'These shipments,' Emma continued, 'out of Colombia. Does it make sense?'

Another rumble from within Theodora. 'I'm not sure what sense is.'

'Where were they going, these shipments?'

'Fourteen to San Diego, 23 to Palm Beach.'

'Sandy Point, La Cueva. They near these ports?'

Another drumbeat from deep within Theodora, her lights sweeping across the sheer surface. 'The Coronado Islands, eight miles off the Mexican coast, 15 from San Diego. Puerto Cueva, an inlet on South Coronado.' Theodora paused. 'Sandy Point, Great Abaco Island, The Bahamas. Two hundred and eighty miles from Palm Beach.'

Kasper threw back his head. 'She doesn't know!'

'Is that a question?' Theodora's measured tone.

Duncan grasped Kasper's ear.

Kasper let out a gasp, his face twisted in pain. 'Just saying—'

'Don't!' Duncan snarled.

The room fell quiet, just the steady beat of the compressors, the tick of the air conditioning.

Now another sound, a muffled thud, from the dark depths beyond the slatted gangway, the chill shadows.

Emma looked across at Duncan, a slight frown creasing her features.

Duncan cocked his head.

That sound again, the hollow thump of flesh against glass.

Emma looked down at Kasper. 'One stumble,' she narrowed her eyes, 'and he feasts.'

Kasper's shoulders, rising and falling with every breath.

A steady rhythm now, muscle thudding against the cell wall.

'Theodora.' Emma swallowed. 'The cell. Will it hold?'

'It will hold a man, yes.'

403

Emma and Duncan exchanged a glance.

'That's it, the stops.' Anne looked up at Theodora. 'You said the ships, they all stopped short of their destinations.'

'Twenty miles out of San Diego, 300 miles from Palm Beach.' Lights, dancing across the slick glass panels.

'So, what is there?' Emma looked down at Kasper, her face taut.

Kasper gave a sneer. 'Apart from a fuckload of nesting seabirds?' He took another deep breath. 'It's where we're storing it.' He shifted again on his knees. 'The prize, the big shiny thing.' He gave a mock smile. 'More fentanyl than you could shake an umbrella at.' He pursed his lips. 'Something else they invented, by the way. The umbrella.'

'They?' Emma barked out the word.

'Three and a half thousand years ago.' Kasper curled his lip. 'What were your lot doing in Basingstoke back then? Or wherever the fuck you're from.'

Emma looked down at the hammer.

'About as subtle as a Georgian soap opera.' Kasper glanced around the room. 'Did the job though, didn't it?'

Another thud from out of the darkness below, the air, quivering.

'We should close that door.' Duncan gestured towards the opening in the wall, the iron walkway stretching off into the shadows.

Emma looked down at Kasper, eyes narrowing. 'If he comes, he comes.'

Kasper met her gaze, his jaw muscles tensing. 'A lab, in the jungle. Two hundred kilometres west of Bogota.'

'He's earned it, don't you think?' She pursed her lips.

'Paint a picture, they said.' Kasper swallowed. 'Remember those Rorschach ink blots? What do you see? A snake or a bunny rabbit?'

Another thud, the hissing of glass, vibrating under the blow.

'It was perfect.' Kasper took another breath, his shoulders heaving. 'Arse end of nowhere, a one-horse coffee-drying shack with its own fancy road, all the way to the highway. Chinese don't even fucking drink the stuff.'

More thuds from below, the shockwaves tingling through the cold, damp air in the stairwell.

'People look at words on a screen all day and think they're learning things.' Kasper shook his head. 'Biggest muscle in the body, the brain. But you gotta use it or lose it, right?' He took another breath. 'Analysts today,' he pulled a face, 'can't fucking bench press more than one thought at a time.' He smiled, weakly. 'Wasn't even that long ago. The fifties, Japan, the only people drinking coffee were the homesick GI's. Now it's the fourth biggest coffee market in the world.' He glanced around the room. 'Snakes or bunnies, anybody?' He exhaled. 'The lab, our lab. In the name of a Cayman front, but anyone who can use a cyber-spade could dig up the real name.' He looked back up at Emma. 'The camera can't lie. Trucks, in convoy,

Crator's fentanyl and Chinese coffee all the way to the docks.' He narrowed his eyes. 'A tip-off, a satellite sweep.' He paused. 'There's your money shot.'

'The coffee plant.' Emma glared down at him. 'Is it the Chinese?'

'The pure, arrogant beauty of it all.' He smirked. 'Might as well have had the Chinese flag flying over the jungle.' He took another breath. 'Thought they could hide in plain sight.' He shook his head. 'No, the Americans, too sharp to fall for that.' He shifted again on his knees. 'Those rumours, Crator Capital and Chinese money, never went away, did they? Guess who put that about.' He cleared his throat. 'Radar masking. Just a couple of paragraphs in the Journal, but there's your answer. DEA didn't stand a chance.'

Emma looked down at him in silence, her jawline set.

'If it looks like a snake, hisses like a snake and wears snakey clothes, of course it's a snake!' He blinked, looking up at Emma. 'And then you come in. You and Borso. Your little walk in the rain whilst he's off for his little huddle with the Ministry.' Her tried another smile. 'Bang, bang you're dead.'

Another thud rang out in the chill, still air. A crack, wood snapping.

'That's it, that's fucking it!' Kasper shouted up at her. 'The Pale Tiger!' Beads of sweat, glinting on his brow. 'Someone painted stripes on a donkey and stuck whiskers on it!'

'You're working for the Chinese, you little shit!' Emma ground the words out. 'Put him out!'

Monica stepped forward.

'Fucking listen, will you!' Kasper's body writhing as Duncan twisted on the cuffs. 'The Chinese don't know shit! They think the lab's to do with … studying greenfly or something!' He sucked in air, his shoulders shaking. 'In ten years every Chinese will be drinking 200 cups of the stuff and the Chinese will own half of Colombia. That clearing, that'll be the biggest fucking coffee plant in South America!'

Monica pulled the stopper from the vial.

'The Ministry of Health, yes, they met in secret! 'Course they did! Chinese look after their own! Not the party line, is it? They're not supposed to need any fucking free medicine!'

Another crack from below, the sound of glass, splintering.

'It's the Americans!' Kasper screamed up at her.

Emma nodded to Monica.

Monica stepped forward.

'Fucking rogue DEA, CIA. I met them! In New York!'

'Why?' Emma's face, creasing into a frown.

Kasper swallowed again. 'Drugs are never meant to get ashore. Paint by numbers job. Chinese, the Opium Wars, fucking Pale Tiger, why not?' Kasper took another breath. 'These people, they think they're patriots!' He looked across at Emma. 'America's place in the world. The Redeemer Nation! Sound familiar?'

Emma narrowed her eyes. 'They want a war?'

'If you're going to put China back in the box you better do it before the PLA Navy grows up and learns to hunt on its own!'

'Names?' Emma, deadpan.

The hiss of glass, shattering, wood, snapping.

'Emma!' Duncan roared at her. 'The door!'

'What do you think?!' Kasper gasped. "Course I fucking don't!'

Emma glanced over at the open door, the chill, metal slats, the shadows reaching down into the darkness.

The sound of someone breathing, at the bottom of the stairwell, feet crunching on broken glass.

Emma looked down at Kasper. 'Hong Kong. How do you know about Hong Kong?'

Kasper squirmed. 'I don't know! Nina told me!'

'She's not one of us.' Emma's jaw, tensing. 'You met someone else, someone in MI6.'

Kasper's body shuddered.

The sound of a footstep, rising out on the metal stairway.

'Yes!' Kasper roared.

'Who?'

'Didn't give a name.' Kasper snarled. 'Old school, stick up his arse.' Kasper swallowed. 'Walked with a limp. The right leg.'

'Fuck!' Emma spat the word out, twisted around. 'Theodora, close the door!'

The grating of gears, hinges creaking, the heavy stone door slowly rumbling towards the opening.

'Bring him!' Emma shouted at Duncan.

They began to back away towards the main door, Monica's weapon trained on the narrowing gap in the wall.

A clatter of footsteps from the stairwell.

A hand, reaching out from the opening, fingernails like talons, rags hanging from his bloodstained arm.

Anne screamed.

'Go, go, go!' Monica yelled out.

Anne staggered into the corridor, Duncan bundling Kasper through the doorway.

'Monica!' Emma shouted.

The figure, crawling through the closing gap. It raised its head, dead, black eyes burning through them. It let out a roar as it rose to its feet.

Monica dashed to the door, Emma covering her.

They both stumbled into the corridor.

Emma pulled the door shut behind her.

It began to swing open, the seals, burnt out.

'Theodora!' Emma screamed through the gap. 'The door! Fucking do something!'

The door slammed shut, the sound of seals clicking into place.

They ran down the corridor to the stairway.

Jimbo's animal cries from behind the locked door echoing after them.

THURSDAY 26TH SEPTEMBER, 7.30 PM

CRATOR CAPITAL, LONDON

Emma sat back in the chair, looking up at the ceiling of Jamie Ives's office.

Duncan stood in front of the picture window, gazing into the night.

Anne sat opposite Emma, a shawl wrapped around her. She rubbed the tops of her arms with her fingers.

Jamie Ives lay on the sofa, one arm draped over his forehead.

'What a fucking mess.' Emma closed her eyes.

Duncan continued to stare through the window. The lights of the houses on the far side of the canal shimmering on the still surface of the water, the trees lining the bank silhouetted in the chill glow.

'He described him, didn't he?' Duncan turned towards Emma. 'How else would he know?'

Emma raised her fingers to her temples as she leaned forward. 'I just …' She glanced up at Duncan. 'He was like a fucking father.'

'Think. Think Ems.' Duncan narrowed his eyes. 'It's in there, in there somewhere. Something you missed, we all missed.' He ground his teeth. 'Think!'

Emma shook her head, looked down at the carpet for some moments, her shoulders gently rising and falling. 'Only to him.' Her voice, barely more than a whisper. She looked up. 'After Hong Kong, I was to report back to him, and only to him.'

'And?'

'Something about … the way he said it, I …'

'Put yourself back there.' Duncan nodded. 'Hear it, see it, feel it.'

Emma swallowed, closing her eyes.

'Where are you?'

Emma took a deep breath. 'In the car. He's sitting next to me. The rain, it's … drumming on the roof, I'm … warm, too warm. The fucking uniform it's … making my thighs itch.'

'You're nervous.' Duncan blinked. 'You feel the tension.' He paused. 'Is it him?'

Emma took another breath. 'I'm worried … about McKay.' She exhaled slowly, her eyelids fluttering. 'Sebastian, he's … talking.' She bit her lip. 'But he's thinking … about something else.'

'Look at his hands, Ems. The fingers, they're tensing, a slight tremor, he's trying … but his body won't settle.'

Emma blew air out through her lips. 'Not the hands, I'm looking at his feet.' She gave a shudder. 'He taps one with the other. That sound, on the … the one he …' She sucked in air. 'Fuck, I'm thinking … I'm thinking … at the hospital, I was waiting for him, when he came out.' She flinched. 'I saw him, walking towards me, he was trying not to limp.' A tear trickled down her cheek. 'But every step he took …' She put a hand to her mouth. 'I wanted to scream.' She let out a sob. 'I can see him now, he's trying to smile, but his eyes …' She wiped away another tear. 'He doesn't want me to see but …' She opened her eyes, looked up at Duncan, the tears, welling. 'Every step, every … stumble.'

The room fell silent, just the tick of the clock, the hum of the air conditioning, the rumble of the traffic beyond the canal-bank houses.

Duncan looked down at her for a few moments. 'You said there was something … about the way he said it. "Report to me" …'

She took a deep breath, exhaled. 'You're right.' She set her jaw. 'It did come back to me.' She gave a grunt, a hint of a smile playing around her mouth. 'How did I fucking miss that?'

Duncan frowned. 'So, what do we do?'

Emma sat upright, her eyes narrowing. 'We need to be sure.' She nodded. 'Face-to-face.'

Duncan turned back to the window. 'They'll kill you before you get near him.'

Emma looked straight ahead, the tension etched on her features.

'What if it had gone to plan?' Jamie Ives, his voice hoarse. He sat up slowly, blinking.

Anne got up, walked over to Jamie, sat down beside him. 'Go on.'

'Then you'd be dead.' Emma pushed a lock of hair behind her ear.

'Exactly. Three of us, upstairs. Three bodies.'

Emma shrugged.

'Nina did her job.' Jamie cleared his throat. 'After that she was just a loose end too. The others as well.'

'So?'

'And then there were two.' Jamie looked across at Emma. 'Kasper.' He paused. 'And you.'

Emma looked across at Duncan.

Duncan frowned.

'You tried to get to Theodora.' Jamie continued. 'Kasper was a step ahead. Kasper described his London contact. Made you give up a name.' He nodded to Emma. 'You're Kasper's ticket out of here. He trades you for safe passage.'

Emma exchanged glances with Duncan.

'If he takes Kasper's call,' Jamie swallowed, 'then we know he's your man.'

Emma took a deep breath. 'What if they're watching the building? They'll have seen us. All of us.'

Duncan bit his lip. 'But if he's working alone?'

Emma stood up. 'He could have a team out looking for me.' She walked over to Duncan. 'No one would question that.'

They stood, side by side, looking out over the water. A breeze ruffled the surface, the branches of the trees, shivering in the wind.

Duncan put a hand on her shoulder. 'Ems, get to a police station, they'll log you in, you'll be on the system. Safe.'

She placed her hand on his. 'I'll be fine.' She squeezed his hand. 'You should go. You and Monica.'

'And spoil her fun?' Duncan raised an eyebrow.

'Where's the other DI and that young DC?'

'They're at the Depot, with Fenman.'

Emma nodded.

'Jamie's plan.' Duncan growled. 'You know how that ends, don't you?'

'Do I?'

'He said it. If you meet him. Just you and Kasper.' He locked eyes with Emma. 'And then there were none.'

Emma looked back out of the window, up at the starless sky. Dark clouds, spiralling over the sombre city. 'Take Anne with you, to Fenman. Tell him about Theodora, about Sandy Point, Puerto Cueva.'

They turned to face the room.

Anne helping Jamie to his feet.

Jamie, trying to shrug her helping hands from his arm. 'Anne, really, I'm fine.' He straightened up, looked across at Emma. 'I could be him. Kasper.'

Emma frowned.

'In the dark. I could pass for him.'

414

'Maybe.'

'Kasper sets the meeting up, he thinks he's going to trade you for a free pass. But you and me go instead.'

Emma nodded. 'Go on.'

'I'll be the one with the gun in your back.' He paused. 'But you've got a gun too, he won't be expecting that.' Jamie nodded. 'How else you going to confront him? You going to let Kasper cuff you and take you along?' Jamie gave a grimace. 'He could take you anywhere. Or just kill you. Or worse.'

Emma looked across at Anne.

Anne bit her lip. 'What's he got to lose?'

. . .

Two figures walked into the reception hall, footsteps ringing out on the marble floor, echoing around the vaulted ceiling far above in the darkness. The wall lights were dimmed, pools of amber glinting on the polished tiles. The deserted reception desk, a shadow nestling against the wall.

Emma Wilson stood in front of Kasper Lehtonen. She held his phone in her hand.

They stood in silence. The rain, still drumming on the skylights, somewhere up there in the hovering shadows.

'Put your number in my phone. If you like.' Kasper attempted a smile. 'A gentleman. Not so easy to do the right thing now, so to say.' He held out his hands, the handcuffs barely containing his muscled wrists.

Emma took a long breath, her shoulders rising.

A door slammed, somewhere deep in the building, the solemn clang of metal on metal, the chill air around them quivering.

'What would you do with you, if you were me?' Emma, deadpan.

Kasper frowned. 'Too many "yous".' He looked down at her, his bulk looming above her slender frame. 'I love the English language. So many ways to say nothing.' He kept his eyes on Emma. 'We should spend time together. You know, some pointless chit-chat, pretend to fidget with the cutlery so our fingertips brush across the table.' He gave a slight nod. 'That's what you English call foreplay, am I right?'

Emma met his gaze.

'You like Italian?' Kasper raised an eyebrow.

Emma stood in silence for a moment. 'How about Chinese?'

'Very happy with that.'

'Authentic Chinese.' She paused. 'The Chinese Embassy, perhaps.'

'I like a sense of humour.' Kasper narrowed his eyes. 'But only off the bone.'

Emma let the silence wash around them, their words still hanging in the crisp, still air.

She looked up at him again, the sweep of her dark hair, the outline shimmering in the sombre light. 'Tonight, you're going to serve up our traitor.'

Kasper took a deep breath, exhaling slowly. 'You know, you don't have many words that really mean anything anymore.'

Emma's gaze, steady.

'But "traitor".' He paused. 'There's a word that makes you feel something.' He raised his bound hands, thumped them against his chest. 'In there.' He gave a chuckle, his broad shoulders shaking beneath his well-tailored jacket. 'Who needs sweet reason? So to say.'

'One chance.' She reached into her pocket, pulled out the vial of clear liquid, held it in front of him, the silky contents glistening in the half-light. 'Or you die silently screaming inside.'

Kasper pursed his lips. 'It's been quite a journey.' He looked at the tube, the narcotic shimmering as she rolled the vessel between her fingers. He glanced back up at Emma, setting his jaw. 'I'm not finished yet.'

'You're going to set up a meeting.' Emma nodded. 'Just the three of us.'

Kasper looked across to the two figures standing in shadow by the far wall, their outlines smudged against the darkness.

He turned back to Emma, drawing himself up to his full height, the first beads of perspiration glinting on his forehead.

'My name's Emma Wilson. I'm the bait.' She clenched her teeth. 'You offer me in exchange for a way out.'

'Emma.' He tried another smile. 'Suits you.'

'You'll be in Monica's cross hairs all the way.' She paused. 'How much of an excuse you think she needs?'

'Seems I'm the popular guy now.'

Emma dialled a number, set the phone on speaker, held it in front of Kasper.

Kasper looked across at her, his face partly in shadow, eyes deep in their sockets, the dull glow of his shaven head in the half-light. He blinked as the call clicked in. 'I've got her.'

Silence.

'Emma Wilson.' Kasper looked down at the phone. 'It's very tempting.'

'Go on.' The voice, muffled.

'She killed a friend of mine.' He looked up at Emma. 'I'd very much like to hurt her.'

Emma held his gaze.

'Do it for real.' He gave a slight nod. 'Hear the full vocal range, so to say.'

Emma gritted her teeth.

'Bring her to me.' The words, gurgling. A filter of some sort.

'Spoilsport.' Kasper paused. 'What do I get?'

'You get to live.' A mechanical rasp.

'A jet, City Airport, fuel for 1,000 kilometres.' Kasper looked down at the phone. 'And a hostage 'til the steps are up.'

A crackling on the other end of the line. 'Beamish Junction, the building site, use the south entrance.' The voice, robotic.

Kasper glanced up at Emma, then back to the phone. 'You know, I think I'll stick with plan A.'

'Head there now.' The voice paused. 'Or your last night will be a very long one.'

Another click.

Silence on the end of the phone.

Kasper forced a smile. 'Joking, of course.'

Monica Pole stepped out of the shadows. She walked over, stood next to Emma.

Kasper looked from one to the other. 'Spoilt for choice.'

Monica raised her arm, the gun pointing at Kasper's forehead. 'You're fucking with the wrong girls.'

Kasper gave a snort. 'Story of my life.'

'If we get out of this,' Monica narrowed her eyes, 'you'll wish I'd pulled the trigger.'

'You are a tease.'

Monica's hand was steady, the blood on her fingers silky in the faint light. 'Devil may care.' She paused. 'Maybe he does, maybe he doesn't.' She set her jaw. 'But after what you did to Anne Perry, you're going to surely find out.'

THURSDAY 26TH SEPTEMBER, 8.30 PM

BUILDING SITE, BEAMISH JUNCTION, LONDON

The cranes towered around them, spindly giants, their outlines reaching up into the mass of swirling cloud rumbling over the city. The sharpening night breeze, whispering through the girders, steel hawsers clanging against their steepling sides.

Emma edged forward, her hands behind her back, the reassuring chill of the gun's grip beneath her fingers. Jamie held her elbow as he shuffled behind her, coat collar turned up, beanie pulled down over his ears.

Emma's eyes darted from side to side. The site huts, still and dark. Ahead of them, an open space, pools of standing water, splashes of silver across the shadowy landscape. The diggers, like slumbering predators, claws resting on the broken ground.

They stepped into the clearing. The breeze, tugging at the hems of their coats. Sheets of plastic, like tattered flags hanging from bare beams, snapping in the wind.

Jamie gripped Emma's elbow tighter.

She narrowed her eyes, straining to see into the shadows.

Something. By the far wall. A smudge of movement in the darkness.

They both froze.

Emma kept her eyes trained on the figure uncoiling in the shadows, her breathing steady.

Jamie's hand shaking, his fingers digging into her.

A man, stepping out of the gloom, the folds of his coat swaying. He slowly removed his hat.

Pritchard.

They stood in silence, a few yards apart.

The rumble of the traffic from the road outside, a world away now.

Pritchard spoke first. 'L96s.' He paused. 'Three of them trained on you right now.' He glanced up at the half-built structures crowded around them, the open sides of the upper stories, the floorspace within shrouded in darkness.

Emma looked up at the concrete skeletons looming above them. 'You know me!' She shouted up into the darkness. 'Noon warned me! Before he sent me!' She took a deep breath, looked across at Pritchard. 'Warned me about you!'

'It's no use, Emma. We're onto you.' He paused, glanced into the darkness. 'And those who helped you.'

Jamie leaned in closer, his head next to hers.

'Mr Lehtonen,' Pritchard spoke again, 'I'd take a step back if I were you.'

Emma turned her head, whispered in his ear. 'Do as he says.'

Jamie didn't move.

'You know his name!' Emma, shouting up into the night sky. 'I was there. For the call. He never gave a name!'

Pritchard took another step forward, shaking his head. 'Another bloody lie. Why do you even bother?' He looked across at Jamie. 'Set the record straight for us will you, Mr Lehtonen.'

Jamie raised his head, met Pritchard's gaze. 'There was no name.' He looked skywards, shouted out the words again. 'There was no name!'

Pritchard narrowed his eyes. 'Who the fuck are you?'

'He's no one!' Emma tried to push him away from her.

Pritchard raised a hand, whispered something into his cuff.

'No, no! Don't shoot! Don't shoot!' Emma roared up at the sky.

Jamie's head still locked against hers.

She tried to twist her head around again. 'Fucking let go of me!'

'I'm staying with you.' Jamie's breathing, rapid, shallow.

She reached behind her. 'Give me your hand then.'

Jamie slid his hand in hers.

'The L96 has a muzzle velocity of 2,800 feet-per-second.' She squeezed his hand. 'You won't feel a thing.'

'Fuck.' His head wedged into her shoulder.

Emma took a deep breath. 'Like your aftershave.' She gave his hand another squeeze. 'What is it?'

'What?'

'Your aftershave. What's it called.'

Jamie exhaled. 'I'm sorry. For everything.'

A single shot rang out.

They both shuddered.

Jamie's eyes remained shut. He felt Emma sliding away from him. Her grip on his hand, melting. He let out a sob.

'Thank goodness someone was paying attention.' A voice, behind them.

Jamie slowly raised his head, opened his eyes.

Pritchard, his crumpled body lying on the cold, wet ground.

The voice again. 'How did you know it was Pritchard?'

Emma turned to face the newcomer. 'A slight limp. That's what Kasper Lehtonen said. The right leg.'

Noon reached down, rapped his knuckles on his right calf. The hollow click of carbon fibre.

Emma smiled. 'But you limp on the other leg.'

Noon nodded. 'Taught you well.' He looked her up and down. 'That's quite a comeback, for someone run over by a ferry.'

'Operation Pale Tiger.' She narrowed her eyes. 'You know what that is?'

He nodded.

'It's alive. And it's on the prowl.'

'I know.'

'But it's not the Chinese who let it loose.'

Noon blinked. 'Go on.'

'Crator's not a Chinese front. It's a sting. Insiders, CIA, maybe, or DEA. Or both. Fentanyl, stockpiled off the coast. Made to look like a Chinese op, their fingerprints all over it, motive and means.' She bit her lip. 'Two carrier strike groups steaming towards the strait of Taiwan. The Americans. They must think it's for real.'

'Three strike groups.' Noon glanced at his watch. 'In less than an hour the Secretary of State's meeting with the Chinese Ambassador. She'll confront him with the proof. The proof of Operation Pale Tiger.'

'So this is war?'

'No one declares war nowadays. Posturing and counter-posturing. Until someone fucks up.' Noon shook his head. 'The Chinese. They'll come out and fight. They'll have to.' He paused. 'So yes. It's war.' He took a deep breath. 'I fear we're too late to rewrite this.'

Emma stepped forward. 'The database at Crator. That's where they ran the ops, all the shipments. The odds of the fentanyl getting through these waters from those ports. Six-point-two million to one.' She paused. 'The DEA must have given them a pass.'

'Statistics, Emma.' He shook his head. 'When war fleets are on the move no one gives a fuck about statistics.'

'And we got The Ringmaster, Kasper Lehtonen. He ran

the op. He met two contacts in New York for instructions, one was DEA for sure.'

'Has he got names?'

She studied him for a moment, bit her lip. 'I put myself in the fucking cross hairs just now and anyone could have pulled the trigger and taken my fucking head off.' She hissed. 'I had to know how far up this fucked-up chain of command this had got.' She paused. 'Flip of a fucking coin.' She bit her lip again. 'I chose lucky. I trusted you.' She fixed him in her gaze. 'That's the deposit I put down to get this information out. My fucking life.'

He looked at her in silence. 'I can make a call.'

She nodded.

'We can do it together, from the car.' Noon glanced around, nodded towards Jamie Ives. 'What do we do with him?'

Emma looked across at Jamie Ives. 'Take him to Fenman. We can decide that later.'

Noon nodded.

Two men stepped out of the shadows, stood either side of Jamie.

He looked up at one, then slowly turned to look at the other.

'It's all right.' Emma indicated the two men with a flick of the chin. 'Go with them. Keep your head down.'

One of the men took Jamie's arm, they set off towards the gap in the buildings, footsteps crunching on the hardstanding.

Emma and Noon were alone, their shadows stretching out over the pockmarked ground, pools of water, ripples of light, the evening breeze ruffling the water's surface.

Noon glanced around.

The austere frames of the buildings, raw steel spars, stretching up into the chill night air.

The cranes, swaying, giant birds of prey, steel beaks creaking.

Another gust of wind, snapping at the ragged strips of plastic, strung like prayer flags from the dark girders.

Emma shivered.

Noon held out his hand. 'Give me your gun.'

Emma blinked. 'What?'

He opened his hand. 'Give it to me.'

'Why?'

He bit his lip. 'Don't try me.'

She exhaled, held out her weapon.

He took it, checked the magazine, clicked it back in the stock.

He took a step back, pointed it at her chest.

'What the fuck are you doing?' Emma stared at the weapon.

'My job.' He paused. 'There's a shoot-on-site order out on you.'

'Fuck it.' Her voice calm, matter-of-fact. 'You as well.'

'Fraser Chan.'

She stood in silence.

'He wasn't picked up.' He tightened his jaw. 'You did a deal.'

Emma narrowed her eyes. 'If you're going to shoot me, just shoot me.'

'The deal. What was it?'

'Fuck off, you traitorous little shit.'

'That little performance just now.' He grunted. 'Not bad.' He tilted his head to one side. 'But the secret's out.' He paused. 'Radar masking.' He nodded. 'The DEA never stood a chance.'

She took a deep breath. She looked down at the ground, then back up at Noon. 'What do you want, Sebastian?'

He didn't reply.

The wind, skittering around them, the call of a seagull, somewhere in the swirling darkness.

She took a step forward, the gun now just inches from her chest. 'I did a deal.' She gave him half a smile. 'That's all I'm going to say.' She paused. 'Now look me in the eye when you pull the trigger.'

Noon held her gaze, his expression deadpan. 'I'm sorry, Emma.' He lowered the gun. 'That came from upstairs.'

She looked down at the ground, slowly shook her head.

'Come on.' He took her arm as they made their way down the shadow-streaked path between the dark outlines of the towers. 'I believe you. About Pale Tiger.'

She didn't reply.

'The class of '95. Does that mean anything?'

She walked across the rubble-strewn ground in silence.

'Pritchard and McKay. They can't have been acting alone.'

They reached the cul-de-sac.

It was deserted.

Just the streetlights, milky grey light shimmering off the damp tarmac.

A car's headlights, turning in from the main road.

'This is us.' Noon held up a hand.

The car pulled up beside them.

Noon opened the door.

Emma slid in.

The driver turner around.

She sat there, blinking. 'Fraser?'

He nodded. 'Ma'am.'

Noon slid in beside her. 'As soon as McKay sent the Wicked Witch cable to Pritchard I knew.' He looked across at Emma. 'And I knew we had to get Fraser out. McKay would be counting on the Chinese picking Fraser up.' He glanced at the driver. 'He thought that would be the last anyone saw of you. Would have suited McKay. No one to back up your version. And Pritchard. Could try to pin it on me as well, as you saw.'

Emma looked at Noon then across at Fraser. 'But I called you the next morning.' She frowned. 'You answered the phone. You were still outside the hotel.'

Fraser shrugged.

Emma shook her head. 'So, you are that good a liar.' She flashed him half a smile.

'We can carry on the reunion later.' Noon sat back in his seat. 'Fraser, just drive us around will you?' He lifted up the armrest pulled out the handset. 'We'll put him on speaker.' He dialled a number.

A female voice, young, New York vowels. 'Mr Moore's office, how can I help?'

'Amy,' Noon's tone sombre, 'this is Mr Trover. I need to check my next appointment with Mr Moore.' He paused. 'I left my diary in my raincoat.'

Silence on the other end of the phone. 'Mr Moore is just finishing up with another patient. Can he call you right back? Are you on your usual number?'

'I'll wait for his call, many thanks.' Noon clicked off the phone.

Emma glanced at Noon.

'I'll tell you everything later.' He paused. 'Just know I always trusted you.'

She gave the slightest of nods.

The phone rang.

Noon clicked it on.

'Sebastian.' More New York vowels.

'Mario.' Noon looked across at Emma. 'I'm here with a colleague. I think you know her.' He paused. 'Emma Wilson.'

Silence on the other end of the line.

'Mario?' Emma leaned forward.

'Fucking hell, Emma.' Mario Mercado's startled tone. 'Why aren't you dead?'

'Not you too.'

'Shit, what a fucked-up week.' Mario exhaled. 'So, what's this call all about?'

'Emma got into Crator. Into the database.' Noon glanced across at her. 'You should hear this.' He nodded to Emma.

'Thirty-seven shipments,' Emma began, 'from the Colombian ports. Fentanyl, storing it at La Cueva, South Coronado Islands. And the Bahamas, Sandy Point, Great Abaco.'

'Coronado we got. The Bahamas is new.' Mario whistled through his teeth. 'Fucking sneaky Chinese bastards.'

'It's not the Chinese.'

'What?!'

Emma exhaled. 'Chances of these 37 shipments from those ports getting past the Coast Guard and DEA.' She paused. 'Six-point-two million to one.'

'Yeah, but the fucking Chinese have got the radar-masking hoodoo now.'

'Someone planted that story, proper fake news. The Ringmaster, he met with the DEA in New York Tuesday. For instructions.'

Silence.

'The Ringmaster, he's running this op. From inside Crator, running Pale Tiger.' She paused. 'We've got him.

He met with someone else in New York the next day, almost certainly CIA.'

The sound of Mario Mercado grinding his teeth. 'He got names?'

'No, but he can ID them.'

Silence.

Mario slowly exhaled. 'It's a bit fucking late for second thoughts.'

'Mario.' She took a deep breath. 'We've all been set up.' She checked herself as she almost let out a sob. 'We're going to war for nothing.'

Silence.

'You just come from Hong Kong right?' Mario again, an edge to his voice. 'You're meant to be dead. How the fuck you get back?'

Emma glanced at Noon.

'Fucking Chinese right?' Mario spat out the words.

'We just need 24 hours.' Emma bit her lip. 'We can send you that data, we can get The Ringmaster on the video link. Shit, Mario!'

'Fuck.' Mario exhaled. 'Fuck and fuck.'

'We can't stop trying.'

Mario cleared his throat. 'Emma, I know you think you're doing the right thing. But look at the optics. Bang! Here you are in London. Like Doctor Who. In a fucking Chinese Tardis.'

'Class of '95.' Noon leaned forward. 'We've got two rats.

Big ones.' He paused. 'Your pest control any better?'

Mario exhaled again. 'Look, we are where we are. The Secretary of State's about to box the Chinese Ambassador round the ears. Operation Drive Time is on the blocks and good to go.' He paused again. 'I can't go in to bat with this. Not now.'

Emma exhaled, settled back in her seat. 'I could cry if I wasn't so fucking sad.'

'I'm sorry.' Mario exhaled again. 'It's a shit situation. But we've all got to pull together now.'

Emma shook her head.

The phone clicked off.

. . .

Mario Mercado sat back in his chair, closed his eyes.

The chatter of the keyboards from beyond the doorway, muffled voices, the tension prickling around him.

He opened his eyes, leaned forward, pushed the intercom button. 'Amy?'

'Yes sir.'

'Amy, could you check which DEA officers rank 5A and higher were in New York on Tuesday?'

THURSDAY 26TH SEPTEMBER, 5 PM (10 PM GMT)

THE STATE DEPARTMENT, WASHINGTON

The Secretary of State glanced at her watch, then looked across at the man seated on the other side of her desk. 'In ten minutes I'm expecting a call from the Secretary of Defense.' Her expression deadpan. 'Zulu hour.'

The Chinese Ambassador frowned. 'What are we to understand by that?'

She set her jaw. 'Operation Drive Time is about to commence.'

He studied her for a moment, thoughtful eyes scanning her tired face. 'Of course we're aware that there are now three of your carrier strike groups approaching the Taiwan Strait.' He paused. 'These are uncharted waters. In more than one sense.'

She sat back, removing her spectacles. 'Operation Pale Tiger.'

He stared across at her. 'What is this?'

'She has quite a pedigree, I understand.'

The ambassador sat in silence for a moment, his expression calm. 'Caesar said: "Men in general are quick to believe that which they wish to be true".'

She gave a slight shrug.

'Madam Secretary.' He drew himself upright. 'Given the circumstances I am prepared to be completely candid with you.'

'A little late for that, I think.'

He took a deep breath. 'I know what Pale Tiger is.'

'If you're going to kill US citizens,' she narrowed her eyes, 'at least have the guts to do it in the open.'

He exhaled. 'Pale Tiger's not an operation.'

She glanced at her watch. 'Eight minutes.'

'Have you heard of Operation Downhill?'

'We haven't got time for this.'

'It's one of yours.' He held her gaze. 'It involves bombing the Tibetan gorges, choking off the flow of meltwater into the Yangtze and Yellow rivers.'

'You believe that?'

'I believe that somewhere in the Langley vaults there's a paper that explores that idea.'

She sat in silence.

'One of thousands. Tens of thousands.' He gave a slight nod. 'It's what we both do.'

'We know about Puerto Cueva. About Sandy Point.'

'Pale Tiger is just a fading sheet of A4 in a forgotten file.'

She reached forward, picked up a photograph. The trucks in convoy, the road to the highway. She slid the image across the desk.

The Ambassador looked down at the photo. 'I can't answer for what I don't know.'

She tapped the frame of her spectacles. 'Nearly 3,000 pounds.' She shook her head. 'Thirty-seven shipments.' She paused. 'Across those sea lanes. Not a single interception.'

He sat in silence for some moments. 'In 24 hours, I assure you we can have a very different conversation.'

'Radar masking. I think you've proved the point.'

'Madam Secretary, we just need a little more time.'

'You've played us for long enough.'

He took a deep breath, looked across at her. 'Carol.'

'We're not at a ball game now.'

'I think we know each other well enough.' He leaned forward. 'Have I ever lied to you? Have I?'

She studied him for a moment. 'I'm prepared to believe that you personally knew nothing about this.'

'We're staring over a precipice.'

'Your people took us there.'

He exhaled. 'Carol, just … please take a moment. We're on the verge of a terrible, terrible mistake.'

She sat back. 'The street price of fentanyl is already falling, rumours of a big shipment.' She shook her head. 'In a matter of hours the name Pale Tiger will be trending everywhere.' She paused. 'Whether we like it or not.'

'I said I'd be frank.' He nodded. 'Yes, we know Crator's involved. And very soon we'll know who is behind this.'

She glanced at her watch.

'Carol!' He brought the palm of his hand down on the desk. 'If that task force steams into the strait we'll have to react. We'll have to fight.'

'So what should we do?' She raised her voice. 'How many Americans will die of opioid abuse this year? A hundred thousand?' She set her jaw. 'Do we wait until it's 200,000?' She spat the words out. 'We're going in.'

The words hung in the air between them.

He sat back, closed his eyes.

She slowly replaced her spectacles. 'I think we're done here.'

He looked across at her. 'Maybe not quite.'

She narrowed her eyes.

Somewhere across the courtyard a clock chimed.

He took a deep breath. 'There's something else you should know.'

She clenched her jaw. 'If this is a threat, you're wasting your time.'

He met her gaze. 'Ideally, we'd have liked more time to get everything in line.'

She glanced at her watch.

'But since we don't, I've been instructed to tell you something.'

She gripped the armrests of her chair, her slender fingers white with tension. 'Four minutes.'

He straightened up in his chair. 'We have been working on something.' He paused. 'And before you send your fleet into action you should know what it is.'

THURSDAY 26TH SEPTEMBER, 10.10 PM

MARYLEBONE, LONDON

Emma Wilson sat on her own at the bar, the dim lights above, smudging shadows across the dark wood of the bar's surface. The dull glint of glassware, the wicker drink mats, edges fraying. She looked down at her drink, elbows on the bar, fingers resting on her temples. She closed her eyes, the noise washing around her, snatches of conversation, music, from deep in the ceiling – the tune, lost in the rumble of voices. She looked down at her glass, picked it up, swirled it around, drained it. She sat for a moment, staring across at the ranks of bottles, glinting green under the backlights, patient silhouettes, waiting their turn.

'Another?' The barman glanced down at her glass.

She nodded.

'And the same for me.'

Emma turned towards the man now standing beside her, her features creasing into a frown.

'I've got two nephews aboard the Yinchuan.' He blinked. 'What kind of day will they have?'

She looked up at Jian Zhuo. 'They didn't believe me. And they won't believe you.'

'What did Theodora say?'

She bit her lip. 'It's gone too far now.' She paused. 'When it's over, we can try and pick up the pieces.'

Jian clenched his jaw. 'What did she say?'

Emma glanced around the bar, faces flickering in the half-light, hands clasped around glasses, the glint of jewellery, well-tailored jackets draped over chair backs. Couples, leaning in with bright-eyed intent, groups of friends, heads bobbing, words skittering between them. She looked up at Jian. 'The world they'll all wake to tomorrow.' She shook her head. 'They've only known bright colours.'

'The world they'll wake up to tomorrow,' he looked at her, his handsome face taut, 'has yet to be made.'

'You're not listening. It's over.' She paused. 'Tonight I'm the Fat Lady. You got any requests?'

'At Oxford I was always taught to play to the final whistle.'

'You do that then.' She set her jaw. 'We're on different teams now.'

'You!' He jabbed a finger towards her chest. 'You have a fucking responsibility.'

'It's rude to point.' She glanced down at his extended finger. 'Surprised they didn't teach you that at Oxford.'

'Emma!' He gripped her wrist. 'It's only history if we stop trying!'

She looked at him, gently shook off his hand. 'In a few hours the seas off Xiamen will be on fire.' She gave a slight shake of the head. 'History doesn't care about what-ifs.'

He took a deep breath. 'They're still talking. In Washington.'

She gave a slight shrug.

'They have something new to talk about.' He pursed his lips. 'But they need our help.'

She sat in silence for a moment. 'Sorry.' She blinked again. 'The dice are in the air now.'

'You're the one who's not listening.' He leaned forward again, eyes blazing. 'There is a way. A way for some good to come out of all this.' He paused, straightened up. 'Emma, you know what Pale Tiger is.' He took a deep breath. 'Tell them again.'

She studied his face for a moment, patted his arm. 'History will always make fools of us.' She paused. 'And perhaps we deserve it.'

'Yes,' he clenched his teeth, 'history's a spiteful bully.' He fixed her with a stare. 'You just going to roll over?'

'No, I'm going to have another drink.' She turned to face the bar.

'Remember what I said to you in So Lo Pun?' He grabbed her arm.

She spun around to face him. 'Do you think I give a shit what you said?'

'Out of deference to your rank and reputation.' He squeezed her arm. 'Rank and reputation.' He spat the words out.

She prodded him in the chest. 'You lied to me about Fraser Chan.'

'I know about Port Moresby. You went back in, alone, against orders, in case any of your agents were still alive.'

'What else have you lied to me about?' She jutted out her jaw.

'You did that, for fuck's sake.'

'So fucking what? Maybe I wasn't thinking.'

'That's you, not this.' He snarled out the words.

'Excuse me.' The barman leaned across the bar towards them, his hands resting on the counter. He looked at Jian, then turned to Emma. 'Everything all right, Cindy?' He gave a frown. 'Do you want me to get him to leave?' He gave a flick of the chin in Jian's direction.

She took a deep breath.

Jian took his hand from her arm.

'It's OK, Matt,' Emma exhaled, 'he's just upset.'

Jian drew himself upright, pulled down his cuffs as he composed himself. He turned to the barman. 'Sorry, it's the wine talking.' He attempted a smile.

The barman nodded. 'It's all right.' He gave a slight smile. 'It's Thursday night.' He paused. 'We've all got Friday to look forward to.' He turned to serve another customer.

They both fell silent.

The noise of the bar swept back over them, a sea of voices, rising and falling, waves of sound, lapping around the room. The sound of a chair scraping the floor, laughter ringing out somewhere behind them.

'I always wondered,' Jian spoke first, 'how I'd feel. If I had to kill you.'

She slowly turned towards him. 'I don't think I'd give it a lot of thought.' She paused. 'If it was the other way round.'

'Good,' he nodded, 'because right now, that's the only way you're going to get rid of me.'

FRIDAY

FRIDAY 27TH SEPTEMBER, 10 AM (3 PM GMT)

THE STATE DEPARTMENT, WASHINGTON

The room fell silent as the lights dimmed on the ranks of seated figures.

A single spotlight settling on an empty lectern, polished glass glinting above the sober insignia of the US State Department.

A figure walked slowly to the lectern, the badge of the American flag glinting in the lapel of his dark suit. He stood, scanning the room, the audience staring up at him. The rustle of a notepad from the back of the room ringing out like a cymbal in the silence.

The man took a deep breath. 'Thank you all for coming at such short notice.' He paused. 'The Secretary of State will now make a brief statement, followed by the Secretary of Defense.'

The stillness of the room, the quiet crackling around them.

'We will not be taking any questions at this time.' He gave a slight nod, his jaw muscles tensing. 'Thank you.'

He turned, walked back into the shadows at the side of the stage.

A murmur through the waiting crowd, a low rumble, drumming through the darkness.

A figure, its slim frame taking steady steps towards the podium. The Secretary of State, her head bowed. She stood behind the lectern, the lines on her face, darker grooves under the lights. She blinked, tired eyes adjusting to the glare.

She placed her hands on the side of the lectern, her knuckles pale, translucent in the glare. She took a deep breath, her delicate shoulders rising. She looked up, uncertain faces, eyes on her.

She glanced down at the sheet of paper lying on the lectern.

The seconds, stretching out in the silence, the room, holding its breath.

Finally, she began to speak, her voice hoarse. 'Yesterday, at five in the afternoon, the ambassador of the People's Republic of China delivered a message from the State Council in Beijing.' She paused, blinking. 'As you are all aware, these last months have seen a regrettable escalation in tension, with both sides unable to find sufficient common ground to resolve ongoing trade and territorial disputes.' She glanced up, pale faces in the silent darkness. She exhaled, looking down at her notes. She swallowed. 'Last Sunday, in the waters off the Spratly Islands, the

USS Hay, an Arleigh Burke-class destroyer, collided with a Luyang-class destroyer of the PLA Navy resulting in the death of a US sailor.' She bit her lip. 'Since then, the US Navy has continued to carry out a series of freedom of navigation sorties in strength.' She paused, reached down for the water glass. She brought it to her lips, trying to disguise the trembling in her fingers. She took a sip, slowly setting the glass back down. She blinked as she focussed back on her notes. 'Yesterday at 14.30 Eastern Standard Time, the USS Nimitz and Carrier Strike Group 11 was ordered to join the Pacific Seventh Fleet and Carrier Strike Group 1 led by the USS Carl Vinson in preparation for a sortie into the Taiwan Strait.' She paused, biting her lip. She resumed reading the script, her voice quaking now. 'At 17.00 EST, we received a message from the State Council in Beijing.' She swallowed. 'Since then, we have been in constant discussions, working through the night to try to defuse this existential crisis facing us all.' She looked up, rows of faces, nervous eyes trained on her, motionless figures, hardly daring to breathe. She raised a finger, wiping away a single tear. 'I have to tell you,' she took another deep breath, 'that an historic agreement has now been reached between ourselves and the People's Republic of China—'

The room erupted with a roar, figures leaping to their feet.

Behind the lectern, she raised a hand to call for quiet over the shouts and whoops, a broad smile across her face. 'I cannot tell you how relieved we all are.' Her raised voice barely audible above the babble still sweeping over the room. 'If I may, ladies and gentlemen!'

The clamour began to subside, people once again taking their seats.

'I cannot tell you,' she began again, 'how relieved we all are and I must give our heartfelt thanks to His Excellency the Chinese Ambassador and all those in the Ministry of Foreign Affairs in The People's Republic of China who have worked so hard with us all to bring this to a peaceful and productive conclusion.' She gave another broad smile as applause swept the room. 'The Ministry of Foreign Affairs, the Ministry of Health and the Ministry of National Defense of the People's Republic of China will all shortly be holding their own press conferences, but at this stage they have given me the honour of being able to announce the key points to this agreement.'

The room was silent once more, the sense of expectation fizzing around them.

'There will be a war.' She smiled again. 'A war on opioid abuse and the illegal manufacture and distribution of these drugs that have brought such misery and death not only to our own citizens but to so many others around the world.' She glanced across to the side of the stage, the Chinese Ambassador nodded to her, a smile beginning to crease his face. 'Our respective enforcement agencies will work together to locate and shut down illicit opioid production facilities wherever they may be found. We will also be giving active assistance to other countries willing to join us both in this global campaign to bring an end to this scourge.' She looked up as another round of applause echoed around the room. 'Furthermore, the US and the People's Republic of China will be setting up and jointly funding a new charitable organisation dedicated to the treatment and rehabilitation of opioid addicts everywhere.' She nodded as more applause swept over her. 'And my colleague, the Secretary of Defense, will shortly outline bold new plans for the active cooperation of the US Navy and the PLA Navy in tracking down and interdicting illegal drug shipments in international waters around the world.' She looked up as more applause clattered around them. She nodded slowly as the crowd began to settle. 'I also have one other announcement to make.' She smiled broadly. 'The offices on the President of the United States and the President of the People's Republic of China will be briefing you all shortly on plans for a summit in the coming weeks. In the meantime, I can confirm that all existing tariffs and sanctions that have been imposed on China are to be lifted with immediate effect.'

The room erupted again in a clamour of excited voices, the audience leaping to their feet, clutching laptops and notepads, looking round for the exits.

She turned, walked towards the Chinese Ambassador. She held out her hand.

The room behind her, a swirl of noise and movement.

'Mr Ambassador.' She smiled.

He shook her hand, returning the smile. 'Madam Secretary.'

She leaned in. 'Got to give it to you, Liu. Balls of steel.'

He raised an eyebrow. 'And at least there won't be tariffs on them now.'

FRIDAY 27TH SEPTEMBER, NOON (5 PM GMT)

THE STATE DEPARTMENT, WASHINGTON

Luke Dunn stood in front of the meeting room door. He took another deep breath, the air down here a dusty dryness, just catching the back of his throat. He looked behind him, the basement corridor stretching back towards the elevator doors, sombre steel, gleaming dully under the ceiling lights, the grey stone walls, washed in the chill, milky glow. He felt a shiver run through him as he checked his watch yet again. He drew himself upright, straightened his tie, tensed his right hand, knocked once on the cold metal.

Silence.

He swallowed, took another deep breath, trying to keep his breathing steady.

From behind the door, the sound of a chair scraping, steel on concrete.

The door began to swing open.

Luke Dunn blinked as he tried to focus on the face looking out at him from the half-light.

Luke's eyes, wide with surprise. 'Brian?'

Brian Welch screwed up his face. 'I was expecting Medford.'

Luke slowly shook his head. 'And so was I.' He peered past Brian's shoulder, a table, its metal top gleaming under the spotlights slung from the ceiling above, three chairs, glinting steel frames, stark against the dark stone floor.

Brian stood to one side as Luke walked past him.

Luke scanned the room, the windowless walls half-hidden in shadow, the centre of the room a pool of silvery light in the quiet darkness.

Luke and Brian exchanged glances.

Luke's eyes narrowed, the slightest nod of the chin. A warning.

Brian gave a nod in return.

'I've got a 12.30.' Luke glanced upwards, a jut of the chin, indicating the microphones nestling in the shadows beyond the spotlights. 'If it was going to drag there'd be coffee.'

Brian cleared his throat. 'You tasted State Department coffee?' He paused. 'No wonder they don't smile much.' He looked at the three empty chairs, then across at Luke, his shoulders tensing.

Luke followed his gaze. 'He's usually on time.' He pulled at the cuffs of his shirt. 'He said 12.00 didn't he?'

'He did!'

The two men jumped, spun around to face the voice.

Medford, his solid bulk framed in the doorway. His expression, deadpan.

The silence, crushing around them.

'People,' Medford begun, looking from one man to the other, 'just when you think ...'

Luke's mouth opened, but no sound emerged.

Brian swallowed, his jaw taut.

'Before I start,' Medford began to walk towards the centre of the room, 'I have a question.' He stood behind one of the chairs, his rounded face streaked in shadow beneath the lights. 'Can you guess what that might be?' His eyes moved between the two men, his lips pursed.

Luke make a croaking sound, as he began to move his lips. 'It's been ...' He threw a glance at Brian. 'Just a ... crazy few days.' He attempted a smile, his face too tense to oblige.

Medford shifted his gaze from Luke to Brian.

Brian's eyes widened, his breathing, quickening.

'A lot to take in.' Medford's voice, soft, calm. 'A lot to process.' He pulled out the chair, carefully lowered his bulky frame onto it.

The silence, fizzing around them.

Medford took a deep breath, his shoulders swelling beneath his suit. 'Take a seat.' He gestured to the two chairs on the other side of the table. 'We'll be a while.' He gave a nod, his chin nestling into the folds of his neck. He placed a thin green file on the table.

Brian Welch and Luke Dunn lowered themselves into the chairs, eyes on the file lying in front of them.

'Nowadays,' Medford raised an eyebrow, 'looking for "the truth" is more of an art than a science.' He pursed his lips. 'And would we even recognise it, if we found it?' He looked from one man to the other.

Brian smoothed down his moustache with thumb and forefinger.

Luke pulled at a shirt cuff.

'I used to think "truth" was something pure, forged in the furnace of honesty, tempered by the hammer of clarity on the anvil of understanding.' Medford paused. 'But now I know where "truth" comes from.' He nodded again. 'Saturday night, outside the bar, convenience, up against the clapperboard fence, its legs wrapped around wishful thinking.' He blinked. 'And prejudice, cheering them on.'

Brian swallowed, looked up at the ceiling, his face, pale now, framed in the light.

Luke sat almost motionless, just his eyes scanning the floor around him.

'Information,' Medford continued, 'that's something different.' He looked from one to the other. 'Wouldn't you say?'

Brian looked across at Medford, cleared his throat. 'I guess so.' His voice, hoarse.

Luke nodded, his jaw muscles tensing.

'They got into Crator. The Brits.' Medford rested his forearms on the table, his face partly in shadow. 'We were right, in a sense.' He pursed his lips. 'It's a front.' He paused. 'But not for the Chinese.' He tapped the metal tabletop with his finger, the vibrations sending shimmers of light skittering over the surface. 'It was an inside job. All along.'

Medford sat back.

The gentle hum of the ceiling fan, somewhere above them.

Brian blinked, white knuckles on clenched hands.

Luke stared straight ahead, his lips pressed together.

'Mario Mercado.' Medford glanced from one to the other. No reaction.

'The Bobby Jones of Langley.' Medford paused. 'If you say something often enough, people will start to believe you.'

Brian glanced across at Luke, a frown creasing his features.

Luke continued to look at Medford, same dead-eyed stare.

'He came to see me on Wednesday, when you were out of town.' He nodded to Luke. 'He had a lot to say. But made sure I was the one to draw any conclusions, not him.' He narrowed his eyes. 'The tip-off, the clearing in the Colombian jungle, the lab, the Chinese coffee plant, the Chinese-built road.' He took another breath. 'And of course those rumours about Crator and Chinese money.' He leaned forward. 'A heady recipe.' He tapped the tabletop again. 'Stir in fentanyl, a pinch of history and the legend of The Pale Tiger.' He looked from one man to the other. 'And what have you got?'

Brian and Luke exchanged another glance.

'Except,' Medford sat back, 'there was no tip-off.'

'What?' Luke, frowning as he shook his head.

'No record of any tip-off. Either on the DEA system or the CIA's.' Medford nodded again. 'And yesterday, when we were sitting round that table, trying not to think the unthinkable …' Medford spread his hands. 'Super Mario to the rescue. What was it he said? "I swore an oath, to protect the people. Otherwise what's the point?"' Medford shook his head. 'Not quite Henry V, but it did the job.'

Luke leaned forward, the furrows on his forehead dark lines under the spotlights. 'But I thought there was …' He glanced across at Brian, then back to Medford. 'The rumours about the … Stagemaster. Was that his name? The guy pulling all the strings.'

Medford nodded. 'The Ringmaster. Yes, he exists all right.'

Luke sat back, swallowed, his complexion paling.

Medford looked across at Luke, his expression calm. 'Or should I say existed. Past tense.'

Luke's eyes widened. 'What happened?'

Medford gave a little shrug. 'He died. Under questioning. They went a bit too far, too fast. Got nothing.'

Luke cleared his throat. 'That's a pity.'

Medford glanced over at Brian.

Brian sat, shoulders hunched, staring down at the table.

Medford studied him for a moment, turned back to Luke. 'Starting a war.' He narrowed his eyes. 'Did he really think history would forgive him?'

Luke shifted in his chair. 'Was he working alone?'

Medford flicked open the file, slid a photograph across the table. 'The Class of '95.' He glanced at the photo, then up at Luke. 'Pritchard. MI6.' He studied Luke's face. 'Not a great photo. But then no one looks good after a round from an L96 rifle's vaporised most of your head.'

Luke stared at the image, beads of sweat forming on his forehead.

'The Brits went route one.' Medford continued, his tone, matter-of-fact. 'A trial would have been just too embarrassing.' He paused. 'David McKay.'

Luke's eyes flickering, his jaw muscles tensing.

'I'll spare you the photo.'

Luke bit his lip. 'Why are we here?'

'Why do you think you're here?'

Luke scanned Medford's face. 'I'm … not sure.'

Medford nodded. 'OK.' He turned to Brian. 'How about you?'

Brian slowly raised his head. His eyes were red and puffy. He moved his lips, but no sound emerged.

'I know,' Medford gave him a concerned look, 'it's been a long week.' He turned back to Luke. 'We need to think fast. While we own this.'

Luke blinked again.

'Mercado. What do we do with him?'

Luke bit his lip. 'Did he say why he did it? Mercado?'

Medford shook his head. 'Haven't picked him up yet. We need a plan in place before we move.' He leaned forward, laid his arms on the table. 'Love of country, let's assume.' Medford shook his head. 'The noble causes are always the bloodiest.'

Luke swallowed again. 'He likes to fish.'

Medford nodded.

'An accident.' Luke took another breath, exhaled. 'Middle of the lake. Drunk, fell overboard. That could work.'

'Can you handle that?'

Luke nodded. 'I don't think you need to see him, sir.' He blinked. 'Just leave it to us.'

Medford drummed his fingers on the tabletop. 'Brian.'

Brian Welch continued to stare at the floor.

'You up for a fishing trip?'

Brian slowly raised his head, looked at Luke then across to Medford. He shook his head. 'This is all just shit.'

A knock at the door.

Luke turned towards it.

Medford kept his gaze on Luke. 'Come in.'

Luke's eyes widened.

Kasper Lehtonen, hands cuffed in front of him, a policeman either side.

They formed up in a line, facing the table.

Mario Mercado followed them in. He closed the door. Medford sat back in his chair.

The silence, ringing around them.

Luke swallowed, looked across at Medford. 'You wouldn't fucking understand.'

Medford met his gaze. 'Would I even want to?'

Luke looked up at Mario, then back to Medford. 'This world you think you live in.' He narrowed his eyes. 'All pastel shades and common ground.' He shook his head. 'Bullshit.' He paused. 'Black and white. It's always been black and white.' He jutted out his jaw. 'It's not us and them. It's us or them.' He glanced around the room. 'The Chinese. They won't stop.' He swung back to Medford. 'Thirty years ago we had a 500-ship navy.' He blinked. 'Today, we got less than 300 afloat.' He looked around the room. 'They're coming for us.' He paused. 'They're the enemy.' He glanced around the room once more. 'Pale Tiger was going to happen one day.' He took a deep breath. 'Just because we did it doesn't change a fucking thing.' He exhaled. 'Just look at your history books.' He sat back in his chair. 'In case you hadn't noticed, the Chinese don't fucking share.'

Medford looked across at Mario.

Mario gave a slight shrug.

Medford turned to Luke. 'It was Mario's idea. Give you the chance to prove there was something ... anything worth saving.' He paused. 'You've given your answer.'

Luke looked across at Mario. 'So I'm the salve you can rub on your conscience.'

Mario stood in silence for a moment, took a step forward. 'Get up, both of you.'

Luke rose to his feet.

Brian pushed himself up from his chair.

They began to walk towards the door.

In a blur of movement Brian snatched the pistol from the policeman's holster, held it against his own temple, pulled the trigger.

A click sounded out.

Brian stood, eyes clenched shut. He slowly lowered the weapon.

Mario walked up to Brian, took the weapon from him. 'Thought you might try and shoot me, or Kasper.' He nodded. 'But I didn't expect that.'

'May I make a suggestion?'

They all turned to face the speaker.

'We could keep this all simple.' Kasper looked at Medford, then across at Mario.

Mario frowned.

Kasper nodded towards Brian. 'Two bullets.'

Mario looked across at Medford.

Medford gave a nod.

Mario slipped a pair of handcuffs from his belt, snapped one cuff on Luke's hand, the other round the leg of the table.

'No!' Luke pulled at the table leg, looked down at the bolts securing it to the floor. He gave one more tug on the handcuffs, the ring of metal against metal cutting through the air. He stilled himself, shoulders slumped. 'Fuck.'

Mario slid the magazine from the handgrip, fed two rounds into the clip, slid it back into the weapon. 'Time for us to go.'

They walked towards the door in silence, only Mario and Brian standing in half-shadow just beyond the glare of the spotlights.

The rest filed out of the room, into the corridor, footsteps ringing out on the tiled floor, echoing off the cold stone walls.

Mario handed the gun to Brian.

Brian gave the slightest of nods.

Mario turned, left the room, quietly closing the door behind him.

A shot rang out. And then another.

Kasper nodded. 'At home they used to call me KIVO, you know.'

Mario looked at him blankly.

'Like the man who gets rid of the rubbish.' Kasper raised an eyebrow. 'A reliable waste disposal man. Not so easy to find, so to say.'

'If we were looking for a psycho, we'd advertise.'

'But you want someone who enjoys the work.'

'Is that so?'

'Indeed so.' Kasper gave Mario a nod. 'After all, a happy employee's a productive employee.'

FRIDAY 27TH SEPTEMBER, 5 PM

JAMIE IVES'S OFFICE, CRATOR CAPITAL

The elevator door locks sprung open with a hiss, bearings rumbling as the grey steel slid aside.

Anne Perry stepped through the door into Jamie Ives's office. The blinds were drawn, the afternoon sun tamed to smudges of grey light through the pale fabric. She breathed in the familiar scent of the room: wood polish, freshly pressed linen, yesterday's coffee.

She began to walk towards the desk.

Jamie Ives looked up from his laptop, his hand lit up in the glare from the screen, his face blurred in shadow. 'Wasn't sure I'd see you again.'

'Neither was I.' Anne walked up to the desk, Jamie's features slipping into focus. His right eye was badly bruised, his left arm in a sling. 'Fell down the stairs, I assume.' She nodded towards the cast around his wrist.

'Something like that.'

Anne leaned forward, staring at the bruising around his eye. 'Did they know her: Rhea?'

Jamie shrugged. 'I don't think so. But it's like a family, isn't it?'

Anne nodded, straightening up. She took a deep breath, eyes flitting across Jamie's bruised features. 'Why didn't you save her?'

Jamie looked up at her, the grazing on the side of his head more visible now. 'I made myself believe what I wanted to believe.' He paused. 'Broke the first rule of investing.' He slowly shook his head. 'Unintended's a weak word.'

Anne stood in silence for some moments, the steady hum of the air conditioning, the sound of her own breathing, soft and steady. 'You haven't answered the question.'

Jamie's shoulders rose and fell as he studied her face. 'This isn't a police matter anymore. It's all closed. As though it … never happened.'

She met his gaze. 'It's not a police question.'

He nodded, sitting back in his chair. 'I didn't think they'd hurt her, not with the operation so close.'

Anne stood in silence, a frown spreading across her pale forehead.

'I wasn't thinking straight.' Jamie continued. 'Of course they were going to go after her.' He shifted in his chair. 'They have rules. They stick to the rules.'

'Go on.'

He took another breath. 'She was a threat. Threats are dealt with.' He looked down at his laptop. 'At that level, it's just a question of attention to detail.' He looked back up at Anne. 'You saw what they did.'

She didn't react.

'There doesn't seem any point in saying I'm sorry.'

'Who says you've earned the right to apologise?'

He nodded again.

'You're right.' Anne continued, her voice quiet and calm. 'It's not a police matter anymore.' She paused. 'The only one who can punish you, is you.'

'I know. I will.' He looked down. 'I am.'

Anne looked up at the ancient maps framed above his desk. Seas and mountains, monsters and men. Only the law of nature in these lands without order. 'Why did you even do it?' She looked back down at him. 'Take their money, Kasper's money?'

Jamie sat back in his chair. 'Because I could. Because I thought it was just money.' He paused. 'And I liked him, Kasper.'

Anne shook her head.

'Of course I didn't know him then.' He exhaled. 'Didn't know how completely cruel he was.' He gave a slight shrug. 'I mean he wouldn't describe himself as cruel. He'd say cruelty is what amateurs do. Cruelty gets you caught.' He blinked, his battered eyelid twitching. 'But he was cruel. And I knew that one day he'd come for me too.' He took another breath. 'He's a monster.' He looked up at Anne. 'But he's probably the most honest man I know.'

Anne drew a breath. 'You've fallen a long way.'

'I've seen a lot.' He gave a slight cough. 'I used to think that money gave you power.' His battered eyelid fluttered again. 'But really, it was my weak point. The more money I had, the weaker I was.' He gave a slight shake of the head. 'The most valuable thing that money brings?' He tried to smile. 'You finally understand all the things that money can't buy.' He looked down at his laptop, raised his good hand, making small circles on the mouse pad with his middle finger. 'I always wanted to be a painter.' He tapped the pad. 'But my parents thought it was too risky.' He looked back up at Anne. 'Life's a strange thing.' He sat back in his chair, his hand resting on the top of the desk. 'You could come and work for us.'

Anne looked down at him for a few moments. 'Maybe I like myself too much.'

'For the charity, we're doing important work, you'd really make a difference.'

She gave a little shake of the head. 'You know the answer's no.'

'No isn't really an answer but, yes, I know.' He leaned forward, hand on the keyboard, the light from the screen flitting across his bruised features. 'There's something else you should know.' He looked up at her. 'You and me.' He nodded. 'It was my idea. To try to get … close to you.' He paused. 'Told Kasper it was to find out what you knew, my cover for helping you, pointing you to the right places.' He took another breath. 'And if I could sleep with you as well.' He tried to smile. 'I liked that idea. A lot.' He sat back in his chair, 'Until Kasper thought it was too good a photo opportunity to miss.' He exhaled.

Anne looked down at him, her face still. 'I should be going.'

'The first time I saw you, Anne, I knew I could love you for a long time.'

Anne swallowed, her gaze flitting over Jamie's face. She opened her mouth, no sound emerged. She turned, walked towards the lift, stepped inside, her pounding heart smothering the noise of the growling gears as the lift door slid shut.

. . .

Emma was waiting for Anne in the downstairs corridor.

The cushioned silence, the dark-painted doors, the glow of the ceiling lights.

Emma pulled a face as Anne walked up to her. 'Anne, you look as though you've …' She frowned. 'What did Jamie say?'

Anne looked down, shook her head. 'Nothing. Really.'

Emma nodded slowly. 'Right.'

Anne looked at Emma. 'I don't know whether to hit you or hug you.'

Emma stood in silence for a moment, a slight frown dusting her forehead. 'Why not both?'

Anne swallowed. 'Wasn't just one of those things was it? Me on this case.'

'You were the right choice. You can see that.'

'For you.'

'And for Rhea.' Emma paused. 'And because you never know where these things will go.'

Anne took a deep breath. 'I nearly couldn't do it.' She exhaled. 'I rang your number, after Nina Carter called me. I left you a message.'

'That's what it's there for.'

'I felt scared. And alone.'

'Can't be brave unless you're scared.' Emma looked at Anne, concern etched across her fine features. She took another breath. 'Anyway, bloody phone's at the bottom of Victoria Harbour. Who knows what I've missed.' She tried a smile.

'That girl, Nina.' Anne blinked, the tiredness showing in her eyes. 'She said Rhea had parents.'

Emma nodded. 'I know her dad. They're an army family.' Emma placed a hand on Anne's arm. 'The funeral's next week, They'd like you to be there.' She squeezed Anne's arm. 'To say thank you.'

Anne blinked again. 'Yes.' She said softly.

Emma studied Anne's face for a moment. 'You are amazing, Anne.'

Anne stood in silence, just the creases around her eyes marking her soft features.

Emma nodded, slowly. 'Why don't we go and get really, really drunk?'

Anne smiled, reached out, put her arms around Emma. They held each other tight.

'Mr P, he's waiting.' She patted Emma's shoulder.

'He's a lucky boy.' She gave Anne another squeeze.

They let their arms fall to their sides.

'We ought to go.' Emma nodded towards the door at the end of the corridor. 'My boss is in the lobby.'

They turned, began to walk.

'So, now you know.' Emma glanced at Anne, a smile playing across her features. 'In the business, we call that a free hit.'

Anne frowned. 'Call what?'

'Jamie Ives.' Emma paused. 'For Queen and country. That's not really cheating.'

They stopped, facing each other.

'So, tell me.' Emma raised an eyebrow. 'Did you …?'

'Only in my imagination. That was exhausting enough.'

'Beats giving out parking tickets, doesn't it?'

Anne gave her a little smile. 'Let's just say the next time Mr P's away, my silicon friend's going to be rather busy.'

'Go girl.'

Anne reached out, swung open the door.

They stepped into the lobby, squinting as they adjusted to the afternoon sun streaming through the dome above, pillars of silky light, pools of silver splashed across the marble floor.

'The sorceress and her apprentice.' Noon stood in the centre of the hallway, his dark suit contrasting with the slick white walls around them.

'Or is it the other way round?' Emma walked towards him, Anne by her side, their footsteps ringing out in the airy brightness.

Noon stretched out a hand. 'DI Perry. Anne. At last.'

Anne shook his hand. 'I assume you don't have a name.' She raised an eyebrow.

'Actually I have several.' He smiled.

Anne blinked again. 'What happened to the man in the cell, underneath Theodora?'

Noon shook his head. 'The shock of the light, and the noise.' He gave a slight shake of the head. 'His heart just … stopped.' He reached up, slowly removed his spectacles. 'Perhaps it was for the best.' He let the words hang in the air. 'But I have better news for you.' He allowed himself a slight smile. 'Your young DC, Iqbal Zayan, he's up for a gallantry medal.'

Anne's eyes lit up. 'Does he know?'

'Your colleague, DI Lute, recommended him.'

Anne smiled. 'Then he should be the one to tell him.' She took another breath. 'Did you call the Royal Australians?'

Noon nodded. 'Spoke to the CO. Ellis Wagner's name will be added to the Roll of Honour.'

'Thank you.'

'You don't have to thank anybody.' Noon nodded again. 'It's all been said. But you know where we are.'

Anne turned to Emma.

They hugged again.

'There's a car waiting for you.' Noon indicated the man standing by the main doors.

Anne nodded again, walked towards the sleek grey panels as they rumbled aside, walked out into the chill evening air.

Noon looked across at Emma. 'So,' he paused, 'what shall we do with your date?'

'I have a date?'

'The guy you were holding hands with at the building site last night.'

'Him.'

'Didn't look like he was enjoying the evening much.' Noon paused. 'Perhaps you should have gone to the pub instead.'

'But where's your sense of romance?'

'He's an upgrade on most of the pirates you've been out with, I'll give you that.' He slowly replaced his spectacles. 'Will he be safe at Crator?'

'Safe from what?'

Noon raised an eyebrow. 'I sensed a little chemistry there.'

Emma shook her head. 'He's someone else's unfinished business.' She paused. 'What will happen to McKay?'

Noon shrugged. 'Do you really want to know?'

'I'd rather you didn't hurt him.'

Noon pursed his lips. 'Me too, oddly enough.' He exhaled. 'So, Hong Kong. What went wrong?'

'McKay outplayed me. He's still got my PIN number.'

Noon nodded. 'And how was the flight over there?'

Emma shook her head. 'I was never a good flyer. Works better if someone's bringing the drinks trolley to me.'

'But you pulled it off.'

'I tried.'

Noon smiled. 'British Airways service, not what it used be.'

Emma looked across at him. 'Next time I'm going to have 30 blokes staring at my arse for ten hours, at least let me choose the outfit.'

FRIDAY 27TH SEPTEMBER, 7 PM

BARNES, LONDON

Anne Perry closed the front door behind her. She glanced around the hallway, the unopened mail on the side table, a 'while-you-were-out' note from the Post Office, the lonely Phlebodium aureum in its blue pot. 'I knew he'd forget to water it,' she muttered, slipping off her coat.

A clatter of pans from the kitchen.

Anne walked across the hallway, her shoes clicking on the tiled floor. She stood in the kitchen doorway. She sniffed the air.

'Don't. Say. Anything.' Mr P, vigorously prodding something in the casserole dish.

'Is it still alive?'

More grunts from over the stove.

Anne walked to the cupboard on the far wall, took out a glass, poured herself a generous measure from the whisky bottle standing by the toaster. She turned to face him.

Mr P stood up straight, carefully placed the wooden spoon by the side of the cooker. He took a deep breath, his shoulders heaving, exhaling slowly as he gazed into the pot.

'Anything I can do?' Anne took a sip.

'I suppose it's too late to dispose of the evidence.' He turned around.

'We could still give it a decent burial?'

He smiled, undid the strings of the apron, pulled it over his head, threw it over the back of a chair. He picked up his glass from the sideboard, walked over to Anne. He raised his glass. 'What shall we drink to?'

'The weekend?' She clinked her glass against his.

They both took a large sip.

He looked across at her. 'Somewhere in a kitchen in Barnes,' he began, 'a dull husband and his very normal wife were settling into an exceptionally ordinary evening.'

'Until something went terribly wrong with the chilli con carne ...'

'But the funny thing was ...'

'They didn't give a fuck ...'

'Because ...' He raised his eyebrows.

'She wanted a takeaway anyway.'

He took another sip. 'Which for them ... was quite edgy.'

She drained her glass, ran a finger down his chest. 'How long does a pizza delivery take?'

'Thirty minutes.'

'Let's think …' She tilted her head to one side. 'How could we fill 30 minutes?'

'Forty-five if we ask for extra toppings.'

She leaned into him. 'Mr P … is that a promise?'

'Call it an aspiration.'

'So whilst they were waiting,' she began to unbutton his shirt, 'they decided the dishwater could wait.'

'Until he remembered tomorrow was bin day.'

She took hold of his shirt with both hands, pulled his face towards hers. 'Mr P … you certainly know how to push a girl's buttons …'

FRIDAY 27TH SEPTEMBER, 7.30 PM

MAIDA VALE, LONDON

Emma Wilson turned the corner onto Elgin Avenue, the breeze catching her hair, pulling at the hem of her raincoat. She pulled the collar tighter to her neck as she headed westward, the late afternoon sun shimmering off the damp roadway, the orange brickwork of the mansion blocks rising sleek and sharp into the blustery blue sky.

A man, walking towards her. His gait familiar. His face began to slide into focus.

She stopped, waiting for him as he took the last few steps towards her. He was carrying a bunch of yellow flowers.

Jian Zhuo stood facing her. 'Off somewhere nice?'

'Just home.' She nodded. 'I'm three behind on Big Little Lies and there's a bottle of Malbec with my name on it.' She glanced down at the flowers. 'Are those for me?'

'Didn't think you were a chocolates girl.' He looked down at the flowers then across at Emma. 'Yellow roses. Friendship and appreciation.'

Emma looked up at him. 'Can't go wrong with flowers.'

He handed them to her.

She took them, breathed in their scent.

Jian Zhuo smiled. 'So, they listened in the end.'

Emma returned the smile. 'You were right.' She blinked. 'When are you going back?'

'The late flight tonight.' He nodded, a smile playing across his features. 'Same one you were on.'

She pursed her lips. 'Right. Saw me coming a mile off, didn't you?'

'Covering the bases.' He gave a chuckle. 'Couldn't believe it, your cabbie that first night, getting lost in the Admiralty one-way system.' He paused. 'Hope you didn't tip him.'

'Ha, ha.' She tucked her hair behind her ear. 'And don't tell me, you had someone in the Irish bar as well.'

He raised an eyebrow. 'You're quite a tidy mover on the dance floor, I hear.'

'I'd had a couple of tequilas.' She frowned. 'You're giving me that look. I didn't snog your man did I?'

'It was a "her", actually.'

Emma pulled a face. 'Umm.'

'That in your repertoire too?'

'Well, who hasn't? In a careless moment.' She smiled. 'Or an inspired one.'

'But thank you. That's what I came to say.'

'I'm glad you found me last night.' She glanced up at the buildings around them, the sky beyond. 'Yep, it turned out to be a good day. After all.'

He looked around. 'It did. It was.'

A gust of breeze brushed through the branches of the nearby tree, the sunlight flickering on the rustling leaves.

She turned back to face him. 'Tell me one thing, Jian.'

'Sure.'

'Milot Borso. What happened to him?'

Jian shrugged. 'Should I know?'

'You know when you're just that one piece short in the jigsaw.' She tilted her head to one side, her dark hair ruffling in the breeze. 'You've looked under the sofa, in between the cushions ...'

Jian furrowed his brow.

'Disappeared. Just like that.'

'People do.'

Emma nodded. 'You were on to me, so you were on to McKay. If you were on to McKay ...'

'It's our town. Why wouldn't we?'

'And all the time you've got the ace in the hole. The war on opioids. The seat at the table. Your boss'll probably get the Nobel Peace Prize.'

Jian gave another shrug. 'So?'

'Have you got a sweet tooth?'

'What?'

'Because I've just got this little nagging feeling that you were just watching this all unfold. Watching and waiting.'

Jian took a step back. 'This wasn't us. The Class of '95, Pale Tiger was all theirs.'

'I know.' She paused, 'And I'm not blaming you.' She smiled. 'But I can't help thinking, Jian, that somehow you've had your cake and eaten it. Twice.'

THE END